The Tartan Swap

A Scottish Highlands Romance

Kimber H. Kinkaid

Highland Embers Press

ISBN: 979-8-9999931-0-6

THE TARTAN SWAP

Warnings?
Aye, lass—all of them.
Blades and betrayals,
whiskey and wanton kisses,
clans clashin' and lovers sparrin' as fierce as any warband.
If ye dinnae like yer stories wi' a bite, best leave it be. If ye do—sit close, the tale's just beginnin'.

Chapter One

Tryss

Frost licked at Tryss MacCraith's bones, sharp and unforgiving—like the crown he'd never asked to bear.

He stood at the edge of the training yard, the wind tearing at his cloak like the blaze burning in his chest. His jaw was set, and a low growl vibrated from deep in his throat. Beside him, Fergus knelt, cleaning his claymore, the scrape of steel a dull backdrop to Tryss's storm.

"So, the bride comes the morra," Fergus said, glancing up with a cautious smile. "MacInnes blood. Whit d'ye reckon o' it?"

Tryss's jaw snapped shut with a sharp crack. He spat into the frost-hardened earth, disgust curling his lip. "Aye, a bride. Like a chain wound tight round ma throat. MacInnes blood. Her father's the verra man who pressed my da's hand tae the treaty that chained us years ago. An' now they press mine wi' his daughter. I'm nae a laird—I'm a pawn in their game. My name's been bartered twice o'er." His voice trembled with a dark fury. "I'm laird by name, but a prisoner tae this cursed marriage. Nae matter how many battles I fight, nae matter how many foes I break, I'm powerless tae halt it."

For a bare breath, his anger faltered, and another thought slid in—shameful, unwanted. Once, when he was a lad, he'd dreamed a wife might mean warmth. A fire in the hearth, bairns at his knee, laughter that belonged tae him. But that dream had withered long ago, buried beneath duty's weight. Now it mocked him, as cold and hollow as the frost at his feet.

He slammed a fist into the post, the wood groaning beneath the blow.

"They bind me tae a woman I dinna want, tae a name I dinna ken. A stranger tae claim ma hearth an' ma life like a thief in the night. 'Tis a curse, Fergus. An' I hate it. I hate it wi' every breath in me."

His hand lingered there, red knuckles pressed into the splintered grain. His chest heaved, the fight in him not yet spent.

"Nay—I dinna hate her," he muttered, almost to himself. "I dinna ken the lass. But I hate what she stands for. A bargain struck o'er my head. My blood bartered like coin. I'd sooner face a hundred swords than bend ma neck tae another man's treaty."

Fergus rose slowly, eyes steady but wary and clamped a hand on Tryss's shoulder. "Ye wear yer burden heavy, brither."

Tryss spun to face him, shaking off his hand, rage flaring like wildfire in his eyes. "Burden? 'Tis a noose. A trap. I'm a warhound penned ahint walls I didna build, snappin' at ghaists. Every man that kneels tae me sees strength, but nae one sees the cage."

He exhaled hard, the mist of his breath disappearing into the gray dawn. Just once, he wished someone'd ask whit he wanted. But no one ever had—and he doubted they ever would.

Fergus placed his firm hand on his shoulder again, a silent anchor. "Mind, strength isna only in the sword. At times the fiercest fight is tae endure."

Tryss's shoulders shook with the weight of his fury and frustration. A bitter smile twisted his lips. "I'll learn tae swallow the poison, but mark ma words—this laird's a tempest waitin' tae break free. An' that wumman... she'd best be ready for the storm."

He looked eastward, toward the MacInnes lands cloaked in mist, and his glare darkened. "The morra, I meet ma fate. A stranger, a treaty, a curse. I hae power, but nae control—and it'll burn me alive."

The words hung in the frosty air, heavy as chains. The hills crouched in silence, hidin' the keep where his doom waited, a place that would ne'er be his home though they'd name it so. His stomach knotted, every nerve straining wi' the impossible fight he couldna win.

Fergus said naught, only set his blade aside an' watched wi' the steady eyes o' a man that kenned storms break whether ye wish it or nae. Tryss drew a long breath, the cold bitin' sharp in his lungs. "Let them think me bowed," he muttered, voice low as thunder on the horizon. "But this laird's nae tame beast. The storm bides its time... an' when it breaks, the MacInnes will feel its teeth."

He turned from the yard, cloak snappin' behind him, leavin' the mist an' the mornin' tae bear witness tae his vow.

Chapter Two

Alyssa

The gown didn't belong tae her. Neither did the bedchamber, the jewels, or the laird waitin' at the chapel door. But by the time the candles burned low the nicht, Alyssa MacInnes would belong tae him.

Alyssa stood in the chamber, half-laced intae a gown finer than anything she'd ever touched. The silk clung tae her skin like armour, stiff and biting, pearl-studded and unforgiving.

She drew a sharp breath, tasting the weight of what she was about tae do.

Behind her, Elsyn moved with precise, practiced grace, fastening the last row o' buttons. Every gesture was deliberate, laced wi' quiet cunning.

"Ye ken whit this means," Elsyn said, voice soft but sharp. "He expects a MacInnes. That's a' he'll ken until the vows are done."

Alyssa's eyes met hers in the glass, steady, measured. "Aye. I step into this, an' it's nae pretend. I'll be his wife. Forever."

Elsyn's lips curved faintly, calculating. "Exactly. Forever. An' I walk away free, safe. But ye... ye take the risk. Ye carry the name, the bed, the story no one else can undo."

Alyssa's jaw tightened. "I ken the danger. I ken the price. But I'll do it. For ye."

Elsyn's gaze sharpened, almost cruel. "Aye. For me. Speak the vows. Move as I would. Keep yer mouth closed, yer face steady... an' ye survive. Fail, an' it burns us both."

Alyssa let her hands brush over the stiff silk, feeling the weight press against her chest. Her pulse thudded, heavy wi' dread, but her voice stayed calm. "I'll take the vows. But mark me, Elsyn... I'm nae yours to command."

Elsyn's eyes glimmered, sharp as a blade. "Never claimed ye were mine. Only that, by the time he discovers the truth, it'll be too late tae undo whit's been done."

Alyssa turned, catchin' Elsyn's reflection in the mirror as she adjusted the fall o' her bodice. Her cousin's hand lingered low, brushin' lightly across her stomach—quick, almost unconscious—before she seemed tae realize whit she was doin' and dropped it tae her side.

"Ye look pale," Alyssa said, narrowin' her eyes. "Are ye no feelin' well?"

Elsyn's smile faltered for only a heartbeat. "Ah'm fine. Just the thought o' bein' sent off tae marry a man Ah've never met. It puts a flutter in ma stomach."

Alyssa chuckled. "Ye never get fluttery."

"Nay," Elsyn murmured, eyes droppin' briefly. "But Ah suppose... things feel different now."

A long beat passed. The fire snapped in the hearth. Wind whistled faintly beyond the stone walls. Something unsaid hung in the air between them, thick and sharp-edged.

"D'ye think a man like Tryss MacCraith would treat me kindly? He's a war hound dressed in tartan. He wants a wife wi' steel in her spine and dirt under her nails. That's no me. That's ye."

Alyssa swallowed hard. She'd heard the stories—o' blood on his blade, o' a voice like thunder and eyes that could silence a room. She imagined him towerin', all shadow and scar, and her stomach twisted.

"Elsyn, he's a laird."

"And ye're the best woman Ah ken." She smiled now, tender, like they were still girls by the burn, sharin' scraps o' bread and braidin' wildflowers intae each other's hair. "Dinnae look at this as a betrayal. Look at it as the only way either o' us gets free."

Alyssa's chest tightened, a small fire kindlin' deep inside her—defiance, raw and tremblin'. She wanted tae scream, tae refuse, tae run far frae this gilded cage. But the intensity o' Elsyn's gaze held her still, cold and unyieldin' as stone.

"And whit happens after?"

Alyssa's mouth parted, a protest on the tip o' her tongue—but it caught there, strangled by somethin' heavier than fear. She looked at Elsyn's reflection in the mirror, searchin' for the girl she'd grown up wi'. The girl who once pulled her out o' the burn when she'd fallen through the ice. Who had taken the blame for sneakin' intae the stores when it was Alyssa who had stolen the honey. Who held her hand through her mother's burial, whisperin', "Ye're no alone. Ah'm yer sister in everything but blood."

Elsyn had always been the clever one, the bold one. And Alyssa, the one who followed—loyal tae a fault.

"Ye owe me nothin'," Elsyn had whispered that day by the grave. "But Ah'll always be here. We look after each other."

That memory rose now like smoke, sharp and stingin'. And

this—this deception—was just another fire Elsyn needed savin' frae.

Alyssa's stomach twisted. Her instincts screamed tae flee. Tae rip off the gown, burst through the door, and damn the consequences. But Elsyn's eyes, dark wi' secrets and auld loyalties, pinned her in place.

The fire crackled, spittin' sparks intae the dark. The wind moaned soft through the shutters, a thin lament that seeped intae the chamber's stillness.

And still she stayed.

Beyond the stone walls, the bells would soon toll, callin' folk tae the chapel. The door would swing wide, an' the lie would be nailed fast as law. Alyssa felt each tick o' silence as though it were a hammer strikin' her chest.

Elsyn leaned close, her whisper brushin' Alyssa's ear—warm an' cold both at once. "After? Ye belong tae him."

The words coiled like iron bands. Alyssa's chest tightened, breath catchin' sharp, her panic risin' hot an' bitin' like brandished steel. Yet Elsyn's eyes—dark pools, heavy wi' secrets—never wavered. There was nae plea in them, nae regret. Only a grim certainty. This was nae jest, nae foolish scheme. 'Twas barter. A bargain struck in shadows. An' whit Elsyn had sold, she would ne'er seek tae buy back.

Alyssa's tongue stuck fast. She didna move. The weight o' it pinned her still. Somewhere deep, deeper than panic, a small spark burned—fear sharpened tae somethin' mair dangerous. For it wasna only her fate at stake. It was Elsyn's silence, Elsyn's secrets—the things left unsaid.

This wasnae choice. This wasnae will. This was surrender, dressed in Elsyn's face, an' it would damn them both.

Chapter Three

Tryss

Tryss stood rigid beneath the gray Highland sky, the stone chapel's ancient walls towering around him like silent witnesses tae his fury. The mornin' wind bit at his cheeks, but his irritation burned hotter than any cauld. He wisnae waitin' for a bride—he wis waitin' for the damn ceremony tae end. And yet, a part o' him, begrudgin' and wary, wondered whit eyes stared back at him frae beneath that veil, whit fire—or fear—might lie hidden.

The great hall at Dun Craith wis quiet save for the distant murmur o' clan folk gathered beyond the doors, their eager whispers barely reachin' the stones. Inside, flickerin' candles threw wavering shadows across the smooth wooden pews. The altar lay bare, waitin'.

He kept his gaze fixed on the entrance, fingers twitchin' at the hilt o' his sword—not that he had any thought o' drawin' it today.

Still, something in the sway o' the silk, the way the figure moved wi' measured grace, caught his attention. A flicker o' curiosity sparked, quickly smothered by impatience, yet it lingered like embers under frost. Even the faintest shift o' her breath beneath the veil made him notice, though he wouldnae admit it, a heart-beat oot o' rhythm wi' his ain. The laws o' the Highlands were ironclad: a man claimed a wife once vows were exchanged, and nae veil could hide the truth. But today, the face behind the veil was a stranger tae him, and that made the waitin' unbearable.

"Why must the wumman remain hid?" Tryss muttered under his breath, voice rough like gravel. "If she's tae be ma wife, then she should hae the courage tae meet me—not hide ahint silk an' lies."

Behind him, Fergus's calm voice broke through the haze o' his impatience. "Tradition binds us a', brither. The veil is honour, nae deceit."

Tryss snarled softly, the muscles in his jaw twitchin'. "Honour. A cruel jest."

A hush fell over the hall as the doors creaked open, and the flicker o' the veiled figure's movement caught his eye. For the briefest instant, the world narrowed: the line o' her shoulders, the tilt o' her head, the curve of her wummonly body, and something unspoken in the way she carried herself made him pause, a pulse o' curiosity threading through his controlled fury. Who was she, hidden behind silk and shadow, darin' him tae see past the ceremony and into the truth beneath?

Tryss's gaze burned into the figure wi' nothin' but fierce defiance. He would claim his bride today, aye. But this was nae marriage born o' desire. It was a battlefield, and the first strike had just been made.

Alyssa

The warm air o' the chapel pressed heavy against Alyssa's chest as she stood a hint the carved oak screen. Her heart hammered like a wild drum, each beat echoing sharp in her ears. Fingers trembling, she gripped the edges o' her cream veil, the delicate lace scratchin' soft against her flushed cheeks. She drew a quick breath, then another, shallow and ragged, as if the air itsel' were thick wi' the weight o' the lie. Her shoulders stiffened, a small shiver running through her, pricklin' her skin like sparks o' ice—but she forced herself tae step forward, one careful footfall at a time.

Through the slit in the veil, she glimpsed the room beyond—stone walls draped in clan banners, flickerin' candlelight casting long, quiverin' shadows, and the gathered crowd waitin' like silent judges. At the front, the laird stood rigid, broad and unyieldin', a fortress o' muscle an' expectation. She knew his eyes would burn through the veil, searchin' for the wumman behind it. But he would see only silk and shadow.

Still, Alyssa's breath caught. He was taller than she'd dreamed, his frame cut wi' the hard lines o' a man who'd kenned battle an' conquered it. Dark hair brushed broad shoulders, catchin' the candlelight, and his jaw—square, scarred, yet striking—spoke o' strength that could crush or protect. His hands, restin' on the hilt o' his sword, looked built for war, yet steady enough tae steady the world itself.

He was dangerous, aye—but he was handsome too, the kind o' handsome that burned, that demanded notice.

This was nae a man ye lied tae lightly. This was nae a man who forgave. An' yet, in a heartbeat, he would be hers.

Alyssa's gaze flicked up as Elsyn slipped quietly inside, eyes sharp, cold, unreadable. For a long heartbeat, their eyes met—hers wide, wild wi' fear, Elsyn's calm and calculatin'. Silent and loaded wi' threat: nae mistakes, nae betrayals. The gamble was on.

Elsyn's lips curled into a faint, almost cruel smile before she melted back into the crowd, a ghost among the flickerin' candles. Her presence lingered like smoke, clawing at Alyssa's skin.

The priest's chant rose, low and solemn, each word fillin' the chapel like lead. Alyssa drew a shudderin' breath and stepped forward. Every step toward the altar felt heavier than the last, as though the weight o' the lie pressed straight into her spine, sinkin' into her bones. Her knees trembled beneath her gown, but she forced her heels to hold, forcing her body tae obey a will that felt half hers and half Elsyn's command.

She thought o' the life waitin' beyond this moment—the freedom Elsyn promised, the danger she invited, the uncertain future tethered tae the man she was about tae claim as husband. Her stomach twisted, the air turnin' thick an' bitter. Guilt pricked sharp—what right had she tae steal a place that wasna hers? What would he think when he found out, for she kent he would? Rage, betrayal—aye. But worse still, perhaps, the cold disdain o' a laird who'd been bound tae a lie.

Her breath caught. There was still time—still the chance tae turn, tae flee, tae cast off the veil an' leave Elsyn tae face her own bargain. One step, and she could vanish frae this chamber, frae this fate.

But her feet didna move. Beneath the ache, a spark o' resolve flared, stubborn an' fierce. She drew herself straighter, the veil heavy on her shoulders like chains she'd chosen tae bear.

When the priest intoned the ancient vows, her voice wavered, caught between dread and defiance. She steadied it, slow and careful, each word a rebellion hidden behind her veil. The lace hid her trembling lips, but not the fire clawin' its way up her chest, nor the heartbeat that refused tae yield.

At the moment for the kiss, she tilted her face just so—veiled and shadowed—hopin' tae keep her secret safe in the briefest, ghost-like touch. The laird's lips brushed hers, a spark o' heat that threatened tae betray more than her eyes allowed.

Her gaze flicked again toward Elsyn in the crowd, searchin' for reassurance. But Elsyn's eyes were steel, as distant and cold as the stone walls themselves. The warning was clear: the game was nae done, and failure wouldna be forgiven.

The die was cast. And wi' it, Alyssa stepped into the storm.

Chapter Four

Tryss

Tryss stood at the altar, every nerve aflame wi' fury. The vows still rang hollow in his ears. He had just pledged his life an' honour tae a wumman he didna ken—a stranger cloaked in a veil that dared tae hide her face frae him. Every heartbeat thudded like a drum in his chest, loud an' maddening, a constant reminder that he hadna chosen this.

What kind o' laird was shackled tae a lie? What strength could his clan see in a man robbed o' his own will? The weight o' their eyes pressed heavy, a thousand judgments hidin' in the silence.

Yet a flicker o' doubt stirred, sharp an' unwelcome. His anger wasna wi' her alone—how could it be, when she was as bound tae this bargain as he? Plenty o' men had been wed by arrangement an' found peace, even happiness. Could he no do the same? Could he learn tae live wi' the stranger behind the veil?

The thought twisted in his gut, leavin' him more unsettled than the fury itself. *Mayhap, but Ahl be damned if I kiss her through that cursed veil.*

Wi' a sudden, furious motion, his hand shot out an' ripped the silk an' lace away. The chapel fell intae stunned silence, the scrape o' torn fabric hangin' thick in the cold, flickering candlelight. Every eye turned toward him, some mouths partin' in shock, some frozen wi' disbelief.

He leaned in, lips crashing hard against hers—claimin' whit was his. Fire surged through his veins, wild an' untamed, as though the gods themselves had lent him the storm in his chest. When he pulled back, the gasps that rippled through the crowd weren't only frae shock—they were confusion, disbelief, a murmur o' scandal that prickled the nape o' his neck.

A voice, sharp an' loud, cut through the murmurs like a blade.

"Alyssa!"

Tryss whipped his gaze toward the sound, eyes narrowin', every muscle taut wi' anger an' disbelief. His brow furrowed, jaw clenching as he took in the figure standing there in the crowd. *Alyssa? Nay, tis wrong.* The blood in his veins roared.

"I thocht yer name was Elsyn," he spat, voice low an' harsh, words like jagged stones. "Whit in a' that's holy is gaun on here?"

The hall sank intae deathly silence again, all eyes lockin' on the veiled wumman standing unflinching beneath the altar's stone arch. She didna falter, didna blink, and the brazenness of her defiance stoked the fire in him further.

His blood boiled, rage ignitin' like wildfire. Every oath he had ever taken, every insult he had suffered, every bone in his body demanded action. This was nae an affront tae courtesy—this was war. And Tryss MacCraith didna yield.

"This is nae weddin'—'tis a lie! A mockery! Who dares—who

dares tae steal ma name, ma honour, ma life?" His hand rested on the hilt of his sword at his hip. Every muscle, every instinct in him driving him to unsheathe it.

The murmurs erupted intae chaos as the clan gathered, shocked an' outraged. The fragile peace shattered in an instant.

Her eyes met his, steady an' unyielding. Her chin tipped a notch higher in defiance.

"I stand here by choice, by necessity. I am the one who will bear yer name."

His shoulders stiffened, every muscle coiling like a spring ready tae snap.

"Nae! Ah willna be bound by deception! This ends—here an' now!"

The hall stirred wi' murmurs, voices rising an' crashing against the stone walls. Candles flickered in wrought iron sconces, throwing jagged shadows across the elders' faces. The smell of smoke an' beeswax mingled wi' the cold bite o' wind that seeped through the high windows.

But the elders raised their voices, callin' for order. Their hands lifted, gavel-like and commanding, and the clan council was summoned immediately tae decide the fate of the marriage an' the truth hidden beneath the veil.

Tryss's chest heaved, every nerve alight wi' hope an' dread. Perhaps this was his chance—his escape from the chains forged by lies, the tangled web that had snared him wi' words an' vows not of his choosin'. He could see it: the council's judgement swingin' in his favor, the veil torn away, freedom snatched frae the jaws of deceit.

But a darker thought pricked at him. Should the council dissolve this union, the clans' delicate alliances would crumble. MacInnes loyalties might falter, auld rivals would seize the chance, an' the blood o' kin would be weighed against a single veil. His wrath sharpened—not just for himself, but for the fate o' every family who'd pay for a choice he didna make.

The chamber was thick wi' expectation. Elders leaned forward, eyes sharp an' unyielding, fingers drumming on the polished oak table. Candles guttered wi' the movement of the crowd, shadows dancing like spirits waitin' for the verdict. Elder MacInnes's hand twitched ever so slightly, the faintest sign o' doubt, and a hush slid between two cousins whisperin' at the back. Every eye seemed pinned tae him, watchin' for weakness, for rage, for the slip o' a single word.

And then—the hammer fell.

When the verdict came, it struck like iron tae his chest. The vows had been spoken. The law was clear. The marriage was binding. Every hope he'd nursed flared briefly, then shattered wi' a roar in his mind.

An elder's voice cut through the clamor, firm an' echoing in the vaulted chamber:

"The law is clear. The vows bind, no matter the veil or face behind it."

He felt the words like fire in his veins, burning disbelief an' fury alike. His jaw clenched, knuckles whitening against the edge of the council table. The hall seemed to shrink around him, the weight o' the law pressin' down, cold an' merciless. Rage, sharp as a blade, flared within him, and yet the council's authority held him in place—at least for the moment.

He drew a hard breath, nostrils flaring. Nae amount o' fury could rewrite what had been done. Nae oath, nae blow, could yet undo the chain that now bound him. And yet, Tryss MacCraith wouldna kneel quietly. The fire in him would wait, patient an' dangerous, for the hour when the scales could be tipped back in his favor.

His anger twisted intae bitter helplessness. He blinked once, slowly, as if tryin' tae shake the fire frae his chest. The war hound was caged, fists unclenching just slightly, his rage still sharp but tempered by the weight of ancient customs.

As the council dispersed, his eyes burned intae her unshaken form. The war was only beginnin'—an' this bride, this stranger, was nae easy foe.

The great hall was charged wi' silence, broken only by the low crackle of the fire in the hearth. Tryss stood near the long wooden table, the weight of the council's verdict pressin' on him like a stone.

For a heartbeat, frustrations gave way tae a hollow ache—the fear that he might never reclaim the life stolen frae him. Every muscle in his body trembled wi' it, though he forced his stance solid as stone.

She stood opposite him, calm an' unwavering, her eyes locked on his wi' a quiet challenge that cut sharper than any blade.

His voice broke the silence, rough an' jagged, carrying the weight o' every insult, every slight, every stolen choice.
"Ye dared tae stand afore ma clan an' claim ma name. D'ye ken whit ye've done? Whit ye've stolen frae me?"

Her gaze didna falter. "Ah took whit was offered, Tryss. The chance tae live. Tae survive."

The instant her voice spoke his name, somethin' inside him shattered. His breath hitched, his chest tight, like the air itself had betrayed him. Heat coursed through him, sharp an' unyieldin'.

His hands clenched intae fists so tightly his nails dug into his palms. His eyes darkened wi' storm-cloud rage, a tempest that made the hall shrink round him. For a terrifying moment, it seemed he might lose himself entirely, let the violence he barely restrained loose on the world.

He swallowed hard, fightin' the tempest rising within, muscles taut, breath jagged. His voice came out low, fierce, trembling wi' barely restrained violence.

"Dinna use ma name—no like that. Ye've nae right. No yet." *Nay, not yet. Not ever.*

She met his glare without flinchin', steady as a mountain, pulse thundering beneath calm exterior.

"I speak the truth, Tryss. Whether ye like it or no, we're bound." Her fingers curled tightly around the folds of her gown, knuckles whitening. She drew a shallow breath, steadyin' it against the tremor that threatened tae betray her own courage. "An' Ah willna be broken by yer anger."

He paced the length of the hall, boots thudding softly on stone, hands still clenched at his sides. His anger flickered wi' somethin' darker—frustration, confusion, an uneasy respect. His mind raced, thoughts jagged, a thousand scenarios crashing against one another like waves on rock.

"Survive? By weavin' a web o' lies? Ye've made enemies o' a thousand eyes an' tongues. D'ye think Ah'll accept this? That ma clan will accept this?"

She took a measured step closer, dared to step within his reach—her fingers brushing the veil as if to remind him.

"This cloth didna speak for me—I did. I stood, I vowed, an' the law binds us now, whether ye'd see me or nae."

He stopped mid-step, jaw tight, nostrils flaring. His voice dropped, edged wi' grudging admission, reluctant but honest. The lass was either verra braw or verra daft—he wasna sure which. He hoped, for her sake, it was the first.

"Ye dinna fear me?"

Her eyes sparkled, fierce as the Highland fire, unyielding.

"Fear has nae place here. Ye couldna do whit's worse than Ah've already borne."

He laughed, bitter an' harsh, the sound bouncing off stone,

echoin' like a warning.

"Ye dinna ken whit ye're walkin' intae, Alyssa."

"Then teach me," she said quiet, shoulders stiff, fingers brushin' against her sides as if bracin' herself, pulse thuddin' sharp wi' the weight o' the moment. Then, wi' renewed courage, she squared her shoulders an' met his gaze. "Or get out o' ma way."

The room seemed tae hold its breath as the two clashed—not just wi' words, but wi' the raw power of wills unyieldin'. Every eye, every shadow, seemed suspended, waitin' tae see which fire would give way first. The air was thick, almost cracklin' wi' the unspoken challenge, the heat o' defiance pressin' against stone walls and flickerin' candlelight.

He let out a harsh breath, nostrils flaring, eyes narrowin' for a heartbeat as if measurin' the force before him. Then, wi' a low, grudging rumble, he drew her name out slow, dangerous:

"Alyssa... that's yer name? Alyssa..." His voice was low, rough, each syllable deliberate, heavy wi' threat. "Ye're a storm, an' Ah'll nae doubt ye'll try tae stand against me—but mark me well... Ah'll be the one tae break ye, if ye push too far."

Her eyes flared, bright an' steady, lips tight wi' defiance, pulse thrummin' wi' the force o' her will.

"Ah'll nae break," she said, voice low but unyielding.

He studied her for a heartbeat, a ghost o' a smile tuggin' at his mouth, eyes glintin' wi' challenge.

"Then we'll see, Alyssa. Bend too much... an' fire dies, even in the heart o' a storm."

The silence that followed was thick, charged wi' unspoken war and the beginnings o' respect. Even the shadows seemed tae lean closer, watchin' the storm of wills, knowin' neither would yield easily.

CHAPTER FIVE

Tryss

WRATH HAS A WAY o' wearin' a man doon. Not this yin.

Tryss stormed oot o' the great hall, boots poundin' the cold stone floor like thunder. The iron-bound doors slammed behind him, a final punctuation tae the chaos left inside. The chill Highland air bit at his face, sharp an' clean, but didna dull the heat thrummin' through his veins. Every step rang wi' questions he hadna answers for: *Whit in the gods' name just happened? How could she stand there, claimin' ma name, wi' nae a flicker o' fear?*

He didna stop till he reached the trainin' yard. A handful o' warriors sparred beneath the pale mornin' sun. The clash o' steel rang sharp in the air, but their movements froze when they caught sight o' him. Tryss's jaw clenched, a low hum of frustration coil'n deep in his chest. .

Without a word, he drew his sword wi' a hiss, steppin' into the circle like a predator claimin' its ground. Every muscle coiled, every nerve taut. His eyes flicked over the men around him, but saw only the blur o' the morning, the echo o' vows spoken, the weight o' the veil still pressin' against his memory. *Whit kind o' man doesna break at such betrayal?* he thought, but even as the question formed, he knew there would be nae answer, nae respite in thought alone.

Tryss's opponent—a broad-shouldered man wi' a squared jaw and steady stance—stepped forward, meetin' his gaze. The man braced, muscles coiled like steel springs. Tryss didna hesitate.

Steel bit steel wi' a scream, ringin' sharp through the frosty air. Dirt spattered, frost kicked up under churnin' boots, breath hissin' and cloudin' in ragged puffs. Each strike tore through the cold like fire, too fast, too savage, too alive tae be tamed by form or rhythm. Every hit drove the man backward, sparks flyin' off the blades, teeth grit against the chill.

A few of the other warriors froze mid-spar, eyes wide, grips tightening on hilts. One let out a soft, startled hiss; another's hand hovered above his weapon, hesitatin', pulse jumping at the storm Tryss had become. Even seasoned men shifted uneasily, leaning just slightly back as if the heat of his fury might singe them from afar.

A flicker o' her face—veiled, stubborn, unyieldin'—stung behind his eyes. He shoved it down, pushin' harder, every swing laced wi' the fire she had lit in him, the betrayal burnin' in his gut and fists alike.

Fergus stayed silent, eyes narrowin', body calm as stone. Lines deepened round his eyes, studyin' Tryss like a man who knew the violence o' a storm couldna be tamed by talk. Sometimes a man had tae bleed his fury oot before reason could reach him.

Tryss surged wi' reckless ferocity, arms and shoulders drivin' like hammers, the motion unyieldin', unstoppable. His body was fire and steel, each flurry a message o' the rage that no words could touch. Wi' a final, brutal twist, he splintered the guard and drove the tip o' his sword upward, haltin' just shy o' the man's jugular. The yard held its breath, the echo o' steel and intent hangin' thick in the air.

The yard went still. Only his ragged breathin' cut through the frozen air. He held the moment, clingin' tae it like the last thing he could command. Fingers ached round the hilt—not from battle, but from the desperate need tae grip somethin' still his.

Slowly, he stepped back, muscles still taut, blade lowering like it weighed a ton o' iron. The fighter gave a tight nod, shiverin', breath ragged, eyes avoidin' his, and stepped away, shaken tae the bone.

Tryss's chest heaved, every inhale a hiss, every exhale a growl. Sweat prickled at his temples, cold air stingin' against the heat that refused tae fade.

His gaze flicked up—and there was Fergus, still, silent, eyes sharp as blades, takin' measure o' him.

Always there. Always waitin'.

Tryss felt the familiar coil in his gut tighten. He didna need Fergus tae move; he knew what was comin' before a single step was taken, before a word was spoken. The man had always been the calm eye in the storm, the one who let a man bleed oot the fire inside before it could burn anythin' else.

"Ye done scarin' the men then?" Fergus asked, voice low and steady—his meaning impossible to miss.

Tryss didna answer. He just raised his sword again and pointed it at him. His chest heaved with the force o' a man caged by his own rage, every muscle strung tight as a bow. The edge in his eyes was darker than fury alone—it was hurt, betrayal, and the bone-deep ache o' a man who no longer knew where tae place his trust.

Fergus didna flinch. "Ye want a real fight?" He uncrossed his arms, steppin' into the circle like a man who'd seen the storm before and wasna afraid o' it.

Tryss's gut tightened. He wanted it—needed the clash o' steel tae carry the fire burnin' in his chest—but every fiber o' him groaned wi' exhaustion he didna yet admit. His shoulders ached, each strike singin' through muscles stiff wi' tension. Sweat ran down his temple, drippin' into his eyes, stingin' sharp, but he didna falter.

Their blades met wi' a shiver o' steel, ringing loud and cruel against the frozen morning air. This wasna chaos—nae flailing, nae reckless fury—but clean, precise, each strike demanding all the strength he could muster. Fergus moved like he knew exactly what Tryss needed: not victory, not pain, but a channel for the fire he couldna yet name.

Fergus gave him nae quarter. Each swing bit deep, unforgivin', heavy wi' truth. Tryss felt it in his bones—every block, every counter, a reminder o' the storm in him that nae amount o' force could douse. His arms trembled, fists slick wi' sweat, muscles knotting and aching wi' effort. The cold bit at his skin, but it didna matter; the heat in his veins drowned out frost.

He drove his opponent back wi' raw, reckless force, body movin' like wildfire even as his legs threatened tae buckle and his lungs burned. He sought relief, release, a fleeting sense o' control—but the steel, the rhythm, the weight o' his own fury, pressed on him harder than any foe.

Each clash hammered a truth he didna want tae face; each block reminded him that fury alone couldna undo what had been done. His breath came ragged, nostrils flaring, chest heaving like it would split from the strain, yet still he pressed on—muscles screaming, sweat dripping, heart pounding, every nerve aflame.

Finally, their blades locked, faces inches apart. Tryss held the final pose, chest heaving, sweat pricklin' at his brow. For a heartbeat, his fury faltered—a fleeting weakness he almost didna acknowledge—before he straightened again, shoulders rigid, lettin' the illusion o' control mask the exhaustion clawin' at his muscles. He lowered the blade, chest heaving. A quiver ran through his arms, from the sheer weight o' fury spent.

Tryss's voice came rough and low. "This isna fixin' it."

Fergus met his gaze. Calm. Steady. "It's no meant tae."

Tryss shoved off, breath ragged, boots scraping stone an' dirt. His chest heaved, muscles taut an' trembling wi' the aftershock o' the fight. "Blast it all!" he roared, the words tearing frae his chest, carried off by the wind, each syllable a hammer against the walls. "Nae oath, nae steel, nae law can set this right!"

He turned frae the circle, storm still alive in every fiber—shoulders stiff, arms aching, sweat drippin' down his spine, pulse drumming like a war drum. And still, it didnahin'—rage couldna undo vows, couldna reclaim what had been taken from him.

He sheathed his sword wi' a slow, deliberate motion, fingers raw from the hilt, knuckles white. Boots thudded against packed earth, each step a drumbeat o' frustration an' despair.

Alyssa

Alyssa stood near the hearth, its flickerin' firelight castin' long, restless shadows across her face. The warmth did little tae ease the chill burrowed beneath her skin. Her fingers twitched at her side, betrayin' the steady voice she forced.

Before her loomed Lord Callum MacInnes—her uncle, Elsyn's father—his jaw set like stone, eyes burnin' with cold fury.

"You have brought ruin upon my house," he said, low and lethal. "Do ye think this deception will go unanswered? Do ye even understand the storm ye've invited?"

Alyssa held his gaze, spine straight though her knees ached from standin' too long. "I did whit I had tae do. There was nae other way."

His hands clenched at his sides, thick fingers curlin' into fists. "No other way? Ye risked the honor o' our name—for yersel'."

"For Elsyn," she corrected, her voice quiet but firm. "Ye ken as weel as I do, she ne'er intended tae follow through."

His expression twisted, equal parts disgust and reluctant truth.

"You stand on the edge o' a blade, girl," he growled. "One wrong move, and ye'll be cast out with nothin' but shame. Do not mistake yer current status for safety. Ye are a pawn wi' nae title, nae land, and nae shield but the man ye tricked."

Alyssa's jaw tightened, but she didna waver. "Then I will bear that burden. If it means survival, I will carry it alone."

Callum stared at her for a long moment. Then somethin' shifted—just slightly—in his expression. Less rage, more... recognition.

"Reckless," he muttered. "Foolish. But perhaps..." His eyes narrowed. "Perhaps there is more steel in ye than I gave ye credit for."

He turned on his heel and stalked away, leaving only the crackle o' fire and the weight o' his judgment behind.

A hand touched her arm—gentle, groundin'. Alyssa turned and met the calm, lined gaze o' her aunt, Lady Morag MacInnes.

"Come," the older woman said softly. "There's somethin' ye

need tae see."

Lady Morag led her through the dim corridors, cloaked wi' shadows and whispers, to a tall window overlookin' the training yard. The flickerin' torches outside threw long, restless shadows across the stone courtyard.

Alyssa pressed close tae the glass. Her breath caught. Her fingers twitched against the window frame, pulse racin' at the raw force she'd married.

Below, Tryss stormed among the warriors, his boots poundin' the earth like thunder. His sword flashed in the firelight, each strike driven by raw, burnin' fury. His face was a storm—tight jaw, fierce eyes blazin' wi' betrayal and rage.

The warriors dared nae meet his gaze, steppin' back as he unleashed his wrath on the nearest opponent.

Alyssa's breath caught. The man she'd married was a tempest, a force o' nature far wilder than she'd imagined.

Lady Morag's voice came low, steady beside her.

"This is the man ye married. A man forged in fire and battle. His anger is fierce, and his temper quick. Ye will face nights where his fury burns hotter than any hearth. His words will cut deeper than blades. Ye must be ready."

Alyssa whispered, "Hou can I stand against that?"

Morag's gaze held hers. "By findin' yer own fire."

They stepped away from the window into a shadowed alcove tucked behind a massive tapestry. The murmur o' clan voices faded behind them, replaced by the quiet hush o' stone walls.

Lady Morag turned to face her fully. Her gaze softened just for a moment, as if rememberin' somethin' far away.

"I ken the lass, sharp an' clever, nae one's fool. This... tis her doing, through an' through." She let her gaze linger on the hall, measuring the weight of the clans' eyes, before letting out a faint, deliberate sigh. "But mark me—just because tis her plot, dinna think it bears nae benefit tae those who see it through wisely." Her lips pressed thin, a glimmer of something more behind the words—ambition, careful an' quiet, like a blade hidden in velvet. "Ye didna ask for it... but nae one can say how the winds might shift in yer favor if ye hold steady."

Her eyes met Alyssa's, steady and knowin'.

"Elsyn has her own shadows tae wrestle wi'—things she keeps locked away, even from those she loves. Ye took a path she couldna walk, and that choice has placed ye both in peril."

Lady Morag's voice dropped tae a whisper. "Yer loyalty tae her is a fierce thing, but remember—this is yer life now. Ye must find yer own strength tae face the storm ahead."

She reached out, layin' a gentle hand on Alyssa's arm. "I see the fire in ye, child. Dinna let it be consumed by another's flame."

Alyssa swallowed hard, the weight settlin' like a stone in her chest.

"Ye married a MacCraith," Morag continued, voice low and deliberate. "Not just any Highland laird, but that one. Tryss is nae soft man. He was born in blood and forged in fire. His temper is a blade honed on betrayal."

Alyssa nodded, her chin liftin' wi' a flicker o' determination.

"I've seen that look in his eyes," Morag said. "Fury and pride. He'll not forget this slight. Not soon. He'll test ye. Push ye. He may try tae break ye."

"I willna let him." Alyssa whispered.

"Good." Morag's nod was slow, certain. "Because in the Highlands, a wife is as much a warrior as any man. Ye will fight every day for yer place. Wi' yer words. Wi' yer silence. Wi' yer spine."

"I've been fightin' all ma life." Alyssa's voice was barely a whisper.

Morag's gaze softened, and for a heartbeat, the hard lines of her face eased. She saw it then—the grit, the weariness, the weight o' a life spent on survival. Even within her own halls, she knew the girl hadna had it easy.

"Aye... I ken it's been hard for ye," Morag admitted, her voice low but steady, carrying both understanding and quiet respect. "But dinna stop now."

Fergus

The clang o' steel still hummed faintly in Fergus's ears as he sheathed his sword, the sharp scent o' sweat and churned earth clinging to him like a second skin. Tryss's fury had been a torrent unleashed, a force nae man could hope tae hold back—not even his closest brother. Every blow, every flurry had carried fire, pain, and raw defiance, and Fergus felt the echo o' it deep in his bones.

Fergus didna call after him. Just watched him move, body heaving, coat tugged by the wind, shoulders tight wi' all the wrath even steel hadna bled dry.

Always the calm tae Tryss's storm—but never had the storm burned so fierce. Concern pricked at him; he hadna seen this fury since Tryss was a lad. So he let him go.

He wiped a thin sheen o' sweat from his brow and let his gaze drift toward the castle's tall windows. There, bathed in the flickerin' glow of firelight, stood the veiled woman. Pale, aye, but steady, watching the yard below. Fergus didna ken her, and yet he could see the ripple she'd left in Tryss—a storm unsettled, unpredictable.

She watches him, aye, like she's tryin' tae reckon the heart o' a storm—or maybe she's the cause of it. But Fergus knew better.

Tryss didna bend for anyone, nor would he. The man would tear the world apart before he let it shape him, and Fergus's chest tightened wi' quiet worry.

The weight o' it pressed on him—the fire still cracklin' in Tryss's limbs, the raw, unspent wrath still simmerin' under the surface. He had seen the storm many times, but never like this. A stranger had stirred him, shaken the balance, and Fergus knew the consequences wouldnae be small.

He let out a slow breath, letting the tension ease just enough to take stock. Tryss was alive, unbroken, but barely. The man's fury had been spent, but he wouldnae stay caged long. And Fergus—best friend, witness, brother—could do nothing but watch and wait.

His gaze drifted inward, tae years past—the long, harsh winters, the battles they'd fought side by side, the times Fergus had pulled Tryss back from the edge o' ruin. They weren't born brothers by blood, but by fire and loyalty forged in the darkest moments.

Tryss had always been the harder man tae reach, the one whose temper could turn a feast into a battlefield. Yet Fergus had been his anchor—the quiet presence who stood firm when the world threatened tae tear them apart.

I've seen him broke, aye, an' I've seen him stand unyieldin' as stone. I've fought at his side, blade in hand, bled wi' him in the dirt an' the rain. He bears the weight o' it all, an' still he willnae bend. A man like that... ye cannae help but give him yer respect, though it near kills ye tae watch him bear it alone.

A sharp breath pulled Fergus back tae the present. Tryss had vanished toward the stables, his back stiff wi' pain and fury.

Fergus's voice dropped low, almost a whisper meant only for himself. "He needs time. An' she'll need steel in her spine if she's tae stand beside him."

Alyssa shifted at the window, her breath foggin' the glass. Fergus's chest tightened—for her, aye, but more for the man below. Two strangers caught in a cruel twist o' fate, and the weight o' it hung heavy in the yard.

He paused—should he speak? Offer counsel, warning, some bridge between the chaos and reason? But the creak o' leather, the distant drum o' hoofbeats, reminded him the world moved on, even when storms raged.

Wi' a final glance toward the window, Fergus squared his shoulders. Tryss walks a lonely path the night, aye—but I'll follow him, aye, step for step, till he kens he's nae alone.

Some bonds, forged beyond blood, forged in fire and fury, demand loyalty that words can never honor—but action will.

As the fading light dimmed outside, Fergus cast one last glance toward the great hall where the feast awaited—but his thoughts stayed fixed on Tryss, whose fire still burned fierce and untamed. Without hesitation, Fergus pushed open the doors o' the stables and stepped inside, followin' the inferno that was his friend.

The doors o' the stables groaned as Fergus pushed them open, steppin' into the cool, dim space thick wi' the earthy scent o' hay and horses. Tryss stood near his favored mount, shoulders hunched, fists clenched tight around the saddle horn, his rage barely restrained.

Fergus stepped forward, voice calm. "Ye're nae fool, Tryss. Ye carry the weight o' a laird—and I ken well it's nae light a burden tae bear."

Tryss's jaw ticked tighter. "They ca' her ma bride—but I dinna ken wha she is, or whit she wants."

"She stands wi' ye now, dinna she?" Fergus said quietly.

Tryss's eyes snapped wi' fire. "Wi' me? She stands again' me." Without warnin', he grabbed Fergus's shirt collar, yankin' him close. His voice was a low growl, edged wi' raw fury. "Ye think she deserves yer respect? Ye think I should trust her?"

Fergus's expression never changed—calm, unshaken. "I ken ye, Tryss. An' I ken anger like yours can burn a man doon if he lets it."

Tryss's grip slackened. "Gah!" and he shoved Fergus away, voice sharp as stone. "I'm nae done wi' this yet."

He turned and stomped away, boots thundering against the stone floor.

Fergus watched him go, eyes steady and knowin'. The fire in Tryss's chest still raged—but it was nae longer a danger tae anyone but himself.

The great hall awaited, its walls hummin' wi' anticipation. The wedding feast was about tae begin, but Tryss's storm had not yet passed.

Chapter Six

Alyssa

THE FEAST BLAZED WI' laughter an' music, but at the head table, the air was thick wi' smoke, silence, an' fury.

Alyssa sat beside Tryss, the rich colors o' MacCraith tartan draped behind them like a curtain o' fate. Trenchers overflowed wi' roasted meat, spiced apples, an' barley stews, but neither o' them touched the food. They sat like statues, carved frae stubborn pride.

He hadna looked at her since they entered, his gaze sweepin' walls, torches, an' the gathered men—but never her.

He spoke tae nae one unless forced, drank heavily when a toast was raised, an' ignored her wi' such precise malice it was near impressive. He was stone an' steel—like a dam under pressure, seconds frae burstin'.

She refused tae be cowed. Her spine was a steel rod, shoulders squared as though she bore a crown o' her ain. Her mouth was set in the faintest curve o' a smile—not mockin', but calm, resolute, as if darin' ony tae test her resolve. The firelight caught in her eyes, unblinkn', unyieldin', an' for a heartbeat she looked less like a lass cornered an' mair like a queen holdin' court.

She sipped her wine when he did. Turned her head when he refused tae look at her. An' when the music swelled an' laughter rippled through the hall, she even smiled—for the benefit o' the crowd, nae him.

But the Highlanders were nae fools. They watched every breath atween the newlyweds, waitin' for the next spark.

It came wi' cruel inevitability.

A voice rose frae the lower tables, rough an' eager:
"A kiss for the bride!"

Laughter erupted. Then another cheer:
"Aye! Let's see if she can tame the war hound!"

Tryss's knuckles tightened round the goblet, the iron ring o' his grip sharp against the wood. She felt the tension roll aff him, subtle at first, then gatherin', coilin', like a blade slidin' free o' its sheath. The air seemed tae shift wi' it, a taut thread stretchin' thinner wi' every heartbeat. She turned her head just enough tae glance at him—calm, steady, unflinchin'—her presence beside him a quiet refusal tae yield.

He moved then, slow an' deliberate, his shoulders squarin' as though he bore the weight o' every eye upon him. The scrape o' the bench legs echoed like thunder in the stillness. One by one, voices faltered, the laughter died, till only the low crackle o' the fire dared tae speak. The hall quieted.

His voice was low, just for her.
"Ye wanted this," he growled. "Let them see it."

Then he seized her mouth wi' his ain.

It wasna a kiss. It was a warnin', a storm wrapped in flesh. His mouth struck hers wi' the force o' a reprimand—punishin', furious, meant tae silence an' shame.

Each motion sharp, demandin' submission, darin' her tae falter. But Alyssa didna flinch. She didna yield. Her lips met his wi' equal fire—not soft, not yieldin', but hard an' unrelentin', an assertion that she was neither broken nor afeart.

The world narrowed tae the clash o' their mouths, the heat o' the fire behind them, the tension in his body, an' the grit o' her determination. He pulled back first, a blink o' surprise flashin' across his features, as if the sheer force o' her defiance had knocked him off balance. For a moment, the hall—the men, the torches, the silence—ceased tae exist. Only the raw, undeniable truth o' her courage an' his fury remained.

She hadna crumbled.

She smiled at him—faint, defiant. Then sat doon, composed an' unbothered.

The crowd roared wi' laughter an' approval, satisfied.

But atween bride an' groom, a different war had begun. One nae fought wi' blades—but wi' breath, an' will, an' the refusal tae yield.

Tryss

He kent it was comin'. It was expected. It was tradition.

The weddin' feast would end, the toasts would fade, an' he'd be required tae take his bride tae his bed.

The thought festered like rot in his gut.

It wasna that she was horse-faced—far frae it. When he'd torn the veil frae her face, he'd been momentarily staggered. Raven-black hair framed skin like cream, an' those eyes—deep, violet, far too knowin'—had stared up at him like she already understood what kind o' man he was. A wee bit slender for

Highland tastes, perhaps, but there was cushion where it counted. He'd noticed, despite himself. Against his better judgment, a pull stirred—a flicker he didna welcome, a heat he couldnae name. He shoved it down. He was angry, nae blind.

But it was the lie.

The damned, deliberate deception that curdled every thought he had aboot her. A weddin' built on treachery was nae marriage at all, an' Tryss MacCraith was many things—but dishonorable wasna one o' them.

An' yet here he was. Bound by law. By clan. By oaths spoken afore God.

The feast blurred round him, colors an' noise lost beneath the churn o' his thoughts. He could feel her beside him, feel her heat like a brand. She hadna backed doon. Not in the chapel, nae at the council, nae at the table.

She kissed him back.

He hadna expected that. Not wi' fire. Not wi' pride. It took every ounce o' control nae tae shove her away—because he feared the way his chest ached at the taste o' defiance.

He dragged a hand across his mouth an' doon his jaw, muscles tight as steel. His life had been aboot control, war, an' loyalty—but this woman had cracked somethin' inside him, an' he hated it.

Honor demanded he fulfill his role. He could nae mair refuse tae bed his wife than he could walk away frae his title. The folk had seen the vows, the kiss. If he didna consummate the union, the questions would come—first whispered, then shouted.

His faither had once warned him: a man who canna trust his wife will never sleep easy in his ain bed. That warnin' echoed noo, low an' gnawin'.

He was cornered.

When the time came, he would bed her. There was nae other

path. But it would be out o' duty. Not desire.

Not until she earned the truth o' his name.

Alyssa

She had never felt sae acutely aware o' her body—o' how close she sat tae a man who radiated fury like a furnace. He hadna spoken tae her since the kiss. Not a word. Not a glance. Yet his presence was a storm pressin' against her skin, pullin' at her spine.

She needed tae prepare.

Not just for the expected intimacy—though that alone made her stomach knot—but for the sheer force o' the man who would come tae her bed. She needed a moment alane, tae catch her breath, tae find her footing afore steppin' intae the fire again.

But tradition demanded his leave.

She swallowed an' turned toward him, gatherin' the tatters o' her courage.

"Try—" she began, but caught herself. No. Not noo. Not here. Not wi' him already sae close tae snappin'.

"Laird, if ye would be sae kind," she said, voice even, respectful but clear, "please announce my departure. I'd like time tae prepare for the rest o' our evenin'."

He didna respond.

His eyes stared forward, unfocused, the tick in his jaw jumping, caught in whatever dark thoughts clutched at him. She could feel the pressure o' his silence—the restraint, the fury, the conflict.

Her fingers hesitated, then reached across the table an' laid gently atop his.

It was like touchin' a coiled beast. She rested her hand

there—silent, deliberate, a quiet defiance in a world that expected her tae lower her eyes.

"I'd like tae be ready," she repeated, softer this time.

His eyes flicked doon tae her hand, then slowly up tae her face. His gaze burned—but it wasna his fire that singed her. It was the sheer force o' will held barely in check. His teeth ground, muscles tight as steel... an' yet a flicker o' fatigue crossed his shoulders, unnoticed by all but her.

Without breakin' eye contact, he stood.

The hall fell intae curious silence.

"My wife," he said, voice clipped an' cold, "will take her leave tae prepare."

He didna touch her. Didna offer a hand or even a glance once the words were spoken. But she stood all the same, spine straight, chin high.

The weight o' a hundred eyes followed her as she left the table—not as a liar, not as an imposter, but as the wife o' a laird.

Her palms were damp beneath her sleeves, but her spine stayed straight. If he wanted a show o' strength, she'd give him one.

An' if her legs trembled slightly beneath her gown, nae one needed tae know.

He remained seated, jaw clenched, starin' at the place she'd stood. Tonight, duty would be done—but the cost o' defiance had only begun. If she thought she'd warmed his bed without consequence, she'd mistaken firelight for flame.

Chapter Seven

Tryss

SHE DIDNA FALTER. NOT once.

Tryss watched Alyssa's figure retreat frae the hall, her head held high, every step measured like she owned the MacCraith tartan wrapped aboot her shoulders. The firelight caught in her hair, dark and gleaming, sharp as a blade—and damn her, that steadiness unsettled him more than ony insult, ony slight, ony blow ever could.

His hands clenched intae fists beneath the table, nails bitin' into his palms. Victory should taste sweeter, but all he felt was a knot tighten' in his gut—anger tangled wi' somethin' raw an' unfamiliar. Respect. Admiration. A spark he didna care tae name.

She'd kissed him back.

Wi' fire.

Wi' defiance.

Wi' a certainty that dared him tae break first.

Her strength... her steel... it mirrored his own, in ways that made him uneasy. She held herself like a warrior, like a queen, like a woman who couldnae be cowered by threats, by custom, by a man bred tae command. Every measured step, every set jaw, every blink unwavering in the firelight—it was a challenge, subtle and deliberate, and it drew him in whether he liked it or no.

What kind o' firebrand was this, who could stand before him, match his storm, and not waver? What fire would she bring tae his keep? Would she forge it stronger, or burn it tae ash? His mind churned wi' questions he hadna dared ask any woman before—questions born of awe, respect, and a grudgin' fear o' what she might make him feel.

He let out a bitter laugh, low an' sharp as steel scrapin' stone. It wasna pride that stirred beneath his skin—it was wariness. She was a storm unleashed in borrowed silk, an' he was a man bred tae tame storms. Yet for the first time, he wondered if some storms were meant tae run wild—and if he was willing tae watch, to learn, or tae be undone by one.

The hall's noise swelled again—laughter, toasts, the clang o' cups—but Tryss heard none o' it. His world had shrunk tae the weight o' the comin' night. The weddin' bed loomed like a shadow at the edge o' his mind, twistin' his thoughts wi' dread.

His faither's warnin' flickered in the back o' his mind, faint an' fragmented: "A man wha cannae trust his wife'll ne'er sleep easy in his ain bed." The memory wasna a comfort—it was a challenge.

Tryss rose abruptly, muscles coiled tight beneath his fur-lined cloak. He needed control. He needed certainty. But all he had was this lie, this bindin' oath spoken under false pretenses.

Tonight, he would face the impossible.

He would take his wife tae his bed.

An' may the gods have mercy on them both.

Alyssa

The great doors thudded shut behind her, muffling the din o' laughter an' music that still spilled frae the great hall. Her steps were steady as she climbed the stone stairs, every inch the poised bride who had just stared doon a warlord's fury—and lived. But once she reached the landing, her knees trembled beneath the weight o' the borrowed gown an' the night's unbearable heat.

She pressed her back against the cold wall, the rough stone bitin' into her skin—an unyieldin' reminder that nae matter how fine the silk, this was still a cage. Whit have I gotten myself intae? The thought flickered, sharp an' unwelcome. A rush o' doubt clawed at her resolve, whisperin' o' failure, o' the man's wrath she'd seen in his eyes. Can I really survive this?

She swallowed hard, the poundin' in her chest threatenin' tae betray her. But I won't show it. Not here. Not noo.

Inhaling slowly, she willed herself steady. *Ye can do this. Elsyn's plan will carry ye through.* Though the lie tasted bitter on her tongue.

But the knot o' nerves tightened with every breath.

The weddin' feast had been a battlefield, an' though she'd stood tall, the war was far frae over. Her mind flicked tae the looming hours ahead—the marriage bed, the man whose eyes still burned wi' fury an' somethin' she dared nae name.

She needed air.

Fresh, sharp Highland air.

Descendin' quickly, she slipped through a side door leadin' outside, the cool night wrappin' around her like a cloak. The stars above glittered cold an' distant, but here—beneath the vast Highland sky—she found a fragile kind o' peace.

The restless whinnies an' shiftin' hooves frae the stables drew her forward, their impatient energy strangely comfortin'. Horses did nae judge. Horses did nae lie. Their steady breathin' an' soft snorts soothed her ragged nerves.

She pressed a palm against the rough stable door, feelin' the warmth o' the animals inside. Just a moment, she thought. Just enough tae catch her breath afore steppin' intae the fire again.

But then a shadow moved in the flickerin' lantern light—familiar, brooding.

Tryss stepped out frae the darkness, his stride echoing against the stone floor. His eyes locked on hers, blazin' wi' a fury that crackled like wildfire.

Without a word, he closed the distance between them in long, thunderous strides.

His hands closed around her upper arms like steel clamps, fingers diggin' through the thin silk, rattlin' her tae the bone. Her heartbeat thundered in her ears, wild an' erratic, matchin' the ragged rhythm o' his breath, which came in sharp, angry bursts against her cheek.

Muscles coiled beneath his grip, tense as drawn bowstrings, an' she could feel the raw power tremblin' through his arms, the furious heat radiatin' off his body. The scent o' leather, sweat, an' the faintest hint o' pine smoke clung tae him, overwhelm'g her senses.

For a terrifyin' moment, she feared the storm within him would spill over.

Then, his voice tore through the tension—harsh, desperate, demandin' answers.

"Alyssa," he snarled, voice rough an' low, "whit in a' the gods' names are ye daein' here?"

Before she could answer, his hands gripped her upper arms like iron bands. The strength behind the grasp was unyieldin', shakin' her—not cruelly, but wi' a harshness meant tae wrench her frae whatever calm she'd summoned.

His breath was hot against her face, words tumblin' out in ragged bursts.

"Ye stand beside me, bound by vows ye dared tae steal—yet ye wander aff like ye own nae part o' this marriage! Now that ye've got me, tell me—d'ye even ken whit tae dae wi' a man like me?"

She met his glare, defiance flickerin' in her violet eyes. "I ken enough tae survive. That's whit I've been doin' since the day I was born."

He let out a bitter laugh, a sound without humor. "Survive, eh? Ye think survivin' is enough tae keep ye safe in my halls? Ye've played a dangerous game, lass."

She straightened beneath his grip, refusin' tae back doon.

"Better tae face the fire head-on than be burned alive in silence."

He shook his head, voice low an' cold as steel. "Ye've made yer bed, lass. Now ye'll burn in it—God help us baith."

Chapter Eight

Alyssa

ALYSSA STOOD ALONE BENEATH the Highland sky, the night pressing cold through her gown. Laughter still echoed faint behind her, muffled by stone, but here there was only her breath and the relentless pound of her heart.

She wasna afraid o' Tryss. Oh, he was angry enough—beautifully angry, if she was honest. But it was what came next that made her chest tighten. To endure the night without losin' herself... without yieldin' to a man who might give her everything but his heart.

Her hand brushed her bodice. Beneath the lace, the scar. A whip's mark meant for Elsyn, borne on her shoulder instead. Proof that even as a lass she had chosen tae carry more than her share. She hadnae flinched then. She wouldnae flinch now.

Still, her fingers trembled. Still, her mouth was dry.

Elsyn's voice echoed: *"Hold yer ground till he sees the truth o' ye.*"But so far, the only truth Tryss kenned was that she was a liar an' thief o' his name.

But she did ken men like him didna respect weakness. If he was goin' tae touch her tonight—if he was goin' tae take her—it would be wi' the knowledge that she wasna some pawn tae be moved across a board.

She would meet him as an equal, or not at all.

He would nae break her. If he touched her tonight, it would be as an equal—or not at all.

The stable door creaked. Memory of his grip, his anger, still lingered on her skin. Yet he had not hurt her—only faltered, as if uncertain whit tae do wi' her fire.

Lifting her chin, she turned toward the manor. Whatever storm waited on the other side, she would face it head-on.

Just as she always had.

Tryss

He stood like a statue at the center o' his chambers, fists clenched at his sides, breath too shallow, too fast. The fire in the hearth roared unchecked, castin' wild shadows across the stone walls. It felt too hot in here—too close. Like the night itsel' was pressin' doon on him, demandin' a decision he wasn't ready tae make.

Fergus leaned against the doorframe, arms crossed, eyes narrowed in that maddeningly calm way o' his.

"You're lookin' more like a storm than a laird."

His jaw tightened until the muscles twitched beneath his skin. His eyes narrowed, sharp an' cold, fixin' Fergus wi' a silence that said more than any words. "Aren't Ah?"

Fergus shrugged. "Depends. D'ye mean tae kill her? Or just scare the wits oot o' her for breathin' yer air?"

He turned away, pacin' tae the window an' back again. "She lied tae me, Fergus. Lied tae a' o' us."

"Aye, she did, an' we dinna ken yet why. Whate'er the reason was, she's yer wife noo," Fergus replied, voice sharp. "Which means she's yer responsibility as well."

"Dinna need remindin'." He ran a hand through his hair, jaw clenched tight. "Every step she takes feels like a challenge. Every word, a test."

"Aye, an' maybe it is," Fergus said, pushin' off the doorframe an' steppin' inta the room. "But ye're the one wi' all the power now. If ye walk inta that room breathin' fire, ye'll only prove her right tae fear ye."

Tryss stopped cold. "She disnae fear me."

Fergus raised a brow. "Na? Then why was she oot there alone, shakin' in her boots afore she'd even crossed the threshold tae yer bed?"

Tryss's hands twitched. Aye, there was gentleness in him—he kent it, though few ever saw it—but just now the anger raged too hot, smotherin' every softer thought. Fury was the armor he kenned best. Still, Fergus's words cut close, stirrin' a hesitation he didna want tae claim.

"Ah'm no soft," he muttered.

"Na," Fergus said. "Ye're no. But ye are a man who disnae want tae spend the rest o' yer life bein' hated by the woman who shares yer bed."

Tryss exhaled sharply, tension bleedin' aff him in gusts. "Ah did na ask for any o' this."

Fergus's voice lowered, firm but not unkind.

"Maybe she chose the lie, but she's still walkin' intae yer fire, same as ye."

Silence pressed in, thick wi' unspoken words.

Fergus softened, his voice quieter now.

"She's in yer keepin', lad. Whate'er she's done—whate'er she is—ye still hae a choice. Ye can take her like a brute an' make her dread every nicht that follows... or ye can show her exactly who ye really are, a man o' honour. Dinnae go tae her bed angry."

Tryss stared into the fire. Somewhere beneath the fury was a sliver o' somethin' else—shame, perhaps. Or hope. He wasn't sure which terrified him more.

Fergus turned tae go, pausin' at the door.

"She's waitin'."

When Tryss looked up, the room was empty.
An' he was alone wi' the fire.

Chapter Nine

Alyssa

THE DOOR CREAKED OPEN—SOFT, deliberate. Tryss stepped inside, his presence fillin' the room like a gatherin' storm. He moved without haste, each step measured an' controlled. Then, wi' a quiet click that sliced through the stillness, he turned an' locked the door behind him.

The air shifted, thickening wi' unspoken threat. His anger simmered just beneath the surface, taut an' contained, like a blade held at the ready.

Alyssa's breath caught, her heart quickenin' as the weight o' his silence pressed doon on her. This was no reckless outburst; it was a cold, calculated warnin'.

The faint scent o' pine an' cold stone lingered in the air. The room felt smaller somehow, the shadows deepenin' in the flickerin' candlelight.

No turnin' back now.

The soft click o' the lock echoed in the stillness, sealin' them inside. Alyssa's fingers curled into fists at her sides, nails diggin' into the smooth fabric o' her gown. The room felt smaller now, every shadow an' whisper magnified.

Tryss stood close behind her, the heat o' his presence pressin' against her back like a livin' thing. She could hear the slow, even beat o' his breath, restrained but raw beneath his controlled exterior. Reachin' for her, he turned her tae face him, pent-up frustration evident in his features, but under that somethin' else she couldnae name.

He didn't say a word. Instead, his eyes—dark, fierce, an' unreadable—caught hers in the dim light. For a moment, the fire in those eyes softened, flickerin' wi' somethin' almost like regret or maybe resignation. She wasn't sure which was worse.

Alyssa swallowed the lump form'n in her throat. This was the moment she had feared an' anticipated. The moment everything would change.

She lifted her chin, meetin' his gaze steadily. If he wanted anger, she would hold her ground. If he wanted war, she would nae back doon.

Tryss

He stopped close behind her, the heat o' him rollin' against her back. His jaw worked, muscles strainin', as though the words he meant tae speak fought for release. Instead, silence pressed down—thick, suffocatin'.

When at last he reached for her, he spun her gently but firmly tae face him. His hands, rough as carved stone, closed round her arms, the strength in them unyieldin'. His eyes burned wi' fury—fury held too long, fury that wanted loose.

"Ye think ye can play games wi' me?" His voice was low, each word clipped, ragged wi' the storm that churned beneath. "That ye can steal vows, a name, an' walk away wi'out cost?"

Her chin lifted, defiant. Her silence was an answer in itself.

His fingers tightened. Then stilled. His nostrils flared as he dragged in a breath, fightin' the urge tae shake sense intae her. He hated the tremor he felt beneath her skin—hated more that it stirred somethin' other than victory.

Damn her, she didnae break. Didnae cower. She looked at him like she dared him tae prove he was more beast than man.

He swore, low an' sharp, and released her. His boots struck the floor as he turned away, every line o' him stiff wi' restraint. Pacing, fists clenching, unclenching. A warlord wi' no war he kenned how tae fight.

Men were easier. Ye fought men. Broke them. Commanded them. But this woman? She met his fire wi' her own, an' it unsettled him more than any blade at his throat. Fergus's words came back hauntingly *"Dinnae go to her bed angry"*. He dragged in a breath and let his rage boil doon to a' simmer.

"I'm no here tae break ye," he ground out at last, voice rough as gravel. The words tasted like surrender, though the storm still swirled in his blood.

He scrubbed a hand doon his face, shoulders sagging as if the weight of his own fury pressed him low. *Damn it,* he thought, *Ah ken the words tae break men, tae command respect... but what kind o' man am Ah if Ah cannae meet her halfway?* The thought scraped at his pride, unwelcome and sharp. He wanted to be gentle—needed to be—but the anger still churned, bitter and raw beneath the surface. Could he even do it without losing himself in the attempt?

Then, wi' a muttered curse, he crossed tae the hearth. He dropped intae the chair. Elbows braced on his knees, he stared at the flames, wrestling the storm inside. Finally, he let a shaky exhale slip past, acknowledging—if only to himself—that some battles were not won with force.

When he finally lifted his head, she was still there. Still standin' tall, violet eyes wide but unyieldin'.

Something shifted. No' peace, no' forgiveness—but a grudgin' respect that scraped against the raw edge o' his pride. An' a temptation, unwelcome an' undeniable, tae reach for gentleness instead o' rage.

His hand dropped to his knee. Rough, dismissive in appearance, but his eyes met hers with something softer, something cautious. "Come now, lass," he said, the corners of his mouth twisting into a crooked, tired smile. "Let's see if we can get through this nicht wi'out burnin' doon the keep—or each other."

Alyssa

It took every ounce o' courage she possessed, but after a long moment's hesitation she eased doon onto his lap, the warmth o' his body pressin' against hers both a comfort an' a challenge. Her heart fluttered, raw an' exposed beneath the steady weight o' his gaze.

"Thank ye," she murmured, voice tremblin' just enough tae betray the storm o' emotions within. "For no breakin' me."

Tryss's eyes narrowed, flickerin' wi' something softer than anger—surprise, maybe even reluctant admiration. His hand found the small o' her back, fingers curlin' there wi' quiet assurance, groundin' them both in the moment.

She swallowed hard, gatherin' her courage. "It wasn't just me who planned this." Her fingers twined nervously in the folds o' his tunic, knotting and unknotting as if the motion could steady her. “Elsyn... she believed this was the only way tae save me. Frae a fate far worse than this.” Her voice trembled slightly, but she forced herself to meet his gaze. “A life wi’out a man tae stand for ye... no kin, no fortune, no one tae shield ye from the world. Low-born women like me... we’re left tae scrape and starve, tae beg or be sold or worse. Ah couldnae... Ah couldnae let that happen.”

Her chest rose and fell rapidly, and she drew a shaky breath. “Ah thought... if Ah told ye the truth, ye’d nae have any use for me. That ye’d send me away, or lock me in some convent tae rot. But... Ah couldnae stay silent, nae longer.”

Tryss’s gaze sharpened, but he said nothing, his silence coaxin’ her tae continue.

“I never wanted tae lie. I was desperate, alone... afraid. Afraid if I told ye the truth, ye’d never accept me. That nobody would accept me.”

Tryss’s gaze was piercing through her wi’ quiet resolve. “Ah’m no cruel man,” he said slowly, voice low an’ steady. “But Ah demand honor an’ truth frae every one o’ my men. An’ we cannae build a life—no matter how long or short—on lies. Frae this moment forward, there’ll be nothing but truth between us.”

She searched his face, hesitant. “Then...ye won’t turn me away? Or lock me in a convent? I couldnae blame ye if ye did so.”

Without a word, Tryss’s fierce gaze softened just enough. He reached oot, pullin’ her against his chest, his strong arms wrappin’ around her as if tae keep her safe frae the world. His lips brushed gently against her temple in a tender kiss.

“Nay, my bonnie lass,” he murmured, voice husky, low an’ wicked, “what fun would there be in that? Ah did promise ye’d burn in yer bed tonight.”

A slow, dark smile played on his lips, the heat o’ his breath warmin' her skin. The promise hung between them—dangerous, electric, an' utterly irresistible.

Chapter Ten

Alyssa

The firelight danced across the chamber, throwing flickering shadows across the walls. Alyssa pressed herself close, trembling—not from fear, but from the ache of anticipation she didn't yet understand. His hands were everywhere at once, confident, commanding, moving along her arms, her waist, her back, grounding her while setting her alight.

He captured her lips in a kiss that was firm, demanding, insistent. His tongue nudged past hers, claiming her mouth in a way that made her breath hitch and her knees feel weak. Every nerve in her body hummed with heat as his hands roamed with purpose, exploring the curves and planes of her untried form.

A shiver ran through her when his lips trailed down her jaw, along her neck. Each kiss, each brush of his mouth, each stroke of his fingers against her skin was deliberate, coaxing the unexperienced fire inside her into something consuming. When his teeth grazed her collar bone she nearly whimpered. She didn't know what to do, but she knew to follow, to respond, because every movement he made demanded surrender and drew her further into him.

Her fingers clutched at his shoulders, at the folds of his tunic, unable to steady herself as heat raced through her body, and desire built with every press of his lips, every glide of his hands. She felt alive in a way she had never known—raw, tender, and utterly consumed by him.

He pulled back just enough to watch her, dark eyes blazing with hunger and control, and she felt the truth of it in every taut line of his body: he would guide her through this fire, and she would follow willingly, losing herself in the inferno of his making.

His hands were sure, deliberate as they slipped beneath the edges of her gown, peeling away layers until skin met skin, warm and trembling beneath his touch. "Ah want tae see all o' ye," his hungry words unguarded, vulnerable, yearning.

Her breath catching, shallow and quick, as he traced slow, reverent paths over the bare curve of her shoulder, down her spine, and along the swell of her hips. He leaned close, his mouth ghosting over the sensitive skin behind her ear, tasting the heat there, his voice a low murmur only she could hear.

“Every inch o' ye" a flick of his tongue, "is mine tae discover," he promised, “an' Ah'll take ma time makin' sure ye ken it.”

She melted against him, the silk gown falling away piece by piece until only the softest whisper of fabric clung to her. He denied his eyes no part of her —the pale curve of her neck, the rise and fall of her chest. She could feel the new sensation, desire pooling between her thighs.

His fingers found the delicate velvet there, teasing, coaxing, pressing just enough to draw a soft, desperate sigh from her lips.

She was wet and wanting, trembling beneath his touch, every nerve ending aflame and alive.

Shifting, he gathered her into his lap more fully, and pressed his body flush against hers, she felt a shiver at the heat of him. His hands moved with growing confidence— exploring, worshiping — awakening her to a new language of pleasure.

"Let me show ye whit touch can be," he whispered, lips brushing the shell of her ear, "whit it means tae be desired, tae be worshiped."

She tangled her fingers in his hair, clutching tightly as waves of warmth rolled through her, the ache deepening, demanding more.

His hands slid lower, his touch teasing, coaxing, ensuring she was ready — fully, utterly ready — before he would claim her in the bed waiting just beyond the curtain.

His breath mingled with hers, slow and warm, a dare in every lingering touch and every whispered word: tonight, she knew she would learn the power of pleasure, the depth of tenderness — and how fierce her body could burn.

He lifted her effortlessly, the heat of her body pressed close against his as he carried her across the room. Every step was deliberate, measured—an unspoken promise in his touch that sent shivers through her spine. He settled her gently on the edge of the bed, the soft linen cool against her bare skin.

His lips descended slowly, worshiping the peaks of her breasts, teasing her nipples with tender, heated kisses that sent ripples of pleasure cascading through her. Her breath stopped all-together, her fingers clutching at the sheets as her insides became molten.

His mouth chased a burning path down her waist, tongue brushing the sensitive skin there, then traveled lower, trailing feather-light kisses along the inside of her thighs. Shock tore through her. *Surely...nay!* "Tryss!" Her body trembled beneath him, the hunger building, a wildfire stoked by every soft caress.

Then, lifting his gaze, Tryss looked up at her, eyes dark and wicked. "Pleasure," he murmured, voice low an' promisin', "is a language. An' Ah'll speak it tae ye, till ye understand every word."

Without hesitation, he pressed his mouth to her most intimate place, tasting her need, drinking in her want. Alyssa gasped, the slick heat of his mouth sending jolts of electric bliss spiraling through her. The ability to think fled. Her hips arched, instinctively seeking more, demanding more, the trembling in her limbs growing impossible to contain.

Every nerve sang, every inch of her alive with need and delicious surrender. She was utterly exposed to him, body and soul laid bare—and in that raw vulnerability, she found something fierce and unbreakable.

His tongue and tender lips coaxed moans from deep within her, unraveling her with every flick and press. The ache inside her blossomed, a sweet torment she hadn't known she craved. She was lost to the exquisite torment of his touch, learning a new language spoken in sighs and gasps.

His mouth never left her, his tongue tracing slow, deliberate circles that made her breath catch and her pulse race. Every flick of his tongue, every press of his lips was a sweet torture she never knew existed, a secret meant only for her. Her body responded without hesitation, hips tilting upward, seeking the exquisite warmth and skill of his touch.

She quaked beneath him—half-shy, half-bold—drawn into a world where only sensation mattered. Her hands slid from his hair to the smooth, muscled planes of his shoulders, fingers digging in as she clung to him, grounding herself in the overwhelming flood of pleasure.

The heat pooling between her thighs grew thicker, a delicious ache that tightened with each teasing glide of his tongue, each patient stroke coaxing her further toward the edge, of what she didn't know. His hands roamed upwards, cupping her breasts, thumbs circling her nipples until they hardened beneath his touch, a sharp contrast to the softness of his lips.

Her breaths came in ragged gasps, her body bucking, urging him on, desperate for the release she hadn't even known she needed until now. The world had narrowed to the sound of their mingled breaths, the slick press of skin against skin, and the electric hum of rising desire.

Tryss's voice, low and intimate, brushed against her ear. "Lass, ye're sweeter than honey an ye're mine the nicht," he murmured," an' Ah will make sure ye remember whit it means tae be claimed by a storm."

She shivered. Her defenses melted away, leaving only a raw, trembling need. Every nerve ending ablaze, every inch of her alive to the sensation of him.

He paused briefly to look up at her, eyes dark and blazing with hunger and tenderness. Then, slowly, he rose, fingers still tracing lingering paths of fire along her skin as he leaned in to capture her mouth in a kiss that was both gentle and demanding.

Alyssa surrendered fully, lips parting, body pressing closer as the simmering tension between them tightened like a coil ready to snap. The promise of more, of something deeper and more profound, hung in the charged silence—a delicate balance between restraint and surrender.

His hands moved with purpose, lowering her shift until it pooled on the floor, leaving her bare and vulnerable beneath his touch. His fingers traced every curve, every hollow, as if memorizing the landscape of her skin and committing her to memory.

Tryss's lips trailed a slow path up her inner thigh, fingers teasing just beyond where she ached for more. He lifted his gaze, dark eyes sparkling with wicked amusement. Her moan begged for more. More of this. More of everything.

"Aye, lass," he murmured against her skin, voice low an' rough, "aye, are ye burnin' yet?"

A shiver ran through her, part laughter, part want, as the heat between them flared sharper. His fingers danced, coaxing, teasing, making her pulse thunder beneath his touch.

Alyssa's breath left her completely.

"Tryss," she whispered—only his name. A breath, a plea, complete and utter surrender.

He stilled for just a moment, lifting his gaze to meet hers. What passed between them in that silence wasn't spoken—it didn't need to be. She was ready, not just in body but in the aching trust that shimmered in her eyes.

His expression shifted, wickedness melting away leaving only concentration and restraint.

With a murmur o' something in Gaelic, low an' soft, he gathered her into his arms and carried her the rest o' the way onto the bed. The linens were cool beneath her back, a sharp contrast to the heat of his skin as he knelt above her, bracing himself on one arm as his other hand swept along the curve of her waist.

"Last chance tae run, bonnie," he murmured, a half-smile playing at his lips, though his voice had lost all its teasing edge.

She reached up, fingertips brushing his jaw. "I'm not going anywhere."

Tryss

His mouth found hers, the kiss deep an' slow, sealing the moment between them. He moved wi' care—anchored not in hesitation, but in purpose. His touch was a tether, grounding her as he lowered himself tae her body, the solid press of him warm an' sure—a shelter from every fear that had ever haunted her. Grasping her hips, he pushed her knees apart. God, she was magnificent.

When he entered her, he thought he might give it up right then an' there. She was so tight. So wet. So hot. *Not yet man, not yet.*

She tensed, breath catching, soft whimpers escaping, and he pressed closer, grounding them both with the firm weight of his hands. Forehead against hers, voice low and rough: "Steady... steady, bonnie... just like that." Wi' one deep stroke he bore through her maiden head.

"I'm sorry, love," he whispered, voice rough. "It will pass. Tell me when."

Wi' as much restraint as he could muster, he held utterly still, his body trembling wi' the effort. His forehead pressed gently tae hers, their breaths mingling in the charged stillness. She clung tae him, fingers tightening at his shoulders, her breath shaky but steadying. Then, after a heartbeat... another... she gave the smallest nod, her hips rising ever so slightly in answer.

Each tiny gasp, each hitch of her breath, stoked the fire roaring beneath his skin. Her fingers dug into his shoulders, nails grazing the hard planes of his back, and he groaned softly, the sound raw, unrestrained. She moved slightly, testing, feeling... and he whispered against her temple: "Ah... gods, ye feel... so bloody perfect."

The small shiver that ran through her, the tremble of her thighs, the soft gasps she made—he memorized them all, letting each tiny sound pull him deeper. Her body yielded in parts, hips tilting, breath deepening, fingers sliding from his shoulders to clutch the nape of his neck. She was with him now, not hesitating, but learning, following his lead.

His rhythm grew, deliberate, firm, commanding—teaching her, guiding her, setting her body alight while he wrestled with the fire it stirred in him. Her soft cries, the trembling of her legs, the gasps escaping her lips—they drew low, guttural sounds from him, rough with exertion and something he couldnae yet name.

"Ah... ye move like a dream... sweeter than Ah could've imagined... gods, ye feel... perfect..." he murmured against her hair, lips brushing cheek and temple, voice rough and urgent. Every small whimper, every gasp, was a revelation, driving him harder, deeper, demanding and claiming.

She clung to him, her body warm and yielding, and he knew—this night, this fire, it was hers as much as his. Every tremble, every sound, every new gasp etched itself into him, and he couldnae stop, nor did he wish to.

He murmured her name against her skin, again an' again. And when the rising tension finally shattered within him, when he finally allowed himself release it's intensity forced a hiss an' then a roar from the deepest part of him, the collapse of a man utterly undone.

He buried his face against her shoulder, heaving, the aftershocks rolling through him like the last waves of a storm. She held him through it—arms winding around his back, anchoring him in a way nae battlefield ever had.

"Ye're mine," he murmured, teeth brushing her skin, breath ragged. "Every part, every breath... mine, Alyssa. Ye... ye were perfect... every inch, every sound... Ah've never felt..." His hands slid along her sides, memorizing the shiver that ran beneath his touch. "The way ye move... the way ye respond... every quiver, every gasp... ye set fire tae me, lass. Perfect, so perfect."

He pressed her closer, resting against her, voice low, rough, and utterly reverent. "Damn, but ye feel... ah... like the world itself could burn an' Ah'd care not, as long as it's wi' ye."

The fire had burned low, its golden light flickering lazily across the tangle of sheets an' limbs. Alyssa lay curled against Tryss's chest, her breathing soft an' steady, one hand resting over his heart as if tae anchor him in the stillness, while his whispered praise lingered in the room like a spell, settling over them both.

He brushed a strand of hair from her temple, marveling at the softness of her skin, the way she fit against him like she had always belonged there. Her lashes fluttered as she drifted on the edge of sleep, lips parted in quiet contentment.

He had never touched a woman like that before—not wi' so much care, not wi' so much restraint. Not wi' so much of himself laid bare.

An' yet...

Tryss stared past her into the shadows beyond the bed, his arm tightening slightly around her. He'd taken her body, aye, but had he truly claimed her trust? Or she his?

His jaw tightened as the thought rose, unwanted but insistent. Could he ever truly believe every word that left her mouth? Or had tonight's sweetness only softened the truth—that she'd lied from the start?

Alyssa stirred against him, murmuring his name in sleep, her breath warm where it brushed against his chest. His hand rested between her breasts, softly stroking the underside.

He didn't know the answer yet.

But gods help him, he wanted tae believe.

An' for tonight... he would let that be enough.

CHAPTER ELEVEN

Tryss

THE MORNING BROKE COOL an' grey, mist clinging tae the moors like breath held too long. The courtyard echoed wi' quiet motion—boots on damp stone, the stamp of hooves, an' the occasional barked order from stable hands preparing the hunt.

Tryss strode through it all wi' the weight of something unfinished pressing between his shoulders.

Fergus matched his pace, falling in step beside him, eyes sharp beneath the curl of his beard. "Is it done then?" he asked, voice casual, but not careless.

Tryss didn't look at him. "Aye. It's done."

They turned toward the stables, boots crunching over gravel an' straw.

A long beat passed before Fergus spoke again. "An' is all forgiven then?" His tone lightened slightly. "She's quite bonnie, might be hard tae stay mad at that one."

Tryss stopped. Just for a moment.

The breath he drew was short an' sharp, his jaw tightening as he turned his head just enough to meet Fergus's eye. "Nay," he said. "Accepted. Not forgiven. They are not the same."

The words cut through the air, leaving a stillness in their wake.

Fergus gave a slow nod, the lines around his eyes tightening. "No, Ah reckon they're not."

They kept walking.

Tryss's mood was a storm, rolling an' unpredictable. One moment silent, the next bristling wi' the edge of some unseen storm. Fergus said nothing else, sensing that tae press further would be tae poke the wolf before breakfast.

At the stables, Tryss reached for the bridle of his stallion, checking the straps wi' a practiced hand. The beast snorted, stamping it's hoof, sensing its master's unrest.

Fergus glanced toward the keep, where a flicker of movement at the upper window hinted at Alyssa's silhouette behind the glass.

"She ken she's not invited?" he asked quietly.

Tryss didn't answer at first. Just cinched the saddle tighter than necessary.

Then: "She'll figure it out."

Fergus raised a brow. "A hunting party without the bride? Bit cold, even for ye."

Tryss swung into the saddle in one smooth motion. "Ah need the ride," he said. "Ah need tae think."

Fergus snorted but swung onto his own mount. "Aye, ye think. I'll just keep us from getting killed."

Tryss didn't respond. His gaze was fixed on the horizon, where the morning mist had begun tae lift, revealing the jagged outline of the hills.

Alyssa

Behind him, up in the chamber they'd shared just hours before, Alyssa watched him prepare tae hunt—without her.

Alyssa's blood burned hot beneath her skin, fury clawin' its way up her throat, twistin' her stomach into tight, angry knots. The weddin' day was over—yesterday—but the sting o' bein' sidelined still tasted bitter an' raw. Left behind while Tryss rode aff without her wasn't just a slight. It was a damn humiliation, a mark o' how little she mattered in his eyes.

She was his wife. His bride. An' yet here she stood, fully dressed an' ready tae ride, an' he'd made it clear she wasna welcome. Like she was naught but a task completed, a box ticked, a burden tae be discarded once done.

Her fists clenched so tightly her nails bit into her palms. How dare he? How dare he presume she'd stand idle, silent, obedient? A storm raged inside her, fierce an' unforgiven, wind an' fire twistin' together until she felt she might explode.

Nay. She wouldna be the forgotten shadow trailin' behind. She wouldna be the woman cast aside once the vows were said. Not today. Not ever.

Her mind sharpened, focus narrowin' on a single truth: he had tae see her. Really see her—not as a possession, not as duty, not as a mark o' pride or obligation, but as a force. A fire that would burn if ignored. She would make him acknowledge her, or he would rue the day he ever thought tae leave her behind.

Boots thudded hard against the stable floor wi' every step, each strike echoin' her determination. The smell o' leather, hay, an' horse sweat mingled wi' her own risin' pulse, fuelin' the fire within her chest. Her fingers brushed along the hilt o' her dagger, not in preparation for battle wi' him, but in readiness tae meet the world on equal terms. She would ride, she would command, she would be seen.

An' when she finally caught sight o' him, mounted an' poised, she let her gaze lock on his. Every line o' his posture, every movement, every taut muscle would bear witness tae the storm she carried. He might have thought he could leave her behind—he'd be mistaken. She was his wife, aye, but she was also her own woman. An' she would make sure he understood that before the day was done.

CHAPTER TWELVE

Tryss

TRYSS STOOD STIFF, THE morning chill doing little tae cool the heat o' his frustration. Then the door swung open, an' there she was—his wife—stridin' in like she owned the place, her copper hair coiled up neat on her head. Alyssa's sharp voice rang oot clear, cuttin' through the morning air.

"Guid mornin', dear husband!" she called, loud enough for the entire courtyard tae hear. "It was so considerate o' ye tae let me sleep just a wee bit longer this mornin', after all—you did keep my attentions very late intae the wee hours, didnae ye?" She reached up and planted a kiss firmly on his mouth—unapologetically bold.

Tryss's anger wavered, a reluctant smile tugging at the corner o' his mouth. *Cheeky lassie*, he thought, shakin' his head in disbelief even as blood raced through his body an' found purchase in his cock. He leaned in, lips reaching for hers, but she flicked back just in time, grin daring him. Heart hammerin', he lunged again, and again she slipped out of reach, laughter dancing on the wind. Memories o' last night flooded every sense, but the thrill o' the chase—her boldness, her fire—made his pulse sing sharper than any battle ever could.

Aye, a lass could vanquish a man's anger with nae more than a daring kiss and a teasing smile. *Gods help me, she's got me undone already... and she's not even tryin'.*

Beside him, Fergus threw back his head an' roared wi' laughter, slappin' Tryss hard on the back. "Aye, my Laird, brither, not the same at all."

Tryss shot him a sharp look, grin tugging at his lips. "Brither, eh? Keep laughin', an' I'll nae let ye near my ale tonight."

His gaze flicked past Fergus, and there she was—Alyssa, standing proud and bold, hair catching the morning light. A heat sparked low in his chest, coiling tight, stirring something dangerous and delicious. Just a glimpse of her smile, the tilt o' her chin, and the world narrowed to the sway o' her body, the sway o' her confidence. Aye... cheeky lassie, indeed.

Alyssa wasted nae time. Her horse was soon tacked an' waitin'. Wi'out a hint o' hesitation or need for assistance, she swung herself onto her steed wi' the grace an' confidence o' a woman who refused tae be diminished.

Tryss arched a brow, his gaze sharp but carryin' an unspoken acknowledgment. He gave her a slow, deliberate nod, then urged his mount forward, the thunder o' hooves answerin' the risin' sun.

The hunt had begun—and so had their new dance o' power an' passion.

Tryss urged his horse forward, the steady rhythm o' hooves poundin' against the earth groundin' him in the present. The crisp mornin' air bit at his face, but it was naught compared tae the fire Alyssa ignited within him — a spark o' somethin' unpredictable an' fierce that unsettled his careful control.

How in God's name had she done it? He'd left her behind, certain she'd stew in his silence, certain he could ride on with his fury as his only companion. He'd meant tae. He *needed* tae. Yet here she was, ridin' bold as any laird's son, eyes bright wi' defiance, réfusin' tae be cast aside

His eyes flicked tae her silhouette ahead, her posture proud an' sure as she rode wi' a wild grace that both challenged an' captivated him. She was a storm hersel', unpredictable an' sharp-tongued, her cheeky remarks slicin' through the usual quiet o' the hunt.

Tryss gritted his teeth, knowin' full well how distractin' she could be — a constant tug on his focus. His doubts whispered at the edges o' his mind, shadows frae the past he wasn't ready tae fully confront. Could he trust her? Could he truly let his guard down an' welcome her intae the fierce, unyieldin' world he inhabited?

Yet, despite the unease twistin' inside him, her laughter rang oot like a bright bell, slicin' through his stormy thoughts. Her wit was sharp, her spirit unbroken, an' somethin' in that stubborn spark called tae him more fiercely than he expected.

Tryss allowed himself a fleeting smile, a rare crack in his battle-hardened armor. For all the questions an' fears swirl'n beneath the surface, he found himself drawn tae her — intrigued, even hopeful.

Fergus rode alongside Tryss, a wicked grin tuggin' at his lips as he jabbed, "Wee hours o' the mornin' then, was it? She rides that horse like she's been deflowered by a pimply-faced lad o' fourteen, nae the man I ken ye tae be."

Tryss's growl was low an' amused, a spark o' mischief lightin' his eyes. Wi'out warnin', he leaned ower, fingers snatchin' Fergus's cinch loose in one swift motion. Fergus let out a startled yelp, nearly tumblin' frae his saddle as his horse jolted.

"Careful there, brither," Tryss chuckled, pullin' back on his reins as he surged ahead, heart poundin'—nae wi' anger, but wi' fierce desire. The chase was on, an' he was racin' not tae catch, but tae either join or perhaps tame his fiery bride.

His laughter echoed through the trees, wild an' free, as he closed the distance—ready for whatever this storm o' a woman would throw at him next.

Alyssa

Well... he hadna refused her after all. She could hear his laughter carried on the crisp mornin' air, sharp and clear as a blade. Turnin' her head, she caught sight o' him thunderin' up beside her, that roguish smile curlin' his lips as if the whole world bent tae his will.

"Ye think tae best me, lass?" he called, voice roughened wi' mirth and challenge both.

Matching his grin, Alyssa flashed a sassy smile o' her own. "Och, Tryss MacCraith, I was bestin' ye afore ye ever set eyes on me." Then she leaned forward an' gave her mare a hard kick, sendin' the beast intae a furious gallop, mane and tail whippin' like streamers in the wind.

The land rose an' fell beneath her, heather blurrin' purple an' green at the edges o' her sight. The wind roared past her ears, near tearin' the breath from her lungs, but it made her blood sing. She threw back her head and laughed, wild and unbridled, the sound carryin' across the moor.

Glancin' over her shoulder, Alyssa caught the sight o' Tryss risin' eagerly tae her challenge. His stallion's muscles bunched an' strained, every stride eatin' the ground between them. His eyes locked on hers wi' a heat that made her stomach tumble and her chest tighten.

Her heart fluttered wi' a queer mix o' dismay an' thrill. Was this what it meant tae be wanted by a man like him? No soft words or tender promises, but a chase fierce enough tae steal the very air from her lungs?

"Ya!" she cried, legs grippin' tight, breath comin' in sharp bursts as she urged her mount faster still. Her laughter spilled out again, bright as sunlight through storm clouds, and for one blazin' heartbeat she forgot the weight o' clans, bargains, an' betrayals.

Tryss

She didnae see it.

Panic surged through his chest like lightning, searin' straight through the haze o' amusement that had clouded his thoughts only moments ago. The ravine cut across the field like a wound, sudden an' unforgivin'—too close.

"Pull up!" he roared, but the wind tore the words frae his mouth.

No. No, no, no.

His boots slammed intae his horse's flanks, an' the beast surged forward beneath him, muscles strainin', hooves tearin' up the earth. He leaned low, urg'n more speed, prayin' he could reach her in time.

Alyssa was flyin', wild an' beautiful, an' completely unaware o' the danger ahead.

Closer.

Her braid whipped past him. Her laugh—he could still hear

it—turned intae a gasp as the ground broke open ahead o' her.

He reached. Wi' a desperate lunge, Tryss stretched out his arm, heart thundering, fingers snatchin' at her reins.

Got them.

Wi' a brutal jerk, he yanked her horse tae a stop, both mounts skiddin' in a spray o' torn grass an' dirt just feet frae the edge o' the ravine. Alyssa reeled, barely keepin' her seat as he hauled her back frae the brink.

Her eyes met his—wide, terrified, breathless. Her face was all fear an' panic an' confusion.

An' Tryss saw red.

"Of all the irresponsible, dangerous, fool-headed—" He was off his horse an' at her side in an instant, rage pourin' frae him in a roar. "Ye could've been killed!"

His chest heaved in rhythm wi' the horses, fury mixin' wi' the last dregs o' sheer terror.

Alyssa blinked, color floodin' back intae her cheeks as she snapped, "Like ye would care!"

Tryss's jaw clenched. That was it.

Wi'out a word, he reached up an' yanked her frae her seat in one swift, seamless motion. She let out a startled cry as he spun her just enough tae bend her ower his knee.

His palm landed once—firm an' unmistakable—against the curve o' her backside. The crack echoed, the sting burnin' sharp through her skirts.

Alyssa gasped, every muscle lockin' in place. Heat flooded her cheeks—part humiliation, part outrage, part somethin' she dared no' name. *Saints above... did he truly just do that, here, before them all?*

Her heart thundered, her pride screamin' for her tae strike back, yet traitorous fire raced through her veins, settlin' low, makin' her knees threaten tae give. The shame of it near undid her as much as the act itself.

“Enough!” he roared.

He set her on her feet again, holdin’ her steady before she could stumble. Her eyes were wide, brimming wi’ disbelief and fury, her humiliation complete—yet her pulse still beat wild, betrayin’ her.

Before she could speak, Tryss’s hands framed her face, an’ his mouth crushed hers in a kiss that stole her breath. She jerked back, gaspin’, “Nae—” the word sharp wi’ fury an’ fear both.

But he wasna finished. The raw edge o’ panic still ripped through his chest, an’ his lips claimed hers again, harder, hotter, demandin’ she feel the truth he couldnae speak. This time she pushed against him, fists poundin’ weakly at his chest—until her hands curled in his tunic instead, clutchin’ as though she couldnae let go.

He tasted the salt o’ her tears, the bite o’ blood where she’d caught her lip in her teeth, the wild storm o’ her breath minglin’ wi’ his. Every clash o’ their mouths was battle an’ surrender both, his fury tangled wi’ somethin’ far more dangerous—need.

When he tore himself back, breath ragged, her eyes were wide, cheeks ablaze, lips bruised an’ swollen. Rage still burned there—but so did somethin’ else. Somethin’ that made his knees near buckle wi’ the weight o’ it.

“I guess I care enough not tae see ye splattered at the bottom o’ a ravine, ye foolish, stubborn lass,” he growled, his voice low an’ rough wi’ emotion. “Ye cannae just act on every fool idea that enters that pretty head o’ yours,” he raged. “Trickin’ me intae a marriage, nearly killin’ yersel’ cause ye hae nae care for what’s in front o’ ye. Hae ye a death wish then, lassie?”

Still panting, Alyssa stood frozen, lips tingling, cheeks blazin’. Tryss turned wi’out another word, seized the reins o’ her lathered horse, an’ started walkin’.

"This hunt is over," he barked, nae lookin' back.

The ravine was behind them, the danger past, but his blood was still thunderin'. Alyssa's eyes blazed, her lips swollen from his kiss, her pride cut tae ribbons.

Hoofbeats pounded closer. Fergus reined in, his face pale beneath the beard. His usual grin was gone, jaw tight as he took in Alyssa's disheveled seat and Tryss's hand still firm on her reins.

For once, the man had nae jest. Only a slow shake o' his head, the weight of it speakin' louder than words. Then, wisely, he said nothin'.

The other men in the party watched in stunned silence as Tryss strode past them. When he reached the stables, he handed the reins off tae a gaping stable boy wi' a look that dared him tae ask questions.

An' then he kept walkin'—head high, shoulders tight, fury rollin' aff him in waves—as he made his way back toward the keep.

Alyssa

Alyssa stood alone, still as stone, heat lickin' at her cheeks an' a sharp twist o' somethin' raw curlin' in her chest. Around her, the huntin' party began tae stir, shiftin' awkward-like, their sidelong glances and muttered amusement pricklin' at her skin. She scarce noticed them.

Her gaze clung tae him—tae the long, broad back that had just turned away, tae the rigid set o' his shoulders, every inch o' him screamin' fury held tight. Och, but it was deliberate, that turn, that dismissal in full view o' every eye. He'd meant tae put her in her place, tae show them all she was naught but a foolish lass playin' at games she couldnae win.

Her throat burned wi' the humiliation of it, sharp an' bitter. Anger lashed through her veins, quick as a whip, flayin' at the ache threatenin' tae weaken her knees. She wanted tae shout after him, tae tear at his pride as he'd torn at hers.

And yet—curse the man—he set her alight all the same. A look, a word, a single motion, an' she was lost tae the fire of him.

The truth struck cruel as a blade: she hadna wanted him tae leave. Not even a little. Her chest ached wi' the shame o' it, longin' twined hard wi' fury until she scarce kenned which cut deeper.

Better his back turned than his eyes on me, she told herself—though the lie tasted bitter on her tongue.

She pressed her palms intae her skirts, knuckles white, holdin' herself rigid lest she betray what raged inside her. *Humiliate me, will ye, Tryss MacCraith?* she seethed silently. *We'll see who yields when next ye try.*

CHAPTER THIRTEEN

Alyssa

SHE WOULDNAE CRY.

Dinnae dare cry, she scolded hersel', bitin' the inside o' her cheek tae will the tears back. But it was useless. Even as the words rang in her mind, a single, traitorous tear slipped doon her cheek. She dashed it away wi' the back o' her hand, hard an' fast, turnin' her back on the huntin' party afore any o' them could see.

Humiliation burned hotter than the sting on her backside.

How dare he?

She hadnae kent about the ravine. He'd never said a word. It had been a game—a chase. She had smiled at him, challenged him, an' he had risen tae meet it. They had been laughin'. He had been laughin'. How could it turn frae breathless joy tae blisterin' shame in the span o' a heartbeat?

She felt every eye behind her, felt their judgment an' their smirks. The slap had been fast, just one, but it echoed louder than a shout. An' that kiss—possessive, searin', meant tae silence her an' remind everyone whose she was.

Her hands balled intae fists.

He had embarrassed her. In front o' everyone.

An' yet... an' yet...

Alyssa drew a shaky breath, draggin' hersel' upright, forcin' her chin tae lift. She wouldnae cower. She wouldnae be the tearful wee bride left behind like a scolded bairn. He might hae walked aff in a storm cloud o' fury an' command, but he hadnae broken her. Not even close.

She turned toward the stable, ignorin' the shifty glances o' the men who still lingered. Her eyes were fixed ahead, her steps steady, her heart poundin' wi' somethin' wild an' unsettled.

If he thought the hunt was over...

He was sorely mistaken.

She turned on her heel, fury risin' anew as her sights locked on the distant shape o' her husband retreatin' toward the keep.

But a hand, firm an' calloused, caught her arm—haltin' her. She twisted sharply, ready tae scold whoever dared tae stop her.

"Aye? What is it?" she snapped, breath still sharp frae the force o' her indignation.

Fergus stood there, unruffled as ever, his expression neither mockin' nor reproachful. If anythin', there was somethin' gentle in the way he regarded her.

Her pride bristled. She had nae patience for riddles or kindly eyes, not when her backside still stung an' her pride burned raw. Did he think tae soothe her wi' platitudes? Tae play the wise clansman while she stood humiliated afore them all? She near laughed in his face at the thought.

Her chin lifted, defiance sparkin'. For a heartbeat, she near wrenched hersel' free, ready tae march past him, chin high, heart hammerin'.

But his gaze didnae waver. Calm, steady, unmovable as the stone beneath their feet. It wasnae pity in his eyes, nor judgment—it was somethin' else. Somethin' that made her breath catch despite hersel'.

Slowly, warily, she stilled.

"Mistress," he said evenly. "If I might offer some....insight."

She blinked, surprised by the unexpected civility in his tone. He extended his arm, an' though part o' her wanted tae brush past him, somethin' in his steady gaze gave her pause. Slowly, warily, she accepted.

They walked in silence through the outer yard an' intae the fringe o' the gardens, the early sun warmin' the stone path beneath their feet. At a weathered bench tucked beneath a windswept rowan tree, Fergus motioned for her tae sit.

"Mistress Alyssa," he said, lowerin' himsel' beside her wi' a quiet grunt, "if ye'll let me, I'd like tae tell ye a story."

She narrowed her eyes, in nae mood for stories, but nodded.

"There's a reason Tryss doesnae take kindly tae reckless ridin'." Fergus's voice was low, careful, as though each word were weighed afore spoken. "A reason burned intae him so deep he scarce speaks of it."

Alyssa folded her arms, the sting o' her pride still hot, but somethin' in his tone made her breath slow.

"He had an older brither. Gavin." Fergus's mouth twitched, half a smile, but it faded almost afore it formed. "Och, that lad... reckless as the day is lang. Could charm the wings aff an angel an' make the devil hissel' laugh. Tryss worshipped him. We all did."

His words faltered. He cleared his throat, rough, eyes fixed on the distant hills as though the sight anchored him. Alyssa noticed the cords in his neck tighten, the bob o' his swallow, an' felt her ain mouth go dry.

"One summer mornin'... nae so different frae this... Gavin challenged Tryss tae a race." Fergus rubbed a hand ower his jaw, the silence stretchin' afore he forced the words out. "Same path. Same ravine."

Alyssa's heart skipped, a cold prickle crawlin' doon her arms.

Fergus's throat worked. He swallowed hard, a long pause stretchin' afore he spoke again, softer now. "Only Gavin didnae see it in time."

The words landed like stones between them. Alyssa's chest tightened, a sick lurch turnin' her stomach.

"He went ower," Fergus said at last, voice thick. "Horse an' rider both. When we found him..." His voice cracked. He broke aff, shook his head, an' started again. "When we brought him back, there was nae bringin' him whole again."

Alyssa's fingers dug intae the edge o' the bench, knuckles white. She couldnae breathe for a moment, her lungs refusin' tae fill, as if the weight o' the story pressed straight against her ribs.

"Tryss was seventeen." Fergus's gaze dropped, an' for the first time Alyssa saw his eyes glisten. His hands clenched once on his knees, then stilled. "He rode after him. Too late. He spent hours in that ravine, diggin' wi' his bare hands, draggin' bones an' shattered hopes oot o' the dirt. Near broke himsel' wi' the weight o' it."

Alyssa's throat closed tight. Tears stung her eyes, hot an' unbidden. She bit the inside o' her cheek, hard, but the taste o' iron filled her mouth anyway.

"So ye see, lass," Fergus said, his eyes kind, "what ye heard in his voice wasnae fury. It was fear. Terror, more like, buried under the only armor a man like him kens how tae wear."

Alyssa's lips parted, but nae sound came. Her cheeks flushed wi' shame.

Och, but she had mocked him. Doubted him. Cruel words flung like daggers, each one striking where she hadnae seen the wound already layin' open. She had thought tae make him smart wi' her defiance, never kennin' she was cuttin' deeper than any blade.

Her throat worked hard as she forced the burn o' tears back. She'd called his care cruelty, and now she saw the truth of it—a brither's ghost in every shout, a grave in every sharp command.

Fergus gave her a moment, then stood. "Go tae him now. Wi' this knowledge. Make peace, an' forgive him. He's no' a brutish man, Alyssa. Not by nature. But he carries ghosts. Dinnae let today be another."

Wi' a nod, he left her there beneath the tree, stridin' back toward the stables as quiet as he had come.

Alyssa lingered, her mind whirlin'. Tryss—furious, unyieldin' Tryss—had carried such ghosts in silence, an' she hadnae seen it. Perhaps nae one had.

She sat, frozen, her hands smoothin' the creases frae her skirts though her heart still beat uneven. Her gaze fixed on the path he had taken. Not tae beg forgiveness, not yet—but tae learn the man behind the armor, the brither still buried in his heart.

If he is bound by ghosts, she thought, *then I must learn how tae walk beside them... or they will always stand between us.*

Tryss

His heart wouldnae slow. Not after the long, furious march tae the keep. Not after slammin' his chamber door so hard the iron latch rattled in its hold.

He stood, chest heavin', every muscle coiled tight, then turned tae the hearth like a man beggin' the flames for absolution. Firelight licked the stone, spittin', cracklin', shadows twitchin' along the walls—yet still his pulse pounded, deaf as war drums in his skull.

Gavin.

The name tore through him like steel.

His brither's face flared in his mind—laughin', wild-eyed, fearless in the way only first sons could afford tae be. Reckless. Beloved. Gone.

Tryss's jaw locked. His fists curled hard enough tae ache, knuckles white as bone. He hadnae said Gavin's name in years, had buried it deep—yet the memory rose now, unbidden, searin' bright as the day it happened.

He saw the hooves again, thrashin' in empty air. Heard the scream strangled by the gorge. Then the silence—och, God, the silence. Louder than any cry, it had pressed the life from his chest, left him kneelin' in blood-soaked grass, hands raw, nails split, draggin' bones an' shattered hopes frae the dirt wi' naught but his own fury an' grief.

His breath hitched. He dragged a hand doon his face, but the grief clawed free, savage, unrelentin', as if the years had been naught but a brittle coverin'.

An' today... today it near happened again. Another rider. Another plunge. Another body lost tae the ravine.

Only this time, it would hae been his wife.

Alyssa.

Her name burned different. Not the blade o' Gavin's memory, but somethin' more dangerous—an ache.

Her eyes had blazed defiance, her laughter wild on the wind, oblivious tae the drop. He had wanted tae throttle her, shake sense intae her bones. He had wanted tae crush her against him, shield her frae every edge an' shadow. He hadnae kent which hunger would win—until his palm cracked against her backside, the sound sharp as his terror.

The kiss that followed—Christ, he'd been lost in it. Not thought, not reason, only proof she was safe, breathin', alive in his arms.

Yet the image lingered. Her laughin'. Her ridin' away. Blind tae the brink. It haunted him still.

He'd nearly lost her. It would hae been his fault. Again.

An' worse—it wasnae only fear that gutted him. It was want. It was need. The ache of her already woven deep where he couldnae bear tae cut her loose.

Tryss let out a ragged breath and dropped heavy onto the bed's edge, elbows on his knees, starin' into the flames like they might sear the memory frae him.

He didnae ken if he could trust her.

He didnae ken if he could trust himsel'.

She was cheeky. Untamed. Bold. A storm he couldnae command. An' yet... she was his wife.

His.

For the first time since Gavin's fall, Tryss didnae ken which fate he dreaded more—losin' someone again...

...or lettin' someone in deep enough that he had somethin' tae lose.

Alyssa

She sat on the cauld stone bench beneath the rowan tree, her hands clasped tight in her lap. Fergus's words echoed in her mind, unravelin' the anger knotted in her chest, replacin' it wi' a tangled mix o' sorrow an' understandin'.

She had been sae quick tae judge Tryss—too quick, mayhap,

blinded by pride an' hurt. But now she saw the shadow he carried, one she had never kent, one that explained the fierce protectiveness behind his anger.

A weary sigh escaped her lips as she tilted her gaze skyward. The sun was climbin', bright an' bold, but the chill inside her lingered—a quiet ache o' regret and hope tangled thegither.

He's no' a brutish man. Just a man wi' ghosts.

She rose, brushin' dirt frae her skirts, resolve hardenin' like steel fresh frae the forge. It was time tae stop hidin' frae the man she had wed—the man who feared losin' her more than anythin'.

Wi' steady steps she turned toward the keep, each footfall a vow tae hersel': tae face him honestly, tae forgive, tae bridge the distance that still gaped between them.

Her heart fluttered wild, a storm o' nerves an' courage churnin' in her chest. But beneath it all, fierce determination burned—she would be more than a bride set aside, more than a game tae be won or lost.

She would show him the woman he had tae trust, the woman he had yet tae truly ken. And when she reached him, there would be nae more runnin'—not frae him, and not frae hersel'. Either way, she'd no' yield. Not to him. Not to anyone.

CHAPTER FOURTEEN

Tryss

TRYSS STOOD BY THE hearth, the fire's flicker castin' restless shadows across the stane walls. His hands clenched an' unclenched at his sides, the mornin's chase still thrummin' like a bruise he couldnae shake. Each breath scraped shallow, the air heavy as if his ribs couldnae stretch wide enough tae draw it in. The fire's heat pressed against his skin, but it was the ghost o' Gavin's fall that haunted the room.

He had locked the door behind him, desperate for solitude, yet the silence only sharpened the ache inside. Could he truly forgive her? Could he trust this wild, fierce woman who had kindled a fire in him an' threatened tae burn everythin' tae ash?

The knock on the door startled him, quick an' gentle.

Alyssa's voice, soft but steady, followed. "Tryss... may I come in?"

His throat tightened. Part o' him wanted tae say nay, tae retreat intae the fortress o' his fears an' pain. But another, deeper part—buried beneath years o' loss an' guarded scars—yearned for somethin' mair. For peace. For understandin'.

Wi' a slow breath, he stepped aside.

"Come in," he said, voice rough but low.

Alyssa stepped inside, eyes searchin' his face. Her voice was quiet, almost fragile.

"I didnae ken."

Tryss's chest tightened. The weight o' Fergus's words echoed in his mind—how she couldnae hae kent, how fear had driven him, no' anger. Yet his pride bristled beneath the surface, still raw frae the mornin's clash.

He watched her approach, slow an' deliberate, yet she kept a careful distance. Her hands stayed at her sides, nae reachin' out, nae attempt tae close the space between them too quick.

She's wary, he thought, like she fears what might come next. Afraid o' wakin' the storm in me again.

Tryss's jaw clenched, but he nodded once, silently urg in' her forward. Nae words came yet—only the silence between them, charged wi' everythin' left unsaid.

She stood afore him now, close but no' touchin', eyes flickerin' wi' uncertainty an' somethin' deeper—hope, mayhap.

Tryss's gaze lingered on her, dark eyes steady yet softened by the unspoken weight between them. The tension in his shoulders eased just a fraction as he lifted a hand slow, fingertips brushin' the air near her arm—a silent question, a tentative offerin'.

Alyssa held her breath, the faintest flicker o' hope stirrin' deep inside her. She didnae move away. Instead, she reached oot, her fingers tremblin' slightly, an' let her hand fall light intae his.

Tryss caught her hand gentle, his rough palm enclosin' hers wi' a tenderness that surprised even him. Wi'out a word, he turned toward the oversized chair nestled afore the hearth, its leather worn smooth by years o' use an' firelight.

He lowered himsel' first, lean frame sinkin' heavy intae the seat, then reached back, palm open in silent invitation.

Alyssa lingered a heartbeat longer, her gaze flickin' toward the door, the notion o' escape stirrin' in her chest. She could leave. She could turn back. But her hand trembled in his, an' the warmth o' it pulled her in, steady as a tide.

Slowly, she chose. She eased hersel' onto his lap, breath caught tight in her throat, head instinctively tuckin' beneath his chin. The crackle o' the fire filled the quiet between them, castin' a golden glow over their joined hands.

Neither spoke at first. Instead, she let her palm glide slow across the broad expanse o' his chest, feelin' the steady beat o' his heart beneath the worn fabric. The solid warmth beneath her fingers anchored her.

At last, her voice came, low an' hesitant. "Will ye tell me about him?"

Tryss inhaled deep, the name on her lips stirrin' a pain he had long kept buried. His eyes fixed on the flickerin' flames, memories washin' ower him like smoke curlin' through the night air.

"He was reckless," Tryss began, voice rough but steady. "My brither. Gavin. Always chasin' somethin' just beyond reach." He paused, swallowin' the tightness in his throat. "We were close, closer than most brithers. He had a fire in him... wild an' untamed." His hand tightened round hers ever so slightly.

She was quiet a moment, then lifted her gaze tae meet his. "What happened?"

Tryss's jaw clenched, the muscles tremblin' wi' the effort tae hold himsel' thegither. His gaze didnae waver frae the fire, but his eyes darkened wi' the weight o' memory—sharp an' raw, like a wound that never healed.

"One day," he began, voice low an' rough, "he lost that chase. I was wi' him." His breath hitched, throat tightenin'. "We were ridin' fast—too fast. The world a blur around us... then sudden, the edge o' that cursed ravine." His hands clenched hers tight, knuckles pale beneath his rough skin. "He misjudged the turn, an' then... he was fallin'."

Tryss swallowed hard, the image vivid as if branded on his mind—the way Gavin's horse's hooves kicked wild in the air, the sharp, gut-wrenchin' sound o' flesh an' bane against stane. The silence that followed was worse than any scream.

"I saw it all. Heard the crash. Raced doon after him, heart poundin' like a war drum in my chest." His voice cracked, raw wi' the years o' pain buried deep. "I found him... broken. Pieces o' him scattered in the dirt. An' I held him till the light left his eyes."

He traced slow, tremblin' circles on her palm, like he was tryin' tae soothe a ghost. "That day... it changed everythin'. Made me who I am. I carry it wi' me, every moment, every breath." His voice dropped tae a near whisper. "That's why I feared today—because I thought I was losin' ye the same way. That's why my anger took ower. It wasnae anger at ye... it was terror."

He swallowed hard, lettin' the words fall plain, wi'out flourish.
"Alyssa... I wronged ye. No' only in the fear I showed, but in the way I bore it. I laid hand tae ye afore my men, an' I kissed ye like a gaoler silencin' his charge. It should no' hae been so."

Her eyes flashed, chin liftin'. "Aye, ye did humiliate me, Tryss. Ye shamed me afore them all. The sting o' it still burns, an' I'll no' forget it easy."

He held her gaze steady, unflinchin'. "I ken it. An' I'll carry that shame, for it was mine tae earn. But hear me plain—I'd sooner see their scorn heaped on me a hundredfold than watch ye fall tae the same fate as Gavin."

The silence stretched, heavy but no longer raw. Her breath eased, though her shoulders stayed squared, proud still. She didnae forgive him outright, but she had her say, an' he had answered it wi'out falterin'.

Her lips curved then, sly as a spark catchin' tinder. "If that was meant tae be a husband's chastenin', I'll tell ye plain—it fell sore short o' the mark."

He huffed a rough breath, a sound half snort, half laugh, though the ache in his chest lingered. "Impudent lass," he muttered, shakin' his head. Yet the edge in his eyes softened, some o' the storm breakin'.

For a moment they sat close, her hand still warm in his, the fire cracklin' low. What had been grief an' fury bled intae somethin' else—somethin' lighter, warmer. No' peace, no' yet, but the first taste o' it.

"And what pray tell, wife o' mine, would ye ken o' such matters?" he asked at last, his voice rough but touched wi' wry humor.

Her brow arched, eyes glintin'. "Mair than ye'd credit, husband."

Afore she could say mair, he leaned in, brushin' his lips against hers. Gentle at first, aye, but the heat caught quick between them, simmerin' like the hearth at their backs.

Alyssa broke away, breath tremblin', eyes dark wi' challenge. "Tell me your fancy, Tryss," she whispered, voice husky. "I would be all for ye—if ye'll let me."

He kissed her again, slower, drawin' it oot till her lips parted on a sigh, then pulled back just enough tae murmur against her mouth. "I fear ye're no' up tae the task, lass. Nay—I could no' ask it o' ye."

Her eyes widened, curiosity sparklin' wi' the firelight. "Tell me," she pressed, lip caught between her teeth, gaze searchin' his.

His smile turned wicked as he kissed her once mair, his words low, conspiratorial. "If ye truly wish tae ken... my greatest fancy is for a wife meek, mild, an' biddable tae my every command."

Her mouth fell open, eyes flashin' wi' fierce fire, a spark that dared tae burn hotter than any obedience.

Tryss's grin deepened, wicked an' certain. "I did warn ye, I ne'er thought ye up tae the task. So I'll content mysel' wi' my fancies—for now."

Afore she could answer, his lips claimed hers again, sealin' the unspoken challenge between them.

Chapter Fifteen

Alyssa

"Laird, what ye do tae me," Alyssa gasped between kisses, her fingers curled tightly intae the thick folds o' Tryss's linen shirt.

Tryss growled low in his throat, his lips claimin' hers again wi' a hunger barely restrained. His body pressed intae hers, slow an' deep, each motion a silent declaration—one she answered wi'out hesitation. Her breath hitched as her hips rose instinctively tae meet him, drawn intae the wild rhythm only they could make. It wasnae just passion—it was power shared, claimed, an' given freely.

The world had narrowed tae this: the heat o' the hearth, the tangled sheets, the sound o' her name broken frae his lips like a vow.

Then—a knock.

Tryss froze. Alyssa, wide-eyed beneath him, gave a soft, startled laugh.

"Gods' teeth, man! No' now!" Tryss roared toward the door, no' botherin' tae lift his head.

Another knock.

Alyssa bit her lip tae stifle her giggle, her hands slidin' up his back. "Should we answer it?"

His eyes blazed doon at her, voice low an' dangerous. "They'll be lucky if I dinnae answer it wi' my sword."

She laughed again, breathless, an' Tryss claimed her mouth in another kiss—rougher this time. "They'll wait," he muttered against her skin, determined tae finish what the knock had tried tae steal.

But the knock came again.

Tryss groaned an' collapsed beside her wi' a thud, arm thrown ower his eyes. "There's nae justice in this world."

Alyssa rolled tae her side, proppin' hersel' on one elbow. "Shall I answer it for ye, husband? Mayhap they've come tae inform ye o' a sheep stuck in a ditch."

He peeked at her frae beneath his arm, smirkin'. "If there's a sheep involved, I'm sendin' ye tae handle it."

She tossed a pillow at his head an' slipped oot o' bed, wrappin' hersel' in a throw. Tryss sighed an' rose wi' far less grace, pullin' on his trousers just as the door creaked open.

It was Fergus.

"Ye're a dead man, Fergus," Tryss growled, voice still rough wi' frustration.

But Fergus only crossed his arms an' leaned one shoulder against the doorframe, entirely unfazed. "Aye, well, I've died a hundred deaths for worse offenses than interruptin' yer bed sport. I'll add it tae the tally."

He didnae apologize. Not even a flicker o' remorse.

"There's trouble," Fergus said, tone shiftin'. "Ye'd best come doon an' hear the word."

Tryss stiffened. The last remnants o' his humor drained frae his face. He swung a shirt ower his head an' began lacin' his boots, urgency cuttin' through his movements. Alyssa stood behind him, her arms wrapped around the throw blanket, watchin' the tension settle like armor across his shoulders.

"What kind o' trouble?" he asked wi'out lookin' up.

Fergus shifted his weight an' said grimly, "It concerns M'Lady as well. I'll wait for ye in the hallway."

Tryss's head snapped up, eyes narrowin'. "Alyssa?"

Fergus gave a curt nod, eyes flickin' past him tae where Alyssa stood wrapped in the blanket, cheeks flushed but gaze defiant. His expression was unreadable—half accusin', half wonderin'—but no' unkind. Then, wi'out further explanation, Fergus stepped back an' pulled the door shut behind him.

Tryss turned slowly, the tension already curlin' beneath his skin.

"Well," he muttered, his voice a rough blend o' frustration an' reluctant amusement, "if ye were willin' tae wait, ye might hae stayed oot the door another five minutes."

Alyssa raised a brow, completely unrepentant. "Ye'd hae needed ten," she said primly.

He barked oot a sharp laugh despite himsel', shakin' his head. "Cheeky."

But the humor faded quickly as he moved toward her, already reachin' for her discarded gown. "Whatever this is... I dinnae like the sound o' it."

She took the dress frae his hands an' began slippin' it ower her shoulders. "Ye dinnae suppose someone's challenged the marriage?"

"No' unless they're daft," Tryss said, voice clipped. "But Fergus looked unsettled—and he doesnae rattle easy."

She fastened the last ties an' turned tae face him, all the

playfulness frae moments ago gone, replaced by the steel she wore when risin' tae a challenge. "Then let's go find oot."

Tryss took a moment tae study her, this woman who had upended his world an' now stood beside him like she'd always belonged there. Then he gave a single nod, set his jaw, an' opened the door.

Fergus straightened frae where he leaned against the wall. Wi'out a word, he turned an' began doon the hall, Tryss an' Alyssa followin' close behind, shoulder tae shoulder.

They took the turnin' by the great stair. Boot leather scuffed stone; a maid dipped her head an' fled. Word had run faster than they did.

They descended the stone stairs intae the main hall, the early sun slantin' through the high windows in golden bands. Alyssa's heart thudded hard against her ribs, but her stride never faltered. Tryss was at her side, tall an' silent, his expression carved frae granite. Whatever awaited them below, they would face it thegither.

The doors tae the hall stood open, an' Fergus stood just inside them, eyes sharp.

"They're waitin'," he murmured, steppin' aside.

Alyssa barely had time tae see who "they" were afore a whirlwind o' pale silk an' honey-brown curls launched across the room.

"Dear cousin!" the lass cried, eyes wide an' shimmerin' wi' excitement. "Thank ye!"

Alyssa blinked as the lass grabbed her hands wi' both o' hers, breathless an' beamin'.

"When ye suggested marryin' Laird Tryss by proxy sae I could get ower my nerves an' fright, I thought ye daft," the lass babbled, her voice pitched tae carry. "But here I am—brave an' ready tae take my place!"

Alyssa didnae speak. She couldnae. She just stared at the lass—Elsyn—whose soft features an' gilded curls mirrored a version o' hersel' Alyssa had once overheard described as "the more proper match." Her cousin. Her rival.

Behind Elsyn, her faither—the Marquess o' Briarhaven—stood tall an' thin, hands clasped behind his back, his expression utterly unreadable.

Tryss didnae move either. His body went still as stone beside Alyssa. But she felt the power in his silence, the storm brewin' behind his eyes. He said nothin' yet. He didnae need tae. Alyssa could feel it in the air—somethin' dangerous, just barely leashed.

Elsyn mistook the silence for approval.

"Oh, I'm sae grateful ye went through wi' it on my behalf, truly," she went on, clutchin' Alyssa's hands tighter. "An' no' tae worry—we'll make sure everyone understands the arrangement noo. I'm ready tae stand as the proper Lady MacCraith. I've practiced curtseyin' in the mirror an' everythin'."

Alyssa's eyes narrowed, her voice cuttin' cool an' clear across the hall. "A curtsey costs less than courage, Elsyn — an' ye've naught but the one tae offer."

Tryss finally took a step forward, voice low an' deadly calm. "Ye married me by proxy?" he asked, gaze like ice.

Elsyn blinked. "Well, no' legally, o' course. I was too nervous, mind ye?" She turned back tae Alyssa wi' a giggle. "But she stood in for me. Ye ken, tae keep up appearances. So nae one would question it until I found my courage."

Fergus choked on somethin' that sounded suspiciously like a laugh. Alyssa shot him a look. He composed himsel' quickly.

Alyssa found her voice, cool an' measured despite the fury risin' inside her. "I said nae such thing. Ye're lyin', Elsyn."

Elsyn gasped. "Cousin!"

Tryss's eyes whipped tae Alyssa, his stare sharp as a blade, disbelief carved intae every line o' his face. His voice came low an' hard. "Is it true, Alyssa? Did ye ken o' her intent tae claim her place?" He took a step closer, betrayal flickerin' behind his eyes. "Ye said she wanted ye tae wed me because she didnae want tae be wed. Ye said..."

He trailed aff, the unspoken weight between them thick an' bitter.

Alyssa opened her mouth, but nae sound came.

"I—Tryss, I didnae ken she would say this. I swear it." Her words were breathless, tangled in shock an' fury. "She didnae want tae wed ye. She said she couldnae, she was afraid—she gave up her claim. She—"

But he wasnae lookin' at her noo. No' fully. He was lookin' through her, tryin' tae sort truth frae memory, frae doubt. She had lied tae him once afore. He hadnae forgotten.

Murder burned hot behind Alyssa's eyes as she turned back tae Elsyn, voice shakin' no' wi' fear—but wi' barely contained rage. "Tell him the truth, Elsyn. Ye were the one who said ye couldnae go through wi' it. That yer faither would ne'er force ye. That marryin' a Highland laird would destroy yer future."

Elsyn blinked, pale lashes flutterin'. "I said I was scared," she whispered, all innocence an' wide eyes. "But that ye would help me. That's what ye said, Alyssa. That ye would help."

"I did help!" Alyssa snapped. "I saved ye frae the very match ye begged tae escape. An' noo ye stand here in my hame an' lie through yer teeth?"

Elsyn clutched her chest like she'd been slapped, twistin' slightly toward her faither for effect. "Ye said ye were doin' it for me," she said again, louder this time, lettin' the words carry through the hall. "Ye said ye would stand in until I could find my courage. I thought ye were my friend..."

The breath caught in Alyssa's throat. For a moment, the room spun.

Tryss's jaw clenched, his body a still wall o' silence. He turned slowly back tae Alyssa, every movement deliberate, tight wi' the restraint o' a man caught between fury an' disbelief.

"Alyssa." His voice was quieter noo, but nae less dangerous. "Did ye lie tae me again?"

She shook her head, mouth dry, her pride crumblin' under the weight o' everythin' unspoken between them.

"I told ye the truth," she whispered, voice raw. "I am yer wife. I wanted tae wed ye, e'en if I didnae ken it then. I never meant tae deceive ye."

But doubt had already taken root. She could see it. Feel it.

"I trusted ye," he said low. "After everythin'—after this mornin'—I trusted ye."

Tears burned in Alyssa's eyes, but she refused tae let them fall. No' in front o' Elsyn. No' in front o' her faither. No' here.

"She's lyin'," she whispered.

Tryss turned his gaze on Elsyn, an' for the first time since the lass entered the room, the mask slipped frae his face. Disgust. Cold, sharp, an' unmistakable.

"And you," he said, voice noo flint on steel. "Ye're a fool tae think ye could twist yer way intae a bond already sealed."

"But—" Elsyn's words faltered.

"Ye were no' at the altar. Ye were no' at my side. An' nae matter what cowardly fancy ye've spun, ye were no' the one I kissed when the vows were spoken." His voice thundered noo. "I ken who I married."

Alyssa's breath caught, hope darin' tae take tender hold in her chest.

Tryss turned back tae her—eyes still stormy, but different noo. A flicker o' somethin' else in them. Pain, aye. But belief was tryin' tae claw its way back in.

“Get oot,” he growled, voice flat an’ final. “The both o’ ye.”

The marquess sputtered, but Tryss stepped forward, towerin’ an’ unrelentin’. “I willnae say it again.”

Elsyn’s lip trembled, but her faither caught her by the arm, an’ they turned, sweepin’ frae the room in stunned, stutterin’ silence.

At the threshold, the Marquess leaned doon tae murmur sharp in his dochter’s ear, his words meant for her alone yet carryin’ just enough tae reach Alyssa. “Make this play work, bairn—or ye’ll nae hae a place left in Briarhaven tae crawl back tae.”

Elsyn’s face blanched, her lips partin’ as if tae protest, but no sound came. Her eyes flicked, wide and desperate, frae her faither tae Alyssa—pleadin’, accusin’, beggin’ all at once, as though her cousin might yet shoulder the burden she couldnae carry alone.

Alyssa’s chin lifted, her voice low but cuttin’. “Dinnae look tae me, cousin. Ye chose this lie yersel’.”

The Marquess’s mouth hardened tae a thin line. Wi’out another word, his grip clamped firmer on Elsyn’s arm, haulin’ her off like a man draggin’ tainted wares from market. Their steps echoed across the stone, then the doors boomed shut behind them, leavin’ only the crackle o’ the hearth in their wake.

Alyssa stood frozen, her hands curled intae fists at her sides. Her legs felt boneless, her chest hollow.

Tryss didnae move. He was starin’ at the closed doors, his shoulders heavin’ once afore he exhaled.

“I dinnae ken what tae believe, Alyssa.” he said quietly—too quietly—an’ then turned on his heel, stridin’ frae the hall wi’out another word.

The echo o’ his boots faded doon the corridor, each step feelin’ like a hammer against her ribs.

He was gone. That thread o' hope, that he would believe her, trust her, snapped.

Alyssa stood frozen, the breath caught in her throat. She stared at the door he'd vanished through, willin' him tae return. Tae say onything. Tae look at her the way he had only hours ago by the hearth—when she'd been safely tucked in his arms, her head beneath his chin, the past beginnin' tae lose its hold.

But he didnae come back.

An' she couldnae blame him.

She had lied once—just once. But it had been enough. Enough tae make him question everythin'. Enough tae cast doubt ower every truth she noo offered. That lie, that single thread pulled in desperation tae protect her cousin, had unraveled all the trust they'd slowly begun tae weave between them.

It would be like this their whole marriage, would it no'?

That single deception would hang ower them like a storm cloud, shadowin' every touch, every word, every vulnerable truth that followed. Nae matter how much she loved him—nae matter how fiercely she tried tae prove hersel'—he might ne'er trust her again. An' it was all her fault.

The thought hollowed her.

She turned slowly an' looked around the grand hall. The fire still crackled in the hearth. The chairs sat in quiet witness tae her shame. The stone walls, sae grand an' ancient, felt suddenly too tall, too cauld, too unforgivin'.

There was nothin' left tae do.

Nae speech tae offer, nae gesture tae fix it, nae vow she could make that would no' sound like another trick.

Alyssa walked numbly toward one o' the long benches along the wall an' sank doon, her hands folded in her lap, shoulders bowed.

She tried tae keep her chin high. She tried no' tae tremble.

But her heart had finally shattered.

An' when the first tear slipped free, she didnae stop it.

She sank intae the emptiness. Grief settled ower her shoulders like a shroud. She wept. When the weepin' ebbed, she wiped her cheeks clean. If truth couldnae stand alone, she'd haul it by the scruff an' set it afore him.

Chapter Sixteen

Tryss

"Nae, Fergus!" Tryss snapped, his voice like thunder in the corridor. "They're both liars. I'm bound tae a liar for the rest o' my years."

Fergus stood firm in his path, arms crossed, jaw tight wi' frustration. "Ye dinnae ken that."

"I do," Tryss growled, turnin' away, pacin' like a caged beast. "She lied once, she lied again. Lied tae her cousin, lied tae me. Gods, she might hae been lyin' this whole time."

"Are ye hearin' yersel'?" Fergus shot back, voice low but hard. "Ye sound like a man wi' nae sense left in his head. Aye, she lied. Once. But are ye sae perfect ye never would hae done the same?"

Tryss rounded on him. "I trusted her. I let her in, Fergus. I let her in."

"And ye think she didnae do the same?" Fergus countered, steppin' closer. "Ye think that lass in there didnae hand ower her whole heart tae ye this mornin' by that fire? Ye think she wanted tae lie tae ye frae the start?"

Tryss's face twisted wi' fury an' pain. "She made me believe I was chosen. That she wanted me. That it was her choice, no' some tangled game wi' Elsyn behind it. I thought..." His voice broke. "I thought I had somethin' real."

For a moment, silence pressed between them like iron.

Then, quieter, Fergus said, "Ye do."

Tryss flinched, his jaw clenchin' again, but he didnae respond.

Fergus stepped forward, voice gentler noo. "She never planned tae wed ye. Aye, that's the truth. But once she did... she fought for ye. Every damn step o' the way. Ye ken it. She could hae walked awa' when Elsyn came. She didnae. She stayed. She faced it. She faced ye."

Tryss turned back toward the stone wall, pressin' a hand against the cauld surface like it could ground him, calm him, make ony o' this make sense.

Alyssa

She pushed the door shut behind her wi' a soft click, the sound far too final for her likin'. Kickin' aff her slippers, she climbed onto the bed an' curled intae hersel', draggin' the coverlets ower her head like they could block oot the world—or the memory o' his face when he asked if it was true.

He hadnae believed her. No' really. How could he? She had lied afore.

An' noo that one moment—that one mistake—had wedged itsel' between them like a blade. Tryss had left her standin' alone in the hall wi' that same hollow expression Gavin must hae worn when he fell.

Her throat burned all ower again. "I didnae lie tae him... no' this time," she whispered intae the blankets.

But what was the use in sayin' it? The truth didnae matter when trust was gone.

She didnae ken how long she cried this time, only that the ache in her chest didnae dull wi' the tears. Eventually, exhaustion pulled her doon intae fitful sleep—tangled sheets, muffled sobs, an' the empty echo o' a marriage unravelin'.

Some time later—minutes? hours?—the door creaked open.

Alyssa sat bolt upright, her hair a tangle, her heart thunderin' in her chest. "Tryss?" she breathed, hope flarin' like a candle in the dark.

But it wasnae Tryss.

There, standin' by her hearth, calmly warmin' her hands as if nothin' in the world had happened...

...was Elsyn.

Tryss

Tryss had heard enough for one day. The words still echoed in his mind—Fergus's stubborn defense o' Alyssa, the blind loyalty in his brother's voice. Why? Why did Fergus keep takin' up for her, when Tryss could see the truth plain as day? They were both liars—each hidin' their ain secrets beneath well-worn smiles an' half-truths. But Tryss refused tae believe Alyssa's lies. No' noo. No' ever.

He walked intae their chamber wi'out ceremony an' flopped doon intae the sturdy leather chair beside the hearth. The fire's glow flickered across his face, but Tryss barely noticed. His mind churned, rage an' doubt twistin' intae a knot o' frustration an' despair.

Did she laugh at me the whole time? Think me a fool tae be led by a bonnie face an' a bold tongue? Gods, had I been so blind?

The silence pressed against him, unbearable. After only moments, it felt as if the chair had burned him. Wi' a sharp breath, he rose an' began pacin' the room—back an' forth, the weight o' the past an' present draggin' at his shoulders.

I gave her my trust. I let her see what none else could. An' what did she gie me back? Lies. Lies wrapped in fire an' laughter. Och, Gavin, ye warned me well enough—dinnae let the heart rule the hand. An' yet here I stand, broken open like a lad at his first tilt.

His gaze fell on the empty bed—where Alyssa should be—and the ache in his chest deepened.

It should hae been Elsyn here. Elsyn, prim an' proper, the match that made sense. Instead I've Alyssa—wild, defiant, a flame I cannae quench. She's mine by vow, mine by law... but was it ever hers tae gie?

He dragged a hand doon his face, breath harsh. *Did she steal what she ne'er wanted tae begin wi'? Or has she spoken true at last, an' I'm the blind fool who cannae see it?*

The doubt cut deep, sharper than anger. *Och, Alyssa... if ye lied again, I'll break on it. An' if ye didnae—then God help me, I've already broken all the same.*

Alyssa

Alyssa's eyes blazed as she rose frae the bed, the thin coverlets fallin' forgotten tae the floor. "Enough, Elsyn." Her voice was low, steady, but filled wi' a fury that surprised even hersel'.

Elsyn's smile widened, confident an' cruel, as she stepped closer, unaware o' how much Alyssa had changed. "Ye think ye can still stop what's comin'? Ye've been my pawn frae the start, dear cousin. Just like when we were bairns—always coverin' for me when I caused trouble, always forgiven while I let ye take the blame."

Elsyn's eyes gleamed wi' a mix o' desperation an' defiance as she paced the room afore turnin' sharply tae face Alyssa.

"Ye think I wanted tae wed Tryss? Ne'er," she spat, her voice sharp as a blade. "I needed someone tae stand beside him—someone tae wed him—so I could keep my ain plans."

Her fingers twisted in her skirts, wringin' the silk as though she could strangle her shame out o' sight. "Ye were perfect. The veil would hide ye, an' the clan would believe I'd taken my rightful place. All the while, I was chasin' after another."

Her face soured, bitterness curlin' her mouth. "I had already lain wi' him—the one I truly wanted tae wed. I believed he would do the right thing, that he'd wed me." She gave a sharp, humorless laugh. "But he didnae. He abandoned me."

When her gaze rose again, it locked on Alyssa, cold an' unblinkin'. "Noo I'm wi' child an' need a husband. If I can convince them I always intended tae wed Tryss an' ye wed him by proxy for me, then I'm saved."

She leaned forward then, her eyes glitterin' with a sly, desperate edge, noddin' slow as though willin' Alyssa tae bend. "I can bed him the nicht, an' everyone will just think the bairn is early later on."

Alyssa's breath caught. Her eyes flashed wi' a fierce, unwavering resolve. She shook her head slowly, voice steady but charged wi' conviction.

"Nay. Nay, Elsyn. Nay."

She took a step closer, voice firm, every word a declaration. "I refuse tae do this tae him. I am his wife. That bairn is no' his—and I willnae give him up."

Her gaze locked on Elsyn's, unyieldin'. "Nay."

The room fell intae a tense silence as Alyssa stood her ground—strong, determined, unbreakable.

Tryss

Tryss sat stiffly in the chair, the weight o' the day pressin' doon on him like stone. Then came the voices—low at first, then sharp an' angry—echoing through the thin walls o' the adjoinin' chambers. Alyssa's voice, fierce an' resolute, an' Elsyn's, smooth but bitin'.

His eyes snapped toward the door connectin' their rooms. The walls were thin—far thinner than he'd imagined. If they could hear each other this clear, then ony near at hand could as well. A flush o' discomfort heated his cheeks. Och, the things they might hae heard—his ain anger, his whispered regrets, the tangled mess o' his heart an' hers laid bare.

Tryss leaned forward, the knot in his gut tightenin' as he strained tae catch every word. Alyssa's tone shifted, a quiet strength risin' beneath the fury. He heard her refuse, firm an' unyieldin', a stand she'd ne'er taken afore.

Wi'out thinkin', wi'out pause, Tryss shoved back frae the chair an' strode toward the door, his heart hammerin' loud enough tae drown oot everythin' else. He flung it open an' stepped intae the room, eyes blazin', voice rough but low:

"Enough."

Both women turned, surprise flashin' across their faces, but Tryss was done wi' silence. He stood there, solid an' unmovable, the storm o' the day settlin' intae a single, undeniable truth—he would face whatever came, an' nae lies would come between him an' Alyssa.

CHAPTER SEVENTEEN

Tryss

TRYSS'S BOOTS POUNDED AGAINST the stone floor as he stormed intae the room. His eyes blazed wi' fury, dark an' unrelentin', fixed on Elsyn wi' a predator's intensity. The air grew thick wi' his wrath afore he spoke—a low, cuttin' roar that filled the chamber.

"Elsyn," he spat, voice tremblin' wi' rage, "I hae ne'er met such a brazen, cruel, an' dishonourable woman in all my days. Ye come here wi' lies drippin' frae yer tongue like poison, weavin' deceit against yer ain kin, against me—against her, yer ain cousin!"

He took a step forward, every word a hammer strikin' doon. "Tae sit here an' plot this vile charade—tae claim what isnae yers, tae forge false bonds an' tarnish the sacred trust o' marriage—do ye hae ony notion o' what ye've done? Ye risk shatterin' lives, draggin' us all intae disgrace because o' yer selfish hunger for power an' position!"

His voice rose, echoing aff the cauld walls. "Ye think this is some game? Some bairn's scheme tae be swept aside when exposed? Nae. Ye hae stabbed me in the back, betrayed the woman who trusted ye, an' mocked the very bonds o' family an' honour. Ye hae nae only insulted me—ye hae insulted the legacy I bear, the blood o' my house, an' the woman I vowed tae protect."

Tryss's hands clenched intae fists at his sides, veins bulgin' wi' the force o' his anger. "Ken this—there is nae place for yer treachery here. Ye are poison, an' I willnae suffer it tae take root. I command ye—leave this place. Remove yersel' frae my sight, my halls, an' my life. If ye hae ony shred o' decency left, ye'll take yer lies an' yer false claims elsewhere an' ne'er return."

He stepped back, breathin' hard, his eyes blazin' as he glared at her. "Mark me well, Elsyn. I am nae man tae be played for a fool. An' I willnae hesitate tae cast oot onyone—family or nae—who dares threaten what is mine."

Elsyn's face blanched, but her chin lifted, eyes sparklin' wi' defiance. "Ye think ye've won, cousin? This isnae over. A MacCraith laird may cast me oot o' these halls, but ye cannae silence the tongues o' court. I'll see ye choke on the gossip afore I'm done."

Her laugh was brittle, edged wi' desperation, but she flung it at them like a weapon, sweepin' her skirts as if retreat were victory.

Alyssa didnae move. She stood rooted, chin high though her hands trembled at her sides. Tryss saw the sheen in her eyes, pride holdin' the tears at bay, defiance an' hurt warrin' in her face. She looked less like a lass caught in shame an' more like a queen who refused tae bow.

Tryss's fists clenched sae tight his knuckles ached, the storm no' near spent. Rage still roared in his blood, pride demandin' he turn his back, hold fast tae anger rather than yield. *She lied. She cut me deep. Am I a fool tae bend sae quick?*

But Alyssa's eyes held him—nae defiance noo, only the raw hurt he himsel' had carved there. The sight hollowed him. His jaw worked, the fight in him wrestlin' wi' the truth, until at last his shoulders sagged. The blaze in his gaze faltered, shamed by the weight o' what he'd loosed upon her.

The battle rage still roared in his blood, but another war stirred—one wi' pride. His tongue wanted tae cut, his chest wanted tae break. Apology tasted like surrender, yet her eyes demanded it. "Alyssa... please. Forgive me. For doubtin' ye, for my harshness this morn, for the storm I set loose when all ye wanted was tae be near me. I was blind wi' mistrust, but that doesnae excuse how I treated ye."

He reached oot, fingers tremblin' slightly, hopin' tae bridge the distance that had grown between them.

Alyssa's eyes flickered wi' a mix o' sorrow an' resolve. She swallowed hard, the weight o' everythin' pressin' doon on her chest. A single, unbidden tear threatened tae spill, but she blinked it back, her jaw tightenin' just enough tae hold the pain in check.

"I understand why ye're angry," she said softly, voice steady but tinged wi' quiet hurt. Her fingers curled briefly aroond his hand, then slipped awa' like a whisper o' loss. "I dinnae blame ye... no' truly."

She paused, searchin' his face as if tryin' tae convey everythin' words couldnae. Then, wi' a slow, almost imperceptible shake o' her head, she stepped back.

"But right noo... I need tae be alone. Tae find mysel' again beneath all o' this."

Her gaze held his for a long moment—equal parts apology an' quiet strength—afore she turned an' walked tae the door.

Wi'out another word, she opened it, offerin' him one last look, eyes brimmin' wi' unspoken promises an' fragile hope.

Then, wi' deliberate calm, she closed the door between them, leavin' the silence tae settle like a soft, achin' wound.

Her retreat felt like the clash after silence, the final blow struck when the foe was already gone. He'd raised his shield too late.

Alyssa

Pain shuddered through Alyssa like a relentless tide, cold as the North Sea, batterin' her frail defences an' leavin' her hollow. The spark between them—the fierce fire that had once roared—felt fragile as glass noo, cracked an' quiverin', ready tae shatter wi' but the lightest touch. Her heart ached wi' every beat, each thrum echoin' the widenin' gulf that yawned between her an' Tryss.

She crawled intae her bed alone, the coverlets clingin' tae her like a shroud, the silence loud as a dirge. At last, the tears came—silent, bitter, an' salt-sharp wi' regret. This bond, once wild wi' promise, once a vow she dared believe unbreakable, seemed tae be siftin' through her fingers like sand frae the shore, nae matter how tight she clenched her hand.

He will ne'er truly trust me, she thought, the bitter truth settlin' heavy in her chest. *Nae matter how oft I swear, nae matter how fierce I prove it—he will aye mistrust first, an' seek forgiveness later.*

Her fingers curled hard aroond the blanket, knuckles white, as if holdin' herself together could mend the cracks already carved deep. But the fractures ran wide, an' she kent it. She had lied once—*once*—an' that single deceit had unfurled like shadow across every tender truth they'd since shared.

"Is this the end?" she whispered intae the dim stillness, the words hangin' heavy, unanswered, hauntin'.

Her throat burned, her eyes sore wi' weepin', yet still her heart wouldna' rest. It beat on, ragged an' sore, trapped in that twistin' reel o' love an' doubt—wantin' tae believe in him, yet certain she'd lost him all the same.

Her breath broke on a sob, exhaustion draggin' her doon at last, though nae peace followed. Even in the grip o' sleep, her chest ached raw, an' her soul lay wide awake, tremblin' wi' the fear that the love she'd found had already slipped beyond her reach.

Tryss

Tryss remained rooted in the shadowed corridor, the door's soft click sealin' the distance between them like a wound he could neither see nor heal. His chest tightened, a familiar ache that had whispered beneath the surface afore—but this time it roared wi' undeniable blame. His fists clenched, nails bitin' intae the palms o' his hands as if punishin' himsel' for every fractured moment.

He swallowed hard, jaw clenched sae tight his teeth ground thegither, fightin' the sting o' shame that burned behind his eyes. The fire that once fueled his anger noo smoldered low an' cauld, replaced by a churnin', hollow weight in his gut.

Tryss's gaze fell tae the floor, tracn' the worn stanes beneath his boots as if seekin' for footin' in a crumblin' ground. The fault line in their marriage—once a whisper o' tension—noo yawned wide an' deep, an' for the first time, he couldnae deny that it was his ain hand that had cracked the foundation.

A bitter taste filled his mouth, no' frae fury, but frae regret sae raw it near choked him. The silence pressed close, thick an' suffocatin', broken only by the faint echo o' the door's final closin'—her choice made clear, the distance atween them suddenly impossible tae bridge.

He stood there, breath shallow, shadows gatherin' tight, feelin' the weight o' a truth he could nae longer avoid: this fracture wasnae just theirs—it was his alone.

If the heart was a battlefield, then he was naught but the wounded, seekin' fire an' whisky tae cauterize what blade had carved.

Turnin' sharply, Tryss stalked doon the dim corridor, each step echoing his mountin' frustration. The weight o' the silence behind him pressed unbearably, an' his mind raced wi' bitter thoughts an' sharp regrets. He needed tae drown the storm ragin' inside—needed somethin' strong enough tae blur the edges o' his guilt an' weariness.

His boots thundered across the stane floor as he made his way tae the great hall. There, by the hearth's fadin' embers, Fergus was sure tae be waitin'.

Tryss entered, all tension an' purpose. "Fergus," he growled, voice rough wi' raw emotion. "Fetch me a drink—or twenty. I need tae forget... or at least remember less sharply."

Tryss sank heavily intae the worn wooden chair, the firelight flickerin' across his tense face. Fergus moved aboot the room wi' practiced ease, uncorkin' a second bottle o' whisky an' fillin' their cups again. The warmth o' the drink was a sharp contrast tae the cauld weight pressin' on Tryss's chest.

"Drink up, laird," Fergus said wi' a knowin' smile, settin' a full cup afore him. "It's been a lang day, an' sometimes the heart needs a bit o' coaxin'."

Tryss lifted the cup but hesitated afore drinkin', as if wary that the whisky might loosen mair than just his tongue. Finally, he swallowed, the burn settlin' deep in his belly.

"It's no' the drink I'm wrestlin' wi'," Tryss muttered, starin' intae the amber liquid like it held answers. "It's the truth. The bloody truth I've been buryin'."

Fergus settled beside him, leanin' forward, eyes sharp but patient. "What truth's that, lad? Ye're no' one tae hide much."

Tryss shook his head, jaw tight. "I'm no' sure I want tae face it. The fault lines atween us keep shiftin'. I thought it was her—her lies, her defiance. But maybe... maybe it's me. Maybe I'm the one who's been breakin' beneath the weight."

Fergus nodded slowly, pourin' another round wi'out askin'. Tryss accepted, downin' it mair quickly this time.

"Tell me what's on yer mind. Nae judgment here, only ears."

Tryss let oot a harsh breath. "She's fire—wild an' untamed. An' I... I'm a man who's used tae controllin' the storm, no' dancin' wi' it."

Another sip, then a longer silence filled the room.

"D'ye think ye're ready tae gie her the freedom she needs?" Fergus asked softly.

Tryss's hand clenched the cup, knuckles pale. "I want tae. I want tae believe I can. But fear grips me—fear o' losin' her, fear o' no' bein' enough."

Fergus's voice was warm, steady. "Aye, love's a dangerous thing. It strips us bare, makes us vulnerable. But it's also the strongest shield we'll e'er carry."

Tryss looked up, eyes dark an' haunted. "Love... I've ne'er been certain o' what it means for me. No' since... since Gavin."

Fergus's expression softened. "We all carry ghosts, laird. But ye cannae let them define yer present."

The fire crackled as Fergus poured yet another drink. Tryss took it, swirlin' the liquid as if weighin' it against his fears.

"It's no' easy tae say," Tryss confessed, voice barely abune a whisper. "But… there's a pull inside me for her—a fierce, stubborn pull I've ne'er felt afore."

Fergus's grin widened. "Aye? Sounds like somethin' mair than a simple pull. Love isnae safe, lad. It demands mair than pride—it demands surrender."

Tryss's eyes flickered wi' reluctant admission. "I… I care for her mair than I want tae admit. Mair than I thought possible."

Fergus chuckled, a low, knowin' sound. "Aye, laird, ye do. Noo the question is—what will ye do aboot it?"

Tryss set doon his cup, determination hardenin' in his gaze. "I'll fight for her. For us. For the chance tae make this right."

Fergus clapped him on the shoulder. "That's the spirit. Let's drink tae that."

The fire had burned low, castin' a warm amber glow as the empty bottle sat heavily atween them. Tryss's eyelids drooped, words slurrin' intae soft mumblin'. Fergus watched quietly, lettin' the silence stretch, knowin' the laird's walls were finally crumblin'.

He leaned back, rubbin' the back o' his neck as if tryin' tae loosen the weight on him. His gaze, unfocused yet sincere, settled on Fergus.

"I… I love her," he said, voice rough, barely mair than a breath. The words landed atween them like a dropped sword—irrevocable.

Fergus's eyes twinkled wi' quiet triumph. "Aye, laird. Ye do."

Tryss blinked, the weight o' his ain words sinkin' in. He pushed himsel' up frae the chair, swayin' slightly.

"I'm gonnae go tell her… right noo."

He lurched forward, catchin' the armrest for balance, then tried again, legs unsteady beneath him.

Fergus chuckled, steadyin' the empty bottle on the table. "Maybe best wait for mornin', laird. Declarations o' love are aye sweeter in the daytime, dinnae ye think?"

Tryss frowned, aboot tae argue, but the warmth in Fergus's tone an' the slow creepin' weariness in his limbs made him sigh an' sink back doon.

"Daytime, then," he muttered, a reluctant grin tuggin' at his lips.

Fergus raised his cup in a quiet toast, a knowin' smile on his face.

"Good man." Fergus hoped the laird would remember his words proclaimin' love when he woke in the mornin'. That headache was goin' tae be a fierce reminder o' the night's honesty—the kind that only came after too many drinks an' a burdened heart.

Tryss let oot a long, heavy sigh, his head lollin' back against the chair, lids half-shut as if even the weight o' breath was near too much tae carry.

As Tryss slumped back intae the chair, mumblin' somethin' unintelligible aboot fightin' for what was his, Fergus shook his head wi' a smile. "Love isnae safe, lad. It demands mair than pride—it demands surrender. If ye cannae lay doon yer sword for her, ye'll lose her wi'out a battle."

Chapter Eighteen

Alyssa

THE PALE MORNIN' LIGHT seeped through the dark curtains, spillin' in wan bands that cast long, restless shadows across the chamber where Alyssa lay still beneath the blankets. The door tae the adjoinin' room remained shut tight—a wall o' oak an' iron that felt heavier than stone, a barrier keepin' her from Tryss. Her fingers curled loosely on the quilt, twistin' the weave as if the cloth could anchor her, but she made nae move tae reach for the handle. Her heart felt leaden, every beat draggin', weighed doon by the gulf that had opened between them like a chasm cut deep through the earth.

She swallowed the ache that threatened tae climb her throat, willin' hersel' no' tae be the wife who begged, the lass who pleaded for peace where suspicion waited ready tae wound again. *Hold yer chin high, Alyssa. Guard what's left o' yer heart. If he doubts ye still, let him wrestle wi' it alone.*

With a breath that shivered more than she liked, Alyssa slid frae the bed. The rush o' the cold stone floor bit at her bare feet, remindin' her she was flesh an' bone an' stubborn will—no' some ghost driftin' in sorrow. She dressed quiet as a thief, each layer o' wool an' linen cinched tight as armor. Then, wi'out a glance back at the silent door, she slipped doon the stair toward the great hall.

The keep already buzzed wi' life. Servants hurried through the chill, skirts swishin', voices low an' clipped. The scent o' fresh bread mingled wi' woodsmoke driftin' frae the kitchens, an' the smith's hammer rang in sharp rhythm frae the courtyard beyond. The noise washed ower Alyssa like a tide, drownin' the stillness she carried frae the chamber aboon. She breathed it in like air she had been starved o'.

She wasted nae time lingerin'. Her voice cut clear through the bustle as she summoned the steward, checked the stores, tallied the oats against the livestock. She sorted quarrels wi' a brisk word, smoothed disputes ower firewood an' wages, an' walked the length o' the hall wi' a step that brooked nae challenge. Her sharp eyes missed little—nae a loose latch, nae a carelessly stacked barrel.

Each task seized, each detail mastered, each decision rendered wi' swift authority—this was how she held hersel' thegither. *Dinnae falter. Dinnae bend. Let the keep see a mistress wi' steel in her spine, no' a woman hollowed by doubt.* The endless demands o' the hall filled the emptiness inside her, dullin' the sting o' the loneliness that threatened tae spill oot if she ever dared stop movin'.

Tryss

Frae the shadows near the hearth, Tryss watched her. His gaze followed her strong, measured movements, but a distant glaze in her eyes kept her just beyond reach. It had been days and her silence remained vigil.

She can command a hall o' men but winna spare me a word. Gods, hae I truly fallen sae far?

He tried tae catch her attention, offerin' a soft word as he passed, a brief smile meant tae bridge the silence—but she met him only wi' polite nods, neutral an' cool, as if he were a stranger passin' through the keep.

Days slipped past this way. Tryss's attempts grew mair frequent—mair desperate. A fresh wildflower left on her desk. A wrapped loaf o' bread tucked near her chair. A hand-carved wooden whistle placed gently on a table. Each time, Alyssa accepted the tokens wi'out a word o' thanks, warmth never sparkin' in her gaze.

Frustration twisted in Tryss's gut like a knot drawn tight wi' every failed attempt. One evenin', a minor dispute ower the harvest festival boiled ower.

"Why d'ye shut me oot, lass?" he demanded, voice sharp an' raw, eyes flashin' in the dim torchlight. "Are ye sae angry ye cannae even speak?"

Say somethin'. Shout. Scream. Anythin' is better than this damned silence.

Alyssa met his gaze steady, calm but resolute. "I am no' angry," she said softly, "only cautious. I cannae bear tae be broken again."

The words landed heavier than any harsh rebuke.

An' yet I was the one who did the breakin'.

Tryss's jaw clenched, muscles twitchin' as he fought for words, but afore he could speak, Alyssa turned awa', shoulders squared, disappearin' intae the shadows an' leavin' him alone wi' the flickerin' flames.

In the days that followed, they drifted like two shadows on the edge o' the same sunbeam—close enough tae feel warmth but never close enough tae truly meet. Their exchanges grew clipped, functional. Silence stretched thick atween them, heavy wi' everythin' left unsaid.

Tryss found her often in the courtyard, overseein' workers wi' a hard set tae her mouth an' eyes that held nae invitation. He'd approach, hopeful smile ready, but she met him wi' a polite tilt o' her head an' distant look afore turnin' back tae her duties.

One cauld night, beneath a sky strewn wi' stars, Tryss stood on the battlements, shoulders tense, breath foggin' the air. His voice was a low whisper carried awa' by the wind. "Alyssa..."

She willnae come. An' if she does, she'll look at me like she's still weighin' the odds. Maybe she should.

He leaned on the stone, starin' intae the distance. *What's left o' a man when the only soul who sees him winna even look at him anymore?*

Inside the keep, Alyssa sat by a dyin' fire, flickerin' flames echoing the turmoil inside her. Her hands clenched tight, nails bitin' intae her palms. She didnae want tae close her heart—but after lies, betrayals, shattered trust, how could she risk openin' it again?

Their love—fierce, wild, untamed—now hung by a thread stretched thin, strainin' atween silence an' shadow.

Fergus strode intae the great hall, his broad frame fillin' the space. His usually bright eyes were clouded wi' worry; he had seen the slow burn o' distance atween Alyssa an' Tryss, an' despite his best efforts, it showed nae sign o' coolin'.

He found Tryss near the hearth, fists clenched sae tight the knuckles whitened. The laird's dark eyes flicked up as Fergus approached, haunted an' restless.

"Laird," Fergus said cautious-like, "ye've been lockin' yersel' awa' mair than the keep's gates."

Tryss exhaled heavy, the tension in his shoulders loosening just a fraction. "Aye, Fergus. But the key... I cannae find it."

Fergus stepped closer, voice low an' firm. "Ye're missin' the truth, lad. She's no' turnin' frae ye tae spite ye. She's hurt—deep, deep doon. Same as yersel'. But the pair o' ye... ye're like two blades in the same wound, twistin' an' cuttin' where ye should be mendin'."

Tryss's jaw tightened again. "She winna speak—no' truly. Flowers, gifts, words... all in a cauld-arsed tone. Whit else am I tae do?"

"Ye broke mair than trust," Fergus said, sympathy weighin' his voice. "She's guardin' her heart noo. The shards cut sharp."

Tryss slumped intae a chair, head bowed. "I fear it's mair than trust. I fear I've lost her heart."

Lost it? Nay. I threw it awa' like it was nothin'. An' noo I'm scramblin' in the dirt tae find it.

Alyssa

Later, Fergus sought Alyssa in the bustling courtyard. She stood tall among workers, issuing orders wi' precise authority, but beneath her steel demeanor, exhaustion lingered in her eyes.

"Alyssa," Fergus said softly, steppin' beside her, "I've tried tae reach him, but ye both are lost in silence."

She glanced at him, lips pressed tight. "It's no' silence, Fergus. It's fear. Fear o' bein' broken again."

Fergus studied her, the lines o' her face drawn tight though her chin never wavered. "Aye, I ken it. But lass, I've seen him broken already—an' it's no' his pride that haunts him. It's losin' ye. The man bleeds in places nae blade could reach."

Her breath caught, though she turned her eyes back tae the bustle o' the yard. "I want tae believe him. God's truth, I want tae. I want us tae be what we were that first night, wi' nae doubt between us. But how do I open my heart when it feels sae fragile?"

Fergus nodded slowly. "Fragile? Aye, but even cracked stone can still stand. I see the way he looks at ye—like ye're the last light in a world gone dark. An' the pain in his voice when he speaks yer name... it near breaks a man tae hear it. He doesnae ken how tae mend this without ye."

She swallowed hard, the first tremor in her mask showin'. "I cannae make myself trust again sae easy."

"Then dinnae force it," Fergus said gently, his voice low enough for her ears alone. "Ye dinnae have tae open yer heart all at once. Sometimes, a crack is enough tae let the light in. But if ye never lift the latch, lass, ye'll both freeze behind doors ye've locked yerselves."

His words struck deep, a blunt kindness she couldnae turn aside. For a moment, Alyssa stood silent, the shouts o' workers an' clang o' iron drownin' beneath the thud o' her heart. She wanted tae run tae Tryss, wanted tae let him hold her like before... but fear clung sharp as briars.

Fergus laid a steady hand on her arm. "He's up there waitin', though he'd die afore he said it plain. Dinnae leave the man tae stew in his own doubts. Ye've more courage than most warriors I ken, Alyssa. Use a breath o' it now."

Alyssa's throat burned. She gave a small nod, gratitude catchin' in her chest. Without another word, she slipped away frae the steward's chamber, the weight o' the day pressin' heavy on her shoulders. The stone corridors o' the keep felt colder noo, the silence thicker as she made her way toward the shared chambers she had avoided for sae long.

Her hand trembled as it brushed the handle. For a moment, doubt fluttered like a sparrow in her chest. *Is this the right thing?* But she steeled herself, rememberin' Fergus's words—she didnae hae tae open everythin' at once. Just a crack, enough tae let the light in.

But God help her, she wanted more than a crack. She wanted tae fling the door wide, tae run intae his arms an' let him hold her until the world made sense again. She missed his rough laughter sparkin' across the hall, the warmth o' his hand claimin' hers in a crowd, the weight o' his gaze when it softened only for her. She missed the way his voice dipped low when he whispered her name, the safety o' his chest beneath her cheek, the fire they built together that chased every shadow away. Without him, the days dragged hollow, each task a march wi' nae music. Nights were worse—long an' cold, her body ache-in' for the heat o' his.

She loved him. God's truth, she did. An' the love was a hunger, sharp an' desperate, gnawin' through every wall she tried tae raise.

Still, fear clung. Her heart was tender, cracked like thin ice in spring, an' one wrong step could send her plungin' under.

Slowly, she pushed the door open and stepped inside.

The room was dim, lit only by the dyin' embers in the hearth. Shadows danced on the walls, soft an' flickerin' like the first glimmer o' dawn after a storm. The scent o' leather an' cedar lingered—familiar, yet distant.

She moved quietly tae the edge o' the bed, hands folded tight in front o' her. For a moment, she stood there, the hush near unbearable. Then, a soft creak frae the bedframe betrayed Tryss's presence. He stirred, eyes openin' slow, meetin' hers wi' guarded surprise.

Tryss

Gods above. She came back.

No words passed between them. Alyssa simply gave a small, tentative nod—an unspoken promise that she was willing to try.

Say nothing. Don't ruin it. Just - Be still. Let her stay.

She turned then, crossin' tae the window, her silhouette etched against the gatherin' dusk. Tryss watched the way her shoulders lifted, the faint tremor in her breath. She stood wi' her back tae him, but even in silence he felt it—some small shift, fragile as dawn through storm clouds. Hope stirred in his chest, faint but real, as if she were lettin' the light in, just enough tae reach him.

Tryss dragged the home-spun quilt behind him like a battle standard as he swung his legs over the side of the bed. He moved silently across the room, eyes fixed on Alyssa standing by the window, her silhouette outlined by the fading light. His cheek came to rest softly atop her head, his breath slow and steady against her hair.

If this is surrender, then let it be the last damn war I lose.

For a long moment, they stood like that—still, silent, the quiet only broken by the faint crackle of the dying hearth. Slowly, Tryss felt the tight coil of anger and hurt begin to unravel, the tension melting away beneath his touch.

She whispered, her voice trembling, "I didnae ken my heart could break like that, Tryss." A sob wrenched from her chest, fragile and raw.

Tryss tightened his hold, his voice low and earnest. "Alyssa, I'm so sorry. When we first consummated our love, we vowed tae be truthful tae each other all o' our days. The very first time that vow was tested, I forgot—you made that same promise too. I let my fear an' pain blind me, an' I failed ye. But I swear, from this moment on, I will remember that vow every day, an' I will honour it, for ye an' for us."

Another sob wracked Alyssa's chest, trembling through her frame as she turned and buried her face against Tryss's chest. Her fingers clutched at the fabric of his tunic, seeking the steady beat of his heart.

Tryss stilled, lowerin' his cheek tae her hair, breath minglin' wi' hers. The storm inside him eased—not gone, but tempered by the simple weight o' her in his arms. *Gods, she came back.* He hadnae earned this grace, yet here she was, giftin' him it anyway.

They stayed like that, silent, the crackle o' the hearth the only sound. Every rise an' fall o' her breath seemed a vow in itself. His hands tightened at her back, no' in hunger, but in awe—holdin' what he had near shattered.

When the trembling finally eased, he gently lifted her, his hands steady and sure, and carried her tae the worn leather chair nestled beside the hearth. Settlin' her onto his lap, he wrapped the quilt around them both, drawin' her closer until she felt the warmth o' his body against hers. His arms curved protectively around her, a steady anchor in the storm o' her emotions.

Her tears finally stilled, Alyssa lifted her head an' seized his mouth in a fierce, desperate kiss—fire flarin' frae sorrow, pourin' her hurt an' hunger straight intae him. Tryss felt the hollow places she carried crash against his own, the raw edge o' her need burnin' through the grief between them. He didnae pull awa'; he couldnae. Instead, he met her fire wi' his ain, grippin' her tight as if the strength o' his arms alone might hold the both o' them together

He waited on her lead, every movement slow and reverent. Pressin' her chest firmly against his, Alyssa lifted her gaze tae meet his dark, searchin' eyes, then raised her arms above her head—an unspoken invitation shimmerin' in her touch. Wi' deliberate care, Tryss peeled the soft fabric o' her sleep dress frae her skin, revealin' the warmth beneath. He buried his face between her breasts, breathin' in the scent o' her, his lips and tongue tracın' fiery paths across the tender skin.

Alyssa's fingers tangled in his dark curls, pullin' him closer, her body archin' as she pressed hersel' deeper against him—breast tae mouth, heart tae heart. Her hands slid doon between them, seekin', findin', an' strokin' him wi' gentle urgency. *For a heartbeat she hovered, eyes locked on his, as if daring him tae turn her awa'—then she lowered hersel', claimin' him wi'out hesitation.* Then, wi' a slow, controlled grace, she settled hersel' astride him, feelin' the solid heat o' his manhood press intae her.

Tryss ground out her name, breath ragged, "Alyssa... slow down, love."

But Alyssa's eyes burned with fierce determination. She slowed just enough, rising and falling along him, rocking gently until the pressure coiled deep inside her. Ignoring his whispered warnings, she picked up the pace again, urgency flooding every movement, the need too fierce to deny. He kent then it wasnae only passion drivin' her. Each fierce rise an' fall felt like defiance, a wild vow that she'd no' be cowed by doubt nor silence. She was burnin' through the hurt, claimin' him as surely as he claimed her. *This wasnae surrender—it was a battle cry, every thrust a demand that doubt yield tae her will.*

Tryss's hands clenched her hips, guiding her with raw strength, driving deep time and time again. Each thrust built the tension higher, until Alyssa cried out his name, her voice trembling with surrender as the wave crashed through her—consuming, powerful, and finally free.

Still joined, her legs wrapped tight around his waist, Tryss lifted her effortlessly and carried her to the bed. His body hardened anew, desire surging as he took his time—tracing slow, tantalizing rhythms, bringing her to the edge again and again, until she was wild with need, trembling beneath him. At last, with a fierce, shared surrender, he sent them both tumbling over the cliff—panting, spent, and utterly satiated. Holding her close, his breath warm against her ear, he vowed low and raw, "I'll ne'er let doubt stand between us again." Her only answer, fierce and simple, was: "Love me."

Chapter Nineteen

Fergus

IT WAS EARLIER THAN he usually rose, but Fergus had aye been a light sleeper. The moment the sun licked the rim o' the distant mountains, he was up, stretchin' the tightness frae his shoulders as he padded doon the hall toward the main chamber. The keep was quiet—the kind o' hush that follows a storm, when tension still clung tae the air like mist.

He took his usual seat near the hearth in the great hall, where the mornin' meal was already bein' set oot. The kitchen lasses moved brisk, placin' steamin' loaves o' bread, boiled eggs, an' slabs o' salt pork on the lang wooden table. The scent o' oatcakes an' smoke drifted through the air, settlin' in Fergus's lungs like an old comfort.

He poured himsel' a cup o' dark tea an' leaned back, lettin' the heat seep intae his hands as he stared intae the fire. His thoughts, as they had for days, hovered around the chaos Tryss had only just begun tae unravel.

Elsyn.

Tryss had telt him everythin'—aboot the deception, the betrayal, the near-weddin'. An' Fergus, gods help him, couldnae make sense o' it. No' entire.

He'd figured she'd be gone by noo. After bein' telt tae leave—by Tryss, nae less—he assumed pride alone would've carried her oot the gates. But there she stood.

The doors creaked open.

She stepped inside like a ghost, her presence somehow both muted an' strikin'. Elsyn.

Fergus blinked, caught aff guard by the sheer presence o' her. No' painted or polished, but devastatin' bonnie in a way that wasna tryin' tae be. Her dark hair hung in a thick braid ower one shoulder, an' though her dress was simple an' worn frae travel, she moved like one used tae bein' obeyed. Aye, shame bowed her head, but it hadna broken the spine o' her.

He stood afore he meant tae.

"Lady Elsyn," he greeted, his voice quieter than usual.

Her eyes met his wi' guarded calm. "Fergus. Ye're up early."

He gestured tae the table. "So are ye. Sit, then?"

She hesitated, then nodded an' moved tae sit opposite him. She tore a piece o' bread frae the loaf but didna eat, just turned it in her hands.

He watched her a lang moment, then asked, "Why are ye still here?"

Her fingers stilled on the bread. "It was too late tae leave last nicht."

Fergus raised a brow. "That's no' all o' it. Tryss made himsel' clear. If ye truly had somewhere else tae go, ye'd be gone."

She looked doon, her lashes castin' dark shadows on her cheeks. Her voice, when it came, was quiet an' brittle. "I dinna."

He waited. When she said naething mair, he leaned forward slight. "Elsyn. Speak plain. Why are ye really still here?"

She swallowed hard, the movement visible in her throat. Her voice trembled. "Because I've nae home tae return tae. My parents hae turned me oot."

Fergus frowned. "Why would they—?"

She cut him aff, her words tumblin' oot fast an' low. "Because I am wi' bairn. Seven months frae noo, I'll hae a babe..." Her grip shredded the crust tae crumbs. She didna look up. "...an' the man I loved—he left me."

A heartbeat o' stillness pressed atween them.

Elsyn's hands clenched roond the torn piece o' bread. She kept her eyes fixed on it, her voice thick wi' shame. "I thought we'd wed. He said he'd speak wi' my faither. But when the time came, he vanished. An' when my parents found oot... they were furious. Disgraced. They telt me I'd ruined ony chance o' a match an' that I was nae longer welcome in their hame."

Fergus leaned forward, brows drawn. "An' that's why yer faither dragged ye here—so ye might reclaim the ladyship, mend the shambles ye'd made o' their name an' reputation."

Her lashes flickered, a flash o' pain cuttin' through the shame. "Aye. He said if I couldna set it right, I was naught but cast off. This was my last chance—his command, no' my choice."

Her voice gave oot. She lowered her face intae her hands. "I hoped Alyssa would forgive me in time," she whispered through a sob. "But noo I've nae place, nae prospects, an' in a few months, a bairn I must somehow bring intae this world alone."

Fergus could see the way o' it noo. She looked hollowed oot by shame an' desperation. Wretched as she had been the day afore, her position noo was naught short o' ruin.

He leaned forward, elbows firm upon the board. "Hear me, Elsyn. I ken Tryss, an' I'm beginnin' tae ken Alyssa. They're no' cruel folk, no' unless cause is gi'en. If ye're sorry—as it seems ye are—then speak it plain. Confess, beg pardon. I doubt either would cast ye oot, no' at this hour."

Elsyn looked up at him, eyes brimmin' wi' tears.
"Ye think there's hope?"

He gave a half-smile. "I think there's aye hope, if ye're brave enough tae ask for it."

She swallowed hard an' gave a shaky nod.

Fergus didna reach for her hand, didna offer grand comforts. He simply poured her a second cup o' tea an' pushed it gentle across the table.

They sat like that in the silence, steam curlin' atween them, as the first warmth o' mornin' finally touched the stones aroond them. *Hope was a poor meal, but sometimes it was enough tae keep a soul standin'.* An' if there was one thing he'd learned, it was that truth—sharp an' bare—was the only weapon that ever mended more than it maimed.

Tryss

He woke wi' a lightness in his chest—a foreign, fragile thing that made him wary o' even breathin' too deep. A new start. Again. But maybe this one would hold.
Tryss blinked at the low mornin' light softenin' the edges o' the chamber. Beside him, Alyssa lay curled on her side, her back pressed intae him, hips nestled perfect against his. Her lashes lay like fans against her cheeks, her breathin' steady an' warm.

Gods, how can she look like peace an' trouble both in the same breath?

He wrapped his arms around her, gatherin' her close until her spine fit the line o' his chest. He nuzzled the back o' her neck, whisperin' words o' love an' lust intae her skin—words that belonged tae nae one else.

"Mornin', my storm," he murmured.

She stirred but didnae speak. Instead, her fingers closed around his hand, guidin' it up ower her ribs, where she kissed his palm wi' a sleepy softness that undid him. Then, still silent, she pressed his hand flat ower her breast, holdin' it there like a seal.

Tryss could just see the curve o' a smile—wicked an' unmistakable—tug at her lips. Little minx. Her bottom gave a teasin' wriggle against his already hardenin' shaft.

"Alyssa." he whispered intae her hair, draggin' his callused fingers across her breast until her nipple pebbled hard beneath his palm. He rolled it gentle, felt her shiver.

She's tryin' tae slay me. An' I'd die willin'.

His mouth found the spot just behind her ear, suckin' soft, markin' her as his even now. She arched back intae him, a soft sound catchin' in her throat as his other hand slid lower, ower her belly, doon tae the wet heat waitin' for him.

"Already ready for me," he whispered, groanin' as his fingers slipped atween her folds. "Have ye been dreamin' o' me, lass?"

Alyssa tilted her head tae grant him better access, a low hum o' agreement escapin' her lips.

"I kenned ye'd be trouble the moment ye opened that mouth," he muttered. "I just didnae reckon ye'd ruin me."

Her only reply was tae press her hips backward, grindin' intae him, her body wordless beggin' for mair.

Tryss hooked a leg atween hers, spreadin' her slow as he kissed the back o' her shoulder. He slid intae her in one long, reverent stroke, his breath catchin' at the heat that welcomed him in. Alyssa gasped, her hand reachin' behind tae grip his thigh.

"Gods above," he hissed. "Ye feel like sin an' sanctuary."

They moved thegither in slow rhythm, bodies tangled beneath the soft sheets, the world narrowin' tae naught but shared breath an' slick heat. Tryss held her close as he thrust deep an' slow, his hand cuppin' her breast, thumb strokin' lazy circles as her moans grew louder.

She turned in his arms, facin' him noo, her cheeks flushed, eyes dark wi' desire. She climbed atop him wi' a graceful swing o' her hips, bracin' hersel' against his chest as she began tae ride him—slow at first, torturous-like.

Tryss's hands clutched her thighs, his jaw clenched as he tried tae hold on.

"I am undone," he groaned. "At yer mercy entire." *Pride had warred wi' fear for days, but in her arms he found neither—only surrender sweet as breath.*

"Good," she whispered, leanin' doon tae kiss him deep. "Then I willnae go easy."

She quickened her pace, hips rollin' wi' deliberate, devastatin' rhythm. His head fell back against the pillow, teeth grit as pleasure coiled deep inside him. Her name fell frae his lips like a curse an' a prayer.

When release overtook her, she shattered wi' a cry, nails bitin' intae his chest. Tryss followed, his body buckin' beneath hers as the world broke open in a white-hot wave.

They collapsed thegither in a tangle o' limbs an' laughter, their breath ragged, hearts thunderin' in sync.

Later, still wrapped in her warmth, Tryss stroked her back, his voice husky against her temple.

"Ye ken," he said, "I dinnae care whit storm comes next. If I hae this every mornin', they can take the rest."

Alyssa chuckled sleepily, fingers splayed across his chest.

"We'll see how smug ye sound when the bairn wakes us at dawn someday."

Tryss froze for half a heartbeat, then grinned slow an' wicked. "A bairn, is it? Then as many as yer heart desires, I'll gie ye—one for every dawn I draw breath at yer side."

Her sigh sank deep intae him, an' in that moment—twined in sweat an' silk an' promises unspoken—they belonged wholly tae each other again.

Fergus

Elsyn paced back an' forth across the dim room, her hands clenched tight at her sides. Fergus sat quiet in the worn chair, watchin' the storm gather on her face—the mix o' fear an' defiance that flickered wi' every step she took.

"What if they say nay?" she finally broke the silence, her voice barely abune a whisper.

Fergus met her gaze steady. "An' what if they say aye?"

Her head snapped up tae lock eyes wi' him, then fell back doon, the weight o' doubt draggin' her gaze tae the floor. "They're goin' tae say nay. Why wouldna they? If I were them, I'd say nay too."

Fergus nodded slow, hearin' the truth buried deep in her words.

He patted the chair beside him, a silent plea. "Sit yersel' doon, Elsyn. Rest a moment."

She eased intae the chair but barely caught her breath afore poppin' right back up, pacin' again.

"Do they normally sleep this late?" she asked, brow furrowed wi' curiosity. "What on earth could they be doin' at this hour?"

Fergus chuckled, fully aware o' what they might be doin'—an' what he hoped they were doin'.

Elsyn caught the mischievous glint in his eye, her own flashin' wi' sudden understandin'. "O-oh. Aye. Um..." She spun on her heel, cheeks flushin' a deep crimson as she hurried awa', leavin' Fergus smilin' tae himself.

He watched her retreat, the color in her cheeks impossible tae miss. Turnin' ower the contradiction laid bare afore him. Why is she sae shocked? he wondered. She's wi' child, has lain wi' a man unwed—yet her cheeks burn like a maiden caught in her first kiss.

He caught himsel'. When she said they were lovers... could she hae meant they were lovers the once? One time? A fleeting moment, no' a tangled affair? Nae way tae ask outright wi'out soundin' a fool. But it might explain the flush, the hesitation—the strange mix o' shame an' defiance.

His gaze drifted back tae the chamber door, still closed but faint sounds—murmurs, a soft laugh—seepin' through the barrier.

"Gods help them," Fergus mused. "If they survive this, they'll hae a tale worth tellin'."

The thought made him grin. For once, he was glad tae be the watcher on the sidelines, the steady hand ready tae catch a brother should he fall.

Alyssa

Her body was still hummin' wi' warmth an' life in the soft aftermath o' their night thegither. She lay quiet, watchin' Tryss dress, a slow smile tuggin' at the corners o' her lips. The firelight flickered against his strong features, an' for a moment, all the worries o' the world slipped awa'.

Wi' a contented sigh, Alyssa sat up, the weight o' the day callin' her back tae duty. The keep wouldna run itself. She moved tae the small mirror, plaitin' her hair careful afore slippin' intae her mornin' dress, the fabric cool against her skin.

Tryss settled by the fire, his eyes never leavin' her. As she finished, he crossed the room an' pressed his lips tae the hollow o' her neck, his voice low an' rough wi' desire.

"We need tae go... nae more time for play the now."

Alyssa giggled, the sound light an' true, an' they left the chamber thegither, the ease atween them a balm tae frayed souls.

Peace in a Highland keep was as fleeting as mist on the moor. Shadows waited just beyond the door.

As they moved doon the hall, speakin' o' the tasks ahead, Alyssa near collided wi' a figure lurkin' in the shadows.

Her breath caught. What was she still doin' here?

Tryss's hand shot oot, grippin' Alyssa's tighter than she expected—sae tight it made her squeak in pain.

She looked up an' saw the storm whirlin' in his eyes—lightnin' flashin', thunder buildin' just beneath the surface. Alyssa felt his grip tighten again, no' frae cruelty, but frae sheer restraint.

Why could she no' hae just left as he'd ordered?

Tryss stepped forward, each word clipped an' lethal. He pointed toward the door wi' a hand that trembled wi' fury.

"I thought I made mysel' clear last night, Elsyn."

Elsyn shrank beneath the heat o' his wrath, her eyes wide, her shoulders curlin' as if the verra walls would crush her.

But Fergus stepped in, plantin' himsel' like a stone in the path o' a flood.

"Tryss." His voice was calm, steady. "Elsyn has somethin' tae say tae ye."

Then, turnin' tae Alyssa, Fergus added gently, "Tae ye baith. I told her ye'd hear her oot."

Alyssa glanced between them, confused, but gave a single nod.

Tryss said nothin'. His jaw clenched tight, muscles twitchin' at the edge o' violence. But he didna move. Didna roar again.

He waited.

An' all eyes turned tae Elsyn.

Her breath hitched. Her fingers twisted in the folds o' her skirts, knuckles white.

"I... I didna leave last night," she began, her voice fragile as spun glass, "because I had nowhere tae go. It was too late tae find shelter, an'—" her throat worked hard around the words, "—I was too afeared."

Tryss said nothin'. His silence was mair dangerous than shoutin'. His jaw worked once, twice, but no sound came. The silence was a blade pressed tae her throat. Alyssa's hand found his again, squeezin' soft. She felt the tension in him coil tight as a drawn bow, certain if it snapped, the whole keep would shake. He didna return her touch.

His eyes never left Elsyn.

Elsyn's gaze flicked tae Fergus for strength, then fell again. "But that's no' the whole o' it."

The pause stretched lang. The chamber seemed tae hold its breath, the fire hissin' low as if it kent a secret was about tae be bared.

"I've been turned oot," she whispered. "My parents... they ken about the man I loved. About what we did. They cast me oot when I told them the truth."

Alyssa's brows lifted in surprise. Tryss's face didna shift, but she felt the tremor in his arm.

"I thought we were tae wed," Elsyn pressed on, her voice shakin' now. "He said—he said he would come for me. But he never did. An' noo I'm wi' bairn."

The chamber stilled.

Elsyn's eyes brimmed wi' tears, but she forced the rest oot in a rush. "I came because I had nowhere else tae go. I was desperate. An' what I did yesterday... tryin' tae take what wasna mine... it was wrong. I see that noo. I hoped Alyssa would forgive me in time—we were as sisters, an' I betrayed ye." She sobbed, shoulders curlin' inward. "But noo I hae nae place, nae prospects, an' in a few months, a child. Cast me oot if ye will—but ken this, I'll carry the shame, no' hide it."

Tryss exhaled—sharp, slow—like a man holdin' back a tide that threatened tae drown him.

Fergus stepped forward, his voice softer noo. "I see the way o' it. An' I think ye do too. Ye've been a fool, aye—but ye were trapped as well. If ye're truly sorry, an' ye speak it plain tae them baith, I've nae doubt they'll listen."

Alyssa's face softened, but Tryss stood like stone.

Elsyn lifted her tear-soaked gaze tae him. "I am sorry. Truly. I never meant tae ruin anythin'. I was just... lost."

Tryss stared at her a lang, lang moment. Then, wi'out a word, he turned an' strode past her, tugging Alyssa gently wi' him. His voice was low, meant only for her.

"We'll hear her oot. But forgiveness is earned."

An' as they stepped intae the hall, Fergus lingered behind, offerin' Elsyn a seat an' a cloth for her tears.

Chapter Twenty

Tryss & Alyssa

THEY WALKED IN SILENCE.

The corridor stretched ahead, empty but for the flicker o' torchlight playin' across the stone. Tryss's hand still held hers, firm but gentler now, his thumb movin' in slow, unconscious circles against her skin. His jaw was tight. Thoughtful.

Alyssa didnae try tae speak at first. The quiet felt too full—like one wrong word might bring the whole moment crashin' doon.

Then, softly, she said, "Weel. That was a mess."

Tryss huffed a breath—not quite a laugh, not quite a sigh. "Aye. An' it's far from done."

They stopped just before the turnin' tae the great hall. Alyssa turned tae him, tippin' her chin tae catch his gaze.

"Are ye angry still?" she asked.

"Not like I was." He met her eyes then, tired an' unguarded.

"But I dinnae ken what tae do wi' her. Wi' all o' it."

Alyssa's mind churned. The image o' Elsyn cryin', her voice shakin' as she confessed everything, played again behind her eyes. The desperation, the guilt. The shame.

"She's lost," Alyssa said quietly. "An' afraid. She made a terrible choice, an' then another, but... I saw nae lie in her eyes the day."

Tryss nodded slowly, jaw flexin'. "Still doesnae undo what she did."

"I ken." Alyssa looked doon. "An' I willnae forget that. But I cannae hate her either. Not anymore."

Tryss grunted. "Ye always seem to the guid in folk. Even when they stab ye in the back."

"That's not what this is," Alyssa said, her voice firmer noo. "I dinnae excuse it, Tryss. But I understand it. She came here wi' nothin', nae one. She's broken. An' her da pressed her tae it besides. I ken what it is tae be a daughter wi' little power, pushed by the will o' men. She tried tae make somethin' for herself oot o' the only thing she thought might still be within reach."

"Ye mean me," he said, bitterness threadin' the words.

Alyssa hesitated. "Nay. I mean safety. A name. A future. Ye were her last gamble. She wasnae tryin' tae hurt me. She just didnae see me."

Tryss raked a hand through his hair an' turned away, his jaw tight as he stared at the stone wall. "Ye ken I dinnae forgive easy, Alyssa. Least o' all when someone's played me false." He paused, breath sharp. "I still dinnae trust we've heard the whole truth. What if it's just more games?" He shook his head, his voice low an' clipped. "That's what burns. That she might make fools o' us both—again."

Alyssa reached oot, placin' her hand on his arm. "She threw everything away for a man who left her. That shame... I think it's eaten her alive."

He was quiet for a long while, the fire in his eyes dimmed noo tae embers. Then, in a voice low an' strained, he asked, "Do ye think ye owe her somethin' after all o' this?"

Alyssa didnae answer right away. She looked doon at their joined hands, then back up at him. "Maybe I do. Not everythin'—not trust, not friendship. Not after what she tried tae do. But I kent her once, afore all this. An' if there's still some part o' that lass left... maybe I owe her enough not tae turn my back when she's already fallen."

She drew in a breath. "That doesnae mean we make her part o' our lives. Just that we dinnae become the kind o' folk who throw someone away when they're broken."

Tryss's mouth pressed intae a thin line. "Ye would forgive her?"

"I think I already have," she whispered.

Tryss turned tae her, studyin' her face like it held the answer tae some riddle he couldnae solve. "Ye amaze me, Alyssa. After everythin'..."

"She was never my enemy."

He wrapped his arms around her then, pullin' her in tight. His voice brushed her hair. "I'm so glad it was ye behind the veil."

Alyssa shot him a sideways grin. "Ye should be glad it was me. Someone else might've made a right mess o' things."

Alyssa gave a sly grin an' turned on her heel. "Come on, afore ye start thinkin' I'm too much trouble even for ye."

Tryss caught her by the waist an' gave her bottom a playful swat. "Trouble's exactly what I signed up for."

Laughin', they walked back toward the great hall together, the mornin' light spillin' in as the smell o' breakfast called them hame.

Fergus

Fergus watched Tryss an' Alyssa's backs vanish doon the hall, their footsteps swallowed by the stone walls. Silence settled ower the chamber, broken only by the soft crackle o' the dyin' fire.

Would they let her bide?

Why should he care? What did it matter tae him if they sent her packin' this very moment? She wasnae his concern. No his burden tae carry. Yet... there was somethin' in her, somethin' stubborn, desperate, that gnawed at the edges o' his mind.

Her een. Those cursed, haunted een. The same shade as mornin' glories after a night's rain. They held shame, aye, but also somethin' fragile, somethin' askin' silently tae be seen. He hadnae thought o' aught else since he first looked on her. Not the scandal, not the folly of her schemes—just the lass herself, standin' there in the ruins o' her own mistakes.

Elsyn's confession had been raw, desperate. No pride left in her voice. Fergus kent Tryss well enough tae know the storm still simmered behind that clenched jaw and taut shoulders. And Alyssa... aye, she had the heart tae see what others overlooked, tae find the girl behind the lies.

But it wasnae that simple. Fergus leaned back, fingers drumming against the chair's arm, a slow rhythm o' doubt an' thought. Could she change? Could she learn tae stand beside them without bringin' ruin again? Was it mercy—or sense—that whispered tae him now?

He recalled darker days in this keep. Families broken, stitched back thegither. Loyalties tested an' reforged. He knew the weight o' second chances. He had seen it fail, aye, and he had seen it work. And yet... this was different. This was a young lass thrown into a world far beyond her ken, guided by no one, forced tae grasp at survival in ways most wouldnae understand.

His gaze returned tae her, curled by the hearth, eyes fixed on the flames as if seekin' a future that didnae exist. The shame and fear were written on her, aye, but so was somethin' else—an honesty in her desperation that even Tryss might nae yet perceive.

Fergus drew in a slow breath. Mayhap... mayhap she could bide. Mayhap it wasnae charity he was feelin', but recognition. Recognition that a girl like her, lost and frightened, had done the only thing she knew how tae do. That she deserved a chance, even if it wasnae a guarantee she wouldnae falter again.

And maybe, Fergus admitted quietly tae himself, that chance was as much for them as it was for her.

Let her stay, he thought, though the words werenae firm, nae yet. They were a question still, an open-ended promise, born o' caution an' hope alike.

Elsyn

Elsyn stared intae the flames, barely feelin' their heat. The flickerin' light seemed distant, like a world she no longer belonged tae. If they sent her away now, where could she possibly go? The cauld night outside felt less cruel than the rejection she feared.

But if they let her bide—could she truly find a life here? A place tae belong? The thought was fragile, almost laughable, yet somethin' in her chest stirred at the mere hope.

She sensed Fergus's eyes on her again, steady and searching, burnin' quietly into her. There was somethin' in the way he watched, somethin' that made her heart twist wi' unease and curiosity alike. He cared... but why?

Maybe it was the way a man like him saw the helpless, forced into choices nae one would wish on a soul. The world had pushed her—her da's cruel designs, the life she hadnae asked for—and Fergus, he understood, even if he wouldnae say it plain. She imagined his voice, quiet and measured, mumblin' truths to himself as he weighed her worth: *'Tisnae entirely her fault... she's but a lass thrown inta the tide... yet there's courage here... worth seein', worth guardin'.*

Fatigue tugged at her mind, softenin' the edges of her thoughts. She wasnae sure which way tae turn—home, hope, or somethin' in between. And deep down, she knew this truth: she didnae deserve Alyssa's love, nor her forgiveness. Maybe she never would.

But she couldnae allow herself tae dwell on that. Not when every fibre o' her bein' screamed out for sanctuary, for a place where missteps could be forgiven, if only quietly, wi' understanding.

Please... let me stay, she thought, whisperin' it tae herself, a plea borne o' fear and hope alike, feelin' Fergus's quiet judgment and hidden sympathy pressing on her soul.

Chapter Twenty-One

Alyssa

Alyssa stepped quiet intae the chamber. Fergus stood by the window, his silhouette framed by the saft dawn light, while Elsyn sat near the fire, lookin' utterly desolate. Guid. She ought tae feel the weight o' this—nae easy refuge for those who stir storms.

A soft sigh slipped frae Alyssa as she crossed the room. She stopped just in front o' Elsyn, who didnae lift her gaze. Tryss came tae stand beside her, his presence a steady anchor at her side.

Alyssa's voice was low but firm, carryin' the sharp edge o' hard-won authority.

"Elsyn, 'tis the debt o' my childhood that finds ye safe an' wi' shelter for noo. Dinnae make me regret it."

Silence followed, heavy as stone. Elsyn didnae move, only stared deeper intae the fire, her shoulders hunched as though the words had struck her through. Fergus's face was unreadable in the half-light, his gaze shiftin' between them as if weighin' the silence itself.

Alyssa drew in a breath sharp enough tae sting, then turned on her heel. Tryss fell in beside her, his footfalls echoein' hers as the chamber door creaked shut behind them, cuttin' aff the crackle o' the hearth an' the weight o' Elsyn's despair.

Only when the cauld air o' the garden brushed her cheeks did Alyssa allow herself tae sag against Tryss's chest an' breathe.

As far back as she could mind, between her an' Elsyn, Alyssa had been the follower. Always trailin' in her shadow, aye, like the lesser light to her star

But nae anymore.

Tryss's arms wrapped roond her without question, cocoonin' her in warmth an' safety. She leaned heavy intae him, lettin' hersel' fold intae that steady presence, his heartbeat a calm against the whirlwind still spinnin' inside her.

Elsyn

Elsyn's mouth opened an' closed, once, then again. Alyssa's footfalls still echoed doon the hall, fading slow like a song cut short. A bolt o' lightning straight tae the chest would've startled her less than those words.

She stared at the door the couple had just passed through, half-expectin' Alyssa tae return, tae take it back. Her ears rang. The fire crackled softly behind her, its warmth nae match for the chill disbelief twisting through her chest.

"She said I could bide," she whispered, voice trembling more tae herself than anyone else. "She actually said it."

Slowly, she turned toward the window, her een finding Fergus.

He stood where he had, solid as a stone pillar, shoulders broad, feet planted steady. His gaze didnae waver, yet neither did it soften. It held somethin' else... that quiet reckoning that couldnae be named aloud.

"Did she... really just say I could bide?" Her voice grew louder, disbelief threading through every syllable, her throat tight around a lump o' emotion she hadnae expected. "After all I did?"

Fergus pushed off the stone ledge with deliberate calm, crossin' the room like a man who moved only when the weight o' it demanded. Arms folded loosely, expression unreadable, he stopped a few paces frae her.

"She did," he said, slow and measured. "But I'd no take it lightly, if I were ye."

Elsyn swallowed hard, fingers curling tight at her sides. "I dinnae. I swear I dinnae."

"Good," Fergus replied, voice low, steady. "Because shelter's been offered, no absolution. An' Alyssa's kindness... it's nae a well ye want tae drain, mark my words."

His words weren't cruel, yet they struck her true, hittin' with the force o' plain truth. She flinched, then nodded, once, sharply.

"I never expected this," she murmured, voice breaking slightly. "Not after the way I behaved. Not after... what I tried tae do."

"No," Fergus agreed, slow and thoughtful. "But it's nae about what ye expected. It's about what ye do next."

Elsyn's gaze drifted tae the fire, blinking rapid as the first swell o' tears stung her lids. Her thoughts were a tangle—relief, shame, disbelief, fear—all fighting like caged beasts. Why had Alyssa offered mercy? Why had Fergus spoken on her behalf? She didnae deserve any o' it. She kent that.

Yet gods help her, she wanted it. She wanted tae prove them right. Wanted a chance tae be someone different, someone more than the girl forced tae gamble with the only options offered by her da's cruel will.

Her voice dropped, barely a whisper. "I willnae waste it."

Fergus gave a single, deliberate nod, tone calm, resolute, yet lined wi' that unspoken weight o' caution. "See that ye dinnae."

Elsyn straightened, slowly, as if each breath pulled her upright. She drew her hands tae her lap, pressed her fingers together, the rhythm grounding her. The firelight danced across the stone, casting long shadows, yet the warmth from Fergus's presence felt steadier than any flame.

She glanced again at him, uncertain if it was encouragement or judgment that lingered in his gaze. Perhaps both. Perhaps it wasnae for her, entirely. Perhaps it was for the keep. For Alyssa. For the rightness o' seeing a girl survive when she'd been cast into impossible tides.

And for the first time in hours, she believed—nae, dared tae hope—that she might just manage it.

Fergus

Hope flared in Fergus's chest, swift an' unexpected. He didnae ken why. Maybe it was the way her een had shifted, just slightly, when Alyssa spoke. Maybe it was the sheer disbelief etched on her face—as though she had braced for the gallows an' been handed a pardon instead.

He turned frae her, boots echoing dully on the stone floor. Relief settled ower his shoulders, but he wasn't sure it belonged tae him.

For her? he wondered. *Why?*

Shaking his head, Fergus muttered under his breath an' made for the door. Whatever strange twist o' fate had just played oot, he wasn't about tae let it fracture the fragile peace inside these walls. The last thing this keep needed was another war between its laird an' lady—or worse, whispered divisions spreading amang the household like rot.

He stepped oot into the garden, the morning sun already warmin' the flagstones, though the air still held the sting o' Highland chill. It didnae take long tae find them.

Tryss an' Alyssa stood near the rose trellis, arms wrapped loosely aroond one another. It wasnae an intimate embrace, not in the passionate sense—but it was close. Protective. Steady. The kind o' closeness built frae survivin' something thegither.

Fergus hesitated, then cleared his throat wi' a pointed cough.

Tryss turned first, one arm still looped aroond Alyssa. She peeked aroond him tae see who had interrupted. At the sight o' Fergus an' the glint in his een—half amusement, half business—her brow lifted.

"I suppose that's my cue," she said dryly, steppin' back frae Tryss wi' a faint smile.

"Just a word," Fergus said, hands folded behind his back.

Alyssa nodded, brushin' her skirts as she moved past them. "I'll see tae a room bein' prepared for Elsyn. Somewhere..." She paused, lips twitching inta a look that was half mischief, half warnin'. "Far. Far. Away frae ours."

Tryss grunted his approval. Fergus watched her go, the tension in his shoulders easing just slightly. Then he turned tae Tryss, jaw tightenin' wi' what needed tae be said next.

Tryss didnae speak at first. Just stood there, arms folded, watchin' the path Alyssa had taken. The garden had a stillness aboot it noo, save for the rustle o' leaves in the breeze an' the faint creak o' the gate swingin' on auld hinges.

Fergus joined him, hands braced behind his back. "That went better than it could've."

Tryss grunted. "Ye mean no one threw a punch or got thrown

oot on their arse?"

"Exactly," Fergus said wi' a nod. "Progress."

They stood in silence for a beat.

"Her confession," Fergus added, glancin' sidelong at Tryss. "Ye believe it?"

Tryss shrugged one shoulder. "I believe she's desperate. I believe she's ashamed. An' I believe Alyssa saw somethin' in her that made mercy the right choice."

"And ye?" Fergus asked. "Ye're all right wi' it?"

Tryss's jaw worked for a moment before he answered. "Alyssa made the call. An' I stand wi' her. I won't pretend it doesnae burn a wee, but... I trust her. That's the line."

Fergus nodded slowly. "She made the right call."

Tryss gave him a sharp look. "Ye sound surprised."

"I'm not," Fergus replied. "Just relieved."

There was a pause. Then Fergus added, "Elsyn didnae expect it. That look on her face—like someone had handed her the sunrise an' she wasn't sure it was real."

Tryss didnae respond.

Fergus glanced at him, tryin' again. "She's not what she was yesterday, Tryss. Ye saw that, didnae ye? That tremblin' thing by the fire wasnae the same woman who strode in an' tried tae—"

Tryss raised an eyebrow an' turned tae him fully, one hand gesturin' lazily. "Ye plan tae keep talkin' about Elsyn, or are we just makin' this an ode?"

Fergus blinked. "What?"

"Ye've said her name five times in two minutes," Tryss said dryly. "An' that's five more than I ever thought I'd hear ye say. Especially wi' that tone."

Fergus's brow furrowed. "What tone?"

"That tone," Tryss repeated, voice flat. "The one that sounds like ye're halfway between plannin' her future an' writin' her poetry."

Fergus scoffed. "Ye're imagin' things."

Tryss gave him a long, slow look. Then tipped his head. "Did ye bang yer head?"

Fergus rolled his een, but colour had crept intae the back o' his neck.

Tryss's mouth twitched. "Ye've got a look."

"What kind o' look?"

"The kind a man gets when he sees somethin' broken an' decides it's his job tae fix it."

Fergus gave a sharp breath through his nose. "She's a mess, Tryss."

"And there we are. Talkin' about her like she's already yer mess."

Fergus said nae a word.

Tryss just smiled, thin an' knowin'. "Ye're in trouble, auld friend."

Fergus muttered, "Don't start."

Tryss clapped a hand tae his shoulder. "Wouldnae dream of it."

Wi' a low grunt, he turned an' headed back toward the keep.

Fergus didnae follow. Not right away.

He stood there in the garden, the sun catchin' on dew-laced roses, the breeze stirrin' the edges o' his coat. Across the courtyard, Alyssa had disappeared through the far door.

He could still hear Tryss's voice echoin' in his mind. You're in trouble, auld friend.

Fergus blew out a slow breath an' muttered tae no one, "Aye. I think I am."

Chapter Twenty-Two

Alyssa

By the followin' mornin', the keep had settled back tae its usual rhythms—or so it seemed at first glance.

The halls bustled wi' servants carryin' baskets o' linens, kitchens clattered wi' pots, an' the courtyard echoed wi' the metallic ring o' sparrin' blades. But underneath the everyday din pulsed somethin' else. A murmur. A thread o' unease.

Alyssa stood near the hearth in the great hall, scannin' the list o' provisions needed for the autumn fair. Tryss sat across from her, one boot propped on the bench, a mug in hand, watchin' the flow o' bodies through the corridor.

"They're talkin'," he murmured without lookin' at her.

"I ken," she said, flippin' the parchment ower wi' more force than necessary. "They started afore the ink was dry on my decision."

He arched a brow. "An' ye're surprised?"

"Nay," she admitted. "But I hoped they'd hae the decency tae wait till I left the room."

Tryss grinned faintly. "Ye're laird's lady now. Ye dinnae get the benefit o' polite whispers."

The door opened an' three servin' women walked in, arms laden wi' table linens. They stopped short at the sight o' Alyssa an' Tryss, eyes goin' wide afore quickly dippin' into curtsies an' murmurin', "M'laird, m'lady." But Alyssa didnae miss the sidelong glance one gave the other—or the way their voices dropped the moment they left the room again.

"She's still here, then?" came a voice near the far table. Low. Male. A young steward, nae more than nineteen.

"She is," someone muttered back. "Saw Fergus order a chamber made up for her this mornin'. Thought he might be losin' his mind."

"She nearly took her place," another voice hissed. "An' now she's got a bed an' food in her belly?"

"Must be nice," the steward said under his breath. "Make a fool o' the whole clan, then get coddled for it."

Alyssa's spine stiffened. Nae. I willnae let their whispers dictate what justice looks like here.

Tryss caught her eye an' gave a subtle shake o' his head. Not yet, his look warned. Let them talk. Let it run its course.

But Alyssa didnae want tae wait for silence tae grow frae scandal. Not when every whispered word chipped at the tenuous peace she an' Tryss had fought tae reclaim. If I dinnae stand firm, the keep willnae respect mercy—it'll see weakness instead.

She rose frae her chair wi' deliberate calm an' walked toward the murmurin' table. The young men scrambled tae their feet, eyes wide.

"My lady," one stammered.

Alyssa smiled—but it was the sharp, glintin' kind. "The next time I hear yer thoughts on a matter not yers tae judge," she said, voice smooth an' cold as river stone, "ye'll be sent tae scrub the stables. Wi' a broken broom."

Silence.

The boys nodded stiffly, their faces pale, an' made a swift retreat out the door.

Tryss leaned back on the bench, grinnin' behind his mug. "Remind me not tae cross ye afore breakfast."

She returned tae her seat, cheeks flushed. I did what needed tae be done. "I'm not proud o' it," she admitted.

"Ye should be," he said. "They'll think twice afore lettin' their tongues wag like fishwives."

She leaned forward, droppin' her voice. "We made the right call, Tryss. I ken we did. But I need yer council tae stand behind me. I cannae hae this festering through the ranks."

Tryss's smile faded. "Ye were nae wrong. Ye showed mercy."

Alyssa exhaled, grateful—and still uneasy. She had kent it wouldnae be simple. Letting Elsyn bide might hae been the merciful choice. But mercy never came wi'out a cost, and she felt it pricklin' at the edges o' the keep already.

Elsyn

The room set aside for her was modest but clean—a small chamber with a narrow window overlooking the cold stone courtyard. She'd been spared the common servants' quarters, but the distance from the main household was a clear message: she was tolerated, not welcomed.

Elsyn moved slowly, her fingers trailing over the rough wooden table, the worn chair. A hush settled over the room, alive wi' quiet wonder an' unspoken curiosity.

She caught a glimpse of herself in the cracked mirror above the washbasin—pale, tired, wi' dark circles shadowin' her eyes. How could she claim a place here, when every whispered word marked her as a traitor, a beggar who had tried tae steal what wasn't hers?

The faint sound of footsteps echoed outside. Elsyn froze, heart pounding.

A soft knock.

"Come in," she whispered.

Fergus stepped inside, his expression unreadable but gentle. "Ye're not as invisible as ye think," he said quietly.

Elsyn met his steady gaze. "I expected nothing less."

He crossed the room an' set a small bundle on the table—fresh linens, some bread, and a flask of water. "For ye and the bairn."

She swallowed hard, fighting the lump in her throat. "Thank you," she managed.

Fergus hesitated, then said, "It won't be easy. There's talk. Doubt. Fear. But ye've been given a chance—dinnae waste it."

Elsyn nodded, determination flickering behind her weary eyes. "I won't."

As he left, she pressed her hand to the doorframe, feeling the weight of the keep settle around her like a shroud. But beneath that weight, a fragile seed of hope took root. Perhaps, here—among the wary, the broken—she could begin to rebuild what had been lost.

Tryss

The council chamber smelled o' burnin' pine and aged stone, thick wi' the weight o' unspoken worries. The low murmur o' voices flickered out as Tryss strode in. Heads turned, some noddin' in greetin', others stiff an' wary, eyes sharp beneath furrowed brows.

He took his place at the head o' the long oak table, hands folded afore him. Aroon him, familiar faces gathered: Fiona, the clan's fierce battle strategist; Murdoch, the grizzled steward; Duncan, a voice o' cautious wisdom; an' others whose loyalties balanced on fragile edges, ready tae shift wi' the slightest wind.

Fiona was first tae break the silence. Her eyes flicked up, dark an' serious, an' she tapped a finger against the table—a quiet habit when she weighed odds. "The raidin' clans grow bolder. Just yesterday, the MacGowan warbands struck near Glenbrae. They've taken livestock, burned two outlyin' cottages. It's the third strike this moon. They're pushin' closer, testin' our reach."

Murmurs rippled through the room. Murdoch slammed a gnarled fist on the table, smudge o' soot markin' the wood. He muttered under his breath, shakin' his head as if the verra notion o' chaos gnawed at his bones. "This willnae be the last. The MacGowans dinnae strike at random—they measure, they probe. An' they ken we're distracted wi' weddin's an' whispers."

Duncan cleared his throat, nervously tuggin' at his tunic cuff, crease deepenin' in his brow. "'Tis true. Supplies are stretched thin, men restless. If they mean tae drive deeper, they'll wait for us tae falter—inside or out. We cannae show fracture in our ranks."

Tryss's jaw clenched. The revelations about Elsyn, the whispers threadin' through the halls, the uneasy alliances—it all threatened tae unravel the fragile peace. External threats were one thing; internal divisions, fed by gossip an' suspicion, could be far deadlier. But the MacGowans... they wouldnae wait for the dust tae settle.

"We'll increase patrols along the northern ridges," Tryss said, voice low but sharp. "Men will rotate shifts—nae gap in watch.

I want scouts reportin' daily, nae excuses. If a MacGowan sets foot on our soil, I want ken o' it afore his boot hits the earth."

Fiona nodded sharply, fingers drummin' the table's edge as she weighed contingencies. "An' what o' the harvest festival? Could be the perfect chance tae show strength an' unity. A display for the clans—and a reminder we remain unbroken. Let the MacGowans hear our horns an' ken we are ready."

Tryss glanced at Alyssa, sittin' quiet beside him, her eyes steady despite the storm o' events. "Aye. The festival goes ahead. Every banner flies, every horn sounds. We show them the MacCraiths are nae easy prey."

Murdoch muttered, rubbin' the back o' his neck where white hair jutted at odd angles. "Aye, let it remind those would-be raiders that we stand ready. But banners alone dinnae stop steel. They'll be back, an' harder next time."

A pause settled. Duncan's gaze shifted, crease in his brow deepenin'. "One other matter—Elsyn. The household whispers grow louder. Some question her place here."

Tryss's eyes narrowed. The room seemed tae tighten wi' the weight o' expectation. "She remains under our protection. But I expect loyalty an' discretion. This clan survives on trust... no' rumors."

Fiona gave a grim smile, lip twitch betrayin' both approval an' impatience. "We'll watch carefully. But for now, the greater threat lies outside our walls. Mark me, Tryss—if the MacGowans mean war, this is only the openin' note."

The council nodded, the meetin' turnin' tae the finer points o' festival preparation—the feast, the games, the invitations tae neighborin' clans.

Tryss leaned back, thoughts circlin' like hawks ower the ridge. The comin' weeks would test them all. Between enemies at the gates an' fractures within, leadership demanded mair than strength; it demanded cunnin', foresight, an' a steady hand.

But for noo, there was a plan.

An' in the Highlands, plans were the difference between survival... an' ruin.

Elsyn

Elsyn knelt on the cold stone floor o' the kitchen scullery, scrubbing at a stubborn patch o' grime she'd nae been asked tae clean—and sure as the gods, there was nae expectation for her to be workin' at all. She was a guest here, albeit a reluctant one. Her hands were raw, ache burnin' through her fingers from the cold water, yet she welcomed the distraction. Better tae be busy than tae feel the weight o' unseen eyes judging her every move.

The worn wooden bucket beside her held water, its surface shimmerin' faintly in the dim light, catchin' what little warmth the hearth offered.

From the corner o' her eye, Elsyn saw one o' the kitchen maids bustling past—skirts sweepin' too close, foot catchin' the bucket's edge. The water leapt out with a sudden splash, soaking Elsyn's skirts and spattering across the stone floor.

"Watch it!" Elsyn gasped, scrambling to keep her balance. The maid barely spared her a glance, lips twitchin' in that sharp little smirk she knew all too well.

"Oh! So sorry, Elsyn!" the maid said, voice sugary sweet, but the eyes... aye, the eyes were sharp, cold, like a knife hidden in cloth.

Elsyn's throat tightened. She wanted tae spit back some biting words, demand respect, or at least a scrap o' courtesy—but the words lodged tight, refusing tae come. She lowered herself, gatherin' the bucket, the cold seeping through her soaked skirts, biting at her skin.

She could feel the other kitchen hands' eyes on her—silent witnesses tae the small humiliation she had nae power to stop.

Later, she stood by the hearth. The heat offered little comfort; her breath came shallow, ragged. Why was she even tryin'? Aye, why indeed?

Fergus

Fergus lingered just inside the doorway, his boots muffled by the thick stone floor. Elsyn was on her knees, scrubbing the scullery floor wi' a desperate kind o' stubbornness that twisted somethin' in his chest. Why was she doin' this? It wasn't her place. No one had asked her. Maybe this was the only way she could feel useful — the only way she could earn a scrap o' belonging.

His gaze sharpened as the kitchen maid stepped past, deliberately draggin' her foot along the rim o' a nearby bucket. In a heartbeat, the bucket tipped, sendin' a cascade o' icy water splashin' across the stones — soakin' Elsyn's skirts and drenchin' the spot she had just cleaned.

Fergus's eyes locked onto the maid's face. Her lips curved into a small, tight smirk. It wasn't an accident. It never was. But no one else noticed — they were caught up in their own busy chatter and tasks, oblivious tae the silent cruelty just played out.

A cold wash o' helplessness swept over Fergus. He clenched his fists, his breath caught in his throat. What could he do? Step in and defend her? That would only stir resentment, make enemies in a household already fraught wi' tension. Elsyn had to find her own way through this, prove herself in her own time. But watchin' the quiet injustice — it made his skin crawl.

He stayed rooted in the shadow o' the doorway, unseen, his gaze lingering on Elsyn's bowed head as she blinked back tears and pressed her hands harder into the rough stone floor, scrubbing even more fiercely now, as if to erase not only the dirt but the sting o' humiliation.

Later, Fergus found her again — by the hearth in a dim corner o' the great hall. The firelight danced across her weary face, but the warmth seemed to offer no comfort. Her breath came shallow and ragged, her shoulders tremblin' wi' a sadness she tried to hide.

Was she cryin'? He stepped closer, hesitant, as if approachin' a wounded animal. He rested a firm hand on her shoulder. She startled, but didn't pull away.

His voice was low, careful not to startle her more. "Ye don't have to carry it all alone."

She looked up at him, eyes wide wi' somethin' fragile and raw — a silent plea for somethin' she couldn't quite ask for.

His jaw clenched tight, shoulders stiff, toes draggin' a slow line across the stone. He stayed where he was, lettin' her scrubbing go unchallenged. The fire in his chest flared, quiet and hot, but he didn't move—not yet.

Fergus lingered for a heartbeat longer, his hand still restin' lightly on Elsyn's shoulder, offerin' silent comfort. But he knew he couldn't stay. Not yet. Not like this.

He pulled back gently and stepped away, careful not to disturb the fragile quiet that had settled between them. Elsyn's gaze stayed fixed on the flickering flames, lost in thoughts he could only guess at.

Fergus turned and moved away from the hearth, the weight of what he'd witnessed settlin' deeper in his chest. There were battles to be fought here too—ones that didn't require swords, but courage o' a different kind.

His footsteps echoed softly as he made his way through the stone corridors toward Alyssa's chambers. He needed to speak wi' her. Not just as her steward, but as a man who saw the cracks in the walls—and the people behind them.

Alyssa stood at the window, arms folded tight across her chest as she watched the courtyard below. The early light caught in her hair, turnin' the auburn strands to burnished gold, but there was nothing soft about the set o' her jaw.

Fergus knocked once on the open doorframe and stepped in. "Ye've a moment?"

She didn't turn. "If this is about Elsyn, I'm not in the mood."

"It is," he said plainly.

A sigh escaped her. "She's got food. She's got shelter. What more do ye expect me to give?"

"She's got cold stares and silence too," Fergus said gently. "I watched her this mornin'. Scrubbing floors no one asked her to touch. Tryin' to find a place she's not been offered. And the kitchen girl—Mairi—knocked her pail over wi' her boot. Right in front o' her. Ye think that was an accident?"

Alyssa stiffened. "What did Elsyn do?"

"Picked it up. Quietly. Like she expected it." Fergus stepped closer, voice even but firm. "And then she stood by the fire like she couldnae feel it at all."

Alyssa finally turned to him, her eyes sharp. "She betrayed us, Fergus. Lied to all of us, to me. I don't owe her anything. Dinnae expect me to like her," she muttered, "Or to forget."

"I'm not asking ye to forget," he said. "I'm asking ye to lead."

That gave her pause.

He went on, his tone low but sure, the one that never raised its voice but somehow always got heard. "They're watchin' ye, Alyssa. Every one of them. The servants. The council. The guards. Ye may not wear a crown, but make no mistake — ye're the measure by which they weigh everything. If ye treat her like a snake in the grass, they will too."

"And if I pretend everything's forgiven? That it's all behind us?" she shot back. "They'll call me weak."

"They'll call ye fair," he said, wi' that maddening, implacable calm. "And more importantly, they'll follow yer example. If there's to be peace in this keep, it willnae come because Elsyn scrubs a few floors or avoids every eye. It'll come when the woman they do trust shows them how to move forward."

Alyssa swallowed hard, the words hitting where she didn't want them to. She looked away again, jaw clenched. "It's not that simple."

"I know," Fergus said. "But simple or not, the household won't settle until ye do. Ye hold the reins whether ye want them or not."

For a long moment, she said nothing.

Then finally, her shoulders sagged just a little. "And what would ye have me do?"

"Give her something that lets her be useful," he said. "She's not asking for love or forgiveness. Just... let her work. Let her matter. The harvest festival needs hands. Let her help."

Alyssa still looked hesitant, but the fight in her had dulled to thoughtfulness.

Fergus gave a nod, as if sealing an unspoken pact. "It dinnae have to be much. Just a start."

She sighed and shook her head with a wry twist of her lips. "Ye always were good at getting yer way."

"No," Fergus said wi' the barest smile. "I'm good at pointing out the right way and letting ye walk it on your own."

Chapter Twenty-Three

Alyssa

THE FIRE IN THE great hall had long since burned tae embers, castin' a faint orange glow across the stane floor. Alyssa stood just beyond its reach, the shadows wrappin' round her like a second skin. Elsyn sat on the bench closest tae the hearth, her hands clasped in her lap, back rigid, eyes fixed on the floor. She didnae look up when the footsteps approached. Didnae need tae.

"I dinnae ken what I thought I'd feel when I saw ye again," Alyssa said, her voice quiet but cuttin'. "Anger, maybe. Spite. But it's nae that."

Elsyn said nothin'.

Alyssa took a slow breath, forcin' herself forward. "Ye were the only one who ever looked at me an' saw more than rags an' a mouth too quick. When I was a bairn, when my world was naught but stane walls an' cold glances—ye made me feel like I mattered."

Still, Elsyn didnae speak. Her shoulders were tight, her face turned tae the fire, but her throat worked like she was tryin' tae swallow words that wouldnae come.

"I trusted ye," Alyssa went on, voice tremblin' now. "Not just wi' secrets. Wi' the soft parts o' me. The ones I never let anyone see."

She paused, eyes burnin'.

"And when it mattered—when ye could've stood beside me—ye chose yer lie. Ye chose yer future. Ye threw me away like I was naught."

Elsyn's hands gripped tighter in her lap. But she didnae raise her head.

Alyssa waited—for an apology, an explanation, a plea for forgiveness. Somethin'. Anythin'.

But there was only silence.

Alyssa nodded once, sharp an' small, as if that silence confirmed what she already kent.

"Ye dinnae even hae the words, do ye?" she whispered. "Ye were sae bold. But when it's time tae be honest?"

Nothin'.

Alyssa's voice hardened. "I'm nae here tae grant mercy or play the saint. I just wanted ye tae hear it—what ye broke. I wanted ye tae ken ye didnae just lie. Ye ended somethin'."

She turned, the finality in her steps echoin' aff the stane.

Behind her, Elsyn didnae move. Didnae call her back. Didnae say a word.

An' that, more than anythin', told Alyssa the truth.

Whatever sisterhood they'd shared had died lang afore this moment. She was only now mournin' it.

The door closed behind her wi' a soft click, but the silence it left behind roared in Alyssa's ears.

She didnae ken what she had expected—tears, apologies, even

anger. Somethin'. Anythin'. But Elsyn had just stared at her, hollow-eyed an' mute, like there were nae words left tae gie. Like she'd already said too much in her betrayal an' had naught left for the reckonin'.

Alyssa's breath caught in her chest.

She turned blindly doon the corridor, her steps brisk, unfocused. She passed two startled maids an' a dog that yapped once afore dartin' away. Stane blurred. Light flickered past in torches an' sconces. But it wasnae until she stepped intae the cool o' the side courtyard, where the garden wall pressed close an' the air smelled faintly o' woodsmoke an' herbs, that she finally stopped.

An' found Fergus sittin' on the edge o' the auld stane fountain, arms folded, pipe tucked intae the corner o' his mouth—but unlit.

He looked up as if he'd been waitin' for her.

Alyssa stiffened. "If ye're here tae defend her—"

"I'm nae," Fergus said simply.

The words halted her like a hand tae the chest.

"I'm nae here tae speak for her, nor make excuses," he said, standin' wi' a slow grunt. "I'm here 'cause ye've that look about ye. The kind folk wear right afore they put their fist through a wall."

Alyssa huffed, turnin' away. "I thought I wanted her tae say sorry. Or explain herself. But when I looked at her..." She shook her head. "It wasnae anger that rose up. It was somethin' worse."

Fergus was quiet. Waitin'.

"It felt like watchin' someone I used tae ken die," she said at last. Her voice raw an' tight. "She was the one who saw me. When no one else did. When I was just a forgotten wee lass in a loud, cold world—Elsyn looked at me like I mattered." Her voice cracked. "An' now she winna even look at me."

She dug the heels o' her hands intae her eyes, furious wi' the tears tryin' tae come.

Fergus stepped forward, close but nae crowdin' her. "It's a cruel thing," he said softly, "when someone we love goes an' becomes someone we dinnae recognize."

Alyssa laughed bitterly. "She kent what she was doin'."

"Aye. She did," Fergus agreed. "But that doesnae undo what she meant tae ye afore. Doesnae erase it. Just makes it harder tae carry."

A long silence stretched between them, broken only by the creak o' wind through the hedges.

"She didnae even say she was sorry," Alyssa whispered.

"Maybe she doesnae ken how," Fergus said gently. "Nae everyone learns the words for remorse. Specially the ones who need them most."

Alyssa's jaw clenched, but her shoulders had slumped, the fight bleedin' oot o' her in slow trickles.

"She left me once when we were lasses," she murmured. "Ran aff an' never said goodbye. I waited three weeks under that blasted sycamore tree just tae hear why. An' now here we are again."

Fergus nodded, solemn. "Some folk leave ye twice. First in the flesh. Then in the heart."

Alyssa swallowed hard. "What am I meant tae do now?"

Fergus gave a small shrug. "Ye dinnae hae tae forgive her the day. Or the morn. Maybe nae ever. But what ye do hae tae decide, lass..." He paused, tippin' his head so their eyes met. "...is whether ye want tae keep bleedin' for someone who winna stop the cut."

Alyssa's breath hitched. She blinked up at him, throat workin' against a lump that wouldnae move.

"Ye're allowed tae mourn what ye lost," he said gently. "But ye dinnae hae tae carry it alone."

She nodded once, unable tae speak.

Then Fergus reached intae his coat, pulled oot a clean kerchief, an' handed it tae her without ceremony. "Go wash yer face, lass. Then go find yer husband. He's been stompin' roon the keep like a bear wi' a thorn in his paw."

Alyssa let oot a shaky, near-wet laugh an' took the cloth. "Thank ye, Fergus."

Fergus nodded once. "Ye've steel in ye, Alyssa. But even steel needs temperin'."

An' wi' that, he stepped back intae the shadows o' the corridor, leavin' her tae the soft hush o' the garden an' the risin' courage in her chest.

She found him in the great hall, hunched ower the lang table, a goblet untouched beside his hand. The fire behind him threw gold across his shoulders, but his face was all shadow.

He looked up when she entered, an' the lines in his brow softened. "Ye're back."

Alyssa crossed the threshold wi' slow, careful steps, her voice tight. "She didnae say anythin'."

Tryss straightened. "What d'ye mean?"

"I went there ready for a fight. For a reason. Anythin'." Her jaw clenched. "But she just sat there, like the silence could erase everythin' she did. An' maybe it has—for her."

He said nothin', waitin'.

"I dinnae owe her," Alyssa went on, her tone sharpenin'. "Nae my time, nae my patience. She lied. Manipulated. She turned everythin' I thought we had intae a weapon."

Tryss rose slowly frae his seat, the firelight catchin' the flicker o' conflict in his eyes. "Ye dinnae owe her," he agreed, voice low. "An' I'd never ask ye tae. I'd gut anyone who tried."

She blinked, startled by the fierceness in his tone, an' then softened just a fraction.

"But," he added, "there's somethin' ye've forgotten."

Her gaze narrowed. "What?"

"Ye forgave me."

That made her falter. Just a blink, just a shift in her breath—but he saw it.

"I humiliated ye," he said quietly. "I hurt ye. An' still, ye found somethin' in yersel'—somethin' stronger than pride or pain—an' ye offered me grace. Ye didnae hae tae. But ye did."

She looked away, bitin' her lip, her hands curlin' intae the fabric o' her skirt.

"I'm nae sayin' Elsyn deserves the same," Tryss said carefully. "Only... that I've seen what ye're capable of. Ye forgive wi' fire. Nae 'cause ye forget what was done tae ye, but 'cause ye refuse tae let it own ye."

Her throat worked roon a word that didnae come.

Tryss stepped closer, reachin' for her hand. "If ye're nae ready, then dinnae. I'll stand wi' ye either way. But dinnae tell yersel' ye're made o' stane when I ken better."

Alyssa met his eyes. Her fingers found his an' held tight.

"I hate that ye're right," she whispered.

A ghost o' a grin tugged at his lips. "Ye usually do."

Elsyn heard the soft tread o' footsteps lang afore the door opened. She didnae rise frae her seat by the fire, nor did she turn. Let Alyssa find her starin' intae the flames—it was better than facin' whatever storm she'd come tae deliver.

The door creaked shut behind her.

"I'm nae here tae fight," Alyssa said quietly.

Elsyn's mouth twisted, bitter an' sharp. "Ye've said yer piece already. Several times, if I recall."

Alyssa moved tae the edge o' the hearth, arms folded, her voice steady but nae unkind. "An' ye've said naught."

Elsyn finally turned, eyes flashin'. "What would ye hae me say, Alyssa? That I'm sorry? That I regret it all? Fine. I am. I do. But if ye've come for another round o' guilt an' fury, ye'll be disappointed. I'm nae yer whippin' post."

A tense silence stretched between them. The fire cracked, spittin' sparks that seemed tae echo in the stillness.

"Ye hurt me," Alyssa said simply. "Not just wi' the lies. Ye were the one person who saw me when no one else did. When I was small an' scared an' had nothin'—ye were the one."

Elsyn's shoulders slumped, the firelight catchin' on the sheen in her eyes. "I ken."

Alyssa exhaled, a lang breath o' somethin' auld an' brittle finally breakin' loose. "We may never be friends again. I'm nae even sure we should try. But we dinnae hae tae be enemies."

Elsyn's brows lifted, wary. "What are ye sayin'?"

Alyssa stepped closer, her tone softenin'. "There's work tae be done. The harvest festival is nearly upon us, an' the keep is buzzin' wi' preparations. I could use help—trusted help."

That word—trusted—landed like a stane in Elsyn's chest. She looked away quickly, jaw tight.

"I'm nae offerin' forgiveness," Alyssa continued. "Nae the day. I'm offerin' a task. A purpose. A start."

Elsyn blinked hard, starin' intae the flames again. "Ye'd let me help?"

"I'm askin' ye tae."

Slowly, Elsyn looked up. Her voice, when it came, was cautious. "Where do we begin?"

Alyssa gave a small nod, the barest curve o' a truce on her lips. "Wi' the guest lists. An' the flower order. An' whether the lads plan tae brew enough mead tae drown a Highland army."

A faint smirk tugged at the corner o' Elsyn's mouth. "So... everythin'."

"Exactly." Alyssa turned toward the door, then paused. "Ye'll find parchment an' quills in the solar. Come when ye're ready."

Then she left, leavin' Elsyn alone wi' the fire, her thoughts, an' a flicker o' somethin' unfamiliar—

Hope.

Tryss and Fergus

Several hours had passed, and the keep had settled intae the quiet hum o' twilight. The torches in the hallways burned low, their flames gutterin' against the draft, casting long golden streaks across the cold grey stane. The day's bustle had dulled tae murmurs, the clang o' the kitchens replaced wi' the softer sounds o' hearths bein' stoked and shutters drawn against the night.

Tryss and Fergus moved side by side along the passage, their boots echoing in the hush, till they stopped short o' the solar.

Inside, a sight neither man had expected greeted them. Alyssa and Elsyn sat cross-legged on the rug, skirts fanned wide, quills in hand. Sheets o' parchment lay strewn about like autumn leaves—charts, lists, and what looked suspiciously like a seating plan, the ink bold and underlined in places where passion had guided the quill. Between them sat a half-forgotten plate o' cheese and apples, nibbled but abandoned in the heat o' their task.

Their heads bent close thegither, hair brushin', voices risin' and fallin' in quiet debate. Alyssa's hand cut the air once, sharp as a blade, tae make her point, while Elsyn only smirked faintly and scribbled something quick across the page.

Tryss blinked, slow, as though his mind were takin' a moment tae trust his eyes.

Beside him, Fergus let out a low whistle, hardly more than

breath. "Well, I'll be damned."

Tryss leaned against the doorframe, arms folded across his chest. His mouth worked as though he might speak, then closed again. At last, he muttered, "Ye think I'm dreamin'?"

Fergus shook his head, his grin stretchin' wide beneath the shadow o' his beard. "Nay. But mark my words, lad—if those two ever truly join forces again..." He gave a mock-somber shake o' his head. "Ye'll be lost, sure enough. Lost and buried."

Tryss huffed, but the sound carried warmth. It wasnae the smug smile he wore in the hall afore his men, nor the grim line o' battle—it was rarer. Softer. A smile that felt a little like peace.

Inside the solar, Alyssa glanced up then, catchin' his gaze. Her lips didnae curve intae a smile, but she gave the barest nod. A quiet acknowledgment. A thread o' something fragile but strong stretched between them.

Tryss dipped his head back, a nod returned, afore straightenin'.

Maybe they were nae whole yet. But they were mendin'.

He glanced tae Fergus, then inclined his head toward the corridor. "Step outside wi' me a moment," he murmured. Without waitin', he pushed the door to, shuttin' out the murmur o' the two women and the soft scratch o' quills on parchment.

The corridor air was cool, sharp wi' the scent o' stane and smoke. Tryss raked a hand through his dark hair, his thoughts gatherin' heavy as storm clouds.

"I've been turnin' something ower in my mind since I saw them—Alyssa and Elsyn, workin' side by side after all that's passed," he began, his voice pitched low. "I want tae do something for her at the Harvest Festival. Something that speaks more than words could."

Fergus crossed his arms, leanin' his shoulder against the wall, watchin' the younger man wi' patient eyes. Tryss drew in a breath, steadyin' the weight in his chest.

"A shield," he said at last, the word hard as steel. His fists clenched, knuckles pale. "Plain. Nothin' gaudy. Just the clan crest, bold and proud. I want her tae carry it—not only in battle, but in life. A thing she can hold when the weight o' this keep bears down. A mark that she's nae only my wife, but one o' us. Bound tae the honor and strength o' this clan."

Fergus's eyes warmed, gleamin' wi' quiet approval. Slowly, his lips curved intae a smile. "Aye, that's a fine thought, laird. There's a power in plain things. A shield like that says more than any jewel or flourish. It tells the world she carries the heart o' the clan wi' ye—and stands her ground beside ye."

Tryss nodded, the picture sharpenin' in his mind like steel ground on stane. "Commission it. Have it ready for the festival. I want her tae see it then—to ken she's nae alone in this."

Fergus stepped forward and clapped a broad, calloused hand on his shoulder. The weight was solid, sure as the man himself. "It'll be done, lad. And ye're right—there's no truer way tae show her she belongs. That she's valued."

Tryss let out a slow breath, the storm in his chest easin'. For the first time in days, he felt the future openin' afore him, nae as threat, but as promise.

Chapter Twenty-Four

Alyssa

ALYSSA SLIPPED INSIDE THE bedchamber, the faint scent o' lavender and wood smoke wrappin' around her like a comfortin' cloak. The light from the high window was dyin', stretchin' long shadows across the worn stone floor, but Tryss was already there—seated in the leather chair by the hearth, his silhouette still and steady.

She paused for a moment in the doorway, watchin' him. The weight in his broad shoulders was lessened now, though the tension still lingered beneath the surface like a low hum. He looked up as she approached, his dark eyes catchin' the last glimmers o' dusk.

"Alyssa," he said quiet-like, his voice rough but warm. "Ye're late."

She folded her cloak and set it careful on a nearby stool before crossin' the room tae kneel beside him. Her fingers brushed against his calloused hand, seekin' the familiar strength she craved.

"I was wi' Elsyn," she murmured, her voice steady but edged wi' exhaustion. "We spoke. It wasnae easy—more battles o' words than I expected. But..." She hesitated, swallowin' down the lingerin' bitterness. "I think it was a start."

Tryss's gaze softened, the sharp lines o' worry easin'. "Good," he said simply. "This household needs that peace, and so do we."

Her eyes lifted tae meet his, and in that quiet moment, all the walls between them thinned. She eased herself down into the chair, into his waitin' embrace, close enough tae lean her head gently against his shoulder. Tryss's hand came up, fingers brushin' softly through the loose strands o' her hair, a quiet gesture o' comfort and connection.

He cleared his throat, breakin' the silence wi' a teasing grin. "So... is the Harvest Festival all planned, or should I be worried I'll be called tae wrestle a boar again?"

Alyssa's lips curved into a sly smile. "Och, ye'll be doin' plenty o' wrestlin', but it willnae be wi' boars this time. Ye've got coin left, I hope? Or should I start auctionin' off yer best kilts tae cover expenses?"

He chuckled, a low rumble in his chest. "My kilts are nae for sale. But if ye need coin, I suppose I could loosen the purse strings a wee bit. Only if ye promise not tae spend it all on ribbons and pies."

She bumped her shoulder lightly against his. "No promises. Ye ken I have a weakness for ribbons—and pies."

He caught her hand and squeezed it gentle. "Then I'll just hae tae keep ye well supplied."

Her eyes sparkled as she looked up at him. "Tryss, ye do spoil me."

He grinned, a teasing glint lightin' his dark eyes. "And what o' me, wife? Will ye spoil me in return?"

Alyssa sank gracefully tae her knees before him, fingers deft and sure as they traced the laces o' his boots. Each loop undone was deliberate, slow—a promise whispered in silk and leather. Her eyes flicked upward, lockin' with his—dark, smolderin', full o' a hunger that mirrored her own.

Her hands slid beneath the worn fabric o' his trousers, fingers grazin' the hard muscle o' his calf as she pulled the boots free and set them aside. The air between them thickened, charged wi' anticipation, the room closin' around them in a private world o' need.

He caught her wrist wi' a slow chuckle, the heat in his eyes darkenin' as his fingers curled around her slender wrist, holdin' her just firm enough tae make her pulse thunder. The slight pressure sent a shiver racin' through her veins.

"Ye're trouble, Alyssa." His voice was low, rough around the edges, laden wi' a promise that made her breath hitch.

She met his gaze, bold and unapologetic, leaning closer until the warmth o' her breath caressed his cheek. "Only for those who deserve it."

Without breakin' eye contact, she reached out tae the waistband o' his trousers, fingers tremblin' slightly wi' boldness as she tugged them down, exposin' the length she ached tae touch.

His breath hitched, chest risin' and fallin' wi' a ragged rhythm as Alyssa's lips brushed the bare skin o' his inner thigh, warm and featherlight. Her hands roamed up tae his hips, steadyin' herself, before her mouth descended, a soft, reverent worship that left nae doubt where her desire truly lay.

Her tongue traced slow, teasin' circles around the sensitive head, her lips partin' just enough tae take him in, tae savour the heat and weight o' him. Tryss's fingers tangled in her hair, clutchin' at the dark curls as she deepened the kiss o' her mouth against him, drawin' out a low groan that filled the room wi' raw, desperate need.

She moved wi' gentle urgency, every motion an offerin', every touch a vow—to spoil him, tae claim him, tae show him in the quiet intimacy o' this moment just how deeply she loved him.

His eyes fluttered closed, head fell back as his breath hitched in time wi' her lips and tongue, lost tae the fierce, tender worship unfoldin' below.

Alyssa's mouth wrapped around him fully now, warm and wet, the slick heat o' her tongue teasin' and strokin' wi' slow, deliberate precision. She sucked gentle, then harder, coaxin' a guttural moan from deep in Tryss's chest that rattled against her ears like thunder.

Her hands tightened at his thighs, anchorin' herself as she took him deeper, the muscles in her jaw flexin' wi' the effort, every movement charged wi' hunger and fierce devotion. She could taste the salt o' him, the sharp tang o' desire minglin' wi' somethin' far older—trust, surrender, raw need.

His fingers tangled tighter in her hair, his breath ragged, uneven, as the pressure built relentlessly. He wasnae holdin' back anymore—each small gasp, each tremblin' grip was an unspoken plea, beggin' her nae tae stop.

She swirled her tongue around the sensitive tip. Teased the nerves beneath her lips. His hips jerked involuntarily. She felt it—the thick, hot pulse o' his arousal quickenin'—and she pressed closer, deeper, until the harsh scrape o' skin met the soft, wet cavern o' her mouth.

The taste o' him filled her senses, ignitin' a fierce, burnin' need that shot straight tae her core. She swallowed around him, her throat tight wi' the pleasure o' knowin' she was the one who held this power—this gift—over the man who owned her heart.

His groan turned raw, ragged, vibratin' through his whole

body as he tipped forward, givin' himself fully tae her hands and mouth. The fire in his eyes was wild now—untaimed and desperate—and Alyssa matched it, movin' wi' reckless abandon, lost in the primal dance o' givin' and takin'.

When at last he shuddered, his release tremblin' and fierce, she held him fast, drawin' every last inch into her before slowly easin' away, breathless and flushed, her lips swollen wi' the sweet ache o' devotion.

She looked up at him, eyes gleamin' wi' triumph and love—knowin' she had truly spoiled him this night, body and soul.

Chapter Twenty-Five

Alyssa

THE MORNIN' SUN FILTERED through the tall mullioned windaes o' Alyssa's bedchamber, spillin' warm light o'er rich bolts o' fabric and delicate trims strewn across the table. Outside, the keep buzzed wi' life—the steady rhythm o' preparations for the Harvest Festival carried on through open doors an' echoing halls. Voices rose an' fell like a tide, laughter mingled wi' the clatter o' tools, an' the scent o' freshly chopped herbs an' bakin' bread drifted upward.

Alyssa sat at the edge o' her carved wooden chair, fingertips tracing the intricate embroidery along the hem o' the deep forest green dress laid afore her. The threads glinted like wee flames in the mornin' light—gold an' moss an' shadow entwined, a perfect mirror o' the land an' legacy she was beginnin' tae claim.

Her gaze lifted tae the tall mirror propped against the far wall. She saw herself reflected there, poised an' radiant in a moment that felt like the cusp o' somethin' vast an' new. Yet, as she turned away frae her reflection, her mind caught on an image o' Elsyn. She had but the one dress she'd arrived in, an' one scrounged up frae the back stores.

A quiet pang tugged at her chest.

She rose, the weight o' the mornin's excitement momentarily forgotten, an' crossed the room. Elsyn had been tryin' tae redeem herself, workin' tirelessly side by side wi' Alyssa in the Harvest Celebration preparations. A pang o' guilt stabbed Alyssa in the gut. She had been neglectful o' her childhood heroine. No matter what had transpired between them recently, she wouldnae let Elsyn be shamed this way. She was already battlin' so many battles.

That notion pressed itself intae her consciousness. For all the house's preparations, the clansfolk's celebrations, an' the vibrant promise o' the festival—Elsyn had sae little tae claim for herself here.

Wi'out hesitation, Alyssa made her way frae her chamber, through the labyrinthine corridors echoing wi' preparation an' purpose. She sought out Fergus, who was overseeing the stable hands near the keep's outer yard.

"Fergus," she called softly, drawin' his attention.

He gave a smile. "Guid mornin', Alyssa."

Alyssa stepped closer, lowerin' her voice slightly. "I need yer help. It's about Elsyn."

His hands stilled.

"She's nae proper dress for the festival," Alyssa continued. "An' I've nae time tae see tae it masel'. Could ye—could ye see tae gettin' one for her? Somethin' plain, but suitable. She shouldnae stand out like a pauper in the middle o' celebration."

Fergus stared at her, blinkin' once, then again. "Me? A dress? Mistress, how would I even—?"

"Ye'll manage," Alyssa said quickly, already sense'n his reluctance. "Surely ye can ask one o' the seamstresses for help. Just see it done, please."

He opened his mouth, then shut it again, rubbin' the back o' his neck. His usual unflappable demeanor had cracked, just slightly, his ears tinged pink.

"I... aye. I suppose I could."

Alyssa arched an eyebrow. "Ye're blushin'. Gods, Fergus, it's just a dress."

"Isn't the dress," he muttered, then straightened an' cleared his throat. "It'll be done. I'll nae see her shamed."

"Thank ye," Alyssa said warmly, already turnin' back toward the hall. "Ye've a kind heart, Fergus."

He stood motionless for a lang while after she left, hands still at his sides, eyes fixed on nothin' in particular.

"Kind heart," he muttered under his breath. "More like a cursed fool."

Alyssa stood still for a moment, starin' after Fergus as he disappeared down the corridor, lang strides carryin' him toward the village wi' somethin' clipped an' unreadable in his expression. Her brow furrowed.

"Isn't the dress..." he had said.

What wasnae the dress? What in God's name did that mean?

She turned the words over, again an' again, but nae meanin' came clear. An' yet... somethin' wasnae sittin' right. Fergus, usually sae straightforward, had stumbled o'er that reply like a man caught in a snare. There had been hesitation in his voice—an unfamiliar falterin'—as if the request had pierced deeper than it should hae.

Her woman's mind, already sharpened by years o' readin' half-truths an' subtle shifts, began tae whirl. Fergus had refused her, nae once, but twice. Fergus—who would face down a hundred angry clansmen at the gate wi'out blinkin'—had looked positively awkward just now.

An' Fergus was never awkward.

Not unless—

Her eyes widened slightly.

"God's teeth," she muttered under her breath, spinnin' on her heel. Her skirts whispered as she moved wi' purpose through the hallway, slippin' past bustling maids an' chattin' servants who paid her little heed.

There was only one man who might make sense o' this, an' she had a feelin' he was either on the trainin' field... or hidin' in the stables again tae avoid bein' made tae taste the festival's ninth version o' roast goose.

She headed straight for the stables.

Fergus

Fergus walked briskly across the stone-paved yard, Alyssa's words echoin' louder in his head than the clatter o' boots or the hammerin' o' festival banners goin' up.

A dress. She wants me tae get Elsyn a dress.

He could've laughed, if it didnae feel sae bloody personal. She had nae idea, o' course—not Alyssa, not a soul. And that was the only reason he'd agreed in the end. The only reason he could agree.

But God's bones, how in the hells was he meant tae stride inta the seamstress's cottage an' choose somethin'—a dress—for the woman who haunted his thoughts like a stubborn flame in the hearth? Somethin' simple an' fine, somethin' she might wear an' feel...

Fergus's hands clenched at his sides, nails diggin' into the palms as if he could will the answer intae existence. "Damnation," he muttered, rakin' a hand through his hair, tuggin' at the dark curls as though he could wrestle clarity from the mess o' his mind.

He reached the stable doors, meant tae grab a horse an' ride quick tae the village, but paused mid-step. He braced a hand against the post, breathin' hard, ribs straining like he'd taken a blow tae the chest.

It wasnae the dress. That was the cursed truth. It was what it meant. It was seein' her in somethin' new, somethin' beautiful, knowin' she might smile at it—and wonderin' if it would be his undoing.

He swore again, quieter this time, lips pressed tight. His mind replayed the thought o' her, hands delicate as she handled silk an' thread, eyes liftin' with that faint glimmer o' satisfaction. The thought was fire, burnin' across his chest, heat that wouldn't be quenched wi' reason.

He shook his head, scowlin' at the ground, boots scuffin' the stone. "Blast it," he muttered, low an' rough, "this is nae simple task, Fergus. It's nae simple at a'."

A gust o' wind rattled the banners above, carrying the scent o' earth an' hay, an' he closed his eyes, countin' slow breaths, strugglin' tae steady the pulse hammerin' through him. Every heartbeat reminded him o' what he'd agreed tae do, an' every thought o' her made the task sae much heavier.

He gripped the post tighter, knuckles white, and muttered again, under his breath, "Gods help me... if this destroys me, I'll nae forgive it."

The stable doors loomed before him, dark an' still, the horses shiftin' and snortin' within. Fergus let out a long breath, shovin' the panic down, sharin' it wi' the cold stone underfoot. He had a job tae do. A simple thing on the surface—but a storm beneath, the likes o' which he'd nae faced in years.

Finally, he pushed at the door, the hinges groanin', and stepped inside. One step at a time, he reminded himself. One. Step. At. A. Time. And yet, even as the familiar smells o' hay and leather wrapped round him, he knew the weight o' this one task wouldnae be so easily borne.

Alyssa

Alyssa ducked intae the cool shadows o' the stable, her skirts swishin' around her ankles, eyes already sweepin' the stalls. She spotted Tryss in the back, brushin' down one o' the younger colts wi' all the exaggerated focus o' a man pretendin' he wasnae avoidin' somethin'.

"Tryss," she called, stridin' toward him.

He looked up, one brow arched in the manner o' a man caught mid-scheme. "Aye, love?"

She stopped just short o' him, hands on her hips. "Ye're nay goin' tae believe what I just asked Fergus tae do."

He cocked his head, interest glintin' in his dark eyes. "Does it involve livestock, food, or a potential riot?"

"Nay. Worse," she said, narrowin' her eyes. "I asked him tae fetch Elsyn a dress."

Tryss blinked once, then snorted. "An' he dinnae faint dead away?"

"Nay, he dinnae," she said slowly, "but he hesitated. Twice. An' then he said somethin' odd."

Tryss leaned against the stall rail, wipin' his hands on a rag. "Fergus always says somethin' odd. That's part o' his charm."

She stepped closer, lowerin' her voice. "Tryss... he said, 'It's nae the dress.' Whit dae ye think that means?"

Tryss froze.

Then, wi' the casual shrug o' a man who definitely kent more than he should, he muttered, "Damnation."

Tryss's muttered "Damnation" might as well hae been a beacon. Alyssa latched onto it like a hawk on a hare.

Her eyes narrowed. "Ye ken somethin'. Out wi' it then."

Tryss straightened, brushin' off his hands like that might dust away the conversation. "I ken many things. Most o' them nae fit for polite company."

"Tryss."

"That man's a mystery wrapped in a wool cloak an' stubbornness. Let him be."

"Tryss."

He sighed, tiltin' his head back like he could find mercy in the stable rafters. "Alyssa, love, ye're nay goin' tae like it."

She stepped in front o' him, blockin' his escape, chin lifted. "Ye think I dinnae ken that already?"

There was a long beat where they stared at each other, her gaze steely, his hesitant.

Finally, he scrubbed a hand over his face and muttered, "He looks at her like ye look at me."

Alyssa blinked. "Whit?" Confusion, then disbelief flashin' across her features.

Tryss huffed. "Like she's the only bloody thing worth lookin' at. Like she rattles the bones in his chest just by breathin'. Like he'd rather chew off his ain arm than admit it."

Alyssa's mouth fell open.

"But... but she's pregnant," she breathed. "He kens she's pregnant by another man."

Tryss didnae move. His expression didnae even twitch—but that stillness was confirmation enough.

"Oh, gods," Alyssa whispered, backin' up a step like the weight o' it all had shoved her. "He kens."

Tryss finally exhaled, slow an' measured. "Aye."

"And yet... he still offered tae get her a dress."

His brow lifted. "He agreed tae get her a dress. After puttin' up a fight."

Alyssa stared at the door Fergus had disappeared through as if it might somehow explain everythin'.

"She lied tae everyone, she betrayed me, she's carryin' a bairn that doesnae belong tae him—or tae anyone here, an' still... still he's lookin' at her like..." Her voice trailed off, an' she shook her head.

Tryss stepped closer. "I can tell he is strugglin' wi' it. His feelins. He kens she is trouble, but damn if I dinnae think that's part o' the allure."

She didnae answer right away. Her gaze drifted tae the window, where the distant sounds o' hammerin' an' laughter drifted in on the breeze. Her thoughts raced ahead—through the festival, through Elsyn's growin' belly, through the lang winter after.

Then she turned an' looked at him.

Tryss kent that look.

Her chin lifted, her brows drawin' together wi' purpose. Stern. Determined. Unrelentin'.

"Alyssa..." he started, already groanin'.

Her wide eyes met his wi' silent command—pleadin', but nae the kind that could be refused. She didnae speak. She didnae hae tae.

Tryss groaned louder, draggin' a hand down his face. "Nay. Nay, dinnae look at me like that—dammit, woman."

But she'd already turned on her heel, skirts sweepin' behind her as she strode out o' the chamber wi' single-minded fury.

He watched her go, then closed his eyes an' shook his head.

"Fergus," he muttered under his breath, offerin' up a silent apology tae the man already neck-deep in trouble, "I'm so, so sorry."

Then, wi' the slow, doomed resignation o' a man who'd just unleashed a storm, Tryss followed after her.

Fergus

Fergus had just crossed the stable yard, head down, muttering tae himself, when Alyssa's voice cracked like a whip through the mornin' air.

"Fergus MacLeod!"

He flinched. "Damnation," he muttered, then turned slow-like. Alyssa was bearin' down on him like a thundercloud, purpose in every stride. Tryss trailed behind her at a more leisurely pace, arms crossed, expression wary but amused—he kent that tone well.

"Aye, my lady?" Fergus asked, tryin'—and failin'—to sound casual.

"Ye said somethin' back there. About the dress. 'It isnae the dress.' What did ye mean by that?"

Fergus blinked, confused, then flustered. "It's... naught. I meant naught."

Behind her, Tryss snorted. "Lad, ye've kent Alyssa long enough tae know that's a fool's answer."

Fergus glared at him. "Ye're nay helpin'."

"I'm nay tryin' tae," Tryss replied, with a shrug and a grin.

Alyssa stepped closer. "Ye hesitated, Fergus. And nay because it's a woman's task or ye dinnae ken colors. Ye've been on the front lines o' this keep for years—dinnae tell me ye get shy about choosin' a dress."

Fergus shifted uncomfortably. "It's... complicated."

"Try me."

"It's nae my place tae say."

"Then I'll say it," she snapped. "She's pregnant. I can see it, and ye kent it. Which means this—" she gestured between them "—is about more than fabric and lace."

Fergus opened his mouth. Closed it.

"She's pregnant by another man," Alyssa said, her voice softenin', more thoughtful now. "But ye kent that already, didnae ye?"

Tryss went still beside her, arms fallin' to his sides.

Fergus's jaw tightened. He looked toward the hills, stubborn silence stretchin'.

And then Alyssa saw it—right there in the clench of his fists, the way his shoulders curled forward, the faint flicker o' somethin' raw in his eyes.

"Oh," she said softly, stunned. "Fergus..."

He turned away sharp-like. "Dinnae say it, Alyssa. Please dinnae say it."

"Ye care for her."

"I dinnae plan tae!" he snapped, groanin', pressin' both hands tae his face. "God above. I dinnae plan any o' it. I just... watched her scrubbin' floors no one asked her tae clean, gettin' glared at like she was poison. And I thought—damn it, someone ought tae care. And I dinnae think it'd be me."

Tryss, quiet all this time, let out a low whistle. "Well," he said, "that's gonna complicate the harvest seating chart."

Fergus shot him a look that could curdle milk.

Alyssa stepped forward, her voice soft now. "Does she ken?"

"Nay," he said flatly.

"Will ye tell her?"

"Nay, Alyssa. Nay."

Tryss raised a brow. "That's gonna eat at ye."

"Nay as much as it'd eat at her," Fergus growled. "Ye think

she wants some fool trippin' after her like a kicked pup when she's already swellin' with another man's bairn? That's nay kindness. That's cruelty wrapped in affection."

Alyssa stared at him a moment longer, then simply nodded. "Fine. But get her the dress."

He stiffened. "Alyssa—"

"It's nay for ye, Fergus. Remember? It's for her. And if ye care for her, ye'll do this right."

Fergus hesitated. Then, with a defeated sigh, he muttered, "Aye. I'll do it."

He turned on his heel and stalked off toward the village.

Alyssa folded her arms, still watchin' him retreat.

Beside her, Tryss murmured, "Should I offer prayers for him now, or wait till after he hands her a ribbon and accidentally proposes marriage?"

Alyssa didnae laugh. She just stared after Fergus, mind already spinnin'.

"He cares for her," she murmured.

Tryss looked at her sidelong. "Aye."

Her eyes narrowed, suspicion dawnin' again. "And ye kent."

He didnae deny it. Just winced slightly and offered a quiet, "Forgive me, Fergus," tae the wind.

And then Alyssa, with no further warnin', turned on her heel and marched back toward the keep.

Tryss sighed and followed. "I told ye she'd find out."

Chapter Twenty-Six

Alyssa

Alyssa found Elsyn tucked away in the quiet corner of the lower storeroom, sleeves rolled up, sortin' bundles of herbs and twine wi' meticulous care. The room smelled of lavender, sage, and damp stone. For once, Elsyn didnae look up wi' suspicion or scorn—just mild surprise and a hint of tired curiosity.

"I thought ye'd be wi' the cooks," she said. "Or the steward. Or... anywhere else."

Alyssa stepped fully into the room, the door whisperin' shut behind her. "I needed a quiet moment."

Elsyn gave a dry laugh, brushin' her hands off on her skirt. "Well, ye've found the dullest corner in the keep. Congratulations."

Alyssa didnae rise to the bait. She glanced at the shelves and baskets, then lowered herself onto the edge of an overturned barrel. "Ye're organizin' all this on yer own?"

Elsyn shrugged. "It gives me somethin' to do besides bein' glared at. Plus, if I dinnae, the servants'll just let it rot. They still think if I touch the bread it'll turn tae ash."

Alyssa let out a small sigh. "They'll come 'round. In time."

"Will they?" Elsyn didnae say it wi' bitterness—just weary resignation. "They dinnae see me. Not really. Just the shadow o' who they think I am."

A pause stretched between them, filled wi' the sound o' birdsong driftin' in from the open slit o' a window and the faint bustle o' preparations from above.

Alyssa let her gaze wander 'round the room, then asked lightly, "So... anyone in the keep ye *do* talk tae?"

Elsyn cast her a sharp look, suspicious now. "Talk tae?"

Alyssa smiled, as if the question carried nae weight. "Ye must hae noticed someone. People watchin' always notice who's watchin' them."

Elsyn snorted. "That's dangerous talk."

"Only if there's somethin' tae hide."

Another beat. Elsyn returned tae bundlin' thyme wi' more focus than strictly necessary.

Alyssa tilted her head. "Fergus has been kind tae ye, has he no'?"

That got her.

Elsyn's hands froze. Not visibly, not dramatically—but Alyssa saw it: the tiny hitch in her breath, the way her fingers stilled mid-wrap.

"He's been... fair," Elsyn said after a moment, careful. "Not cruel, like some. Not overly warm, either."

Alyssa gave a quiet hum, her face unreadable. "He's nay overly *anythin'*, that one."

That pulled a faint flicker o' somethin' from Elsyn. A shadow o' a smile, maybe. Or a grimace hidin' behind it.

"He sees too much," Elsyn said, still no' lookin' up. "More than he says."

Alyssa folded her hands in her lap. "Does that trouble ye?"

Finally, Elsyn looked up, meetin' her gaze fully. There was challenge in her eyes, but also somethin' deeper—uncertainty, maybe even fear.

"It should," she said. "But it doesnae."

Alyssa studied her. She wanted tae press—wanted tae shake her, maybe—but she saw enough in that single admission tae still her tongue.

Instead, she rose, dusted off her skirts, and gave Elsyn a small, almost imperceptible nod.

"Well," she said casually, "if ye *do* talk tae him again... be kind."

Elsyn blinked. "Why?"

Alyssa's mouth twitched. "Because Fergus deserves a wee bit o' kindness. And maybe so do ye."

Without waitin' for an answer, she turned and swept out the door, leavin' Elsyn alone—her hands hoverin' uselessly over the half-tied bundle, her heart poundin' wi' questions she hadnae dared ask herself until now.

Fergus

Fergus adjusted the collar of his tunic for the fourth time as he strode down the sloping cobblestone path toward the dressmaker's cottage on the edge o' the village. The morning air was sharp wi' peat smoke and damp wool, the kind that clung tae a man's bones. A dozen folk greeted him wi' nods an' half-smiles—recognizing the MacInnes captain, not the reluctant errand boy he currently was.

He kept his face impassive, his gait purposeful, but inside? He wanted tae crawl into a barrel of whisky an' vanish.

This was nae his world. But God's bones, how in the hells was he meant tae stride inta the seamstress's cottage an' choose somethin'—a dress—for the woman who haunted his thoughts like a stubborn flame in the hearth? Somethin' simple an' fine, somethin' she might wear an' feel—

"Damnation," he muttered, rakin' a hand through his dark curls.

Fergus shifted his weight, scowlin' at the rows o' cloth like they were lined enemies. He'd stared down steel at his throat wi' steadier breath than he had now, standin' among silks an' ribbons. A dress. Gods' bones, this was his battlefield? He near laughed at the absurdity—aye, laugh or break.

Damnation.

The bell above the dressmaker's door tinkled softly as he entered, and a wave o' lavender, starch, and old pine greeted him. Bolts o' fabric lined the shelves in rich jewel tones an' soft earth shades, an' spools o' thread danced like soldiers across the counter.

A thin woman wi' sharp eyes and silver streaks in her braid emerged from the back room. "Can I help ye, Captain Fergus?"

He cleared his throat. "I need a dress."

Her eyebrows rose. "Do ye now."

"It's nay for me," he snapped, a touch too quickly. "It's for... someone. A woman. She'll be attendin' the festival. I was told tae fetch somethin'... suitable."

"Mm," she said, folding her arms. "And this mystery woman—tall or short?"

"Average."

"Fair or dark?"

"...Aye."

The dressmaker gave him a dry look.

Fergus exhaled hard through his nose. "Look. I dinnae ken what she'd choose. She's nay the sort for frills or fuss. She needs somethin'... practical. But still fine enough nay tae draw stares."

The woman softened, reading between the lines. "Ah. One o' those."

Fergus frowned. "One o' what?"

"Never mind." She motioned for him tae follow. "Let's see what we've got."

She led him tae a row o' finished gowns hung along a rail. Silks an' satins gleamed in the morning light, flutterin' like moth wings. He scanned them, unsure what exactly he was lookin' for—only knowin', wi' a growin' tightness in his chest, that he'd ken when he saw it.

Fergus scowled at the racks, every gown lookin' dafter than the last. Lace an' ribbons, frills that'd swallow a lass whole. Christ's wounds, he thought, none o' this will do. He shifted, near ready tae storm out an' tell Alyssa she could stuff her schemin'.

And then he saw it.

The green one.

Sea moss, soft as river water in summer.

Sea moss green. The fabric looked like mornin' mist caught in a sunbeam. It was soft an' fluid, gathered gently beneath the bust, wi' long, graceful sleeves an' a neckline that dipped modestly but not too high. The skirt flared just enough tae skim over a swelling belly.

He didn't move for a long moment. Then he touched the fabric. It was cool, smooth—like somethin' Elsyn would scoff at first... but then quietly run her fingers across when she thought no one was watchin'.

"This one," he said gruffly. "Wrap it."

The dressmaker nodded, her gaze thoughtful. "It's one o' my

best. She's a lucky lass."

Fergus looked away. "Just make sure it's ready."

As he stepped outside, parcel in hand, the wind tugged at his hair and cloak. He stared down at the wrapped dress, heart thudding strangely.

Aye, he was doomed.

Alyssa

The door swung open without warnin'.

Alyssa looked up from her writin' desk, quill still poised mid-air as Fergus strode in wi' the full authority o' a battle-worn captain an' the expression of a man who'd barely survived a skirmish. In his hands was a neatly wrapped parcel, slightly creased from the pressure o' his grip.

"Never," he announced, voice dark an' clipped. "Nay ever again."

He marched across the chamber an' dropped the bundle unceremoniously on the bed, as though it had personally insulted him.

Alyssa blinked, then pressed a hand tae her mouth tae hide her smile. "Well then," she said sweetly, "shall I call the physician, or are yer wounds o' a more emotional nature?"

Fergus scowled, crossing his arms. "Yer task was a trap. And I fell right inta it."

She rose from the desk and approached the bed, brow arched. "Let's have a look at yer endeavors, brave soldier. Have ye brought me a prize or a puzzle?"

"I brought ye a bloody miracle," he muttered.

Suppressing a laugh, Alyssa untied the parcel wi' delicate fingers. The fabric spilled out across the coverlet in a gentle cascade o' sea moss green—soft, flowing, elegant in its simplicity. Her breath caught.

"Oh," she whispered.

It was perfect. Exactly right. Not flashy, not gaudy. Thoughtful.

She glanced up at him, something softer in her gaze now. "Fergus... this is beautiful."

He didn't meet her eyes. "The woman said it was one o' her best. I took her word for it."

Alyssa stepped closer, studying his rigid stance, the way his hands fidgeted behind his back like a schoolboy. "Ye chose well. Gallant knight."

He cleared his throat. "I willnae be caught in a dressmaker's again, Alyssa. I dinnae care if Elsyn turns up barefoot in a potato sack next time. That's yer realm, nay mine."

Her lips twitched. "Mmm. Noted."

Fergus shifted, then turned to go—eager to escape before she could poke deeper. But Alyssa's voice stopped him.

"Fergus?"

He paused at the threshold.

"Thank ye," she said quietly. "Truly."

Alyssa ran her fingers gently over the moss-green fabric, a smile curving on her lips. "Fergus?"

He froze in the doorway. "What now?"

"I do have... one more favor to ask."

He turned slowly, eyes narrowing. "Nay, Alyssa. Absolutely not. Whatever it is—I say nay."

She tilted her head, all innocent charm. "Ye havenae even heard it yet."

"I dinnae need tae hear it." He jabbed a finger at her like she was a wasp hoverin' too close. "That tone, that smile—ye're about to ruin my day again."

She only smiled wider.

He groaned. "Alyssa..."

"I want ye to give her the dress."

The look on his face was sheer horror. "Oh nay. Nope. Alyssa... nay."

"It's just a dress," she said sweetly. "A kind gift. That ye chose."

"That I dinnae choose! I stood in a room full o' lace an' lies until some madwoman handed it tae me and I panicked an' paid!"

"But ye did choose it," she said, stepping toward him. "Ye knew it was the one. And that matters more than anythin'. Elsyn will know it too. That's why it should be ye."

Fergus stared at her, mouth agape, as if she'd just suggested he perform a solo at the festival's feast. "I am not... I dinnae do gift-giving. I barely do words."

Alyssa folded her arms. "Ye do loyalty. Ye do kindness. Ye do what's right. And this, Fergus, is right."

He rubbed a hand over his face. "Ye're enjoyin' this."

"Oh, immensely."

He groaned again, muttered somethin' under his breath, then turned for the door like a man being sent tae his execution.

"Fergus," Alyssa called.

He stopped without turning.

"She's goin' to love it."

He didn't answer, but the tips of his ears were red as he left.

Chapter Twenty-Seven

Elsyn

THE LOWER STOREROOM WAS quiet again, the afternoon sun castin' soft light through the high slit o' a window. Elsyn had resumed her sortin', though her motions lacked the earlier precision. Her mind was elsewhere, distracted by the faint echo o' footsteps approachin' down the hall. She didnae look up.

She didnae hae to.

Fergus cleared his throat. "Mind if I step in?"

Elsyn blinked, startled, her fingers paus'n mid-wrap around a bundle o' rosemary. She turned, brow lifted. "Since when do ye ask permission?"

He grunted. "Since now, apparently."

He stepped fully inta the room an' shut the door wi' a quiet click. In his hands, a simple brown parcel—creased, weathered, clearly carried wi' some care despite his gruff demeanor. Elsyn eyed it.

"You lose a wager?" she asked, arms crossin' o'er her chest.

"Aye," Fergus muttered, walkin' forward. "To Alyssa. Naturally."

That earned a flicker o' amusement from her, brief as it was.

He set the parcel down on a clean section o' the worktable, then stepped back, almost sheepish. "She wanted me tae bring ye this."

Elsyn didnae move. Her brows pulled together slightly. "What is it?"

"A dress," Fergus said flatly. "For the festival."

She stared at the package. "An' she sent ye?"

Fergus looked vaguely offended. "Apparently, I hae a talent for fabric now. Or maybe she just enjoys torturin' me."

Still, Elsyn didnae reach for it. She studied his face instead, wary.

"You're givin' this tae me," she said slowly. "Why?"

He hesitated. The silence stretched.

Then he exhaled. "Because she asked me tae."

It wasnae untrue. But it wasnae the whole o' it.

Elsyn tilted her head, the sharpness in her gaze soft'nin' intae somethin' else—confusion, maybe. Disbelief. "I dinnae need charity."

Fergus's jaw tensed. "It's nae charity. It's a dress. One ye might wear. Or nay. It's none o' my business either way."

Her gaze dropped tae the parcel again.

"Why you?" she asked, more tae herself than him. "Why not Alyssa?"

Fergus didnae answer.

Elsyn took a step forward, fingers brushin' the edge o' the wrappin'. Her hands trembled, just a wee bit.

The paper parted wi' a quiet rustle.

She pulled back the fabric, revealin' a sea moss green

gown—soft, flowin', gathered beneath the bust in gentle folds. Her breath caught, an' for the briefest instant, her fingers stiffened on the wrappin', as if the beauty o' it had startled her.

For a lang moment, she simply stared. Then she whispered, "It's beautiful."

Fergus cleared his throat again. "Aye. That's what the dressmaker said. Or somethin' close tae it."

She looked at him. Really looked.

"You picked this," she said.

He met her gaze, his own guarded but steady. "Aye."

"Why?"

He hesitated. Then, softly, "Because it reminded me o' ye."

He looked away. "She asked me tae get one. I got one."

"You picked this one." Her voice wasnae accusin'. Just... curious. And it rattled him more than if she'd shouted.

Fergus rubbed the back o' his neck. "Dinnae seem right, ye goin' tae a festival wi' only what ye arrived in. I figured..." He trailed off, brow furrowed, strugglin' tae find words. "Ye deserve tae nay be... shamed. Or stared at."

Her lips parted slightly, as if she might speak, but nae words came. Instead, she set the parcel gently on the table behind her, then turned back tae him.

"I've never been given anythin' like this before." Her voice was thin, barely more than a whisper. "Not without a price."

Fergus's jaw tightened. "There's nae price."

She studied him then—really looked at him. For the first time, maybe. Past the clipped words an' the stern mouth. Past the bristlin' sense o' duty. And in that silence, she saw it: the storm beneath his calm, the way his fists stayed clenched even when his face stayed composed. A man tryin' very hard not tae care—because carin', for him, would be ruin.

"I dinnae ken what tae do wi' your kindness," she admitted,

voice low. "I dinnae ken how tae carry it."

He met her eyes. "Just wear the dress."

The quiet between them stretched, dense an' electric.

"Fergus," she said, softer now. "Thank ye."

He gave the barest nod, turnin' toward the door.

"And Fergus—" she stopped him again.

He turned just slightly, nay facin' her fully.

She tried for somethin' light. "Next time ye're choosin' for a woman, ye might want tae avoid colors that match the moss on the north wall."

That almost-smile twitched at his mouth again. "Noted."

She watched him leave, the doorway swallowin' his tall frame an' the sound o' his boots fadin' wi' each step. Only once she was alone again did Elsyn let her fingers trail over the wrapped dress. Her breath caught.

For the first time in a lang while, she felt somethin' warm rise in her chest. Not safety, not yet. But maybe—maybe—a beginnin'.

Elsyn blinked hard. Whatever sharp retort she might have conjured melted into silence. Her fingers closed gently over the fabric, pullin' it closer tae her chest.

Alyssa

In the hallway, just beyond the door, Alyssa stood still as stone, one hand pressed over her mouth, heart thudding against her ribs. She hadn't meant tae eavesdrop. But when she'd come tae check if Fergus had delivered the dress, the sound o' their voices had stopped her, frozen her in place. Every word, every pause, carried weight she hadnae expected. She could still hear, in her mind, Fergus's gruff tones, the way he'd cleared his throat before speaking, the stiff way he'd held the parcel—as if it were a wounded beast he dared not touch too tightly. The small quiver in Elsyn's fingers, the short, sharp catch in her breath when she saw the sea moss green fabric... it made Alyssa's chest tighten.

She drew in a slow breath, tryin' tae steady herself, then turned and found Tryss just outside the great hall. The late mornin' sun cast sharp shadows across his face, highlighting the angles o' his jaw and the faint lines at the corners o' his eyes. He was polishin' the pommel o' his sword, posture stiff but watchful, muscles coiled like a spring. Alyssa's feet moved before her mind could catch up, quick steps bringing her tae him, excitement bubbling beneath her calm exterior.

"Tryss," she said, breathless wi' news, cheeks warm.

He looked up, eyes lifting to hers with mild curiosity, head tilting just a bit. "Ye've my attention love—what is it, then?"

"I saw Fergus give Elsyn the dress I had him get. The one from the dressmaker. He gave it tae her himself."

Tryss's expression darkened, shadowed wi' disbelief. "Ye expect me tae believe ye thought that was a good idea? To saddle Fergus wi' an untrustworthy woman like Elsyn?"

Alyssa's eyes flashed, quiet fire sparkin' in their depths. "The heart does what it wants, Tryss. Fergus deserves someone who sees him—not just a servant or a shadow. And Elsyn... maybe she needs someone who will stand with her, even if no one else does."

Her mind flicked back tae Fergus shifting awkwardly, scratching his neck, eyes avoiding Elsyn's gaze. How he'd muttered about not knowing what she'd like, the quiet tension in his shoulders—it showed how much it mattered tae him, even if he wouldnae admit it. Watching Elsyn's soft, trembling fingers on the dress, Alyssa saw Fergus anew: brave not just on the battlefield, but in small, quiet acts no one noticed.

Tryss scoffed, shaking his head, lips pressed into a thin line. "Ye sound like ye're defendin' her. After everything."

She stepped closer, closing the gap, voice dropping softer but no less firm. "And what about ye? Ye're no saint, Tryss. A brute in many ways. But my heart insists on lovin' ye. That's how it works. We dinnae choose who breaks through the walls. Sometimes the heart knows better than the mind."

Tryss met her gaze, the hard lines around his eyes softening just a wee bit, the tension in his jaw easing. "Ye're as stubborn as a Highland storm."

She dared a small, defiant smile, eyes glintin' mischievously. "And just as unstoppable."

He let out a quiet, reluctant chuckle, shaking his head as if fightin' against some invisible tide. "Ye're nae ordinary lass, Alyssa. Ye think and act too much wi' that heart o' yours."

She lifted her chin, eyes steady, voice laced wi' warmth and certainty. "Better tae act wi' heart than tae live a life too careful to care at all. And Fergus... he showed me that. Even in his gruff way, he gave. He risked embarrassment, confusion, maybe even scorn. And Elsyn... she saw it. That's how it matters, Tryss. Not in words, but in actions."

Tryss's gaze lingered on her, a mixture o' admiration, exasperation, and... somethin' softer, quieter, that made her pulse quicken. He finally nodded once, curt but loaded wi' understanding, then returned his attention tae the sword, but Alyssa knew the conversation had shifted something between them. Something unspoken, yet heavier than the words themselves.

Alyssa's lips curved into a subtle, satisfied smile, her thoughts drifting back tae Fergus and Elsyn. The image of him, tall and awkward, clutching the wrapped parcel, the brief flicker o' nerves behind his eyes... she felt a pang of fondness, respect, and something tender she hadn't expected. And for the first time in a long while, she felt the stirrings o' hope ripple through her chest—not just for Elsyn, or Fergus, or even herself, but for the small acts of bravery that made the keep, and the people in it, worth caring about.

CHAPTER TWENTY-EIGHT

Alyssa

THE MACCRAITH KEEP HAD never felt so alive.

Smoke curled from open spits where pheasants roasted on iron hooks, their skins golden an' crisp. Tables stretched in lang rows across the courtyard, weighed down wi' roasted squash, honey-eyed parsnips, fresh-baked oatcakes, an' glazed apples strung together like garlands. Casks o' mead an' spiced cider steamed in great copper pots, fillin' the air wi' warmth an' sweetness that wrapped around the revelers like a second cloak.

Weans darted between the dancers, hands sticky frae sugared nuts an' soft plum tarts. Musicians lined the steps o' the great hall, fiddles an' flutes in hand, stampin' their boots in rhythm as they played lively reels that made even the auld men tap their feet.

Woven ribbons hung frae the trellises, catchin' every gust o' wind an' sendin' flashes o' deep harvest gold an' crimson red through the air. Lanterns bobbed overhead, their glow soft an' amber, swayin' like stars tethered tae earth.

Alyssa stood near the edge o' the crowd, her hands wrapped around a steamin' cup o' cider, the warmth seepin' intae her fingers. She wore soft green velvet tonight, the hem kissed wi' silver thread an' fallin' just abuin her slippered feet. Her hair was braided back frae her face, pinned wi' sprigs o' rosemary an' dried heather.

Tryss had disappeared some time ago, dragged inta a game o' knife-throwin' that had gotten dangerously competitive after the second tankard o' ale. Alyssa had left him tae it. Tonight wasn't aboot displays o' strength. It was aboot joy. An' roots. An' gatherin' what was theirs tae keep.

A gust o' cool wind tugged at her braid just as the music shifted—softer, slower, a new tune carried on lilting flute.

That's when she saw them.

Emergin' frae the side arch near the herb gardens—Fergus an' Elsyn.

They weren't arm in arm, not exactly. But they moved in step, side by side. Fergus wore his best dark wool, a new tunic she hadn't seen before—loose but neat, his shoulders straight, his jaw clean-shaven. His brow looked less furrowed than usual. He even had a ribbon—a ribbon!—tied around one wrist, a pale shade o' green.

But it was Elsyn who stole the breath frae Alyssa's chest.

The sea moss dress fit her as if it had been sewn against her skin. High-waisted, flowin', the colour pulled every glimmer o' green frae her hazel eyes. Her dark hair was half-braided an' adorned wi' wildflowers—white clover an' cornflower blue. She walked as if she wasn't sure whether she belonged here... but the way Fergus looked at her said otherwise.

Fowk noticed.

Heads turned. Some wi' curiosity. Some wi' approval. None wi' open scorn.

Elsyn faltered a step. Just the smallest hesitation. Alyssa saw her fingers twitch at her sides.

An' Fergus—without a word—offered her his elbow.

A beat passed.

Then Elsyn took it.

Alyssa pressed her lips together, a smile bloomin' slow an' satisfied. She sipped her cider an' turned, headin' back inta the festival before either o' them could spot her watchin' like a proud aunt or an overeager conspirator.

But oh, her heart fluttered like a ribbon in the wind.

Let it happen, she thought. *Please, let them baith be brave enough tae let it happen.*

Somewhere behind her, a fiddle soared. The music swelled. An' beneath the flickerin' lanterns an' fallin' leaves, Elsyn an' Fergus stepped inta the light o' the crowd—together.

The sun dipped low behind the heathered hills, paintin' the sky in hues o' fire an' rose. The courtyard o' the keep had been transformed—draped in autumn garlands, sheaves o' golden wheat, bundles o' dried herbs, an' colourful wool ribbons flutterin' frae beams an' bannisters. The air was thick wi' the mingled scents o' roastin' meats, spiced apples, an' honeyed ale. Laughter rang across the stone, weans darted between the legs o' dancin' adults, an' fiddlers kept the beat lively wi' stompin' reels an' joyous strains.

Tables groaned under the weight o' the harvest—fresh breads, wheels o' cheese, crisp pears, an' glazed nuts. A pig turned slowly over an open fire, its skin cracklin'. Wine flowed freely, an' so did stories.

Alyssa stood near the edge o' it all, wrapped in a deep green shawl, her gaze sweepin' across the crowd wi' a quiet satisfaction. She spotted Fergus—lookin' flushed an' uncomfortable—standin' beside Elsyn. The moss-green gown hugged her loosely, but she looked different tonight. Less guarded. Almost... graceful.

A soft smile tugged at Alyssa's lips.

Warm arms wrapped gently around her waist.

Tryss.

He leaned in, pressin' a kiss just beneath her ear. "I was wonderin' where my wife had wandered off tae."

She leaned inta him, his solid frame a perfect shield against the coolin' air. "Just watchin'."

"Mmm," he hummed, restin' his chin on her shoulder. "Ye always did like tae watch before jumpin' in."

"Not always." She turned tae glance up at him, her smile mischievous. "I seem tae recall a night I leapt before I looked."

Tryss chuckled, his breath warm on her cheek. "An' look where that got ye. Spoiled. Loved. Terribly overfed."

She laughed softly. "Ye're not wrong."

They stood for a moment in silence, simply breathin' together, watchin' as torches were lit around the square an' the tempo o' the music picked up. Feet stamped on the stone in rhythm, skirts twirled, an' someone whooped at a particularly darin' spin.

Tryss tilted his head toward the dancin'. "Come on, lass."

Her brows lifted. "Ye? Wantin' tae dance?"

"I dinnae say I wanted tae," he said, already pullin' her toward the gatherin' crowd, "I said come on. There's a difference."

"Ye'll regret it," she teased as she stepped inta his arms.

"Nay a chance," he murmured, his hand settlin' at the small o' her back. "Nay when I get tae hold ye like this."

The musicians launched inta a sweepin' reel, an' they were drawn inta the movement. Alyssa laughed as he twirled her, then caught her again, his smile rare an' dazzlin' under the torchlight. Around them, the courtyard spun wi' colour an' life, but Alyssa only saw Tryss—her brute, her heart, her home.

For a moment, the weight o' the past weeks lifted, carried off on music an' firelight. An' in the heart o' the harvest, wi' her clan all around her, she felt full—not just o' food or warmth, but o' joy.

Fergus

Fergus shifted his weight, suddenly too aware of the way her eyes were still on him—steady, sharp, like she was peelin' him open wi' a look he hadn't learned tae meet so openly. His chest felt tight, and his fingers flexed against the hilt of his hand as if he could summon courage through sheer force.

He cleared his throat, a rough rasp in the quiet courtyard. "I'm nay good at it," he said low, almost harshly, his voice carrying that familiar edge of self-reproach.

Elsyn tilted her head, brows knitting just slightly. "At what?"

"Dancin'."

A beat passed. A long, quiet pause, filled wi' the distant hum of music an' laughter from the festival around them. Fergus's eyes flicked away for a fraction, then back again, caught in the light of her gaze.

Then a slow, skeptical smile curled at her lips, softenin' the sharp lines of her face. "Are ye tryin' tae ask me?"

He shot her a withering look that was meant tae warn, to intimidate—but even he could feel it falter. "I'm tryin' tae tell ye it's a bad idea."

Another pause. Longer this time. His jaw clenched, and he blew out a slow breath, the kind that tried tae push away nerves that refused tae leave.

She stepped a little closer, chin lifted, the firelight flickerin' across her cheekbones like liquid gold. "Fergus."

Her name on her tongue—it nearly undid him. Something knotted in his chest, a mix o' fear an' want he had no right tae admit.

He muttered something low, possibly a curse, possibly an apology, and held out his hand. A small, deliberate gesture. "Will ye dance wi' me then?"

Elsyn blinked, caught off guard for the first time all night. Her eyes scanned his, searchin' for the unspoken, the hidden fears he carried behind that gruff exterior. And for once, he didn't hide. There was no mask. No bravado. Just him, bare in a way that startled her.

With a slow nod, she slid her hand into his. Cool fingers against calloused warmth. A shock ran through him at the touch, almost enough to make him stumble—but he caught himself, muscles tightening to steady the moment.

"You're sure?" she asked quietly, voice soft, curious, hesitant.

"No," Fergus admitted, his voice almost swallowed by the music. "But I'd regret nay tryin' more than makin' a fool o' myself."

The musicians struck up a gentler tune, the fiddles sweet and lilting, the flute carrying notes that made the courtyard feel suspended in time. Fergus led her onto the packed stone, each careful step deliberate, measured. He kept her close enough to feel the warmth of her shoulder, the gentle press of her palm against his, but gave her room enough to breathe, to move.

Around them, the festival carried on—music, laughter, firelight dancin' on every face, lanterns bobbin' overhead. But for Elsyn, there was only the strange warmth of his hand, the tentative rhythm they found together, and the flutter in her chest she hadn't felt in years.

She hadn't been asked tae dance in a long, long time. And

never like this. Never wi' someone who looked at her like she was more than a mistake waitin' tae happen, like she was—somehow—enough.

She stepped closer, just slightly, emboldened by the quiet steadiness in him.

Fergus looked down at her, a hint o' breathlessness under the rough exterior, and muttered, "I think we're baith doomed."

Elsyn's lips curved in a slow, soft smile. "Then let's make it a beautiful doom."

And they danced.

The stones beneath their feet echoed faintly, a rhythm that was part music, part heart. He guided her gently, occasionally brushing her fingers with his thumb, each movement shy yet deliberate, a language neither had spoken aloud. The warmth from her hand spread through him, loosening shoulders he hadn't realized had been holding the weight of weeks, months, years.

Around them, the world spun in lantern light an' laughter, but in that space—between one step and the next—there was only this. Only the press of shoulders, the quiet inhalation o' breath, the unsteady certainty o' being found.

And for the first time that night, Fergus dared tae believe that maybe, just maybe, he could be more than the man he showed to the world.

Alyssa

The music lifted inta a lively reel, fiddles chasin' drums as dancers clapped and turned across the firelit courtyard. Laughter rose like smoke intae the crisp night air. The scent o' roasted apples and honeyed oatcakes still lingered, but most plates had been abandoned now in favor o' feet stompin' merrily on packed earth.

Tryss's arms were still wrapped around Alyssa's waist as the last notes o' their dance faded. She leaned inta him slightly, flushed wi' exertion and contentment. His chin rested lightly on her crown, breathin' her in like she was the only sweet thing left in the world.

Alyssa caught movement from the corner o' her eye—somethin' surprising enough tae make her pause.

She straightened a wee bit. "Tryss," she murmured, nudgin' his arm wi' her elbow.

He didn't move.

"Tryss."

"What?" he grunted, half in a daze o' warmth and rhythm.

She tugged his sleeve and tipped her head toward the crowd. "Look."

He followed her gaze—and there, just beyond the ring o' dancers, was Fergus. His back was stiff, but his hand was wrapped around Elsyn's as he led her into the dance.

She didnae look smug or sulky or defiant. For once, there was nae armor in her posture. She looked... cautious. A little stunned. But her cheeks were flushed, and there was a light in her eyes Alyssa had never seen before. It was as if someone had turned her lantern back on.

"They look—" Alyssa started.

"—like two sheep who wandered onto the wrong side o' the fence," Tryss cut in, foldin' his arms.

Alyssa gasped. "Ye brute."

He arched a brow. "I'm just sayin', this is a terrible idea."

Alyssa narrowed her eyes. "Why?"

Tryss didnae hesitate. "Because Fergus deserves tae find happiness wi' someone he doesnae hae tae doubt at every turn.

Someone who doesnae flinch when offered kindness. Someone who doesnae come wrapped in secrets."

Alyssa stopped movin'.

The music and the laughter swirled around them, but she was suddenly very still. Her hand slipped from his, and she stared up at him—wide-eyed, not wi' anger, but somethin' deeper. A quiet wound he hadnae expected tae reopen.

"Ye once thought the same o' me," she said.

The words landed like a stone dropped in still water. Soft, simple—but wi' ripples reachin' farther than either of them could see.

Tryss exhaled, jaw clenchin'.

"Aye," he admitted after a long moment. "I did."

His voice wasn't defensive—it was low, thick wi' regret. "I looked at ye and saw a woman full o' fire and fury and lies. I thought trustin' ye would be my undoing."

Alyssa tilted her chin. "And was it?"

He looked at her for a long time. The firelight caught the strands o' gold in her hair, and his heart clenched in his chest.

"Nay," he said quietly. "It was the smartest damned thing I ever did."

Her lips curved, slow and sure. "Then maybe Fergus deserves the chance tae be wrong, too. Just once. Maybe she's nay what he needs—but maybe she is. And if she is, he'll fight for her the way ye fought for me."

Tryss didnae answer right away. He glanced across the crowd, where Elsyn's laughter—hesitant and surprised—rose above the music for a heartbeat before disappearin' again. Fergus stood close, not touchin', but present in a way that mattered.

He sighed through his nose. "I dionnae like it."

"Ye're nay meant tae," Alyssa said, linkin' her arm wi' his again. "Ye're just meant tae let it happen."

He grumbled somethin' unintelligible under his breath, but he didnae pull away.

She leaned into his side, smug satisfaction in every line o' her frame.

"And besides," she added airily, "if it all goes wrong, we'll just blame ye."

That earned her a sideways glare.

But he didnae argue.

Elsyn

She had expected the dance to feel awkward. Obligatory. A polite gesture to smooth edges before they returned to whatever roles they'd assigned each other—he, the guarded captain, and she, the fallen daughter of a proud family.

But it didn't feel like that at all.

Fergus's hand was warm against her back, his grip at her waist steady but not possessive. His steps were solid, unhurried, and he didn't flinch when her palm settled against the broad span of his shoulder. He held her like she wasn't fragile. Like she wasn't shamed. Like she was... just a woman, in his arms, at a festival.

The music wrapped around them like a ribbon—soft and lilting, nothing like the firelight reels of her youth. The kind of music that allowed for quiet, for noticing. And she was noticing *everything.*

How his jaw flexed when he concentrated. The way his thumb shifted once, almost absentmindedly, against the curve of her spine. The faint scent of leather and clean linen clinging to him.

She didn't speak. Not at first.

She was too afraid that if she opened her mouth, it would all fall apart.

Too afraid that if she asked him why he was doing this—*why her*—he might say something practical. Something impersonal. Something that would send her back behind her armor.

But Fergus wasn't giving her armor. He wasn't taking it, either. He was just *being there* with her. Letting her exist in his arms like she belonged.

Her dress shifted with every step, sea moss green and whisper-soft around her legs. It wasn't the most beautiful gown she'd ever worn—far from it. But it was the most *important.*

Because someone had picked it for her.

Because *he* had.

Because Fergus MacInnes had walked into a shop, thought of her—*really thought*—and chosen something that might make her feel worthy again. And now he was holding her like she already was.

"I didn't think you danced," she murmured, breaking the silence.

Fergus's brow twitched. "I dinnae. Nay well."

"You're doing just fine."

They swayed another beat before he spoke again. "I dinnae usually do this, Elsyn."

She tilted her head, watching him. "What—dance? Speak to scandalous women in soft tones?"

His lips twitched. Almost a smile. "Ye're not scandalous."

She raised a brow. "Nay?"

He met her gaze, steady and unflinching. His voice took on that low rasp she had come to crave in her short time there. "Nay."

And then, before she could blink, before she could brace herself, he added—

"I think we should put the scandal tae rest."

Elsyn froze, her breath caught between her lungs and her throat.

Fergus went on, voice low but sure, the kind that didn't shout but never wavered. "Marry me. Let me claim the bairn. It'll be mine and only mine. People will think we were lovers before now. That's what they'll whisper. They dinnae know the whole story. They dinnae need tae"

She stared at him, the world tilting slightly beneath her feet—not from the spinning of the dance but from the weight of what he'd just said. No embellishment. No romance. Just truth laid bare, like a sword between them.

Her lips parted, but no words came. Not yet.

Fergus

What did I just do? Fergus's mind raced, heart hammering like a war drum. *Did I mean to say that?* Yes. *Why? Because you love her. Because she's worth more than whispers and shame. Because she deserves a place where no one can touch her—except you.*

He held his breath, waiting for her answer.

But Elsyn pulled away, her eyes darkening. She shook her head, voice barely above a whisper. "I can't let you do that."

Without another word, she turned and began to walk away.

Fergus didn't hesitate. He rose swiftly, closing the distance between them in long strides. "Elsyn, wait."

She paused but didn't look back.

"Nay like this," he said softly. "Nay like a favor or a charity. I'm nay taking ye in out of pity."

Her shoulders tensed, but he pressed on.

"I want to stand beside ye. As yer husband. As the father of yer child. As the man who believes ye."

She stopped, still facing away, but the tension in her body seemed to soften, just a fraction.

Fergus waited, every fiber of him hoping she'd let him in.

Tryss

Tryss stood a wee apart frae the crowd, his gaze casually sweepin' the festival scene—though his eyes kept driftin' back tae Fergus and Elsyn. He tried not tae look like he was watchin', but the tension in his jaw betrayed him.

He nudged Alyssa gently wi' his elbow and nodded toward the pair still dancin', a flicker of curiosity shadowin' his usual stoic expression. "Whit d'ye think that's about?" he asked low enough tae keep it between them, voice laced wi' that familiar mix o' skepticism and concern.

Alyssa's eyes followed his gesture, a knowing smile tuggin' at her lips. "Something... complicated. But maybe also hopeful." She caught his wary look and added wi' a touch o' mischief, "Or maybe I'm just hopeful."

Tryss grunted softly, foldin' his arms across his chest. "Ye've got a knack for meddlin' in things that dinnae always go yer way."

She shot him a playful glance. "And ye've got a knack for pretendin' ye dinnae care."

He smirked, but there was somethin' softer in his eyes as he glanced back at the dancin' couple. "Maybe. But this? This I'm watchin'."

They fell into a quiet moment, both aware that the story between Fergus and Elsyn was far frae over—and that it might just change everythin'.

Tryss's gaze lingered on Fergus, his brow furrowin' slightly as he watched the man move across the dance floor wi' Elsyn.

He had never seen Fergus interested in a woman—not really. There'd been the occasional glance, the polite nod, maybe a shared drink or a passin' flirtation at best. But nothin' had ever stuck. Nothin' had ever softened those iron shoulders or drawn out that flicker o' somethin' almost tender in his eyes.

But this?

This was more than interest.

Tryss could see it in the way Fergus leaned in to catch Elsyn's words, how he didnae crowd her but still hovered close, ready tae step between her and the world if needed. He saw it in the way his hand settled at the small o' her back—not possessive, not commandin'. Just... steady. Protective.

There was care there. And somethin' that looked dangerously close tae devotion.

Chapter Twenty-Nine

Elsyn

SHE KENT HE WAS followin'—his boots didna crunch the gravel like others might, but she kent the rhythm o' his steps now. Familiar. Heavy. Inescapable. She stopped just beyond the lights an' laughter o' the festival an' slipped through the garden gate, where the shadows stretched lang an' the music dulled tae a faint hum.

She sank onto the worn stone bench beneath the arbor, the ivy rustlin' faint abune her in the night breeze. Her back was straight, her hands clenched in her lap, but her voice still trembled when it broke the quiet.

"Why?" she demanded, no' lookin' at him. "Why would ye do that?"

Fergus stood a few paces away, silent, uncertain. She turned tae face him then, her eyes wide an' shinin' wi' somethin' fierce.

"Ye're cruel," she said, the words sharp as glass. "Unfeelin'.

Half the time ye willnae even look at me, an' when ye do, it's as if ye're tryin' no' tae. An' now ye'd offer marriage—claim my bairn? Do ye think I'm that desperate? That pathetic? That I'd say aye just because nae one else would ask?"

She rose in a rush, fire flashin' in her eyes. "That's no' kindness, Fergus. That's pity dressed up like chivalry. An' I willnae take it."

She meant tae storm aff—she aye did when her heart was achin' an' pride fought tae cover it—but he moved afore she could.

"Nay," he said, his voice low, near raw. "Ye're wrong, Elsyn. I didna ask oot o' pity. I asked because I cannae stop thinkin' o' ye. Because every time ye walk past me, I ache tae reach for ye. Because when ye laugh, it feels like the first sunlight efter a long winter."

Her lips parted, but nae words came.

"I dinnae care whose bairn it is," Fergus went on, softer still, eyes burnin' wi' truth. "If ye'll hae me, it'll be ours. That's the whole o' it."

Silence stretched atween them.

Elsyn's chest rose an' fell in ragged bursts, her hand tremblin' as it lifted tae her lips.

An' this time, she didna run.

Fergus

She hadna run.

She hadna said aye, but she hadna run. For a woman like Elsyn, that meant everythin'. She had fire in her, stubborn as the Highlands an' twice as untamed, but she hadna stormed aff. She was still here, starin' at him wi' wide eyes an' parted lips, breathin' like she was bracin' for a blow that hadna come.

There was steel in her spine—he admired that mair than he should. But right noo? All Fergus could think aboot was kissin' her.

So he did.

He closed the distance in two sure steps, an' afore she could second-guess either o' them, his hand rose tae cup her jaw—gentle, but firm. Her skin was soft, her breath caught, an' when his lips found hers, he kissed her like a man anchorin' himsel' tae somethin' he'd long tried tae deny.

She didna pull awa'. She didna freeze.

Elsyn leaned intae it—slow, cautious, like someone steppin' intae a memory they werena sure was real. Her fingers fisted in the front o' his tunic, an' when he deepened the kiss, her lips parted on a soft, startled sound that near undid him.

The taste o' her—rosewater an' resolve—lingered on his tongue. He tilted his head, savorin' the shape o' her lips, the way she trembled just slightly as his other arm slipped roond her waist an' drew her closer.

He could've stayed there forever.

He near did.

But then came the unmistakable sound o' someone clearin' their throat.

Fergus broke the kiss wi' a sharp inhale, still holdin' her close. Elsyn, flushed an' breathless, blinked up at him in a daze. An' then—

Alyssa's pointed voice cut through the silence.

"Well, dinna stop on our account."

Fergus turned, groanin' inwardly. Alyssa stood just beyond the hedgerow, arms folded, one foot tappin' against the flagstones wi' theatrical patience. Beside her stood Tryss, his face unreadable save for the single brow arched sae high it near vanished intae his hairline.

Alyssa gave a wee hum o' amusement. "Saints above, I love a good festival romance as much as ony lass, but I was beginnin' tae wonder if we'd hae tae send someone in tae rescue her frae that kiss."

Tryss finally cleared his throat, voice dry. "She seemed... willin' enough."

Fergus's ears went red. Elsyn made a strangled sound an' turned half intae his shoulder, hidin' her face.

Alyssa's grin only widened. "Och, dinna fash. Just be sure ye dinna leave us all hangin' wi' half a tale. If ye're goin' tae scandalize the garden, at least finish it proper."

Tryss gave Fergus a lang look, the weight in it nae softened by his wife's mischief. "Just be sure ye ken what ye're doin'."

"I do," Fergus said, steady noo, his arm still firm roond Elsyn's waist.

Alyssa sniffed, but her eyes softened just a touch. "We'll leave ye tae it, then. Carry on, lovebirds." She looped her arm through Tryss's, winked, an' pulled her husband awa', their footsteps vanishin' intae the nicht as the music swelled again in the distance.

She winked an' drew her husband awa', their footsteps vanishin' intae the nicht as the music swelled again in the distance.

Fergus looked doon at Elsyn.

She was still pink-cheeked, but she hadna stepped back.

He reached up tae tuck a loose strand o' hair behind her ear. "I dinna regret it," he said soft. "Nay the kiss. Nay the offer."

Elsyn's eyes shimmered, no' wi' tears—but wi' somethin' mair vulnerable. Somethin' like hope, raw an' hesitant at the edges.

For a lang beat, she said naething. Then, slow, she reached up an' covered the hand he still had on her face, her fingers small an' warm against his.

"I dinna ken what I've done tae deserve that kiss," she murmured, "let alone the offer."

"Ye dinna hae tae deserve it," he said gruff. "Ye just hae tae want it."

Her throat bobbed, a faint crease appearin' between her brows as she searched his face. The garden felt hushed aroond them, like even the wind was holdin' its breath.

"I was foolish," she said quiet. "I was cruel. I burned every bridge I ever walked across. But Fergus..." Her voice broke just a little. "Ye make me want tae build somethin' again. Somethin' better."

She shook her head, a bitter laugh catchin' in her throat. "I cannae promise I willnae make a mess o' it. O' us."

"I dinna need promises," he said. "I need truth."

Elsyn stepped closer, the front o' her dress brushin' his tunic. She looked up at him, cheeks flushed, hands tremblin'—but her voice rang clear this time.

"Then here's the truth. I want it. I want ye."

He kissed her again, slower this time, as if makin' a promise. One day—soon—he'd say it out loud. He loved her.

But for the nicht, this was enough.

"I want the bairn tae grow up in a hame, no' a shadow. An' if ye're truly offerin' that—if this isna some fit o' pity or misplaced duty—then aye, Fergus. I'll wed ye."

His breath caught, sharp an' unguarded. For a man who seldom let his emotions show, his relief was thunderous.

She smiled then, small but real. "An' I dinna regret the kiss either."

Fergus dipped his head, pressin' his brow tae hers, his voice near reverent.

"Good. Because I'm goin' tae ask for a thousand mair."

CHAPTER THIRTY

Alyssa

THE KEEP WAS ABUZZ. No' the usual bustle o' chores or the clatter o' festival clean-up—but a bright, flutterin' kind o' hum that drifted through every corridor an' courtyard.

Everywhere Alyssa turned, voices carried the same name.

"Did ye hear?"

"Fergus an' Elsyn."

"They say the bairn is truly his."

"I aye thought she fancied him."

"He's sae honorable."

"He must truly love her."

It should've been maddening. It wasna.

Alyssa couldnae stop smilin'.

No' the smug smile o' victory—though she was tempted—but somethin' softer. Somethin' that curled warm beneath her ribs every time she passed a pair o' gigglin' maids or overheard an auld guard mutter that Fergus "finally found someone who suits him."

She sipped her tea on the east balcony, watchin' the mornin' mist curl awa' frae the hills. Behind her, the kitchens clattered wi' trays an' chatter, an' someone had already set a second loaf o' honey-oat bread tae rise "in case she's feelin' poorly—what wi' the bairn an' all."

Alyssa wrapped her shawl tighter aroond her shoulders, lettin' the breeze tug at the braid that brushed her back.

No' all the whispers were kind.

"I heard she tempted him at the festival."

"Likely wasna even his idea tae wed her."

"She'll ruin him."

But they were fewer. Quieter. An' a select few could challenge the cleaner tale: that the child was Fergus's rightful-born. That he'd loved her in secret. That at last, they had made things right.

Because Fergus would say naething tae the contrary.

He would carry the truth like a shield if it meant gi'en Elsyn an' her bairn peace. An' in doin' so, he had gi'en her far mair. A name. A place. A future.

Alyssa leaned against the stone balustrade, lettin' her smile grow a little. No' all plans bore fruit. She kenned that better than most. But this one—this one had taken root an' begun tae bloom.

She'd seen it in the way Elsyn looked up at Fergus wi' somethin' like awe. An' in the way Fergus hovered, aye a hand's width away, ready tae catch her if she faltered—but never takin' what she didnae offer first.

Love, Alyssa thought, sat well on them baith. Unexpected, rough-edged, but real.

"Watchin' yer victories frae afar again, are ye?"

Tryss's voice broke intae her thoughts like a smile at the corner o' a closed mouth. She turned as he strode toward her, hair tousled frae mornin' drills, shirt damp at the collar.

"I'm just enjoyin' the mornin'," she said prim-like.

He arched a brow. "An' the dozens o' giddy gossips praisin' yer friend-makin' skills?"

Alyssa shrugged, but the light in her eyes betrayed her. "They do make a bonnie couple."

Tryss leaned beside her, his gaze followin' the sweep o' the moor. "Aye. They do. Still..."

She nudged him wi' her elbow. "Dinnae say it."

"She's got fire, that one. But Fergus?" He shook his head. "He's got too much heart tae spare. She'll hae tae mind no' tae crush it."

Alyssa turned tae face him, her expression soberin'. "She kens. An' she willnae."

Tryss studied her face a lang moment, then nodded. "Good. I'd no' fancy killin' anyone on their weddin' day. Hard on the caterin'."

She laughed, leanin' intae his side. "Remind me tae tell Fergus how touched ye are."

"Nay sae touched," Tryss murmured, his voice gone low an' thick, "nay the day."

Alyssa turned, brows arched—but it was the look on his face that stole her breath.

Wicked.

Wicked like storm winds curlin' beneath a kilt. Wicked like a man who already kenned he'd won.

Her gasp was dramatic, scandalized, an' entirely for show. "Och! So it's touchin' ye want, then?"

He didnae blink. "Aye. But only frae ye."

Wi' a delighted laugh, she seized his hand an' tugged him through the archway toward the keep. "Come along, my Laird.

We'll see just how touched ye get."

He let himsel' be led, grinnin' like a man well-fed an' well-loved.

Alyssa wasted nae time. She pressed her body against Tryss, her fingers trailin' deliberate doon his chest, tracin' the taut muscle beneath his shirt wi' a hunger that had been buildin' all evenin'.

Her lips found the hollow beneath his ear, nippin' soft, teasin' until a low sound rumbled frae his throat. Tryss's hands tangled in her hair, tuggin' her closer as she kissed a fiery path alang his jaw—slow, possessive sweetness in every inch.

She pulled back just enough tae meet his dark eyes, her ain glimmerin' wi' mischief. "Ye said ye wanted tae be touched," she whispered, hot against his skin.

His wicked smile deepened, lips curvin' like a vow. "Aye. An' I intend tae be."

Wi' that, she traced a line doon his chest, slippin' beneath his shirt tae feel the steady thrum o' his heart. Her fingers danced bold alang his waist, kennin' well how tae steal his breath an' hold it.

The day stretched ahead, full o' promise an' fire, an' Alyssa was bent on makin' sure neither o' them would forget a single beat.

It was mair than a guid mornin'.

It was a reckonin'.

A blaze.

A celebration o' everythin' they were—fierce, tender, an' utterly, deliciously theirs.

Elsyn

She was a wreck. Every step back toward the keep felt heavier than the last, her heart poundin' like a drum in a war march. What in God's name was she thinkin'? Agreein' tae wed Fergus—acceptin' his kiss, his offer—it felt like steppin' aff a cliff wi'out kennin' what awaited below.

She needed someone tae tell her it was the right thing. Someone who wouldna judge, who could see past the tangled mess o' shame an' hope swirlin' inside her. Alyssa. O' all folk, Alyssa was the one she trusted, even if their paths had rarely crossed afore this nicht.

The halls felt unusually quiet as she moved through them, the usual clatter replaced by the hum o' mornin' chores an' distant laughter. She spotted Alyssa on the east balcony, wrapped in her deep green shawl, gazin' oot toward the mist-cloaked hills.

Elsyn's throat tightened. Gatherin' her courage, she approached slow, unsure if she'd even find the words.

"Alyssa?" she called soft.

Alyssa turned, surprise flickerin' in her eyes, quickly replaced by a gentle warmth. "Elsyn. Whit brings ye here sae early?"

Elsyn swallowed hard. "I... I needed tae see someone. Someone who might understand."

Alyssa's gaze softened. "Come, sit wi' me."

They settled side by side on the stone balustrade, the cool mornin' breeze tuggin' at their cloaks an' loose strands o' hair. For a lang moment, neither spoke.

Finally, Alyssa broke the silence. "Ye're wonderin' if it was the right choice."

Elsyn's eyes drifted again tae the hills, the endless sweep o' gold an' green stretchin' like a promise intae the horizon. The dawn light softened the landscape, but inside her, shadows lingered still.

"For all the finery I was raised wi'," she began hesitant, voice low an' near brittle, "the silks, the jewels, the dinners where I was expected tae smile an' be seen... I never truly felt seen. No' really. No' like I mattered."

Her fingers twisted the edge o' her cloak, knuckles white. "I was admired, aye. But only as a possession, a prize tae be shown off or hid awa' when inconvenient. I learned early that my worth depended on keepin' appearances, on hidin' the parts that were messy or weak. An' when my secrets came tae light..." Her voice cracked, a fragile pause followin'. "I was cast oot, like a broken thing nae one wanted."

Elsyn drew a deep breath, feelin' the pull o' old wounds but also a spark o' courage. She met Alyssa's calm, unwavering eyes. "Do ye truly think Fergus loves me?" she asked quiet, voice barely abune a whisper. "Or is he... playin' the hero? Tryin' tae save me frae the ruin I've fallen intae?"

Her eyes searched Alyssa's face for truth. "I want tae believe he sees me—all o' me. No' just the polished mask the world demands, but the scared, stubborn, flawed woman beneath. The one who's still standin', still fightin'."

Alyssa's smile was soft, tinged wi' understandin' an' somethin' fierce. "That kind o' love... it's rare," she said gentle. "Tae be truly seen, an' still chosen. An' if Fergus is ready tae fight for ye—not just oot o' duty or pity, but wi' his whole heart—tae claim ye an' the bairn as his ain... then maybe this is the kind o' love worth riskin' everythin' for."

A flicker o' somethin' like hope crossed Elsyn's eyes, a quiet relief settlin' ower her. "Thank ye," she said soft.

Alyssa gave a small, encouragin' smile. "Ye're no' alone anymore. An' ye dinnae hae tae face this by yersel'."

Bathed in the soft mornin' light, Elsyn felt her chest lighten, makin' room for breath, for hope, an' for the first stirrin's o' a future she'd never dared imagine.

Tryss

Tryss found Fergus near the stables, where the chill o' mornin' clung tae the stone walls. The other man leaned against a post, arms crossed, eyes narrowed against the low sun.

"Fergus," Tryss called, steppin' closer.

Fergus didna look surprised. "Tryss. Whit brings ye here?"

"I want tae understand," Tryss said, keepin' his tone steady. "I've been thinkin'... aboot Elsyn, aboot ye. Aboot all this." He gestured vaguely toward the keep. "Do ye truly ken what ye're doin'?"

Fergus's jaw tightened. "Aye, I do. Mair than ye reckon."

Tryss sighed, scrubbin' a hand through his hair. "Look, I'm no' blind tae her past. I ken whit folk say, whit she's done. Her past isna exactly the sort o' tale ye brag on at a clan gatherin'. I just worry she might stir up mair trouble than ye're prepared tae shoulder."

Fergus's eyes flashed wi' a rare heat. "Tryss, ye've got this image o' her frozen in the past. She's no' the lass ye think. An' if ye think I'm playin' the hero, rescuin' some damsel, ye're daft. Ye dinna get tae judge her by the worst the gossips whisper. She's mair than that—and I'm no' some fool who cannae see it."

The raw anger in his voice caught Tryss aff guard. It was the same fire he'd only seen once afore—in their youth, on the field, when neither would back doon. That refusal tae yield made Tryss pause.

"I dinna mean tae doubt ye," Tryss admitted, voice low.

"Aye, well," Fergus said, mouth twistin', "ye did a poor job hidin' it."

Tryss snorted. "Och, that temper o' yers. Gods save Elsyn

when ye two quarrel."

"She'll give as good as she gets," Fergus muttered, though a ghost o' a smile tugged at his mouth.

"Good," Tryss said dryly. "If she knocked ye flat, it would save me the trouble."

That earned a proper laugh, rough an' unguarded. Fergus shook his head. "I need ye tae stand wi' me, on the day I wed her."

Tryss frowned. "Aye, but I'll wager Elsyn will want Alyssa as her witness."

"She probably will," Fergus agreed. "But I want ye there too. Someone's got tae keep the peace when the wine flows an' the stories get taller wi' every cup."

Tryss huffed. "Peace? With ye takin' vows? That'll be the day."

"Better ye than half the fools in this clan," Fergus shot back.

Tryss barked a laugh, shakin' his head. "Fine. I'll stand wi' ye. But if anyone throws a punch, I'm blamin' ye—an' I'll make sure the whole hall kens it was yer fault."

Fergus grinned. "Deal. Just dinna fall asleep afore the vows."

Tryss clapped him on the shoulder, smirkin'. "Wi' ye aboot? I'll be too busy makin' sure ye dinna disgrace yersel'. Again."

Fergus's laughter rang oot across the yard, the tension between them breakin' like mist in the sun.

CHAPTER THIRTY-ONE

Alyssa

THE FIRST LIGHT o' dawn filtered soft through the linen curtains, castin' pale gold across the rough-hewn beams o' their chamber. Alyssa lay beneath the blankets, the gentle hush o' early mornin' curlin' aroond her like a tender promise. The room felt too large, too empty wi'out Tryss—he had already risen an' slipped awa', as was his custom afore a big day.

She turned onto her side, eyes flutterin' open, but the weariness clung stubborn tae her limbs. Despite the stir o' the weddin', her body felt slow, her wame unsettled in a way she hadnae expected. She closed her eyes again, willin' the sickness tae pass.

Minutes later, the sharp twist in her belly won oot.

Wi' a groan, she swung her legs ower the side o' the bed an' rose unsteady, the cauld stone floor bitin' at her bare feet. She barely made it tae the chamber's corner afore she bent forward an' was sick quiet intae the basin set there for such mornins.

Catchin' her breath, she sank back against the wall, hand pressed tae her damp brow. The weight o' the day pressed harder than she'd reckoned—the feastin', the dancin', the faces, the expectin'. Everythin' still waitin' tae be done.

Her fingers trembled slight as she wiped at her mouth, forcin' doon a wave o' vexation. She telt hersel' it was only the press o' the day ahead. It had tae be. Onything else was too much tae dwell on.

"Come on, Alyssa," she muttered. "Ye've a weddin' tae survive."

Risin' again, she steadied hersel', bent on facin' whatever the day held—even if it meant doin' sae a little worse for wear.

All through the mornin', Alyssa moved between rooms an' passages, her hands busy but her mind far awa'. She conferred wi' the cooks ower the feast—insistin' they keep the spicin' light an' the meat tender, even as her wame churned at the thought o' rich fare. She consulted the gardener aboot the flowers tae be cut for the ceremony, choosin' sprigs o' rosemary, heather, an' wild thyme tae scatter alang the aisle an' deck the tables.

Mair than once, the sickness surged wi'out warnin', an' Alyssa had tae slip awa' quick, cheeks flushed, breath shallow. She found quiet corners behind stacked crates or ducked through a side door just in time tae steady hersel' afore disaster struck.

She hadna bothered wi' breakfast. The verra thought o' bread or porridge turned her stomach, an' she forced hersel' no' tae think on it. Her appetite had fled, replaced by a hollow queasiness she tried tae ignore.

But as the sun climbed higher an' the keep filled wi' the sounds o' bustle an' clamour, a slow shift came ower her. The dizziness ebbed, replaced wi' a steady warmth. By midday, the tight knot in her belly had eased, an' a real hunger stirred awake.

Alyssa found hersel' drawn tae the kitchens once mair, the

scent o' fresh-baked oatcakes an' honeyed apples beckonin' her gentle. She took a cautious bite, savorin' the crisp sweetness an' soft crumb. Strange, how her wame had turned frae revolt tae hunger in the span o' a few hours. It unsettled her, that sudden change—yet the taste was too guid tae resist.

Steppin' intae Elsyn's new chamber—closer tae the main hall, becomin' her new station as a beloved guest—Alyssa let oot a soft sigh. The space was bright an' airy, sunlight pourin' through the tall windows an' castin' gentle patterns ower the floor.

An' there was Elsyn. She looked like a dream—clad in soft creams an' flowin' fabric that rippled wi' every hesitant move. Every delicate fold seemed tae catch the light just sae, makin' her look every inch the lady steppin' intae a new life.

Alyssa smiled warm, steppin' closer. "Och, love, Fergus willnae ken whit tae think. Ye're radiant."

Elsyn's nerves were plain as day—her hands trembled slight, her breath quickened—but beneath the polish o' a well-born lass, she did her best tae hide it. A small, tight smile tugged at her lips as she met Alyssa's encouragin' gaze, drawin' strength frae the kindness in her friend's eyes.

Fergus

The doors of the great hall stood open, but to Fergus, the world narrowed to the center aisle and the hush that followed his every heartbeat.

Sunlight streamed through the high windows, casting long golden shafts across the floor, illuminating the wild herbs scattered down the aisle—rosemary, heather, and thyme, symbols of remembrance and strength. And when she appeared—

God above.

The crowd faded. Time stilled.

Elsyn stepped into the hall like a prayer answered. Her gown was simple, but it moved like water over her form, soft cream with a hint of gold at the seams, as though sunlight had stitched itself into the fabric. Wildflowers crowned her hair—not perfect, but real, and more beautiful for it.

Fergus felt the air punch from his lungs. His heart kicked in his chest.

She walked toward him not like a bride being led, but like a woman choosing her own fate. And choosing him.

Every step she took echoed with quiet courage. Every breath, every glance—earned.

And when she reached him, he didn't reach for her hand at once. He looked into her eyes instead, giving her one last chance to turn away, even now.

But she didn't.

Elsyn looked up at him with steady eyes, chin high, though he saw the tremble in her lashes, the emotion barely held at bay. So he offered her his hand—not in demand, but in promise.

She placed her hand in his, warm and shaking, and it fit. God help him, it *fit.* A man like him hadna dreamt o' deservin' this—yet here she was, choosin' him before all the world

The officiant began to speak, but Fergus barely heard him. His pulse thrummed in his ears as he turned to face her fully.

And then—*his turn.*

"I've no pretty words," Fergus began, voice low but carrying. "No poems or riddles."

A murmur passed through the crowd, but he kept his eyes only on her.

"I only know this: the day ye walked into my life, everything shifted. Ye were a storm I dinnae see coming—and I never want the calm again."

Elsyn let out a small breath, her fingers tightening around his.

"Ye've stood alone for too long, Elsyn. Fought too hard. And I'll nay let ye do it alone anymore."

He drew her hands to his chest, just over his heart.

"This is yers," he said. "Every day, every hour. For as long as I draw breath, I will fight beside ye, nay in front of ye. I will protect what we build. Ye. The bairn. And the life we make."

She was trembling now—not from fear, but from the enormity of it.

Her voice, when it came, was soft and fierce all at once.

"You saw me when I was hidden. Stood beside me when I was unwelcome. I have doubted many things—but never you."

She reached up, touching the edge of his jaw with trembling fingers.

"I offer you what's left of me, Fergus. And I promise to build something stronger with you."

The officiant nodded. "By the old vows and the new, before God and clan—do you take each other freely?"

"Aye," Fergus said without hesitation.

"I do," Elsyn whispered.

"Then seal it."

Fergus didn't hesitate.

He cupped her face in both hands—strong, reverent—and kissed her.

Not a chaste brush of lips. Not a fleeting press of affection.

This was a *claim.*

A kiss forged in fire and forged in choice. In front of God, and clan, and every whisper that had ever tried to name her less.

His mouth met hers with quiet reverence, then deepened—not possessive, but *certain.* Like a man who knew exactly what he had, and would never, ever let it go.

And she—she rose to meet him.

Her fingers curled into his collar, her body arching into his like a vow all its own.

When they parted, breathless and flushed, the room held still for a beat.

Then the cheer erupted, thunderous and wild. For once, the whispers didna matter. They were drowned beneath the roar o' his clan claimin' them both.

Tryss

Tryss scanned the hall, the feast in full swing—clinkin' cups, laughter rollin' like waves through the crowd, fiddles skirlin' their reels. The ceremony was done; Fergus an' Elsyn were wed, an' the whole keep was roarin' wi' cheer. Yet amid all the warmth an' revelry, Tryss's eyes kept seekin' the one face he wanted maist.

Alyssa was nowhere tae be seen.

A frown pulled at him. He slipped awa' frae the tables, weavin' through dancers an' guests, the scent o' roastin' meat an' spiced ale clingin' thick. He pushed on tae the quiet corners, an' at last reached their chamber. Easin' the door open, he caught the sound—soft, faint—a gag, a weak cough, hid behind the privy screen.

The smile fled his lips. Concern struck like a blade.

He crossed swift, drawin' the screen aside careful. Alyssa was pale, her hand clamped at her mouth, eyes shut tight as sickness wracked her.

Without a word, Tryss dropped tae his knees, gatherin' her hair back wi' one hand, the other rubbin' gentle circles at her back. His voice fell low, a murmur meant only for her.

When the worst eased, he lifted her slow, offerin' a wee cup o' water. She sipped, swallerin' wi' effort.

Guidin' her frae the floor, his hand at her waist, he steadied her steps—tentative, fragile—and led her tae the hearth. The fire crackled, shadows dancin', turnin' the chamber soft wi' glow. He sat wi' her on his lap in their worn chair, holdin' her upright but close, anchorin' her against the storm.

Her breath came uneven, her head nestled at his chest, the beat o' his heart steady beneath her cheek. His fingers threaded through her hair, slow, tender, aye remindin' her she was safe.

He pressed nae questions, lettin' the silence stretch—only fire crackle an' breath shared atween them. His thumb brushed small circles at her temple, feelin' the tremor still in her body, the way she gripped his tunic sae fierce.

"Lean on me," he whispered, voice low an' steady, a vow made soft.

She loosed a breath, long an' weary, an' some o' the weight slipped frae her shoulders. Still, she was pale. Still too still. Alyssa was never this still.

Tryss bent, kissin' her hair, breathin' her in—lavender, cloves... an' somethin' else he couldna name. She'd barely eaten for days. He'd telt himsel' it was nerves—organisin' feasts, keepin' order, always busy as fire. But here, wi' her tucked fragile against him, truth pressed close.

He tilted her chin gentle, thumb grazin' her jaw.

"Alyssa, love..." his voice rasped, rough wi' care. "Has it only been the day ye've felt this ill?"

The words slipped out quiet, unplanned—but they landed heavy as stone.

Her gaze rose, wide, uncertain. She blinked, lips partin', then shut again as thought chased thought. Her pulse raced beneath his palm.

"Tryss..." she breathed, near a whisper. "Ye dinna think..."

He saw it then—the dawning spark, the wonder, the fear.

He nodded slow, reverent.

"Aye, love," he said, his voice raw. "I do think." His throat worked, a smile spreadin' across his face like sunbreak. "I think I'm gonnae be a da."

The world shifted. The fire held, the stones stood—but somethin' in him turned ower, as if the verra stars had moved tae make space for this truth.

She stared, lips tremblin', eyes wide wi' the weight o' it. Then her hands clutched his shirt, tears spillin'—nae o' fear, but awe.

He gathered her close, kissin' her temple, her brow, her hands, again an' again. She clung back, their hearts poundin' the same vow.

An' they stayed that way, wrapped tight as the fire burned low—two souls altered, awed, an' quietly, exquisitely remade.

CHAPTER THIRTY-TWO

Tryss

THE SOLAR WAS AWASH in late-morning sunlight, the hearth crackling merrily though it was more for comfort than warmth. Somewhere below, the last of the guests ambled out with lingering smiles and easy steps, their laughter drifting up through the stone corridors like the final notes of a song.

The wedding was over. The feast devoured. The floors sticky with spilled mead and rose petals.

Peace, one might've called it.

But peace had a peculiar look to it that morning.

Tryss stood with one shoulder propped against the window frame, arms crossed, mug in hand, brows drawn in a line of deep, suspicious thought. Fergus sat beside the fire in the great carved chair that had once belonged to his father, rubbing a thumb slowly along the side of his own mug, eyes fixed straight ahead.

Across the room, on the wide cushioned bench beneath the tall windows, Elsyn and Alyssa were curled up like a pair of cats in a sunbeam—bare feet tangled in each other's skirts, heads leaned close, cheeks flushed with conspiratorial glee.

"God above," Tryss muttered. "Look at them."

"I'm tryin' nat tae," Fergus said flatly. "I dinnae think I can survive what they're plottin'."

Tryss took a sip of his drink. "Do ye think they're talkin' about us?"

Fergus didn't move. "Alyssa just laughed without coverin' her mouth. That's never a good sign."

"They haven't stopped smiling since breakfast."

"Elsyn kissed my cheek and said she *forgives me already,*" Fergus said darkly. "What in God's name am I about tae do?"

Tryss turned, squinting as Alyssa leaned in and whispered something to Elsyn, who gasped and clapped a hand over her mouth. Both women dissolved into silent laughter, their shoulders shaking like girls in a hayloft.

He drew a slow, horrified breath. "We're doomed."

Fergus exhaled through his nose. "There are two of them."

"With *our children inside them,*" Tryss added, tone almost reverent and almost terrified.

Fergus finally turned toward him. "How did this happen?"

"You married her," Tryss said, pointing with his mug.

"So did ye."

"I was drunk on love and her thighs. Ye were just drunk."

Fergus grunted. "Ye're not wrong."

A long pause followed as both men watched the pair of women giggle and lean closer, heads pressed together, a single, shared shawl around their shoulders like a banner of allegiance. Alyssa elbowed Elsyn gently, and Elsyn rolled her eyes with the air of someone perfectly comfortable in their power.

Tryss blew out a breath. "It's started already."

"What has?"

"Their union. Their dominion. We're done for, Fergus. I've seen this before in beasts. When two clever animals learn they can hunt as a pair."

"Do ye think they'll let us keep the keep?" Fergus asked, deadpan.

"I'd settle for a corner of the stable and a bit of leftover bannock," Tryss replied. "Ye think Elsyn'll let you sleep inside once she starts growing?"

"She said I snore."

"Ye *do* snore. Alyssa kicks me in her sleep. Every night."

"Did ye *deserve* it, though?"

"Probably."

They fell quiet again, sipping their drinks, watching the two most formidable creatures they'd ever met bask in sunlight and laughter, and plan whatever war campaign newly married, newly pregnant women with iron wills and clever hands could devise.

Tryss sighed again, but this time there was something softer in it. "Ye know we're never gettin' the last word again, aye?"

"We never had it," Fergus said, shaking his head.

They clinked mugs, solemnly.

Across the room, Alyssa turned her head. Met Tryss's gaze. Smiled slow and wicked.

Tryss choked slightly on his drink. "She *knows.*"

"She always knows. And she's makin' Elsyn worse."

"I know. I love her," Tryss said.

Fergus took a long drink. "Aye. That's the problem."

They both turned back to the fire. Two grown warriors, proud sons of Highland clans, staring down the terrifying certainty that the real battle hadn't even begun.

And they wouldn't win a single skirmish of it.

Steel an' sword had never frightened him half sae much as Alyssa's smile. God help them both.

Alyssa

Sunlight pooled warm aroond Alyssa an' Elsyn as they curled up thegither on the wide window bench, heads bent close in whispered conspiracies. The room smelled faintly o' wildflowers an' honeyed mead—the lingerin' breath o' a weddin' day that had already changed everythin'.

Alyssa nudged Elsyn wi' a grin. "I swear, I caught Fergus watchin' ye this morn like he'd just seen a ghost. Or maybe an angel. Either way, he looked ready tae swear fealty on the spot."

Elsyn laughed saft, jabbin' her back wi' an elbow. "An' Tryss? The man looked like a ship caught in a storm—nae rudder, nae hope, an' terrified oot o' his mind. Honest, I dinnae think he's been the same since ye found oot ye're carryin' his bairn."

Alyssa's eyes sparkled. "Poor fools. Two newly minted husbands, an' already they're at our mercy. They might as well start buildin' bunkers the noo."

Elsyn's smile turned sly. "Ye think the worst is the bairn? Fergus near jumped oot o' his skin when I telt him 'forgive me already.' I swear, the man looked like I'd asked him tae wrestle a bear."

Alyssa burst oot laughin', the sound bright an' free. "I caught Fergus tryin' tae sneak awa' frae ye after ye kissed him. Like a lad caught stealin' honey frae the queen's table."

Elsyn shook her heid, eyes glimmerin'. "He's doomed. An' sae is Tryss. Two pregnant wives means double the demands, double the moods, an' double the mischief. We've got them right where we want them."

Alyssa smirked, leanin' back against the cushions, baskin' in the quiet power o' their shared triumph. "It's queer, is it no'? They look sae big an' strong, all muscle an' bark—but pit two clever women in the same room, baith carryin' their bairns, an' suddenly they're just lads pretendin' tae be men."

Elsyn's laugh softened, warmer noo. "But we love them, dinnae we? These terrified fools who'd move mountains for us e'en when they dinnae ken which way is up."

Alyssa reached ower, squeezin' Elsyn's hand wi' a grin. "We do. An' as much as I'm bracin' for the storms tae come, I wouldnae trade them for onything."

Elsyn's eyes shone wi' fierce affection. "Neither would I. For all their fumblin' an' fear, those two haud our hearts. An' that's the one battle they've already won."

They shared a look then, the kind only women who've stood through fire an' found joy on the far side ken—full o' laughter, love, an' the fierce certainty that thegither, they were unstoppable.

CHAPTER THIRTY-THREE

Tryss

TRYSS STOOD SILENT BENEATH the battlements, eyes fixed on the distant horizon where a faint column of smoke curled skyward. The peaceful life they had fought so hard to build now trembled on the edge of something darker.

Fergus joined him moments later, his stride quiet on the flagstones. He didn't speak immediately, letting the weight of the moment settle between them like a shroud.

"It's the MacGowan raiders," Fergus finally said, voice low and grim. "They've been restless these past moons, growing bolder. This is nay mere skirmish—it's a raid, a warning, and a threat."

Tryss's hands clenched into fists at his sides. "They struck a homestead east of the river at dawn. Took what they wanted, burned what they couldn't carry. The people fled into the woods, terrified, some wounded. Word is they're moving closer, testing our defenses."

Fergus's gaze hardened. "They seek to destabilize us, weaken our hold on these lands. If they breach our borders, it will bring ruin nay just to the clan, but tae every soul in the glen."

Tryss turned to face Fergus fully, the fire in his eyes kindling with determination. "Then we must show them strength they haven't seen before. We cannae wait for their next move—we have tae strike first, prepare every man and every weapon."

Fergus nodded, his mind already racing through strategies and contingencies. "The watchmen will double their patrols. Scouts sent to track their movements day and night. We'll need supplies stocked, arrows sharpened, gates reinforced."

"And the council," Tryss added. "We gather the clan leaders this afternoon. This is more than a raid—it's a declaration. Our response must be swift, unified, and merciless if necessary."

Fergus rubbed the stubble on his chin, his usual dry wit absent beneath the gravity of command. "We fight nay just with our steel, but with the hearts of our people. Fear cannae find footing here. Nay now."

Tryss's voice was steady, unwavering. "We protect our own—our wives, our children, our home. They will see that MacGowan blood does not run free here."

The two men shared a silent moment, the sun climbing higher, casting long shadows over the courtyard. The peace of the morning was a fragile illusion.

Fergus broke the quiet with a measured breath. "We've faced threats before. But this... this feels different. It's a test, nay only of strength but of leadership."

Tryss met his gaze with a fierce resolve. "Then we rise tae it. For the clan. For the future."

Together, they moved toward the great hall with purpose. The time for celebration had passed. Now began the work of defense—of war.

The long hall of the keep was colder than it should've been.

Banners stirred softly in the draft above the hearth, and though the fire was lit, its warmth did little to cut through the chill that settled over the assembled council. The wooden table stretched between them all—scarred from years of use and war councils past—now the center of something none of them had yet named aloud, but all could feel.

Tryss stood at the head of the table, one hand planted on the wood, the other curled around the hilt of his belt knife. He hadn't sat since the meeting began.

Fergus was to his right, arms folded tight, jaw clenched, his gaze sweeping the room with the careful attention of a man who trusted few and expected less.

Alyssa stood between them—tall, composed, her braid looped neatly at the nape of her neck, her hands folded before her. She hadn't spoken yet. She didn't need to. Not yet.

Around the table sat the captains and stewards of Clan MacInnes and its sworn allies: grim men with lined faces and leather-bound ledgers, seasoned warriors with old wounds and sharp eyes. There was no laughter here, no idle talk. Just the scent of oiled steel, smoke, and tension.

Tryss spoke first.

"We've confirmed the MacGowan raid on the eastern holdings," he said, voice clear and hard. "Two farms burned. Three dead. One child missing. They crossed the river and dinnae even bother tae hide it."

A murmur ran through the room, sharp as a blade edge. Someone cursed softly under his breath.

Fergus added, "It wasn't a raid of opportunity. It was planned. They were fast, coordinated. They knew the land."

"Which means they had help," Alyssa said smoothly. Her

voice cut clean through the rumbling. "A guide. Or someone who's walked that stretch before. That puts the danger closer than we'd like."

All eyes turned to her. There was no challenge in their looks—just grim acceptance. Alyssa was no longer just Tryss's wife. She had proven herself too many times. She saw what others missed. She always had.

"We cannae wait for another hit," she continued. "If this was a test, we cannae let them think we failed it. We need eyes along every road. Supply runners ready. Healers gathered and protected. Our vulnerable moved closer tae the strongholds."

"Aye," Tryss said. "The women and children from the outer farms come in by week's end. We fortify the passes. Nay a one gets through unless we say so."

One of the older councilmen leaned forward, brows furrowed. "Do we send riders tae the lowland allies? Call for aid before they press further?"

Fergus shook his head. "Not yet. Not until we know what they're after. If we raise alarm too soon, we look weak. If we strike with clarity and force, we might end it before it becomes a war."

Tryss looked down the table, his eyes steady. "Make nay mistake—we're nay planning for one battle. We're preparing for a siege. A test of patience, supplies, loyalty. We will outlast them. Outthink them."

Alyssa added, "And if we're smart—we outmaneuver them."

Finally, Fergus pushed back his chair, rising to his full height. "Get yer scouts moving. Rotate the watch. Nay a one sleeps easy this week, not until I say so. We'll meet again in two days' time. Dismissed."

Chairs scraped. Boots echoed. One by one, the men and women of the clan rose and filtered out, voices low and movements swift.

When the room had emptied, Tryss finally let out a slow breath, rubbing a hand down his face.

"God above," he muttered. "It's beginning."

Alyssa stepped beside him, her hand brushing his sleeve. "Then we begin, too."

Fergus grunted. "We should get word to the blacksmith. Have him start checking the armory stocks."

Tryss turned to Alyssa. "Ye'll keep eyes inside the keep? If anyone's whispering in the wrong corners—"

"I'll know," she said simply. "And I'll deal with them."

There was no question in it.

The three of them stood together a moment longer—warriors and leaders and something more—facing the shape of a storm not yet formed, but already felt in the bones.

And when they left the room, it was not with fear.

It was with fire.

Chapter Thirty-Four

Alyssa

The courtyard bustled wi' urgency. Barrels rolled toward the cellars, herbs were strung frae eaves tae dry, an' shouts rang aff the walls as sentries rotated an' supplies were checked again. A storm hadna come—yet—but the sky smelled o' it. No' rain. Tension.

Alyssa stood at the center o' it all, givin' orders like breath, efficient an' calm. She held a leather-bound ledger tae her chest an' scanned the yard, her sharp gaze sweepin'—till it landed on Elsyn.

"Elsyn," she called. "Walk wi' me."

It wasnae a question.

Elsyn obeyed, fallin' intae step beside her, already feelin' the eyes that followed. They aye followed. She wasna one o' them—not really. Not yet.

They passed a knot o' women tyin' sacks o' grain, who dipped their heads polite but dinnae stop whisperin' once the pair had gone by. Elsyn's spine stiffened.

"They dinnae trust me," she said quiet.

"Nay," Alyssa answered plain. "No' yet."

The honesty struck clean an' sharp. Elsyn turned tae search her face, but Alyssa's gaze stayed forward, sweepin' the outer buildings o' the village.

"They dinnae trust ye," Alyssa continued, "because ye were brought in like a riddle. They dinnae ken yer folk, nor yer past. An' most didnae like how fast ye went frae scullery tae high table."

"I never asked—"

"I ken. But that's no' the point." Alyssa halted in front o' the long dryin' barn. "The point is, they dinnae trust ye yet. So ye're goin' tae earn it."

Elsyn blinked. "By doin' what?"

"By takin' charge o' the village."

Stunned silence hung.

"Me?" Elsyn whispered.

Alyssa turned full toward her, voice low but sure. "If we're cut aff, this village will need order. It'll need hands an' calm heads an' someone tae tell them what matters first. That cannae be me—I'll be in the war room. It cannae be Moira—she's too weary. An' the men?" Her mouth curved, humorless. "They'll be off sharpenin' blades an' shoutin' at maps."

Elsyn swallowed. "But—"

"Ye're clever," Alyssa cut in. "Ye ken this place. Ye've listened. Watched. Worked harder than most o' them ever did. But none o' that matters if ye cannae show it. This is yer chance. Take it."

Elsyn's heart thudded. Her eyes darted tae the women spooling ropes nearby. One glanced ower. Didnae smile.

"This is a test," Elsyn breathed.

"Aye," Alyssa nodded. "An' the only way tae pass is tae stop waitin' for permission."

She shoved the ledger intae Elsyn's hands.

"Start wi' the cellars. Get Moira tae walk ye through the root stores an' dried meat. Divide the folk intae shifts—food prep, firewood, clean water. Assign one or two women tae each home tae check on the elders. Ye've seen how I run the keep. Do the same. Better."

Elsyn hesitated, starin' at the leather book like it might scald her palms.

Alyssa's voice softened, but the steel remained. "They'll talk either way, Elsyn. So let them talk while ye lead."

A long breath left Elsyn's chest. She glanced back toward the green, where bairns skipped rope, dogs barked, an' men loaded carts wi' pitch an' stone.

Then she squared her shoulders.

"All right," she said. "I'll do it."

Alyssa tilted her head, approval sparklin' like flint. "Guid. Ye've till dusk tae make yersel' indispensable."

As Alyssa strode back toward the hall, Elsyn lingered a moment, clutchin' the ledger, lettin' the weight of it seep intae her bones. Then she turned—not tae the whisperin' women lurkin' in the shadows—but straight intae the heart o' the village.

The war room smelled faint o' smoke, steel, an' old parchment—ghosts o' a dozen past councils, though none had held the same weight as this. The heavy door thudded shut ahint Alyssa as she stepped in, her face all steel now, the warmth o' the yard traded for resolve.

Fergus stood at the map table, arms folded, jaw locked. Tryss leaned ower one side, turnin' a carved token in his fingers—a marker for the southern road. His look was grim, sharpened by duty. Whatever ease the men had shared that morn was gone, buried beneath command.

Alyssa took her place atween them. "Elsyn's taken the village preparations," she said plain. "We're movin' forward."

Tryss gave a curt nod. "Guid. Because if what Fergus heard is true, we've less than a week afore the northern road's cut aff."

Fergus grunted. "Campbell's scouts sent word—fires spotted last night. Far too close tae be chance."

A hush fell, heavy as stone.

Alyssa leaned in. "Walk me through what we ken. All o' it."

Fergus seized a wax stick an' drew a sharp line ower the map. "Here. The Glen Rae pass—narrow, treacherous, but the straightest march if they're travellin' light. We blocked it two winters back wi' a landslide, but if they've cleared it—"

"Or never meant tae use it," Tryss cut in, flippin' the token west. "They could swing toward Braemor fields. Mair open ground, guid for cavalry. Worse for us."

"Do we ha'e enough men tae hold both?" Alyssa asked, her brow furrowed.

Tryss's hand rubbed at his jaw afore he answered. "Nay, no' wi'out thinnin' our walls. We've just recalled men frae the south border. Some willnae reach us for days yet."

Fergus's voice was grim. "We're stretched. Too many roads, too few blades."

"But we ken the land better," Alyssa pressed, tappin' the map. "We force them tae split. Harass their supply lines. If they bog down in Braemor's woods, we cut them off afore they touch the main road."

Tryss gave a slow nod. "It'd take a guid captain tae pull that off."

Alyssa met his eyes. "Then we'd best choose one."

The talk quickened efter that—scouts assigned, patrols re-drawn, provisions shifted tae safer storehouses. The air was tense, but charged wi' purpose. They all kenned: this was bigger than one keep. It was hearth, family, survival.

As the council wound down, Fergus leaned close tae Alyssa. "Ye sure aboot Elsyn?"

"I am," Alyssa said wi'out hesitation. "She needs this. An' sae do we."

Tryss, overhearin', smirked faint. "Ye keep handin' folk rope, they'll either build a bridge... or hang someone."

Alyssa shot him a look. "Then pray they build."

Silence settled as maps were folded, tokens gathered, an' boots scraped against stone.

Chapter Thirty-Five

Tryss

THE FIRE HAD BURNED low. Shadows flickered lang an' thin across the war room walls, tall as sentries standin' guard. The last ember cracked, the only sound left apart from the steady, even breath o' the woman curled in his chair.

Alyssa.

She'd made it halfway through Tryss's last report afore her eyes fluttered shut. Now a book lay forgotten on her lap, her chin tucked intae the collar o' his auld cloak. Her boots were unlaced, curls spillin' loose o'er her shoulders, lips parted as if she might wake any moment tae argue some detail.

Tryss watched her from the far side o' the chamber, unmovin'.

He should wake her. He'd meant tae—an hour past. But each time he took a step forward, somethin' in him held back. Maybe it was the wee sigh she gave in sleep. Maybe it was the way her hand had fallen—not o'er the book—but o'er the soft swell o' her belly.

Their bairn. Their future.

He rubbed a weary hand o'er his face, draggin' it through his hair. Weariness pulled at him, but no' near sae heavy as the thoughts weighin' doon his chest.

War.

He could smell it in the wind. Taste it in the silence at mealtimes, in the way men stood straighter on the walls, women spoke softer by the hearth. The MacGowans hadnae yet crossed the ridge, but they would. The waitin' was near worse than the clash.

An' still—here she was. Asleep. Safe. For now.

He crossed the room at last, kneelin' beside her. Her skin was warm, her breath even. She looked younger like this, softer. But no' less fierce. She was still Alyssa—the firebrand who'd defied him, matched him, loved him. The fiercest soul he'd ever kent, wrapped up in one small, stubborn frame.

"Alyssa," he whispered, brushin' a curl frae her brow.

She didnae stir.

Tryss breathed out—half sigh, half smile—and slid an arm behind her knees, the other behind her back. She curled instinctive intae him as he lifted her, like she always had. Like she belonged nowhere else.

"All right, then," he murmured. "Let's get ye hame."

The halls were dim as he carried her, firelight givin' way tae moonlight spillin' through the narrow windows. The stone was cool underfoot, the silence thick wi' the hush that falls between a day's work an' the harder day tae come.

In their chamber, he laid her gentle on the bed, careful as if she were spun frae glass. She murmured somethin' too soft tae catch, shifted once, then stilled again. He tugged the worn slippers frae her feet, drew the blankets up o'er her shoulders.

For a moment, he only stood there. Watchin' her breathe.

Then he eased doon beside her.

Her warmth found him even afore her body did. He wrapped an arm aroond her, drawin' her close. She fit there as if she'd been carved for it. As if she always would.

His hand drifted slow o'er her side—till it came tae rest on the gentle curve o' her belly.

An' there he stilled.

A life. Right there, beneath his palm. Flesh an' promise. Their bairn. His child.

God above.

It felt impossible an' undeniable at once, as if the very stars had tilted tae make room for it.

How does a man guard a whole clan... an' this? This fragile, powerful bit o' him an' her?

He didnae ken. Not yet. But he'd damn well find the way.

"I'll keep ye safe," he whispered—no' just tae the bairn, but tae her. Tae the woman who'd aye seen too much, carried too much, an' never faltered.

His jaw set. The softness hardened tae steel. "An' I swear it—nae MacGowan dog will e'er lay claw nor blade on ye. They'll break on these walls afore they touch what's mine."

He bent his head, pressin' a kiss tae her bare shoulder. Another tae her temple. Then he let his brow rest against her hair, his hand protectin' the most fragile vow he'd ever made.

Steel, blood, war—aye, they'd come.

But the night belonged tae them.

For this one breath, this one heartbeat, he had everythin' worth fightin' for safe in his arms.

An' that was enough.

Chapter Thirty-Six

Tryss

The gates of the keep slammed shut behind them with a bone-jarrin' thud.

The mornin' was thick wi' smoke an' the stench o' burnin' timber, the once-clear air now choked wi' ash an' chaos. The flames had been a lure—a calculated trick tae draw their forces oot, tae make them scramble. But Tryss an' Fergus werenae the scrambling kind.

They were the reckonin'.

Tryss stood shoulder tae shoulder wi' Fergus just beyond the outer wall, baith men clad in steel an' purpose. Nae fanfare. Nae banners. Just the raw breath o' battle hangin' heavy in the wind.

"There," Fergus growled, pointin' tae the tree line. "Three squads. Archers at the rear. They're waitin' for us tae break rank."

Tryss squinted intae the early light. Shadows moved low tae the ground, careful, silent. These werenae wild raiders. These were MacGowan-trained men—disciplined, deliberate, testin' their strength against the keep's bones.

"We push hard tae the right," Tryss said. "Flank 'em afore they're in range. If we hold 'em here, afore the fire reaches the village, we stand a chance."

Fergus gave a sharp nod. "Nae prisoners."

Tryss drew his blade in answer. His thigh ached fierce where steel had cut him days ago, the bandages already tight wi' blood, but he shoved the thought aside. Alyssa's face flickered across his mind—her eyes sharp, her hand guidin' his tae her belly. Their bairn. Their future. There'd be nae mercy left in him this day.

They moved fast.

Mud sucked at their boots. Shouts rose from the trees as the enemy surged forward. A flash o' movement—then steel sang.

Tryss hit the first man wi' the full weight o' his charge, blade cleavin' shoulder tae gut in a spray o' crimson. Pain stabbed his leg as he landed, near bucklin' him, but rage steadied him. He wouldnae fall. Nay while Alyssa waited behind these walls. Nay while the bairn inside her depended on him.

Beside him, Fergus fought like a storm unleashed. Wide arcs o' his axe broke men in half. The MacGowan line pressed close, tryin' tae swallow him, but he moved wi' a brutal grace—bone-snappin', blood-slick, unstoppable.

"They're drivin' tae the village gate!" Tryss roared, swingin' his sword through another man's neck.

Fergus hurled a fallen shield edge-first, breakin' a gap in the press. "With me!"

They charged.

Others followed—MacCraith men, blades drawn, voices

thunderin'. What had begun as a trap turned intae a melee o' grit an' desperation. Tryss's arms burned, his breath tore ragged through his throat. His wound screamed every time he pivoted, every time his boots slipped in the mud, but he kept swingin'. He had nae choice.

A pike lunged for his chest. Tryss twisted, felt the tear of linen and flesh across his side, and drove his dagger hilt-first intae the man's face. Bone crunched. Blood sprayed. He didnae watch him fall.

The fight was closin' in, bodies crashin', blades screechin' against shields, screams boilin' the air. For every man they cut doon, two mair pressed in.

Then—a horn blew.

The MacGowans faltered, eyes flickin' tae the southern slope.

Riders crested the hill, sunlight glancin' off spearpoints and helms. MacCraith cavalry—the reserve force Alyssa had insisted be held back. Alyssa. Even here, her mind, her foresight, her fire.

Tryss laughed, feral, blood-streaked. "Ye beautiful, terrifyin' woman."

The mounted men thundered doon the slope, crashin' intae the MacGowan ranks wi' the full weight o' vengeance. The tide turned nae gently, nae mercifully—but like a flood that had been waitin' for the dam tae break.

Fergus caught the last man wi' both hands an' drove him tae the ground, blade-first, until his scream choked off intae silence.

Then—silence.

Tryss stood amid the carnage, chest heavin', blood slick on his leathers, mud heavy on his boots. His thigh burned, his hands shook. But his clan still stood. The keep still burned bright against the dawn.

Fergus slumped against the remnants o' a broken cart. "We

hold the line."

Tryss nodded, turnin' toward the village, toward the smoke-stained sky. His grip tightened on his sword, a vow sharp as steel burnin' in his chest.

"And we dinnae give the MacGowans another inch."

Alyssa

The flames were oot. The bodies counted. An' the sun was risin' ower a village that would ne'er forget the nicht.

The air still clung wi' the reek o' smoke, iron, an' scorched thatch. Soot smeared the cobblestones. A broken cart wheel lay where it had splintered durin' the fight, an' blood streaked the edge o' the well where a man had fallen an' rose nae again.

Inside the longhouse, it was quiet noo—only the low groans o' the wounded an' the hurried whispers o' women tendin' them. Alyssa moved atween them wi' steady hands, her sleeves rolled up an' her skirts pinned tae her knees, her eyes sharp wi' purpose.

But her heart was elsewhere.

Tryss had taken a blade tae the thigh—deep an' ragged—and though he'd bound it himsel' an' fought on like a devil, she'd seen the limp after. She'd seen the blood soakin' through.

When she found him, he was seated at the edge o' the hearth, pale an' bare-chested, the firelight glancin' off the sweat streakin' his back an' the dirt ground intae his skin. His hands braced on his knees, but he looked up the moment she entered, like he'd kent the very second she stepped through the door.

"Alyssa," he murmured.

Her throat tightened. "Ye idiot."

He grinned through the pain, but it slipped quick as she knelt in front o' him an' tugged the blood-crusted linen frae his leg.

"I'm fine," he tried.

"Ye're no'," she snapped, rippin' the fabric clean awa'. He flinched, hissin', an' she froze. "I'm sorry," she whispered.

He reached for her hand wi' a grunt. "I'd take a thousand cuts if it means I get tae watch ye care like this."

She glared at him, her eyes stingin'. "That's nae romantic. That's foolish."

"Aye, well. I'm a fool in love."

She pressed her brow tae his knee, just beside the wound, her breath shakin'. "I thought—when I heard the fire, an' they said ye'd gone tae the walls—I thought..."

He cupped her face in his blood-smeared hand. "I'm here, lass. Still breathin'. Still yers."

She nodded once, then set tae work.

She cleaned the wound in silence, her hands swift but gentle. Tryss watched her the whole time—watched the set o' her jaw, the line o' her brow. Watched the rise an' fall o' her belly beneath her dress. Their bairn. Still safe. Still here.

When she finished, she bound his thigh tight, then leaned in an' pressed a kiss tae the inside o' his knee like it might anchor her. After, she settled at his side, her head fallin' against his shoulder. For a lang moment they did naething but breathe the same air, side by side.

Fergus

Across the village green, in what remained o' the gatherin' hall, Elsyn moved like a woman possessed.

There was nae fear in her. Nae hesitance. She cleaned wounds, set bones, barked orders tae the women who had followed her intae fire an' blood. Her cream weddin' sleeves were dark wi' muck an' gore, her hair pinned hastily back wi' a sliver o' splintered bone.

Fergus watched her frae the far corner—his shirt still torn, his sword still bloody at the hilt. His hands were clenched at his sides.

When she finally reached him, she pressed her fingers intae his shoulder wi'out ceremony an' said, "Ye're bleedin'."

"So are ye," he said, rough.

She gave him the ghost o' a smile. "Mine's no' important."

"Elsyn—"

"Nae." She cut him off wi' a fierce look. "Ye need tae be steady when ye speak tae him."

Fergus turned his gaze tae the center o' the room.

The only survivor frae the MacGowan dogs was tied tae a beam, beaten but conscious, blood seepin' frae a split lip an' one crushed hand. His eyes gleamed wi' somethin' between fear an' fanaticism.

Fergus turned back tae Elsyn. "Dinnae let onyone near him but me."

"No' even Tryss?"

"Especially nae Tryss. He's still full o' fire, an' I need answers afore I let the fire burn this bastard tae ash."

Elsyn didnae argue. She turned instead an' began tae clean the edge o' his jaw, where someone's blade had grazed him, blood crusted like rust doon his neck.

Her fingers trembled once. Just once.

"Ye'll be all right?" she asked.

Fergus nodded. "So long as I ken ye are."

"I'm no' frightened," she said, an' it was true.

But she was weary. Sick o' the blood. Sick o' the endless waitin' for the next wave.

"I ken," he said, lowerin' his brow tae hers. "But I still wish ye didnae hae tae be sae damn brave."

Fergus lingered in the warmth o' Elsyn's breath for one more heartbeat, then straightened wi' a soft grunt. The ache in his shoulder hadnae eased since the battle, but it wasn't what pressed against his chest now.

It was what came next.

He glanced tae the far end o' the longhouse where the prisoner was still tied an' bleedin', then back tae the door. He already kent what he'd find on the other side o' it. Tryss MacCraith would never sit out an interrogation. Especially no' after what had just happened.

An' especially no' when it was his wife who could've been caught in the fire.

Fergus made his way tae the hearthside chamber, where Tryss was still restin'. Except he wasnae restin' at all.

He was sittin' up now, elbows on his knees, shirt back on but hangin' open, the bandages aroond his thigh already spotted wi' blood. Alyssa stood beside him wi' her arms crossed tight an' a look on her face that would wither the bark aff a tree.

Tryss was defiant. An' pale. But alert.

Fergus leaned a shoulder against the doorway an' exhaled through his nose.

"I kent I'd find ye upright."

Tryss looked up, his face lined wi' exhaustion but his eyes clear. "Ye think I'm lettin' ye talk tae that bastard alone?"

Fergus let oot a grunt. "Didnae think it. Hoped it."

Alyssa turned her glare on him, sharp enough tae make Fergus's spine go straight. "He shouldnae even be standin'."

"I'm sittin'," Tryss corrected mild.

She whipped her heid tae him, fire in her voice. "Ye need stitches."

He lifted a brow, tryin' tae play it cool. "Then stitch me."

"Properly."

"Quick an' dirty. I'm no' sittin' on a stool while Fergus wrings words frae the man who tried tae burn our hame."

Alyssa looked ready tae argue again, but somethin' in Tryss's face—somethin' resolute, almost haunted—stayed her tongue.

She let oot a breath like she was bleedin' steam frae a kettle an' gathered her supplies wi' short, sharp movements.

Tryss didnae flinch. He only looked at Fergus. "Ye awricht?"

Fergus nodded. "Elsyn's holdin' the village thegither. Ye?"

Tryss smirked. "Nae deid."

"Then that's a win."

Alyssa dropped tae her knees beside him wi' a needle an' thread already in hand. "This is gonnae hurt," she said flat.

"I married ye," he said through his teeth. "I'm familiar."

The first stab o' the needle made his jaw clench, but he didnae move. Alyssa's hands worked fast—efficient an' precise, but far frae gentle. The thread pulled taut wi' every pass, bindin' the ragged wound wi' care disguised as fury.

Fergus watched them both. Watched the way Tryss held still for her, even as his fingers dug intae the chair's arm. Watched the tightness in Alyssa's shoulders, the flicker o' concern in her eyes every time he hissed.

He cleared his throat. "Ye gonnae live?"

Tryss grunted. "Ye plannin' tae do this slow or fast?"

Fergus's mouth twitched toward a smile. "That depends."

Alyssa tied off the last stitch an' smacked Tryss's knee. "Ye're done. Dinnae tear it open again, or I'll stitch it shut wi' yer ain bootlaces."

Tryss flexed his thigh, winced, then caught her hand an' pressed it tae his lips. "Ye've always been a poet, love."

Alyssa rolled her eyes, but her hand lingered.

Fergus stepped frae the wall. "Come on, then. Let's get what we can frae him afore Tryss passes oot or the women find a better use for us."

"Lead the way," Tryss said, risin' wi' a grimace.

The two men walked side by side doon the corridor toward the cell. One battered, one bloodied, baith carryin' the weight o' a clan that needed answers—and the vengeance that would follow.

Elsyn

Elsyn moved among the wounded, her hands steady, her eyes sharper than ony blade. But when she reached a group o' women murmurin' like restless wolves, the challenge came hard an' fast.

One o' them — a tall, weather-beat woman wi' eyes like flint — stepped forward, voice rough as gravel. "Whit right hae ye tae tell us what tae do? Why should we listen tae some soft-faced stranger?"

Elsyn stopped dead. The firelight caught the hard set o' her jaw. Her voice dropped low, ice laced wi' steel.

"By Alyssa's bloody authority. That's whit right."

A hush fell. Every head turned.

Elsyn stepped forward, fierce as a Highland storm, her voice climbin' tae claim the room.

"I'm no' here tae make friends or trade pleasantries. I'm here because Alyssa trusts me tae ready this village for whit's comin'. An' if ye think for one damn second that means ye get tae ignore me, ye're sorely mistak'en."

She locked eyes wi' the woman who'd dared tae challenge her, voice cuttin' like a knife.

"This is war. There's nae room for cowards or doubters. We

obey, or we die. I'm no' askin'. I'm tellin' ye."

The crowd shifted, uncertain, but Elsyn stood her ground, breath slow an' steady — a predator claimin' its turf.

"If ye want tae live through the next moon, ye'll follow orders. Ye'll listen. Ye'll work yer hands tae the bone. Because if ye dinnae — if any o' ye pull yer ain way — I swear on the stones o' this land, I will see tae it ye regret it."

A silence so heavy it pressed in on every side settled ower the longhouse.

Then, a grudging nod frae the woman who'd spoken first. Others followed, slow at first, then aye enough to matter.

Elsyn didnae soften. She didnae offer mercy or smiles. She turned on her heel and strode back intae the chaos, voice sharp once more.

"We start at dawn. Be ready. No excuses — no mercy for slackness. We do this for ourselves an' for those that depend on us. I'm nae gentle lady, an' I'm nae bloody fool. Cross me, an' ye'll wish the war was the worst thing ye ever faced."

Chapter Thirty-Seven

Fergus

FERGUS LEANED FORWARD, HIS dark eyes unblinking, voice low and deliberate. "Yoe've brought Black Rowan's menace to our doorstep. We want to know *everything*—yer strength, yer numbers, yor plans. Speak truthfully, or suffer for yer lies."

The man spat on the dirt floor. "I serve my lord with loyalty no steel can break. Ye'll get nothing from me."

Tryss's hand slid to the pommel of his sword, knuckles white beneath the coarse leather glove. "We don't have time for yer games." His voice was sharp, cutting through the stale air. "How long before Black Rowan rides through those gates?"

The prisoner's eyes flicked nervously between the two men. He swallowed hard, the defiance in his jaw softening just enough to betray the truth. "Two... maybe three days. They ride fast. The Black Rowan's warbands are nay gentle folk—they burn, kill, and take without mercy."

Fergus straightened, voice like iron. "Nay mercy, eh? Ye'll find we don't offer much either." He motioned to the guards, who stepped forward, cracking their whips against the floor. The prisoner's gaze widened, but Fergus held up a hand. "Not yet. We want tae hear what else ye know."

Tryss paced, restless and coiled, as the man coughed violently. The fear was eating at him. "Tell us of your warbands. How many? What's their order? Who leads yer scouts?"

The prisoner licked cracked lips. "Aye, I know it well. Black Rowan commands near two hundred warriors. The fiercest damned fighters ye'll ever see. Scouts move like shadows—silent and deadly. They come with fire and steel."

Fergus's fists clenched. He looked to Tryss—shock at the numbers evident on his face. "Two hundred. That many. And ye expect us to hold against that?"

Tryss's eyes burned with cold fire. "Expectations mean nothing. We will *make* the outcome. Yer lord's arrogance will be his undoing."

The prisoner's breaths grew ragged, sweat mixing with grime on his brow. "I dinnae know yer plans, but I swear on my life, Black Rowan will crush ye unless you're ready."

Tryss moved closer, voice low but fierce. "We are ready tae bleed. Ye will tell us where his forces camp, where his weaknesses lie."

The man's resolve shattered like glass. "The camp lies in the broken valley—past the crags and the old burned forest. Weakest at the north ridge, where the ground is soft, and the sentries few."

Fergus nodded, absorbing the information. "Ye've done well. Perhaps enough to save yer worthless skin. But if ye lie again—"

Tryss interrupted, voice hard as flint. "We'll carve yer tongue out and feed it to the crows."

The prisoner's eyes brimmed with terror. "No lies. I swear it."

Fergus finally stood, voice grim. "Guards. Take him away. We have what we need."

Tryss watched the man dragged from the chamber, the fire of battle lighting his eyes.

"This war will test us all," Fergus said quietly. "But we will stand. For the clan. For our homes."

Tryss nodded, voice low and fierce. "And we'll make Black Rowan regret the day he came knocking."

Fergus stood at the head of the table, eyes sharp and clear beneath his furrowed brow. He traced the lines of the map with a steady finger, pausing at the broken valley—a narrow, rugged gorge carved between jagged cliffs and dense, blackened forest.

"We know Black Rowan's warbands will push hard through the valley," Fergus said, voice calm but resolute. "It's their fastest route, but also their greatest weakness."

Tryss leaned forward, the scars on his knuckles gripping the table's edge. "Ye think we can hold them there?"

Fergus nodded, a slow, confident smile flickering. "More than hold. We will shatter them."

Alyssa's eyes gleamed in the firelight. "How? Their numbers overwhelm us. Five hundred strong, seasoned fighters."

Fergus's fingers tapped the table with deliberate rhythm. "The broken valley is a natural choke point. Narrow paths, unstable cliffs—terrain that favors cunning over brute strength."

He pointed to a cluster of steep ridges and tangled woodland. "We'll deploy three main forces."

"First," he continued, "a small, highly mobile vanguard led by Tryss and his best riders will strike ahead tae harry their scouts and scouts alone. They'll disrupt their information flow—confuse and delay their advance."

Tryss cracked a tight smile. "Sounds like a chase I'm eager for."

Fergus pressed on, voice lowering to a strategic whisper. "Second, we fortify the north ridge—the soft ground where sentries are weakest. Our archers and spearmen will take the high ground. We'll rain down arrows, force their warbands into tight bottlenecks where their numbers count for nothing."

He tapped the map's ridged outline. "We'll dig pits, set traps—hidden snares to cripple horses and men alike. Black Rowan's warbands thrive on speed and chaos; we'll turn that against them."

Alyssa nodded slowly, catching the rhythm of the plan. "And the third force?"

Fergus's gaze locked on hers. "The third will be our reserve—hidden in the blackened forest itself. Warriors who know every tree and shadow. When the enemy is disorganized and broken, they'll strike—cutting off retreat, sowing panic."

Tryss clenched his fists, eyes aflame. "We trap them like wolves in a snare."

Fergus's voice grew fierce. "Exactly. We turn their greatest strength—speed and ferocity—into their undoing."

He swept his gaze across the room. "This will be bloody and brutal. No glory here, only survival. But if we stand as one, the Black Rowan will learn to fear the broken valley—not as a passage, but as a grave."

A silence fell—heavy, charged—with understanding.

Alyssa's voice cut through, steady and sharp. "Then we prepare. Every hand will be ready. Every clanman and woman. There will be nay mistake."

Tryss's jaw clenched. "And when it's done?"

Fergus's eyes narrowed, cold as steel. "Then we strike hard at the heart of Black Rowan's forces. No mercy. We leave at first light."

The council rose, grim but determined. The fight for their lands had only just begun—and Fergus's plan would be their fiercest weapon.

Alyssa

Tryss sat at the edge o' their bed, shoulders bowed, the fire's low glow paintin' his face in flickerin' gold and shadow. Weariness carved deep lines at his brow, but his eyes—God above, his eyes still burned—wi' the resolve o' a man who kenned the battle before him wasnae just for land nor honor, but for the verra soul o' their folk.

Alyssa knelt before him, her skirts spillin' across the stone, hands tremblin' as they sought his—warm, calloused, steady despite the chill that seeped through the chamber. She felt the tension coiled in him, hard as drawn steel, and it pressed cruel against her heart.

"Ye dinnae have tae carry this weight alone," she whispered, her voice soft but unyieldin'. "We're in this fight thegither. Let me stand at yer side. Let me be yer strength when ye falter."

Slowly, Tryss turned tae her, the fierce fire in his gaze gentled by love. "I ken it, lass. I feel yer strength wi' every breath. But this time..." His jaw tightened. "This time I must be both shield an' sword. The clan looks tae me. I cannae falter."

Her breath hitched, sharp as a blade in her chest. "An' if..." She swallowed, her courage frayin'. "If ye dinnae come back?"

He caught her hands in his, rough an' sure, anchorin' her. "Then ye will be the storm that carries us all forward."

The thought near broke her. The world without him was a world hollow and gray. Her voice cracked wi' the weight o' it. "I cannae... I willnae live in such a world."

Tryss pulled her intae his arms, holdin' her close as if he could stitch their souls thegither. His voice was low, urgent, vow an' prayer in one. "Ye willnae hae tae. On every breath, on every beat o' my heart—I swear it—I will come home tae ye. Tae our bairn."

Her hand drifted, tender, over the swell o' her belly beneath her gown. The fragile spark o' life that tethered them both tae hope. Tears shimmered in her eyes. "Promise me," she breathed. "Promise ye'll come back."

"I promise," he said, his brow pressin' tae hers, sealin' it wi' a vow fierce as steel.

Her lips found his in a kiss soft but desperate, pourin' every fear, every love, every unspoken word intae him. She clung tae his shoulders as if holdin' him could keep the storm at bay.

When she drew back, eyes glistenin', her whisper cracked the quiet. "I love ye, Tryss. More than words. More than fear. Come back tae me."

His mouth curved in a small, weary smile, but the fire in it was unbreakable. "I love ye, Alyssa. Always. An' nae MacGowan devil will ever take me from ye."

Elsyn

The moon hung heavy an' low ower the battered village, castin' a thin silver sheen across churned mud an' broken timber. Smoke curled in tired ribbons frae the last o' the smoulderin' fires, an' the air still tasted o' blood, ash, an' sweat. Elsyn moved—slow, steady, stubborn—her skirts muddied tae the knees, sleeves rolled tae the elbows, hands red wi' scrubbing, stitchin', an' heaving whatever wounded still needed her.

She couldnae feel her feet. Nor her shoulders. Nor the sting where she'd sliced her palm earlier. Stoppin' meant thinkin'—an' if she let hersel' think, she might well break.

So she kept movin'.

Until she didn't.

A broad warm hand curled roond her elbow, stoppin' her wi' quiet finality. She turned, blinkin' against the blur in her vision, an' found Fergus standin' afore her like the last tree in a storm—mud-spattered, blood-streaked, unmovable.

"Ye need tae come in," he said, low an' even.

"I'm fine," she shot back too quick. "There's mair tae be done."

"Ye're done," he said simple, nae unkind.

She opened her mouth, but he lifted an eyebrow—just the one—and it silenced her mair than any shout could hae done.

He stepped closer. "Elsyn," he murmured, voice so soft it cut truer than steel, "ye're swayin' on yer feet. If I let ye keep goin', I'll be carryin' ye in—an' nae wi' the dignity ye'd prefer."

Her mouth twitched. Damn him.

"I can still help," she insisted, though her voice lacked conviction. "I'm no'... no' broken."

"I ken ye're no'," he said, finger skirlin' a soot-streaked curl near her temple. "Ye're just too bloody stubborn tae rest. An' I need ye alive mair than I need ye useful the night."

Her jaw clenched. "An' you? Whit aboot ye? Ye're gaun again, are ye no'? Out there. Tae the Broken Valley."

His silence answered.

"Ye'll leave afore the sun rises," she said flat. "An' dinnae think I dinnae ken it."

"I willnae lie tae ye," Fergus said, hands settlin' on her arms, anchorin' her. "Aye, I go. But this is the fight we hae tae bring tae them afore they reach us again."

Her fingers curled in his tunic. "Ye've just come back."

His forehead dipped tae hers, breathin' her in like she was the breath keepin' him steady. "I ken," he said. "An' if I could bide, I would. But the keep will fall if we wait. I cannae protect ye by standin' still."

"I'm no' askin' ye tae stand still," she whispered. "I'm askin' ye tae come back."

He leaned back just enough tae meet her eyes. "I will. On my life, Elsyn—I will come back tae ye."

Her throat tightened; her voice shook. "Swear it."

"I swear it. On the stones, on my name, on everythin' I am."

Her legs gave oot then—not frae sheer exhaustion but frae the unbearable weight o' love. Fergus grunted and caught her, liftin' her easily into his arms.

"Fergus, I can walk," she protested, feebly thumpin' his chest.

"Ye've walked enough for a lifetime the night," he muttered. "Now hush, or I'll drop ye in a mud puddle just tae make my point."

She managed a small, fierce smile. "Ye wouldnae dare."

He glanced down, all mock menace. "Dinnae test me, love. Nae when ye've got the look o' a woman who's held the verra village togeither wi' frayed string an' temper alone."

He carried her through the keep's gate inta the torch-lit corridor smellin' o' herbs an' smoke-warm stone. The air inside was warmer, kinder, but it couldnae melt the cold clingin' tae her chest.

Just afore they reached the stair, she spoke again, quiet as a confession.

"Fergus?"

"Aye?"

"Ye come back tae me... or I'll come find ye masel'. An' I'll no' be bringin' flowers."

He chuckled, but there was nae mirth—just awe an' reverence. “That’s the most fearsome promise I’ve ever heard.”

He bent then, kissed her forehead wi’ a tenderness that hurt. “An’ I’ll keep mine, Elsyn. I will.”

CHAPTER THIRTY - EIGHT

Tryss

THE DAWN BROKE SLOW an' grey ower the Highlands, the sun strangled behind a thick veil o' mist that clung tae the moor like breath on glass. A bitter kind o' mornin', one that tasted o' ash an' endings, as if the very air kent blood would soon be spilled.

The courtyard was near silent when Tryss an' Fergus strode oot, armor buckled, swords belted, faces carved in stone. Horses stamped restless by the gate, their breath puffin' white in the cold. Clansmen stood at the ready—grim, watchful, the weight o' unspoken fear hangin' in the air like smoke after a burn.

An' there she was. Alyssa. Standin' beside Elsyn, both cloaked against the chill, though neither woman seemed tae feel it. Alyssa's eyes found his at once, sharp an' desperate, like she could anchor him wi' a look. Her hand caught his sleeve, fingers curlin' tight, as though holdin' him tethered tae earth itself.

"Ye've done all ye can here," she whispered, her voice fierce though it trembled beneath. "Let someone else lead."

He looked at her, gods help him. At the strength in her jaw, the fire in her eyes, an' the bairn she carried between them. His voice came hoarse, raw frae the truth that burned in his chest. "I am the someone else. If I dinnae go, I'll rot watchin' others bleed for what I swore tae protect."

Her lashes glittered wi' unshed tears, her mouth pressed tight against the terror she wouldnae give voice. "Then swear somethin' tae me now."

Tryss's hand covered hers, rough, scarred, steady. "I'll come back," he said, without hesitation. Nay flinch, nay pause. "However long it takes, however battered I am—I'll come back tae ye. Tae the bairn. Tae the life we've built."

Her breath caught, an' then she pulled him down intae a kiss—hard, tremblin', full o' fury an' fear alike. She kissed him like she could press her demand intae his very bones, seal the vow wi' her lips. When she broke away, her mouth brushed his ear, the words spillin' hot against his skin.

"I love ye, Tryss MacCraith. So bloody much it terrifies me."

His eyes squeezed shut, his forehead restin' against hers, armor cold but her warmth sinkin' intae him like fire. He swallowed hard, his voice low an' ragged. "Good. That fear—yer love—that's what keeps us alive."

For a moment the courtyard, the men, the mist—all of it vanished. There was only her, her heartbeat against his, an' the vow he'd carry like a blade through every breath o' the battle tae come.

Then Fergus cleared his throat, the sound sharp as a blade bein' drawn, an' the spell shattered. Tryss forced himsel' tae step back, though every part o' him screamed tae stay. He mounted his horse, never takin' his eyes frae her until the gates groaned open an' the world beyond swallowed him whole.

Fergus

No' far off, Fergus found Elsyn still in her work tunic, the hem stained wi' blood from wounded men too stubborn tae admit they should've stayed abed. She'd tended them anyway, sleeves rolled, hands red, will hard as iron. She hadnae slept—he could see it plain in the slump o' her shoulders, the purple hollows beneath her eyes, the faint tremor in her fingers as she smoothed her skirt wi'out thinkin'.

"Time tae go," he said soft, though the words weighed like stone.

Her head snapped up, eyes wide, raw. "Ye can't," she whispered, her voice breaking at the edges. "Not wi'out—just—just rest another hour—"

"I cannae," he answered, steady as the earth, an' cupped her cheek wi' a hand still rough wi' callus an' blood. "An' ye ken it."

Her lips pressed intae a thin, shaking line, eyes glimmerin' wi' a storm she wouldnae let spill. "Then at least promise me ye'll no' do anything stupid."

"I'll only stab who needs stabbin'."

"Tryss doesn't count," she muttered, a brittle smile crackin' through, an' a laugh escaped her throat like it surprised her.

His chest eased just a fraction at the sound. He leaned closer, their foreheads touchin', the smell o' her hair—smoke, herbs, an' her—groundin' him harder than any oath. "I'll fight tae get back tae ye," he murmured, voice low, fierce, true. "That's the only damn thing that matters now."

Her breath shook as she kissed him, not soft, but desperate—like a woman who feared the world might rob her of the chance if she waited even a heartbeat longer. He kissed her back, deep an' unyielding, a brand tae carry intae the fray.

When at last they broke apart, he caught her hands in his, pressing them hard against his chest, over the hammer o' his heart. "It beats for ye, Elsyn," he said rough, "an' I'll drag it back tae ye, nae matter the hells I walk through."

Her throat worked, but she said naught. Her hands trembled, but she held on. An' for that moment, it was enough.

Fergus forced himsel' tae let go, to turn, tae mount. The leather creaked, the horse shifted, the weight o' war settling ower him like a mantle he couldnae cast aside.

Tryss swung up intae his saddle wi'out a word, his eyes already on the gates.

They opened wi' a groan o' iron an' wood, spillin' the dawn mist inside.

An' the storm rode out.

The Broken Valley

The sky had turned tae iron by the time they reached the edge o' the gorge. No' just overcast—waitin', like a blade held at the throat. The air was foul, heavy wi' the stink o' sweat, oiled leather, and the sharp, copper tang o' blood nae yet spilled but already promised.

Fergus sat his horse at the crest, starin' doon intae the valley like a man readin' the names o' the dead in the scars o' the land. Jagged walls rose on either side, cliffs steep an' black as if the earth itself had split. The path wound narrow, mean—too narrow for retreat, too steep for mercy.

A coffin. A killbox.

Just as he'd prayed for.

Tryss rode up beside him, jaw locked, shadow beard rough across his face, eyes sharp an' feral. "Scouts say two hundred. Maybe more."

Fergus didna blink. "Let them bring a thousand. We'll send them back in pieces."

Tryss huffed, joyless, like the sound o' steel slidin' free. "Ye always did have a talent for cheerful metaphors."

Thunder cracked—not frae the sky. Drums. Rowan's drums. A death knell, poundin' steady as a heartbeat.

An' then they saw them.

The far ridge blackened wi' movement. A tide o' men spilled ower like maggots pourin' frae a rottin' wound. Their armor was black as pitch, helms carved like snarlin' wolves, hollow-eyed skulls, an' darker things nae meant for prayer. Painted shields. Spiked maces. Axes already gleamin' red, as if they were hungry afore the blood was even drawn. In the midst rose Black Rowan's banner—crimson on black, flayed an' flutterin'. It didna look like cloth. It looked like skin.

Fergus lifted his sword, the edge catchin' the grey light like captured lightning. "Signal the flanks."

Tryss said naething. He only grinned, slow an' savage, unsheathin' his blade. He pointed it doon the gorge, where hell waited.

"Let's make the bastards regret drawin' Highland breath."

Then the crash.

The first collision o' steel on steel, steel on bone, bone on mud.

The battle didn't begin—it detonated.

Rowan's men poured intae the gorge like floodwaters, an' the Highlanders met them head-on—shields locked, blades bared, teeth gnashin' wi' fury. The valley walls rang wi' the shriek o' iron, the wet sound o' blades enterin' flesh, the bellow o' men dying violent.

Tryss was a storm loosed.

He ducked, turned, cut, an' lunged, his sword a streak o' silver death. He slit throats an' opened bellies, hot entrails spillin' doon tae steam in the mud. He shattered ribs wi' a twist o' his hilt, drove steel deep until blood fountained high, sprayin' his face an' hair. Every motion was brutal, honed, nae wasted breath.

Fergus didna dance—he destroyed.

He crushed skulls like eggs beneath his blade, his strikes heavy, merciless. A shield slammed intae him—he drove his elbow back, felt bone snap like dry kindlin', then rammed his sword doon through the bastard's mouth, splittin' teeth an' tongue alike. Another leapt at him, screamin'. Fergus caught him wi' the full weight o' his shoulder, bones crunchin', an' sent him flyin' doon intae the blood-soaked muck.

Back tae back, Tryss an' Fergus carved their way through Rowan's horde like reapers cuttin' tall grain—except here the stalks screamed an' bled.

"Gods," Fergus roared ower the din, "how many have we felled?"

Tryss laughed—laughed wi' blood in his teeth, like a man born for this slaughter. "Not enough!"

Blood was everywhere. Slick an' thick beneath their boots. Spurting hot from slit throats, gushin' frae opened bellies. Men stumbled on the entrails o' their brothers, screamin' as blades hacked them doon tae silence. The valley itself seemed tae choke, rivers o' crimson churnin' wi' the mud.

Tryss took a cut tae his arm, flesh partin' wide, blood pourin'—but he didna flinch. Fergus had blood blindin' one eye, pourin' doon his face, but his sword never faltered.

They were engines o' death, forged in fury, unyieldin'.

The sky dimmed, bruised purple wi' dusk, but still the gorge roared wi' the clash o' steel an' the last cries o' dyin' men.

An' still the Highlanders stood.

Fergus lifted his head, chest heavin', blood pourin' frae his temple. "They keep comin'."

Tryss spat blood, lips curlin' in a feral grin. "So do we."

Steel clashed again, iron on iron, bone on stone, scream on scream.

An' the sons o' the Highlands did not yield.

Chapter Thirty-Nine

Blood and Bone

THE SUN NEVER ROSE on the second day.

It clawed weakly at the edge o' the mist, a dim grey glow behind a curtain o' smoke an' storm clouds, as if even the sky was tired o' the slaughter. The valley stank—o' blood, piss, sodden wool, an' the coppery tang o' torn flesh. It soaked the earth, turned every step tae slick treachery, made the narrow pass a butcher's yard.

Tryss didna ken how long he'd been fightin'.

Minutes. Hours. A lifetime.

His arms felt like lead to the bone. His right hand was wrapped wi' a strip o' torn tunic where a blade had laid his knuckles open. His left leg throbbed from a glancing spear that'd scored flesh above the knee. Smoke an' screams filled his lungs till breath was a curse.

Still he fought.

He drove his sword through a man's gut an' wrenched it free

in time tae pivot an' block an axe that'd come down like a god's hammer. It jarred tae his spine. He kept his feet. He ducked low, slashed out, watched the man crumple, hamstrings giving, lungs gurgling. One more down. One more breath.

Somewhere in the haze Fergus roared, a sound like a war-drum.

Tryss turned, catchin' sight o' him barreling through a knot o' Black Rowan men like a bull through brambles, blade cleavin' through shield an' bone. Fergus limped now—when had that happened?—but he didna slow. His face was a map o' war: blood crusted in his beard, sweat draggin' grime across his brow, eyes alight wi' a terrible, bright fire.

"Ye still breathin'?" Tryss shouted, shields bruisin' as they stood back tae back.

"Just barely," Fergus growled. "Thought they had me an hour ago."

"They dinnae."

"Nay. They will—if we give them an inch."

Tryss spat, blood bitter on his tongue. "Then we dinnae."

They locked shields an' held the line as another surge closed in, tighter than before. Black Rowan was testin' them, feelin' for weakness. An' they were startin' tae find cracks. A few o' the lads who'd broke tae protect the flanks hadna come back.

The worst o' it? The enemy was rested. These waves came fresh, one an' then another, while MacCraith men had fought through the night wi' barely a pause. They were starvin', soaked tae the skin, shakin' wi' exhaustion.

But they didna yield.

Tryss stabbed forward, dragged his blade up through a soldier's ribcage. The man screamed, then gurgled. Tryss shoved the corpse aside wi' his boot.

An' for a heartbeat, his mind slipped.

He saw Alyssa—nae blood, nae tears—laughin'. Sittin' beside Elsyn in the solar, tossin' a grape the way she always did and catchin' it in her mouth, fingers busy at a braid she'd never finish. Lips red wi' wine. A belly just startin' tae swell.

A warmth flared in Tryss's chest, then a hand yanked him back.

"Dinnae drift," Fergus barked, grabbin' him by the shoulder as an axe whistled past the place his neck had been.

"I'm nay driftin'," Tryss growled, settin' his feet.

"Ye were dreamin' o' her again."

"Damn right I was."

"Save it for when we're nae dyin'!"

Tryss cracked a grin through a mouth full o' blood. "I fight better thinkin' o' her."

They pushed forward, step by bloody step, like climbin' uphill through a tide o' knives.

An' the valley kept swallowin' men.

By mid-morn they'd been shoved nearly back tae the second rise. A bairn frae Glen Brae—nae older than a lad about tae shave—took a blade tae the chest while tryin' tae drag a wounded man tae safety. Tryss had screamed for him tae fall back, but it wasnae enough. The boy died gaspin' for his ma.

Tryss didna ken the lad's name. He carved a path through Rowan's men after that that'd've made saints weep.

Fergus took a blow tae the head. A dent in his helm. Blood trailin' an' cloudin' one eye. Still he carried on. Still he led.

By midday they had fewer men than they'd brought. The wounded clogged the hold on the western slope, medics runnin' oot o' cloth an' tincture. The sky closed heavier, like a coming storm—maybe dusk, maybe both.

"Fall back tae the second ridge!" Fergus bellowed, wavin' men while he covered their retreat wi' the other hand.

Tryss limped beside him, blood seepin' through his leggings. "We'll lose the bluff if we do."

"An' we'll lose the whole army if we dinnae regroup. We're stretched tae snapping." Fergus's voice cut hard, but he didna flinch.

Tryss ground his teeth. "We'll nae last another full night."

Fergus's jaw set. "That's why we finish it tomorrow."

That evenin', firelight was weak behind a hastily raised wall o' shields. The wounded moaned in low, ragged chords. Rain spat an' the stench o' rot hung heavy. Tryss leaned back on a stone outhrust, leg wrapped tight, chest burnin', stare fixed on the bruised sky.

Fergus limped over, half his face black wi' soot. He dropped beside Tryss wi' a groan.

"Ye know," Fergus rasped, "we're both too old for this."

Tryss let out a short, bitter laugh. "Ye're older than me."

Fergus snorted. "Still prettier."

Tryss said nothing. He stared at the fire, the crackle like bones in the silence.

"Tomorrow?" he asked.

"Tomorrow we make 'em bleed till they choke on it."

"God willing?"

"Nae. Us willin'."

Tryss drew his blade, restin' the flat across his knees. "We've nae saints left—only stubborn men an' sharper steel."

Alyssa

The storm came like a beast—howlin', batterin' the keep. Wind tore at shutters, rain slashed the windows blind, the world outside a smear o' iron. Far ower the blackened roofs the valley was a smear o' smoke. Tryss was out there somewhere beyond that noise, fightin'.

Alyssa stood at a narrow window in the solar, hands braced on cold stone. She couldnae see the gorge from there—nae line o' sight—but she watched the village roofs, slick wi' rain, watched folk flit like shadows. It was the absence that pulled at her maist: his voice, his presence, the half-ready grin she hated on him.

"I canna feel him," she whispered.

Elsyn, busy at a table gatherin' bandages and tinctures, looked up. "What do ye mean?"

"I usually can," Alyssa said, never takin' her eyes from the wet roofs. "Like a thread. I tug, he tugs back. I know when his anger's hot, when he's glad. Today... the thread's frayed."

Elsyn crossed the room, layin' a hand steady on her back. "That's fear. An' exhaustion. No' some omen."

Alyssa's throat tightened. "There's a shadow at my back, Elsyn. Like the reaper's standin' there, waitin'. No' tae take me—but to reach for him."

The wind keened down the chimney.

Elsyn held her gaze a moment, then spoke soft but steel-edged: "Then we make sure death finds closed gates an' torches lit. Tryss MacCraith's too bloody stubborn tae die. But if he falls, he'llna fall for naethin'. Not while ye breathe."

Alyssa turned, eyes bright as coals. "We cannae let this keep fall. Nay matter what."

Elsyn's nod was hard. "We won't."

They moved doon together—cloaks flingin' like banners. The great hall had become a war-room. Barrels were stacked, doorways reinforced, water boiled, weapons sharpened. Moira moved quick, takin' orders wi' a jaw set.

Alyssa bent over the map spread on the table, held down

by tankards an' a knife. She traced roads, slopes, the second fallback inside the walls. Every line burned into her mind.

She didna feel like a lady. She felt like a drawn blade, waitin'.

Children were shepherded tae the chapel. Old men offered to fashion pikes. The smith burned like a furnace, hammer ringin' through the storm.

Elsyn handed her a cup o' hot broth. Alyssa took it but didna drink.

"Dinnae lose yersel'," Elsyn said, gentle as she could.

Alyssa shook her head. "I cannae risk findin' myself. Not til he comes back."

An' if he didna?

She wouldna let the thought finish. She hadnae clawed tae this keep, nae thrown herself intae this life, nae wanted a bairn—only tae be left holdin' ghosts.

Because he would come back. Because she'd not fought tooth an' nail tae be left standin' in a ruin.

If death came, she'd meet it. An' she'd drag the bastard down with her.

Chapter Forty

By the third day, the Broken Valley reeked o' death. Mud sucked at boots like a grave swallowin' its dead. Blood pooled black in the churned soil. Tryss MacCraith's arms trembled so bad he could scarce keep hold o' his sword, the hilt slick wi' gore an' sweat.

Every breath rasped like fire in his chest. Smoke stung his eyes. His ears rang wi' the screams o' dyin' men an' the ceaseless clang o' steel. For three days they'd fought without pause—steel on steel, flesh on stone—and the valley had turned tae a charnel pit.

He staggered behind a shattered rock wall, the stub o' a barricade already soaked red. Fergus slumped there, one eye swollen shut, his hair matted wi' blood.

"We cannae hold this line," Fergus croaked, each word torn frae him like it cost a pound o' flesh. "One more push an' we're bones."

Tryss barked a laugh that broke on his cracked lips. "Nay shite." His hand shook so bad the blade tip scratched furrows in the stone at his side.

The war drums thundered again. Rowan's men were regroupin'. Tryss felt the sound in his bones—doom, steady as a heartbeat.

He looked at Fergus. Nae jest left. Nae swagger. Just two men, battered an' bled dry, holdin' on tae the last scraps o' will.

"We fall back," Fergus rasped. "Eastern bluff. We die there—or we dinnae."

Tryss's nod was barely a twitch, but it was all he had. He raised the whistle tae his lips—three sharp blasts cut through the smoke-choked air. A horn took it up. The ragged line o' Highlanders broke, draggin' their wounded, stumblin' through the mud wi' the last strength in their bones.

The sky had turned the color o' ash. Men cried out an' fell behind him. Tryss ground his teeth, copper an' grit sharp on his tongue, and forced his legs tae move. When he dared glance back, Rowan's banners loomed closer.

This was it. The end.

And then— Thunder. Not drums. Nay storm. Hooves.

Frae the northern ridge, the mist tore like cloth as riders poured through, green an' silver flashin' in the firelight. Banners crested the rise, a tide o' white stags thunderin' doon the slope. Horns blared, a scream o' vengeance that split the valley wide.

At their fore, a stag-helmed man raised his sword and bellowed:

"FOR HOUSE MACINNESS!"

Tryss's chest seized. His heart slammed so hard it hurt. Fergus blinked blood frae his good eye and rasped, "That's Elsyn's da."

Then the cavalry hit.

It wasnae a charge. It was a reckonin'.

MacInness riders smashed intae Rowan's flank like the hand o' God. Spears skewered men like kindlin'. Swords flashed silver, split shields, split skulls. The sound was sickening—meat an' bone crushed beneath hooves, men screamin' as the tide ripped through them. Rowan's line shattered, broken wide open.

Tryss found his voice—raw, guttural, torn frae the pit o' his chest.

"MACCRAITH!"

Fergus roared beside him, his bellow shakin' the smoke.

"FOR THE HIGHLANDS!"

And the Highlanders rose.

The broken, the bleedin', the near-dead. They surged one last time, fury draggin' them tae their feet. Tryss vaulted the barricade, blade lifted high, an' the charge was born.

He cut without thought. A sword rammed through ribs, twistin' till he felt the snap. A thrust tae the throat, hot spray blindin' his cheek. His world narrowed tae the arc o' his blade an' the beat o' his heart—every strike for Alyssa, for the bairn he prayed tae see, for the keep that was his tae defend.

Fergus carved beside him, shoulder tae hip, cleavin' men apart wi' grim, steady rage. Step by step they drove through Rowan's collapsin' line.

Black Rowan's standard-bearer turned tae flee. Fergus's blade came doon like judgment, shatterin' his spine. The Rowan captain raised his axe tae rally the broken—Tryss split his skull in two wi' a scream that stripped his throat raw.

Men ran. Men begged. Men died beneath hooves an' Highland steel.

By nightfall, silence fell at last—not peace, but slaughter.

Tryss leaned heavy on his blade, too weak tae sheath it, breath sawin' ragged through his chest. Fergus limped tae his side, sword snapped tae the hilt, his hands flayed raw.

"Ye still breathin'?" Fergus rasped.

Tryss gave one small nod. That was all.

The Rowan banner flapped weak in the wind—once, twice—then tore free, fallin' intae the muck wi' a wet slap.

Tryss exhaled, his whole body shakin' wi' the release.

"We held."

Fergus closed his eye, his mouth twistin' into somethin' close tae a smile.

"Aye. We did."

The Broken Valley was theirs.

Chapter Forty-One

THE FIRST SCREAM CAME frae the watchtower.

Alyssa was halfway doon the hall when the horn sounded—one long, low note that rattled the marrow in her bones. She didnae need anyone tae tell her what it meant. The enemy wasnae only in the valley. They were here.

She flew up the stair tae the battlements, skirts hiked, lungs burnin'. The night struck her like a blade—icy wind, the stench o' smoke driftin' up frae the valley, the red glow o' fire lickin' the horizon. Then she saw them: a band o' Rowan raiders breakin' frae the trees, torches raised, chargin' the keep like wolves scentin' blood.

The guards left behind were too few, half-trained lads an' gray-haired men. Fear glazed their eyes.

"Archers tae the wall!" Alyssa shouted, her voice rippin' the night. "Oil! Rocks! MOVE!"

They scrambled at her command, no' because she bore a title, but because her tone left nae room for hesitation.

A crash sounded below—the first ram-strike against the gate.

Wood groaned like it was alive. Alyssa's stomach pitched, but she forced hersel' tae the wall's edge. She seized a bow frae a tremblin' lad an' notched an arrow, her fingers stiff wi' cauld.

Steady. Aim. Loose.

Her shot flew, strikin' a torch-bearer square in the chest. He stumbled, fire lickin' his cloak afore he toppled intae the ditch. The boy beside her gasped.

"That's what ye'll do," Alyssa barked. "Every one o' ye. Now—FIRE!"

Arrows darkened the sky, hissin' intae the raiders. Screams tore the night. The ram struck again, splinters flyin'.

"Boil!" she cried.

Women hauled iron pots tae the battlements, steam billowin' like angry ghosts. The first cascade poured doon, searin' flesh. The stench o' burnin' hair an' skin clawed at Alyssa's throat. She gagged but didnae look away.

Another strike. The gate splintered.

"Brace it!" she ordered, flyin' doon the steps.

Inside the courtyard, Elsyn staggered under the weight o' a beam, hair loose, cheeks streaked wi' soot. She wasnae meant tae be here, but Alyssa didnae have time tae argue. Thegither they heaved the timber intae place as the gate shuddered again.

Crash. Crack. The hinges shrieked.

A lad screamed as the barricade gave way an' Rowan men spilled through like a black tide.

"Form up!" Alyssa roared. "Kitchen knives, pitchforks—onything! Stand yer ground! We'll nay give an inch tae these bastards!"

It was chaos. Steel clashed. Women shrieked. A guard went doon under a blade, blood sprayin' hot across the stones. Alyssa's hands closed on a fallen spear. She thrust—wild, clumsy, but true—catchin' a raider in the belly. His scream was high an' wet. Her arms shook as he collapsed at her feet.

She near dropped the spear. Near.

Dinnae falter. Not now.

Elsyn appeared beside her, knife in hand, eyes wide but blazin'. Thegither they fought, shoulder tae shoulder, sisters an' strangers all at once.

The battle turned brutal. Bairns wept as women dragged them intae hidden cellars. The wounded moaned. Blood slicked the stones beneath Alyssa's boots. She slipped once, caught hersel', then rammed her spear intae another man's throat wi' a cry that was mair rage than fear.

Minutes? Hours? She lost track.

Then—horns.

No' Rowan horns. The MacCraith horns.

A roar swelled frae beyond the gate—the return o' their warriors. The sound crashed ower her like a wave. Relief an' terror tangled in her chest.

The raiders heard it too. Their eyes darted, their line faltered. One bolted. Another followed. Soon, the tide turned—Rowans scramblin', cut doon in retreat.

Silence returned in ragged gasps an' sobs. The courtyard reeked o' blood, smoke, an' boiled flesh. Bodies sprawled like broken dolls. The gate hung ruined.

Alyssa leaned on her spear, chest heavin', arms slick wi' blood no' all her ain. Her knees trembled, but she stayed standin'. She had tae. Every eye in the courtyard was still on her.

Elsyn slumped against the wall, her knife stained tae the hilt. Their gazes met—exhausted, hollow, but alive.

Alyssa raised her chin. "See tae the wounded. Burn the rest. This keep stands."

An' as the women scattered tae obey, she finally allowed hersel' one thought, raw an' desperate:

Hold fast, Tryss. I've kept the walls for ye.

CHAPTER FORTY-TWO

Tyrss

THE PRICE OF HONOR

The battlefield still reeked o' blood an' smoke. The thunder o' hooves had long faded, but its echo lingered in every heartbeat. Men limped among the wounded, blades heavy in blood-crusted hands. Tryss leaned on his sword like a crutch, chest heavin', sweat an' soot smeared doon his face.

Beside him, Fergus stood silent—taller than most, but bowed under the weight o' somethin' mair than battle. His eyes, dark an' unreadable, were fixed on the ridge where the Highland tide had turned.

MacInness was already dismountin'.

The laird o' House MacInness bore the years wi' steel in his spine an' ice in his gaze. He moved wi' the careful grace o' a man who'd seen too many battles an' still chose tae walk intae another. His plaid whipped in the wind, dark blue an' green—colors

Fergus hadnae seen in ower a decade.

Tryss shifted beside him. "That's him, then?"

Fergus gave a low nod. "Aye. That's her faither."

MacInness's boots hit the churned mud wi' a muffled thud. He strode forward, men partin' like water aroond him. His eyes swept the field—takkin' in the carnage, the broken line o' Black Rowan's retreat, the blood an' fire still smolderin' in the valley—and finally landed on Fergus an' Tryss.

Then, wi'out hesitation, he came tae a stop afore them.

The silence was heavy.

Fergus stepped forward.

An' MacInness extended his hand.

Nae words. Not at first. Just that outstretched hand—firm, deliberate, wi'out pride or pretense. Fergus met it. Their grip was hard. Weighted wi' what neither o' them could quite say aloud.

"I'm told ye wed my dochter," MacInness said at last, voice like gravel ower stone.

Fergus nodded once. "I did. I'd wed her a thousand times ower."

MacInness studied him a moment longer. Then, tae Tryss's astonishment, the auld man nodded—once, sharp. "Guid. She deserved better than what I gave her."

Tryss glanced sideways at Fergus, watchin' the subtle shift in his expression. A flicker o' somethin' too deep tae name crossed his face.

"How did ye ken tae come?" Fergus asked, his voice low.

MacInness's jaw flexed. "A rider came. Sent by Elsyn. Nae seal. Just her hand, an' her name."

He looked oot at the battlefield again, where the final wave o' his army was roundin' up the last o' the Rowan survivors.

"She begged," he said quiet. "Begged me tae come. Tae save

the hame she'd made. The man she'd chosen. The clan that had given her sanctuary."

Fergus didnae speak. Couldnae.

"I ignored her once," MacInness said. "I'll nae do it again."

They stood in silence for a beat. The wind tugged at their cloaks. Somewhere behind them, a dyin' man groaned, an' a soldier's voice called for water.

Then MacInness turned tae Tryss. "An' ye must be The MacCraith."

"I am," Tryss said, squarin' his shoulders despite the fire burnin' in his torn leg.

MacInness gave him a nod o' approval. "I've heard o' ye since Elsyn... weel... did what she did."

"I imagine nae all o' it guid."

MacInness cracked the ghost o' a smile. "That's usually the best kind."

Then he turned back tae Fergus. "We ride tae yer keep. I'd see the woman who saved yer lives—an' my soul."

They walked in silence.

Behind them, the battlefield smoldered. Afore them, the road tae the keep stretched long an' broken.

Fergus didnae speak as they rode back. His hands were steady on the reins, but his thoughts were far frae the road. Elsyn had begged the man who'd cast her oot. Had written tae the faither who'd turned his back—and asked him for mercy.

For him.

For all o' them.

Tryss rode in silence too, but he caught the look on Fergus's face, saw the way his jaw clenched an' his eyes burned wi' somethin' mair than exhaustion.

"She saved us all," Tryss said quiet.

Fergus didnae look awa' frae the road.

"I ken."

Alyssa

The Walls o' the Keep

The wind clawed at their cloaks atop the battlements, keenin' like the ghosts o' the fallen. Alyssa stood wi' her hands braced on the rough stone, heart thunderin' like hooves in her chest. The hills stretched afore them in a shroud o' dusk an' dread. Nothin' moved.

Nothin' yet.

"I should hae gone wi' them," she whispered, the words catchin' like thorns in her throat.

"Nay," Elsyn said behind her. "Ye were needed here."

Alyssa's voice turned sharp. "Whit guid is strategy when they're oot there dyin'?"

"They're no' dead." Elsyn's voice had steel noo. "No' those two. Ye'd ken. An' I—" She broke off.

Alyssa turned, eyes narrowin'. "An' ye?"

Elsyn hesitated.

Then she stepped forward, cloak whippin' aroond her ankles. Her face was pale, her eyes fierce.

"I sent a rider tae MacInness," she said quiet.

The words hit like a dropped blade.

Alyssa blinked. "Ye... whit?"

"I wrote him after the first council—when we kent it would come tae war. I didnae ask permission. I didnae tell onyone. I just did it."

Alyssa's breath caught. "Elsyn... he cast ye oot. Ye swore ye'd never speak his name again."

"I also swore tae protect whit I loved," Elsyn said. "An' I meant baith."

The two women stared at each other in silence.

Then Alyssa stepped closer, voice hoarse. "Ye begged help frae the faither who turned his back on ye?"

Elsyn lifted her chin. "I did."

"And ye did it for him?"

"I did it for all o' us," she said. "But aye—Fergus first. Always."

Emotion surged like wildfire in Alyssa's chest. It was too much—too big.

She wanted tae scream. She wanted tae weep. She wanted tae run doon the battlements an' tear open the sky.

But instead—Elsyn gripped her arm.

"There," she breathed.

Alyssa turned.

At first it was only a haze—dust an' gold in the low sun. But then—movement. Rhythm. Steel catchin' light. Banners snappin' like thunder. A wave crestin' the ridge.

Alyssa's breath left her in a single, broken sob.

It wasnae Black Rowan.

It was MacInness.

An' at the front—ridin' like ghosts risen frae the dead—Tryss an' Fergus.

Bloodied. Bruised. Alive.

The MacCraith an' the Fraser.

Alyssa's hands flew tae her mouth. Her knees buckled, an' Elsyn caught her, bracin' them baith as tears poured doon their faces, unnoticed in the wind.

"Ye brilliant, reckless, bloody woman," Alyssa gasped, still starin', "ye brought them hame."

Elsyn exhaled shakily. "Nay," she whispered. "They fought their way hame. I just... gave them a chance tae win."

The first banner crested the hill fully.

Tryss raised his sword—tattered an' red wi' blood—and shouted somethin' that carried across the field like lichtnin' crackin' the sky.

Alyssa didnae hear the words. She didnae need tae. Because her heart heard them. *I am comin' hame.*

Chapter Forty - Three

Fergus

THEY STOOD AT THE crest o' the final rise, just three men atop a bloodied hill, but the earth itsel' seemed tae hold its breath beneath them.

Fergus sat motionless in the saddle, shoulders slumped frae exhaustion but his spine iron-straight, eyes locked on the keep below. He'd dreamt o' it in the blackest hours—walls toppled, banners torn, smoke risin' wi' the wails o' the women he loved. Now, seein' it still standin'—scorched, battered, but standin'—hit him harder than ony blade ever had.

Smoke curled frae its chimneys, soft an' steady, as though the stones themsel's were sighin' wi' relief. Its banners still flew—edges charred, fabric ripped—but aye, they flew. Defiant. Unbroken.

Home.

Behind them, what remained o' their host waited. Men who'd

bled three days wi'oot pause. Highlanders wi' eyes sunk deep intae their skulls, mail split, helms dented, tunics stiff wi' dried gore. Some leaned heavy on broken spears, some clutched wounds bound wi' rags already soaked through. They were mair ghosts than men, yet every chest still rose, every hand still gripped steel. Exhausted. Bloodied. Bone-weary. But alive. Victorious.

Tryss drew in a slow, ragged breath, chest heavin' beneath the dented breastplate, blood still streakin' the line o' his jaw. His voice was hoarse, near-broken. "Ye ever seen onything mair bonnie than that?" he asked, noddin' toward the keep.

Fergus couldnae answer. Not yet. His throat was too tight, his heart poundin' wi' a weight he couldnae loose.

Malcolm MacInness dismounted beside them, boots sinkin' intae the sodden earth, his plaid snappin' in the wind. His gaze fixed on the keep the same as theirs, but his words broke the silence. "Yer women are fierce," he said, gruff, almost reverent. "Both o' them. I'd wager every bastard who crossed that threshold in our absence fears them mair than Black Rowan's whole damned horde."

Tryss let oot a sharp sound—part laugh, part sob, teeth flashin' red wi' dried blood. "Aye. An' they'll kill us for makin' them wait this long."

Fergus's voice came at last, low, rough as gravel dragged ower stone. "We fought three days wi'oot sleep. Ate bark, dirt, an' rage. Bled our verra souls intae the mud. I watched lads die callin' for their mothers, an' I buried men whose names I never learned." His gauntleted hand lifted, tremblin' wi' exhaustion an' somethin' greater, pointin' toward the keep. "An' that—" his voice cracked, then steadied, "—that's what we did it for."

For Elsyn. For every soul behind those walls.

Tryss tilted his head, a ghost o' wickedness twistin' his

cracked lips. "Didn't ye say somethin' about carvin' our names intae Highland legend?"

"I did," Fergus said, voice thick wi' iron an' sorrow.

Tryss bared his teeth in a feral grin, weary but unbroken. "Well then... I reckon we just fookin' did."

The words struck the air like a vow, heavy as steel, as if the mountains themsel's had heard an' would etch them intae stone.

Fergus let oot a long, shaky breath, his grip slackenin' on the reins just enough tae feel the horse shift beneath him. For the first time in three days, the weight in his chest eased. Not gone. Never gone. But eased.

Because the keep still stood. Because Elsyn still waited. Because, God help him, they had lived.

Tryss

Frae somewhere deep in the ranks behind them came the first sound—a single voice raised in wordless triumph. Then another. An' another.

It rolled forward like a storm.

A roar o' Highland pride. A howl o' victory.

Tryss's fingers clenched the reins till his knuckles burned, every nerve alive wi' the surge o' a fire that had smouldered three hellish days. The roar rolled ower the hills, raw an' ragged, shakin' the verra air—no' just the cry o' men, but the soul o' a clan roarin' for its warriors.

He turned, eyes sharp, catchin' Fergus's burnin' gaze, wild an' fierce. "Ye hear that?"

Fergus's jaw tightened, his voice a low growl like thunder beneath the storm. "That's nae just a call for hame, Tryss. It's a war hymn—our war hymn."

Tryss's grin cut through the exhaustion, cruel an' electric. "Then it's time we answered wi' everythin' we've got."

He spurred his horse forward—a sudden eruption o' motion that ripped through the stillness like a bolt o' lightning. Fergus was on his heels, MacInness close behind, the three o' them thunderin' doon the ridge like gods o' war reborn.

Behind them, the earth itsel' trembled as the clan rose as one—a livin' tempest o' thunderin' hooves, flashin' steel, an' fierce hearts poundin' in time tae a savage drumbeat.

The air was thick wi' the scent o' blood, smoke, an' unyieldin' will. Horns shattered the silence, ragged victory songs tearin' intae the sky.

Frae the keep's ramparts, watchmen spotted the tide—the battered but unbroken tide—and raised the MacCraith banner high, flappin' like a promise on the wind.

Tryss threw back his head an' roared, a raw, unchained bellow tearin' frae his chest—every breath defiance, every word a sacred vow.

"MACCRAITH!"

The cry shattered the distance, swallowed an' returned a hundredfold—a mighty chorus o' brotherhood an' homecomin' that shook the stones an' stirred the ancient hills.

They thundered doon the slope like wild spirits freed frae hell itsel'—swords raised, mouths wide wi' howls o' fury an' joy, hooves poundin' a relentless rhythm that echoed in the bones o' every man, woman, an' bairn who heard it.

An' through the swirl o' dust an' shattered light, just beyond the iron gates an' the worn stone walls, the two women waited—Alyssa an' Elsyn—fierce as the flames in their hearts.

Hame. No' just a place. A beacon. A promise.

The roar swallowed the valley, growin' louder still, a storm o' triumph, grief, an' unyieldin' hope.

Because this—this charge—was mair than a victory. It was legend.

As they thundered doon the hill, the gates o' MacCraith swung wide wi' a groan o' ancient iron an' fresh hope.

Tryss didnae rein in—not till the poundin' hooves slowed tae a desperate gallop, an' he was mere feet frae the figure that held his world steady.

The horse's sides heaved beneath him, foam drippin' frae its bit, but Tryss's gaze swept the ground ahead. Bodies littered the yard—men he knew, men he'd trained wi', broken an' stiffenin' where they'd fallen. Blood seeped intae the cracks o' the stone, black in the torchlight. Arrows jutted frae the gate, the walls, the verra earth like a cruel harvest. The keep hadnae gone untested; its stones bore the scars o' fire an' steel.

He swallowed hard, the taste o' copper thick on his tongue. Every ruin he passed—splintered pike, shattered shield, a smear o' crimson where someone had been dragged away—was proof o' how close he'd come tae losin' it all.

But then—he saw the banners still flyin', ragged but unfallen, an' the faint glow o' hearth-fires beyond the walls. Alive. The keep was alive.

Alyssa stood like a stone goddess on the threshold, eyes fierce an' unblinkin', a MacCraith shield clenched in her hand, worn but unyieldin'—just like her.

Her cloak whipped wild in the wind, an' for a heartbeat, time cracked open, the roarin' world shrinkin' doon tae the space between them.

Tryss's breath came ragged, sweat an' dirt streaked across his face, every muscle screamin'—but the weight in his chest was somethin' else entirely.

He swung doon frae his horse, boots strikin' the cobbles hard as he closed the final steps.

Nae words. Nae cheers.

Only the fierce gravity o' all they'd endured—the sharp relief o' survival—and the unbreakable tether o' two souls meetin' again in the storm's eye.

Alyssa's shield lowered slow, her eyes softenin' just enough tae catch his.

Tryss dropped tae his knees before her, the stone cold beneath him but his heart burnin' wi' fierce gratitude. Here stood the mighty woman who had held his keep, carried his bairn beneath her heart, an' anchored his restless soul.

He took her hand gentle, pressin' it tae his lips. "I'm hame," he whispered, voice rough as the Highland wind.

In that moment, every wound, every scar, every vow forged in fire an' blood surged through him like a tide—wild, relentless, unbreakable.

Alyssa didnae hesitate. She dropped tae her knees, meetin' his gaze wi' her ain fierce, shinin' eyes. The shield slipped frae her fingers, thuddin' soft against the stones—forgotten, unnecessary now.

Nae words passed between them. There was nae need. Every battle, every fear, every hope hung heavy between them like sacred smoke.

She reached for him, hands tremblin' but steady, cradlin' his face wi' reverence—as if holdin' the last piece o' her world.

Tryss leaned intae her touch, breath ragged, eyes closed, surrenderin' fully.

Fegus

The gates swung open, welcomin' the weary an' bloodied, but

Fergus's eyes sought only one soul.

There she stood—Elsyn—steadfast an' radiant, the fierce light in her gaze tempered now wi' exhaustion, her belly heavy wi' their bairn, the livin' proof o' all they had endured.

Fergus dismounted quick but gentle, each step measured as he came tae her. He dropped tae his knees before her, hands tremblin' wi' awe an' relief—one restin' soft upon the curve o' her belly, the other clingin' tae hers like a lifeline.

"Ye're the keeper o' my soul," he whispered, his voice thick as peat wi' emotion. "Ye carried me through hell. An' ye carry our future."

Elsyn's eyes shimmered, fierce yet tender, but before words could bind them, Fergus pulled her close, his lips crashin' against hers in a kiss fierce an' desperate—raw wi' every moment o' pain, fear, longin', an' love they'd buried deep these long days apart.

She met him wi' the same fire, clingin' tae him as though he might be torn awa' again in the next heartbeat. The world fell silent aroond them—nothin' but heat, breath, an' the thunder o' two hearts poundin' as one.

When at last they broke apart, breathless, Elsyn's gaze flickered past Fergus.

There he stood—her father, MacInness—stern, silent, the lines o' his face carved by years o' hard choices an' harder battles. Her breath caught as he stepped forward, an' for the first time, the hardness in his eyes was softened wi' a rare, vulnerable light.

"I was a bloody fool tae send ye awa'," MacInness said, his voice rough as gravel, heavy wi' regret. "I let pride an' anger blind me tae the fierce woman ye'd become—and the life ye carved frae nothin'."

His eyes held hers, steady, unyieldin'. "Ye carry my blood, but ye made yer own way. For that, I am proud. Mair proud than I ever said."

Elsyn's chest tightened, years o' rejection an' exile twistin' intae somethin' fragile—somethin' close tae hope.

"Ye cast me oot, but I never lost myself," she answered, her voice low but burnin'. "I forgive ye. Because wi'oot that pain, I'd ne'er have become who I am."

MacInness bowed his head, his voice thick as storm clouds. "Gods forgive me for my blindness. I'm sorry for every moment I made ye doubt yer worth."

Her hand lifted, tremblin', an' settled in his. "Thank ye. For this. For tryin' now."

He gripped her hand wi' fierce tenderness, a silent vow passin' between them—blood made whole again, no' by birthright, but by choice.

Chapter Forty-Four

Alyssa

The war was ower.

The mud an' bloodshed had faded intae memory, leavin' only the silence that follows a storm's passin'. MacCraith Keep, though battered an' scarred, still stood resolute against the Highland sky. Its walls bore the marks o' battle—shattered stone, charred beams, an' the faint tang o' smoke lingerin' in the air—but inside, life pulsed wi' a fragile, determined rhythm.

The courtyard had become a place o' mendin'. Makeshift beds lined the stone, the wounded moanin' soft or starin' quiet at the sky. Alyssa moved among them wi' gentle hands, cleanin' wounds, soothin' fevers, whisperin' comfort. The bairn she carried stirred inside her, a silent promise o' new life amid the ruin.

When her work was done, when the last poultice had been tied an' the last basin emptied, she found him.

Tryss sat by the hearth, his leg still bound tight, his great shoulders bowed, his eyes distant. The ghosts o' the fight lingered there—but beneath them was a steadiness, the resolve o' a man who had given all an' found somethin' worth livin' for.

She knelt in front o' him, her fingers reachin' for his. "Ye're far away again," she murmured.

His rough hand closed ower hers, anchorin' him tae her. "Aye. Countin' the dead. Wonderin' why it's us still breathin' when better men fell."

"Better?" she said, soft but sharp, her thumb brushin' the dirt frae his knuckles. "Nay man better than the one sittin' here wi' me. Ye held the line, Tryss MacCraith. Ye gave us back our lives."

His throat worked, but nae words came. He stared at her, fierce an' undone all at once.

She leaned closer, her forehead pressin' tae his. "Ye made me a vow afore ye rode intae that valley. Ye said ye'd come back tae me. An' here ye are. Bruised, broken, aye—but here."

"I thought o' ye wi' every stroke," he whispered, voice raw. "Every man I cut doon, every breath I near lost—I swore tae the gods I'd crawl back tae ye if that's what it took."

Tears pricked her eyes, but her smile held. "An' if ye'd failed, I'd have dragged ye back mysel', by the hair if need be."

That earned the ghost o' a laugh frae him—ragged, weary, but real. He lifted her hand, pressin' his lips tae the back o' it, lingerin' there. "Ye kept the walls," he said hoarse. "I saw the bodies at the gate. Alyssa... ye fought."

Her jaw tightened. "Aye. I killed. An' I'll no' forget their screams. But I'll no' regret it either. I'd do it again, an' again, tae keep ye, tae keep this bairn, tae keep our clan."

His gaze dropped tae her belly, the faint swell visible even through her gown. His hand slid tentatively, reverently, ower the curve. "That's our future. Our second chance. Our proof that blood an' war cannae take everythin'."

Alyssa cupped his face in her hands, liftin' his eyes tae hers. "Listen tae me, Tryss. We willnae live in the shadow o' this fight forever. We'll raise our child wi' laughter, wi' songs. We'll build somethin' stronger than ony wall—somethin' Black Rowan or ony other bastard could ne'er burn doon."

His eyes softened, misted. "Ye're my heart, lass. My home. I'd fight ten wars if it meant comin' back tae this."

She kissed him then—slow, deep, the kind that held nae fire o' battle, only the quiet ache o' survival, the fierce tenderness o' souls who had near lost everythin' but clung tae each other instead.

When their lips parted, she rested her head against his chest, hearin' the steady drum o' his heart. "Rest now, warrior," she whispered. "The fight's done. For the night, at least."

His arm curled roond her, holdin' her close. "Aye. For the night."

An' for the first time since the valley, Tryss MacCraith closed his eyes wi' peace, anchored in the arms o' the woman who had kept his soul alive.

Chapter Forty-Five

Elsyn

THE STONE WALLS OF the birthing chamber were cold and unyielding, but inside, the air was thick with sweat, tension, and the scent of herbs steeped in boiling water. Elsyn's breaths came ragged and fierce, her knuckles white as she gripped the rough wooden bedpost. Moira crouched nearby, a steady hand on her forehead, murmuring prayers in the old tongue, while Alyssa hovered, soaked with sweat and smelling faintly of sweat herself.

"By the saints, Elsyn, ye've got the stubbornness of a wild goat and the strength of one too," Alyssa said, forcing a wry smile as she pressed a cool cloth to Elsyn's damp brow.

Elsyn groaned, her face contorted with pain, a fierce glare shot Alyssa's way. "If you say goat again, I swear I'll—"

"Calm, lass. Save that fire for pushing." Alyssa's voice softened, but her eyes flicked to the small wooden stool she'd dragged close, reminding herself to keep steady, keep calm. This was far from the gentle births she'd imagined as a girl.

The contractions hit like hammer blows—each one stealing the breath from Elsyn's lungs and twisting her insides raw. Moira adjusted the herbs simmering in a clay pot, the steam carrying faint hints of lavender and rosemary meant to soothe and strengthen.

Alyssa leaned in close, wiping the sweat from Elsyn's upper lip. "Ye're doing bloody brilliant. Every time ye yell, just remember ye're terrifying the hell out of the men in the great hall. Probably making Fergus spill his ale."

Elsyn let out a strangled laugh, grimacing as another wave seized her. "That damn fool. If he drops one more cup, I'll—"

"Save yer curses, mother of mine." Alyssa reached for a cloth soaked in warm water, gently cleansing Elsyn. "We're almost there. But there's still a long road ahead."

Elsyn's grip faltered, and Alyssa caught her, murmuring soft encouragements, hands steady and sure despite the chaos.

Outside the chamber, the distant roar of celebration drifted through the stone walls—men toasting victories, unaware of the fiercer battle being fought here.

Elsyn's eyes locked with Alyssa's, raw and fierce. "No turning back now."

"No turning back," Alyssa agreed, heart pounding. "Just ye and the bairn, and the fire in yer blood."

The room tightened with silence, broken only by Elsyn's ragged breaths and the rhythmic thud of a pounding heart—waiting for the moment when new life would break through the pain and blood and sweat.

Fergus

The great hall buzzed with the dull hum of celebration dulled by worry—ale sloshed in cups, fires crackled in the hearths, but all joy was shallow. Every man knew what was happening behind the thick stone walls above.

Fergus sat at the long table, untouched drink in hand, boots planted wide, jaw clenched so tight it looked like he might crack a molar.

Tryss sat beside him, arm slung lazily over the back of his chair, but his eyes—sharp, watching, waiting—betrayed every ounce of calm.

Then it came.

Another scream—ragged, feral, unmistakably Elsyn. It sliced through the stone like a blade.

Fergus shot up like he'd been stabbed, chair scraping back violently, already half to the door.

Tryss slammed a hand to his chest, halting him with force. "Ye're nay goin' in there."

Fergus's nostrils flared. "She's screaming."

"She's birthing."

"I *know* what she's doing!" Fergus barked.

Tryss didn't budge. "And unless ye've suddenly grown a midwife's hands and Moira's calm, ye'll stay the hell out of it. Ye burst in there and she sees yer fool face? She'll lose focus—or worse, think ye dinnae trust her tae do what she's doing."

Fergus's hands curled into fists. "Ye dinnae get it."

"I do," Tryss said, quieter now. "She's yer whole bloody heart. And she's in pain. And ye can't do a damn thing but wait."

Fergus dropped his head, breath ragged.

Tryss leaned closer. "Alyssa told me once—there's not a war fiercer than what a woman faces bringing life into this world. All we can do is stand ready when she comes out the other side."

A beat. Then another cry tore through the air.

Fergus's jaw trembled. "What if she doesnae?"

Tryss's hand tightened on his shoulder. "Then we raise the earth and sky until they give her back."

For a long moment, neither spoke. Just the fire crackling. The sound of boots shifting. The thundering weight of hope and helplessness.

Then Tryss reached for his drink and took a long swallow. "Now sit yer arse down, Fergus. And pray. Loudly. Because she's gonna need every saint, spirit, and star in the sky—and so will ye when she sees ye paced a hole in the hall floor."

Fergus let out a half-choked laugh and sat.

Tryss raised his cup. "Tae women fiercer than war."

Fergus raised his. "And tae surviving them."

Elsyn

Elsyn was drenched in sweat, her hair matted to her forehead, her shift bunched around her hips and soaked clean through. Her thighs trembled with effort, muscles drawn so tight she could feel them splintering from the inside out.

Another contraction tore through her body like a flaming sword and she screamed—a sound ripped from somewhere deeper than pain, deeper than fear.

"*Yoere doing it, love,*" Moira said, hands firm on Elsyn's shaking knees. "Head's nearly there—just one more push now—"

"One more," Elsyn snarled, teeth bared. "You said that five pushes ago, you lying crone!"

Moira grinned grimly. "Then stop shouting at me and push the damn bairn out!"

Alyssa was behind her, bracing her shoulders with firm hands, pressing cold cloths to her neck, whispering words Elsyn barely heard through the storm of agony ripping her in two.

"Ye've survived worse," Alyssa murmured. "Ye've faced an entire clan with yer chin high. *This*—this is just one stubborn little soul who needs to meet ye."

Another wave hit. This time it wasn't fire—it was *fury*.

She *bore* down, roared like a storm, and something *shifted*. The burn turned to pressure. Pressure to release. Pressure to *let go*—

And that's when the door crashed open.

"ELSYN!"

Fergus was already halfway into the room, wild-eyed and furious with fear, before Moira could throw her arm out to stop him. Alyssa whipped around, hair flying.

Elsyn's head jerked toward him. She was already pushing, face twisted with effort, scream caught in her throat.

Fergus froze, stunned. Not by blood—he'd seen blood. Not by pain—he lived in it.

But by *her*.

The sheer *force* of her.

And then—

A final, primal cry.

And the room cracked wide open.

The child slid into Moira's waiting hands, slick with blood, bawling like the world had offended it already.

Fergus dropped to his knees.

Elsyn collapsed back against Alyssa's chest, shaking, tears streaking her flushed face.

Moira moved fast, clearing the cord, wrapping the babe in clean linens. "It's a boy," she said breathlessly, eyes wide with the thrill of it. "He's *perfect*."

Fergus was still on the floor, unmoving.

Alyssa turned to him, voice shaking. "Fergus—say something."

He crawled to the bedside like a man crawling back to life. Reached out. Touched the tiny, screaming bundle.

Then turned to Elsyn.

"Ye didn't just birth a child," he said, voice cracking. "Ye birthed a bloody warrior."

Elsyn laughed through the sobs. "Then he'll burn his own path through the world"

Fergus leaned in and kissed her—hard, reverent, trembling with awe. "Just like his mother. Ye," he whispered, "are the fiercest thing I have ever known."

And from Elsyn's chest, cradled between them, their son wailed like he already knew he'd inherited the fire.

Alyssa

Alyssa left the chamber without a word. The air in the birthing room had felt too thick, too red. Her limbs moved without permission, her breath hitchin', shallow and sharp.

That had been the most violent thing she'd ever witnessed.

Mair violent than war.

Mair savage than ony battlefield clash.

Her hand drifted tae her ain belly, roundin' now beneath her gown. Still small. Still safe. But a sickening wave rose in her chest, hot and cold at once.

She didnae make it far.

Doon the corridor, past the wide eyes o' servants and through the double doors o' the great hall, Tryss had just turned tae say somethin'—only for Alyssa tae blow past him like a storm wind.

He caught only a glimpse o' her face—ashen, stricken—afore

she was gone.

He followed.

Ootside, she had barely cleared the threshold afore she doubled ower, one hand bracin' against the stone wall, the ither clenched in the folds o' her cloak. Her stomach lurched and turned, and she retched hard intae the frozen earth. Again. And again.

Tryss was beside her in moments, wordless. He crouched and rubbed slow circles atween her shoulders, his calloused hand warm through the fabric.

"There now, love," he murmured. "What ails ye?"

She spat and wiped her mouth wi' the back o' her hand, still breathin' like she'd run a mile. Her eyes shone wi' tears, though none had fallen yet. When she looked at him, her voice cracked like brittle glass.

"The bairn's born. It's a lad." Her throat worked as she swallowed. "And that's... guid. It's guid."

Tryss nodded slow, brows drawn.

"But Tryss..." Her voice dropped tae a whisper, raw wi' fear. "God's teeth, the way he came intae this world... the blood, the screamin'—it wasnae birth, it was battle. I've ne'er seen a woman fight like that. It tore her apart."

She leaned intae him now, buryin' her face against his chest as his arms wrapped roond her, tight and groundin'. "And I keep thinkin'..." Her words came in a rush now, muffled by the wool o' his tunic. "That'll be me. That's where we're headed. And I—I dinnae ken if I'm strong enough. What if I cannae—what if I—"

"Shhh," he whispered, pressin' a kiss intae her hair. "Ye're no' Elsyn. And ye willnae face it alone. Nay for a single breath. Ye've got me, Alyssa. All o' me. Every damned moment."

She pulled back, eyes fierce despite the tears clingin' tae her lashes. "Ye cannae promise tae stop it. Ye cannae make it safe."

"Nay," he said, voice rough as stone. "But I'll be there. I'll sit through every scream, every shudder, every tear if it means ye dinnae face it alone. I'll no' wait behind doors like some coward. I'm no' leavin' ye—dinnae ask me tae."

"Tryss," she gasped, blinkin' hard. "Men arenae— They dinnae— That's no' done—"

"Then let 'em choke on their damned traditions," he said, scoopin' her intae his arms afore she could say anither word. "They can call me mad. I'll still be the one haudin' yer hand when our bairn enters the world."

Alyssa stared at him, stunned, the air knocked right oot o' her.

He looked doon at her, fire in his gaze and reverence in his hold. "Ye carry my bloody soul in that belly, Alyssa MacCraith. Ye think I'd wait on the ither side o' a door?"

She opened her mouth, but the protest died on her tongue. Her fingers curled intae his tunic, clutchin' tight.

Withoot waitin', Tryss turned and carried her up the steps, his stride certain, unstoppable, as though nae power in this world could turn him back.

In their chambers, Tryss settled them baith intae the great chair by the hearth. The embers still glowed, low and golden, castin' soft flickers across the stone walls. Alyssa tucked hersel' intae his chest like she belonged there—and she did. His arms curved roond her, his hand strokin' slow, soothin' circles doon her back.

"Feelin' better now, love?" he murmured against her temple.

She gave a soft, tired huff o' a laugh. "Well, I'm in nae danger o' gettin' sick on yer lap, if that's what ye mean."

He smiled intae her hair.

But then she shifted slightly, enough tae look up at him, her expression growin' serious again. "Tryss… I still dinnae think ye should be there when the time comes."

His brow furrowed. "Alyssa—"

"Nay, just—listen." Her voice trembled, no' wi' fear but wi' honesty. "Ye dinnae ken what it's like. What ye would see. What ye'd hear. Gods, Tryss, it's no' just pain. It's blood. Violence. It's—" Her throat tightened. "Ye'd ne'er want tae touch me again. Nay like that. No' after seein' me… torn open just tae bring life."

He went still beneath her

Then, slowly, he lifted her chin until her eyes met his. His voice, when it came, was low and reverent. "Ye think I love ye for what ye look like in pleasure, Alyssa? Ye think these hands only crave ye when ye're soft and sweet and smilin'?"

He leaned in, his forehead brushin' hers, his breath warm and steady. "I'll love ye wi' blood on yer thighs and curses on yer lips. I'll love ye when ye're scream-swept and wild-eyed and fightin' for every breath tae bring our bairn intae this world. I'll love ye when ye're stronger than me. When ye're braver than I could e'er be."

Her mouth parted, a tear slidin' silent doon her cheek.

Tryss brushed it away wi' his thumb. "I willnae walk away frae that. I cannae. Because what I saw the day, what I heard—that was war. And I've ne'er been mair terrified. But ye?" His voice broke, just barely. "Ye're goin' tae walk through that storm and hold life in yer arms at the end o' it." He swallowed hard. "And I swear, Alyssa, I'll still want ye. Gods help me, I'll likely want ye mair."

Alyssa's breath caught, her lips parted—but Tryss wasnae finished.

A wicked glint flickered tae life in his eyes, sharp as flint and twice as dangerous. "But if ye're truly worried there'll be nae mair after the bairn comes," he murmured, voice low and sultry, "then I suppose I'll hae tae see ye sated now, aye? Properly ruined wi' pleasure, so ye ne'er doubt it again."

Afore she could retort—or laugh, or blush, or do onything at all—he was liftin' her intae his arms, easy as breath, like she weighed nae mair than a sigh. Alyssa squeaked in surprise, gigglin' despite hersel', fear meltin' away in the warmth o' his strength and certainty.

"Tryss—"

"Shh," he murmured, already crossin' the room. "Ye've worried enough for one nicht, love. Let me take care o' ye."

He laid her doon upon the bed wi' achin' reverence, his hands gentle, sure. Her hair spilled across the pillows like flame, her cheeks flushed, her body already hummin' beneath his gaze.

And Tryss—Tryss was all business now. Tryss knelt atween her thighs like a man afore an altar, hands reverent as he parted her legs, eyes drinkin' her in as though she were the very source o' his strength. "Look at ye," he murmured, voice husky wi' want and wonder. "So bloody perfect, love. And ye dinnae even see it."

Alyssa's breath hitched, her body already tremblin' beneath the heat o' his gaze. But then—gods—his mouth was on her.

He didnae rush. He worshipped.

Slow, languid strokes o' his tongue, each one draggin' a shiver up her spine. He kissed her as though she were made o' somethin' sacred, somethin' rare and powerful. His mouth worked her expertly, lovingly, drawin' moans frae her lips that echoed against the chamber walls. Every flick, every press, was purpose-built tae undo her.

Alyssa's hips arched, her hand divin' intae his hair, a whimper escapin' her throat as she gasped, "Tryss—"

He growled low, the sound vibratin' against her. "Let me, love. Let me remind ye what ye mean tae me."

He devoured her like a man starved, like her pleasure was the only thing anchorin' him tae the world. Her thighs trembled, her voice broke, and still he didnae stop—until she was writhin' beneath him, breathless, lost in the waves o' sensation crashin' through her.

When she cried out his name, shatterin' on the peak he'd so carefully built, Tryss finally lifted his head—face flushed, lips glistenin' wi' devotion and desire.

Alyssa was shakin', pantin', her eyes wide and glassy as she looked at him.

But Tryss didnae move. He only looked at her wi' that fierce, wicked gleam in his eyes, his voice low and rough wi' devotion. "I'm no' done wi' ye yet, lovey," he murmured. "Ye'll take yer pleasure again, just like this. Cum for me."

Afore she could protest, afore she could even draw breath tae argue, his mouth was on her again.

Gentle was gone. Now he was relentless. His tongue found the places that made her tremble, the rhythm that made her gasp. One arm snaked under her thigh, anchorin' her tae him, while the ither hand splayed across her belly wi' reverent weight—steady, groundin', his thumb brushin' the soft curve that held their child.

He worshipped her, aye—but this was claimin'. This was a man determined tae show her she could ne'er break the desire atween them, no' wi' pain, no' wi' fear, no' wi' time.

Alyssa's cries rose higher, her hips liftin' in desperation, her hands fisted in the blankets.

He didnae stop. He gave her everythin'—his mouth, his breath, the heat o' his love poured intae every stroke, every flick, every relentless press o' tongue against achin' flesh.

And when she came again, shattered and sobbin' his name, he stayed right there, haudin' her through it, lips still pressed tae the heart o' her, as though he could drink doon every wave o' her pleasure like a vow.

Only then did he lift his head, eyes dark and full o' fierce tenderness.

"Now," he said, voice tremblin' wi' restraint. "Now I'll gie ye what ye asked for."

Slowly, deliberate, Tryss eased hissel' inside her, fillin' her wi' a weight that was baith groundin' and electrifyin'. The warmth o' her pressed tight aroond him was a fierce, pulsin' welcome, and he let oot a low growl as he settled deep.

His hands framed her face, thumbs brushin' ower her cheekbones, anchorin' them thegither as he began tae move. At first, his strokes were measured, savorin' each inch, each shiver that rippled through her body. His gaze locked onto hers, searchin' for every flicker o' need, every breathless gasp, every tremor o' delight. Then the pace quickened—harder, deeper—his hips drivin' steady, relentless, matchin' the thunder o' his heartbeat.

Alyssa's breath hitched, eyes burnin' wi' fierce determination. "Let me ride ye, Tryss," she whispered, voice low and commandin'. Withoot hesitation, she shifted, slidin' up his body until she was straddlin' him, her hands pressin' intae his chest for balance. The heat atween them deepened as she took control, guidin' hersel' wi' slow, deliberate movements that set baith their bodies ablaze.

Tryss groaned, his hands findin' her hips, grippin' firm as she rode him wi' a steady rhythm that teased and tormented, every motion pullin' them closer tae the edge.

Her fingers curved aroond the sensitive swell o' his balls, cuppin' and rockin' them gentle, a delicious torment that sent ripples o' pleasure through him. The contrast—her strength in that tender touch—pushed him closer tae the brink, every movement a balm and a fire.

Alyssa's gaze locked on his, fierce and unyieldin', as she leaned back, archin' her spine, rockin' her hips in a slow, sensual dance that demanded surrender.

Tryss's breath hitched sharply, his muscles tensin' beneath her as the tension inside him spiraled higher and higher. A raw, shatterin' wave o' pleasure exploded through his body, fierce and consumin'. It was as if every nerve, every fibre, ignited in a blaze o' heat that coursed frae his core ootward, electrifyin' and relentless.

His hands gripped Alyssa's hips tighter, clutchin' her as if haudin' on tae the world itsel', his body tremblin' wi' the force o' it. His voice broke free—a guttural, ragged sound torn frae deep within—an echo o' everythin' he felt: release, desperation, and a fierce, unyieldin' love.

Time seemed tae shatter and collapse intae that moment, the thunder o' his heartbeat drownin' oot all else as he surrendered utterly, lost in the wild, fierce connection that bound them. When it passed, the aftershocks rippled through him, leavin' him breathless and tremblin', utterly spent—and completely hers.

Alyssa smirked, teasin', "Is that yer definition o' properly ruined wi' pleasure? I would hae thought it better."

Tryss grinned, shakin' his head. "Cheeky minx."

Chapter Forty- Six

Tryss found Fergus at the long table, shoulders slumped, a mug of ale cradled between both hands like it might hold the last warmth in all the Highlands.

Tryss dropped onto the bench across from him. "Ye look like ten miles o' bad road."

Fergus grunted. "Feels longer."

Tryss grinned. "So… how's fatherhood treatin' ye?"

Fergus lifted bloodshot eyes and fixed him wi' a stare. "Fergie's been screamin' for three days straight. I've nae slept, Elsyn's nae slept, and the bairn's lungs might be the strongest thing I've ever encountered—and I've fought men twice my size."

Tryss chuckled. "Aye, the lad's got fight in him. Came out roarin' and hasna stopped since."

Fergus huffed a tired laugh. "He howls like a battle cry at midnight. At sunrise, it's more of a siege. I tried walkin' him through the halls to settle him—he screamed louder. Swaddled, unswaddled, rocked, sung to, fed—nothin' helps. He just screams."

"Sounds like he takes after his ma," Tryss said wi' a smirk.

Fergus's lips twitched. "And his da."

Tryss raised a brow.

"I may nae have sired him," Fergus said, quiet and fierce, "but that bairn's mine. He's mine in every cry, every kick o' those tiny legs, every time Elsyn lays him on my chest and he settles—for all o' three breaths." His eyes darkened wi' pride and exhaustion. "Elsyn named him Fergus, Tryss. Fergie. After me."

Tryss nodded, all teasin' gone from his face. "Aye. I ken."

"I held him this mornin'," Fergus murmured. "Screamin' like a banshee, red-faced and furious. But his wee fist curled roond my finger, and gods help me, I nearly wept."

Tryss clapped a hand on his shoulder. "Ye're doin' fine, Fergus. And Elsyn?"

"She's a force o' nature." Fergus rubbed a hand across his face. "But I can see the edges frayin'. I'd trade my sword arm to give her one night's sleep."

Tryss lifted his mug. "To Fergie, the fiercest wee warrior this side o' the Highlands."

Fergus raised his own. "And to the lass who brought him roarin' into the world... and still hasna lost her mind."

They drank deep.

Somewhere overhead, a sudden, shrill wail pierced the rafters—followed by Elsyn's muffled voice shoutin' from the solar. "Tell him if he's comin' in here, he best bring a clean swaddle and a miracle!"

Tryss snorted into his mug. Fergus winced, but his mouth twitched wi' pride.

"Think he'll settle soon?" Tryss asked.

Fergus sighed. "I think he'll rule this place by volume alone."

Tryss smirked. "He's got the name for it."

But settle he did.

In the days that followed, Tryss often found Alyssa and Elsyn in the solar, bathed in soft light from the tall windows, wee Fergie nestled in the cradle beside them. The bairn had finally found his rhythm—nae longer a tiny storm o' howls, but a warm, blinkin' bundle o' contentment swaddled in wool and lullabies.

It was a sight that stilled Tryss every time he came upon it: Alyssa bent forward, gently brushin' her fingers along the child's downy hair; Elsyn restin' nearby, her face softer now, less pale, laughter returnin' to her like sunlight after storm. The quiet hum o' womanly conversation filled the chamber, interrupted only by Fergie's occasional snufflin' sigh.

Fergus had once said he'd trade his sword arm for Elsyn's peace. These days, he'd trade both arms for a night o' sleep.

And Tryss... Gods, he'd never kenned he could feel like this.

There was a peace in that room that shook somethin' loose in his chest. A glimpse into what came after—after the war cries faded, after the steel was sheathed and bloodied banners stored away.

Peace.

It was a word he'd ne'er trusted afore. To him, war had always been the constant, the marrow o' a Highlander's life. Battles o'er land, o'er honor, o'er vengeance—it had been endless. Men like him were forged for it, trained to lead others into it, crowned by it.

But now... it was over. For the first time in years, the keep's walls were nae braced for siege. The folk walked the courtyards wi' laughter instead o' fear. Bairns played wi'out watchin' the horizon for riders. His men had gone from sharpenin' blades to teachin' lads to fish, mendin' thatch, plantin' fields.

And him? He was still their laird. Still their leader. Only now, he was nae called to war but to keep them steady in the quiet. To guide them into somethin' he barely kenned how to name:

peace.

It was a heavier crown than war had ever been. Steel was simple. Life was nae.

Tryss leaned a shoulder against the doorframe, watchin' Alyssa. Watchin' them. His fierce, stubborn, sharp-tongued Alyssa—who could command a hall wi' a glance and laugh like a lass in the next breath—cradlin' someone else's bairn like she was born for it. His throat tightened.

A couple o' months, Alyssa had said. Their own bairn would be here at winter's end. Just a handful o' weeks. A breath, a blink.

Was he ready?

He wasnae. But he would be. Because love like this didnae wait for readiness. It demanded risin'.

And he would rise.

For her. For the bairn. For the folk who looked to him not only in war, but in peace. For whatever future lay ahead.

Chapter Forty-Seven

Alyssa

THE CHAMBER WAS DIM, the low fire casting flickering shadows across the rough stone walls. Alyssa sat upright in the broad bed, her hand resting gently on the swell of her belly. The chair beside the hearth, once shared easily between them, was now too small to hold her and Tryss both, so he settled close beside her beneath the thick woolen blankets.

Tryss's eyes were heavy but bright as he leaned in, brushing a stray lock of auburn hair from her face. "MacInness has broken Black Rowan's siege," he murmured, voice rough but steady. "They've taken the pass an' pushed Rowan's men back from our borders. Tae have an ally holdin' that line again—that changes everythin'."

Alyssa smiled, the faint lines of fatigue softened by hope. "It's a relief, isn't it? After all we've been through." Her gaze lingered on the flames, thoughts tumbling faster than her lips could frame them. She'd known fear too sharp tae name, the kind that curled in her chest at night when the sound of steel had echoed across the glen. Now, with Rowan's men driven back, she could almost taste the promise of peace—not only for their people, but for the bairn she carried. "And little Fergie is growing fast. Two months now, and already he's the fiercest wee bairn I've ever seen." Her eyes drifted toward the cradle by the window, the sight of it still tugging at her heart. She had offered Elsyn four hours of sleep and the babe hadn't stirred the whole time. A small miracle. A gift she didnae take for granted.

Tryss chuckled softly. "Fergie's got his ma's spirit—and his da's stubborn streak. That lad's goin' tae shake these hills one day."

They fell into a comfortable silence, the quiet punctuated only by the crackle of the fire and the soft breathing of their keep.

Slowly, Tryss reached out, fingers entwining with hers, resting against the curve of her belly. Alyssa leaned her head against his shoulder, feeling the steady strength of him beside her.

As the night deepened, exhaustion pulled at their limbs. The world outside might still be a storm, but here in the flickering glow, they found a fragile peace.

The night was thick and silent, save for the ragged breaths and quiet groans coming from the bed in the corner of the chamber. Tryss lay behind Alyssa, his strong arms wrapped firmly around her, holdin' her as if he could carry every wave of pain crashin' through her.

Her back pressed against his chest, slick with sweat and tremblin' with exhaustion, but still unyieldin'.

"Damn ye," Alyssa gasped between clenched teeth, her voice sharp as the ache twistin' through her belly. "If I dinnae hate ye by the time this is done, I'll eat my plaid."

Tryss's breath hitched in a laugh. "Well, that's nae very nice. Why say such things tae me when I love ye so?"

"Maybe because I do." She bit her lip, eyes squeezed shut. "But right now? I want tae punch ye through every stone in this blasted keep."

He tightened his grip gently. "Ye'll have tae try harder. I'm no' goin' anywhere."

"Fine. Just don't choke me when I do."

Another contraction hit like a thunderclap. Alyssa gasped, diggin' her fingers into his forearms, nails bitin' into skin. Tryss pressed his cheek tae the curve of her neck, voice low and steady. "There's fire in yer soul, Alyssa. Ye've the strength for this."

She followed, though the air barely reached her lungs. "Ye're lucky I'm in love wi' ye, Tryss MacCraith. Otherwise, I'd swear ye were enjoyin' this."

His grin was a slow burn against her skin. "Ye forget I'm as stubborn as ye. This bairn willnae beat us."

She snorted, bitter and fierce. "It better no' look like ye, or I'll be the one doin' the cursin'."

"Now that's low." He shifted so his hand rested on her swollen belly, rubbin' slow circles. "I'll have ye ken, I'm quite the handsome devil."

"Och, ye're an ugly toad." She smirked despite herself, then her face twisted in pain.

Tryss laughed, a rough, delighted sound. "Better tae be ugly an' brave than bonnie an' useless."

Her breath hitched, voice strained. "Speak for yerself."

The room fell into a rhythm of moans, whispers, and the scrape of shiftin' bodies. Time lost meanin'. Minutes blurred into hours. The fire guttered low in the hearth, castin' flickerin' shadows on stone walls that had witnessed countless births but never one as fierce as this.

Tryss never wavered, never left her side. When she trembled, he held her tighter. When she cursed him, he smiled through the pain.

At last, after what felt like an eternity, the cry came.

A sharp, raw wail cuttin' through the dark like the blade that would one day protect him.

Alyssa's eyes flew open, tears streamin' down her cheeks, mixin' with sweat and exhaustion. Tryss pulled her close, lips brushin' her temple, voice husky wi' awe.

"A son," he whispered.

She gave a tired, triumphant smile. "Aye. A laird for MacCraith."

Tryss laughed softly. "They'll all meet him soon enough."

They stayed wrapped in each other's arms as the world outside held its breath.

The bairn's name would come—but for now, all that mattered was this fierce new life, born of love, pain, and an unbreakable bond.

Tryss

Long after Alyssa had fallen into the deep, ragged sleep of a body that had given everything, Tryss remained awake, cradlin' his son against his chest. A son. Gods, a son. He'd never have believed it, not in all the years o' war, blood, and endless nights o' fightin'. Yet here he was, the bairn's tiny chest risin' and fallin' with each breath, the soft hum o' life steady beneath his hand.

He shifted slightly, careful not to wake him, and studied the wee face. So small, so fierce, already so determined—aye, a MacCraith through and through. Fingers curled round his own, trustin' instinct alone tae hold him safe. Tryss let his thoughts drift, imaginin' the years ahead: the first steps across the stone floors o' the keep, the first laugh that would echo through the halls, the first time he'd ken the feel o' pride that came from fatherhood, raw and sharp as a sword's edge.

A quiet chuckle escaped him, low and rough. "Ye'll be trouble, I ken it," he murmured, pressin' a kiss tae the bairn's crown. "But ye'll be my trouble. Mine tae protect. Mine tae love. Mine tae teach... if ye survive tae teach me in return."

The fire in the hearth had burned low, embers glowin' like tiny coals in the shadowed room, and Tryss allowed himself tae simply breathe. The war was over. The banners were stored, the steel set aside, and the men he had led through blood and fire now walked the keep's halls in peace. Peace. A word he'd never trusted, a concept that had once seemed foreign, almost dangerous. Yet now it settled o'er him, heavy but welcome, like the weight o' the bairn against his chest.

He felt the pull o' exhaustion, the ache o' adrenaline finally fading, and for the first time in years, he allowed himself a moment o' stillness. He whispered tae the child, voice rough and tender: "I'll rise for ye, wee one. I'll rise for yer ma. I'll rise for all o' it—the keep, the people, this life we've been granted. And by the gods, I'll do it with every breath I've got."

Tryss shifted, adjustin' the bairn so he rested more comfortably against his chest. He studied the boy again, commitin' every detail tae memory: the curl o' hair, the tiny fists, the way his lips parted slightly with each sleepy sigh. A son. A MacCraith. The first light o' a future he hadn't dared imagine, now held safe in his arms.

And in the quiet dark, wi' only the hiss o' the dyin' fire and the soft rise and fall o' his son's chest, Tryss let himself finally believe that peace—fierce, fragile, and worth every fight—was real.

Epilogue

Tryss

THE GREAT HALL OF MacCraith Keep had never looked more alive.

Banners fluttered high above the rafters, golden light from the high windows pourin' down over the assembled crowd. The hearths blazed with warmth and welcome, their smoke trailin' gently through the open chimneys like offerings tae the ancestors. The scent of pine boughs, heather, and fresh bread filled the air. Every surface had been scrubbed and adorned. Bowls overflowed with fruit and sugared almonds, casks of ale stood ready tae spill, and tables groaned with roasted meats and honeyed cakes.

But it wasn't the food or firelight that made the place shine.

It was the people.

They came from every corner of the Highlands—MacCraith warriors in their finest plaids, women in rich silks, the village smith with soot still on his collar, Fergus and Elsyn with two-month-old Fergie swaddled tae her chest, and even Lord MacInness standin' with his shoulders squared and chin high, a silent but powerful pillar of approval.

And at the front, on the raised platform beneath the carved MacCraith crest, stood Tryss and Alyssa.

He in his dark green and silver, a polished brooch at his shoulder, the sword of his line strapped proudly at his hip.

She in a flowin' gown the color of storm-lit heather, her long dark hair braided with bits of gold thread, the firelight catchin' on her skin. And in her arms—the bairn.

Their son.

Swaddled in MacCraith green, with a shock of inky hair, cheeks like roses, and a pair of fierce, curious eyes that had been watchin' the world since the day he was born, as if tryin' tae puzzle out how best tae conquer it.

A hush fell as the elder stepped forward, her voice carryin' with the weight of tradition.

"Before all gathered," she said, "we bear witness. This child—firstborn of House MacCraith—is tae be named. Nay as a whisper, nay in secret, but in the full light of kin and kinfolk. A name tae be carried like a banner. A name tae shape the future."

Tryss shifted slightly, his hand restin' lightly at the small of Alyssa's back. He was calm—but there was tension in his jaw. He hadn't asked what name she'd chosen. He trusted her. Still, somethin' in his throat tightened.

The elder turned to them. "By whose will is he named?"

Alyssa looked up at Tryss.

And smiled.

"By ours," she said, her voice steady and proud. Then louder, for all tae hear:

"His name is Trystan MacCraith."

The silence broke like sunlight through fog.

Tryss turned toward her, stunned—eyes wide with wonder, with disbelief, with a kind of joy so deep it hurt.

"You named him... after me?" he asked, voice rough, almost boyish.

Alyssa's eyes shimmered. "Nay after. For. For the man who fought for him before he was ever born. For the one who held me through the storm and never let go."

A murmur rippled through the hall. Smiles bloomed. Moira wiped her eyes. Fergus let out a quiet breath of laughter. Elsyn squeezed his hand and leaned her cheek tae Fergie's soft hair.

Tryss looked down at his son—his Trystan—and somethin' in him broke open. Pride filled him like fire. He took the child gently from Alyssa's arms and turned tae the hall, liftin' him high.

"Trystan MacCraith!" he cried, his voice a roar, a vow, a benediction.

The hall erupted in cheers.

The drums started.

Voices rose in song.

Tankards were raised, and feet began tae stomp. A piper struck a note that soared up tae the beams, and the hearth flames leapt higher as if the stones themselves rejoiced.

But for Tryss and Alyssa, the world had narrowed tae just one thing.

The tiny weight in their arms.

The future of a clan.

A promise born of blood, fire, and fierce, stubborn love.

Trystan MacCraith.

Heir tae a legacy.

Son of the Highlands.

Crimson Tartan – Book 2 – Sneak Peak

Dear Reader,

If you felt the fire of the Highlands in *The Tartan Swap*, I'd be honored to have you return for the next chapter of the MacCraith legacy.

The story continues in *Crimson Tartan*—where Fergus and Elsyn must face the storm that's been building since the day Tryss and Alyssa wed.

The Highlands remember. Wind howls across the glens, carrying whispers of vows once spoken and battles yet to come. Beneath storm-lit skies, loyalties will be tested, hearts will be claimed, and the name MacCraith will be written anew—in blood, in fire, and in love.

The hills lie quiet... but it's the quiet before the blade.

The drums are calling.

With fierce gratitude,

Kimber H. Kinkaid

Crimson Tartan – Book 2

Chapter 1

Fergus

THE AIR REEKED OF smoke and iron, thick and clinging, burnin' the throat with every breath. Fergus's heart hammered like a war drum, each beat echoin' the clash of steel all around him. Men fell on either side, screams and curses tangled with the thunder of hooves and the sharp, cruel cry of the wounded.

He swung his blade, muscles straining, eyes burnin' with fury, and caught a glimpse of Tryss fightin' just beyond the shattered line. The laird was a storm of green and silver, cuttin' through men like he'd been born tae do it, but even Tryss couldnae be everywhere at once. Fergus's fists clenched on the haft of his sword.

"Hold, ye sons of—hold!" he roared, though the words barely carried over the din.

A spear whistled past, buryin' itself in the frozen earth, and

Fergus twisted, narrowly avoidin' a swinging axe that would've cleaved him in half. Blood sprayed, hot and sticky, drippin' down his arm. He gritted his teeth, breath ragged, muscles coiled for the next strike. The Highlands were unforgivin' tonight, unforgivin' as the screams of fallen kin filled the mist.

And then he saw him.

Tryss. His brother in arms. His friend. The heart of MacCraith. Surrounded. Pressed back by men who cared nothing for honor. Fergus's chest tightened, a wild, raw fear clawin' up his throat. He pushed forward, gut instinct takin' over, but the world slowed in that single moment, every sound sharp as a dirk.

A hulking figure loomed above Tryss, broad sword raised high, catchin' the flicker of torchlight like a blade of fire. Fergus's stomach dropped. His throat closed. And then...

"TRYSS!"

The scream tore from his chest, primal, guttural, filled with all the rage, terror, and love he had for the man who had always stood at his side. Time seemed to fracture, the clash of steel, the cries of the wounded, the rush of wind—all of it narrowed to the sight of that sword arcin' down, aimed true at the heart of his laird.

Fergus lunged, but in that heartbeat, in that searing, gut-twisting instant, he knew... nothing could reach Tryss fast enough.

And the world blurred into the roar of steel, the smell of blood, and a scream that would haunt him forever.

The clangor of battle fades to memory—a sound the Highlands will never forget.

The Highlands hold their breath. Across the wind-whipped passes and shadowed valleys, war gathers like a storm, and the keep that has long been a sanctuary stands on the brink. Fergus feels it in his bones—the clash of steel, the cry of men, the sudden hush before the chaos. And he knows, with a dread that tightens his chest, that those he holds most dear are walking a path of peril he may not be able to guard.

Tryss and Alyssa fight as only they can, pillars of strength against a tide that would see them broken. But when the banners of the enemy rise and the first fires ignite, it will fall to Fergus and Elsyn to stand, to act, and to face the darkness that threatens to sweep through the Highlands. They will need cunning, courage, and a fierce bond neither had expected—and even then, it may not be enough.

Through smoke, blood, and the roar of battle, Fergus and Elsyn will discover that survival demands more than sword and skill. It demands heart, it demands fire, it demands choices that could shatter everything they know. And when the first blow falls, the fight for home—and for those they love—will have only just begun.

Crimson Tartan: MacCraith Keep will never be the same. Elsyn and Fergus must survive... and fight to protect a future born of blood.

www.ingramcontent.com/pod-product-compliance
Lightning Source LLC
Chambersburg PA
CBHW010528100726
47903CB00011B/2941

* 9 7 9 8 9 9 9 9 9 3 1 0 6 *